Evo: The Elements

By

D1414336

Nicoline Evans

Author: Nicoline Evans – www.nicolineevans.com

Editor: Andrew Wetzel – www.stumptowneditorial.com

Nicoline Evans, LLC

Cover Design: Odessa Sawyer – www.odessasawyer.com

And a big thank you to everyone who has offered me support (in all ways, shapes, and sizes) during this entire process.

Dedicated to our warring human hearts

Four thousand years from the start…

Chapter 1

Maila Celesse stood at the edge of a cloud. She closed her eyes and dove.

The forceful winds beneath Ayren were harsh, but she remained calm. She was determined to learn how to glide.

Years of doubt placed on her by family and friends were swept away with the night wind. She wasn't fragile or weak; she was capable and strong. Her bravery alone proved that much. Now, she just had to succeed.

She tried to combine her climithe skills with her ability to levitate, but struggled. She couldn't figure out how to harness the wind. Not truly gliding *or* controlling the air, she found herself merely floating and being tossed about at the air's will. The wind was violent, and after a minute of flailing about, Maila started to panic. The current's initial power was much stronger than she imagined. The sensation of falling lingered, but she regained her composure and focused on levitating.

As her gift of levitation saved her life, it finally felt like a blessing rather than a burden. Being the only person in Ayren born with this ability, she spent her entire childhood living in shame and embarrassment. Ayren was a perfect utopia and its citizens were haughty and cruel; they had no room for mutants in their world. The scrutiny she endured was terrible. It took years to overcome their prejudices and become the fearless young woman she was today.

Now that she was successfully floating, it was time to try out her climithe skills below cloud level. She spread her arms wide and seized the current. It shifted to the west and carried her body with it. The air blew through her hair and caressed her cheeks. The sky was infinite and she was part of its unrestrained glory. Being one with this defiant force of nature was liberating. She could not control it, but she could control herself within it, and the sense of independence it gave her was therapeutic.

She was doing it. Her heart leapt with excitement as she imagined how great it would be to show everyone she was a natural at gliding. When she returned to her home above the clouds she'd arrive armed with triumph. The Heads of Ayren could no longer prevent her from learning the mysteries of the world now that she knew how to glide. She'd soar beneath the clouds collecting knowledge, with or without help from Darrow and the other Gliders, and deliver it to the uninformed population of Ayren. She smiled as she imagined changing everything for the better.

A gust of wind smacked her in the face, interrupting her revelry and knocking her off course. It frightened her, but she used her climithe skills to adjust the breeze so she did not fall out of the current. Pride filled her heart as she successfully recovered.

No one ever thought to mix the professions of Ayren together, and if they had, they never followed through. Ayren was regimented and strict; everyone abided by a rigorous set of rules and never strayed from the path they were born into. Maila never fit in because she always craved more, and now that she took that desire into her own hands she was realizing all the ways in which the Ayrenese society hindered itself from greatness. Knowing how to control the winds *and* being trained to glide was a powerful combination. Many of the professions would be better served if individuals knew multiple skillsets. It was just another reason why things needed to change in Ayren.

After accomplishing five minutes of her first glide, she was ready to return home. She was raising herself toward the clouds of Ayren when a strong pocket of air punched her in the chest. It made her black out for a brief moment before hitting her again, knocking her down ten feet and into a new current. Her hollow bones quivered, but she tried to ignore the pain. The new current was volatile and tossed her from side to side. The force gave her whiplash and her previous assuredness disappeared. She no longer had control of herself within the great force surrounding her and though she tried to regain her focus, she was unable to get a firm hold of her center. Too many currents swirled at once and she could not get herself out of the crossfire.

She dropped another ten feet. Attempting to stay levitated, she focused all her energy on maintaining a solid core until the worst of the current passed. Her center remained afloat while the rest of her body hung in the sky from her belly button, arms and legs dangling beneath her.

Calm down, she thought, *regain your levitation, then ride the current.* She tried with all her might, but the strength of the current dragged her along through the sky and she couldn't get upright. The previously controllable winds beneath Ayren were now erratic, and the current she was stuck in hauled her further downward, away from the clouds. It was becoming clear that she was no match for the strength of the night wind. A pain seared through her chest as she realized Darrow was right in his stance during their argument earlier that night; she wasn't strong enough to glide, at least not in anything stronger than a mild current. She felt a surge of disappointment; for failing herself, and Darrow. He would have been happy to be wrong, especially now that the outcome was looking grim.

Her struggle with the furious air was useless. She could not beat it, so she hopelessly clung to her life while her body obeyed whichever direction the wind chose to blow. Her head whipped back while her legs splayed in different directions. The hollow bones in her shoulders threatened to break as her arms swung freely at the wind's discretion.

She was losing. No amount of levitation could alleviate the predicament she placed herself in. Her eyes filled with tears as her certainty for this plan disintegrated. She was about to cry out for help when, out of nowhere, an even stronger gust of wind hit her across the face, sending her spiraling downward.

She flailed desperately, hoping that her refusal to quit would pay off. She called out Darrow's name, praying somehow he might hear her from above, but her voice was lost in the loud howl of the wind. The whistle of her descent was piercing and rang through her skull as the momentum of her fall increased. She was losing this battle. Her mind raced around any last possibilities that may save her, but she could think of none.

The sickening notion of defeat filled her as she buckled under the pressure of the wind and let go. She let go of her breath, of her center, and of any chance that she may still be floating amidst the chaos.

Tears welled in her eyes but were ripped away by the harsh acceleration of her plummet. Pain seared her frail bones. The incoming darkness reared as her fall turned into an uncontrolled dive toward the earth. A moment after she stopped levitating, the air around her disappeared.

She was submerged, unable to breath but still falling downward, only much slower and through a silent mass of liquid. Grief took over as she realized she had fallen into the ocean.

She reached the end; there was no fixing what she had done. Too weak to move and uneducated on how to swim, she could not fathom a solution that might save her.

Conflicting feelings crossed through her heart and the lack of oxygen flowing to her brain blocked the clarity she needed to sort them out. She was mad at herself for acting so foolishly. She was proud that she had tried. She was remorseful that she left her loved ones on bad terms. She had to stop these thoughts because none of it mattered anymore; all these feelings would drown alongside her.

Her eyes closed as the oxygen in her lungs trickled into nothing. Maila's tiny body smoldered a silver radiance in the clear water, like a firefly losing its light as it sank to the bottom of a glass jar. The fists she previously clenched in panic released into open palms.

The descent to the ocean floor was gentle. Her toes touched the sand lightly while her body remained suspended upright with her arms floating at her sides.

Floating, she managed to think to herself, *this feels like floating.* The weightlessness of her body in these last conscious moments felt pure and familiar, like she was home above the clouds. She let the peaceful feeling consume her. It helped ease her dying heart.

Right before losing consciousness, something nudged her shoulder. Blood raced to her brain, setting her nerves back in motion. She looked for the source, but saw nothing.

A firm push from behind came a second time and her right arm was yanked above her head. She was being dragged upward, faster than the free fall that landed her at the bottom of the ocean.

Her mind came back to life and started working overtime, but the lack of oxygen made her delirious. Nothing made sense. A million pictures and thoughts flashed inside her head but they were jumbled together, out of order, like a terrifying hallucination.

She opened her eyes to the sight of an angel, a heavenly creature pulling her toward the light, dazzling in its elegance. But her sight flickered, fading in and out of blackness, and the radiance of the being above her became fuzzy and unfocused.

Her limp body trailed behind her arm as the unknown source towed her upward. It was leading the way toward the sky. Was it an angel? Or was it Death Himself, cruelly taunting her with a last moment plagued by pointless hope? The queries disappeared as her body shut down.

She tried her hardest to hold on for a few more seconds, fighting off death as it tried to take her, wrestling with defeat so she could inhale the air she was heading toward. But she couldn't stretch her lungs any further. Maila's eyes closed and her breath ceased moments before dawn's sunlight hit her face through the surface of the sea.

Chapter 2

There was light beyond the smog—a sign of life from the other side. Though Mr. Lamorte stared into the sky often, this was the first time he ever caught a glimpse of hope that more existed beyond the dome. For a brief moment, a falling star illuminated a small patch of their confinement. It cast a glowing silhouette on the impenetrable walls that kept him trapped. It only lasted a few minutes and the light was now gone, but he continued to lean against the railing of his balcony, plotting new ways to try and exit the smog. His desire to escape the dome was reignited; he would capture that star and conquer whatever lived outside the dome.

"Donovan, don't you want to come and play with me?" Camille stammered with an inebriated slur.

The president of North America took a deep breath through flared nostrils. He snapped his head in anger to find his current girlfriend sprawled across his bed in her lingerie. He had no desire for her. She was his lover, though there was certainly no love involved. He needed her for his image. This relationship was a façade to fool the masses into believing he was normal, that he had regular human emotions and needs. It was all an act. The nerves lining his heart were numb.

He didn't want a companion. There was an empty void deep within his soul that sucked the desire for those natural impulses straight out of his being. The human touch made him cringe, it was entirely too invasive. He feared a simple kiss would let a woman see further into his dark mind than even he dared to go.

These women were dangerous. Every time his lips touched theirs, his immediate impulse was to put his hands around their throat. Over the years, he methodically trained himself to suppress these animalistic urges. He reminded himself how terrifically horrendous it might seem to everyone else if he killed one of his girlfriends. The people he ruled needed to believe he was a normal, morally rigid man. Someone who always chose to do right while the rest of his people chose to do wrong. It kept them believing there was hope, when really, there was none.

To remedy the predicament of his dark fantasies, and to silence his nosy and needy lovers, he gave them heavy doses of painkillers a few times a day. It was the only way to keep these women blind to his complete lack of humanity. They were walking zombies, just as Mr. Lamorte crafted them to be.

"Camille, can't you see I have no interest at the moment. You bore me." Camille sat on his bed, staring at him with glazed eyes. She was oblivious to his cruelty. Her head bobbed back and forth, as if the weight of it was too heavy to hold upright.

"But Donovan," she managed to stammer.

Mr. Lamorte thought to himself that perhaps he slipped her more pills than necessary that evening. She looked at him with a pathetic faraway pout.

"Stop it," he demanded. He hated when she whimpered his name like he owed her something. "I said no. Go back to sleep." Her head wobbled with the weight of concentration she was putting forth to comprehend their conversation. Then her glassy eyes grew wide as she heaved into her bony hands. Her face contorted with horror as she lowered her hands and saw that they were covered in blood. She let out a whimper as she stumbled toward the bathroom, gagging into her bloody hands once again.

Mr. Lamorte left her to handle the mess on her own. He had the disease too, but his medicinal mask helped lessen the pain. He removed the sapphire-satin mask and gently placed his hand on the deteriorating skin that covered his forehead and left eye. It was an infection no doctor was able to cure and it was slowly turning his face raw. The rotting skin, bright red at the center, was slowly worsening into shades of brown and green along its edges.

Japan had a similar contamination twenty years ago. No one survived. Today, nothing remained of Japan's empire except barren land deemed useless due to the poisonous air and destroyed terrain. The earth's foundation in Japan, the Koreas, China, and Mongolia consisted of putty and sand, and all the buildings and highways constructed by the extinct culture were on the brink of collapse. It was a wasteland. Though the demise of Japan's realm should have been a grave warning, Mr. Lamorte saw it as a positive development: less competition to build the biggest, most powerful empire. His only rivalry now was the Capitol le Francais, who moved leisurely in their development of new land, as if time did not tick on that side of the ocean. They both remained imprisoned under domes of smog, but he suspected he'd find a way out of his long before they escaped theirs.

The sound of Camille vomiting in the bathroom was vile, so he closed the balcony door to recapture the silence she interrupted. He returned his attention to the night sky, which was pitch black. The star was gone and there was no light except that which glowed from the buildings in this part of the city. Daytime was a lighter shade of gray due to sources beyond the smog, but no one knew what brought the light. The history archives attributed it to an orb called the sun, but he had never seen it and had little inclination to believe it was anything more than a myth.

Though he had no interest in the sun, he still wished to conquer the unnatural borders that kept him imprisoned. Every night he stared at the ceiling of the dome, wondering what marvels might exist beyond the permanent gray film that obstructed his view. How far could he go if he ever found a way equally. They all felt responsible for the corruption they were privy to but could not change.

The strong winds provided a sense of relief as they hit Darrow's face. He thought of Maila and smiled. His love for her enhanced the way he saw everything: every color, every shape, every moment. Even though their first attempt at ridding the world of the Debauched so the Law of Secrecy could be eliminated failed, he was determined to keep trying. She made him want to change the world.

The meeting today was a regular trade meeting: they'd check in on the status of the Tierannite's jungle to schedule rainfalls and the Tierannites would send them home with baskets full of fresh food. Tensions would be high since it was only a day ago that the gliders tried to get them to agree to war and the Tierannites adamantly protested. Their reaction was mixed with anger, logic, and fear. The failure of that exchange left Darrow in a foul mood, which carried over into his fight with Maila, but he was ready to brainstorm and try again. In a few weeks he'd have a new plan that would fix Ayren for the better.

The gliders approached the coast of Tier, which was once known as South America, and slowed down once they reached the top of the tree line. He saw the Tierannites already standing there, waiting for the meeting to begin. Darrow recognized them all; he dealt with these correspondents on a daily basis.

Lux and Eluno stood tall. Their messy waves of brown hair had random pieces braided and beaded. The men in Tier and Coralen braided their hair, and he wondered if the Ahi did too; he never met one of them. Each of these older Tierannite men had similar tattoos, Lux with a sun on the left side of his chest and Eluno with a crescent moon on his right. They both wore shorts made of leafy hemp and had vines wrapped around their torsos.

Next to them was Relina, the only female Tierannite Darrow ever met. Her long, light brown hair was tangled into a mess of braids and knots that reached the middle of her back. She had defined arm muscles with a vine tattoo that coiled its way from her shoulder to wrist. Her two-piece outfit was made of hemp and exposed her toned abs. The dirt that covered her long legs blended into the dark color of her shorts. Harsh sunlight hit her angular cheekbones and made her look like a divine creature; one of such beauty, he sometimes wondered if he created her image in his head. But every time he saw her again, he was reminded just how real she was. Once again, there she stood, as radiant and serious as ever. Her green eyes shifted up toward him and his fellow gliders as they entered the meeting space.

Darrow noticed Zyleh last. He was silently hoping to be spared from his presence after yesterday's failure. Zyleh was cocky and stubborn and he always gave him a hard time. The dynamic when they spoke was rarely pleasant. Zyleh's shaggy brown hair hung

24

"Sorry, we just came down to collaborate this month's rain schedule and collect some food for the week," Darrow chimed in to relieve the tension.

"Of course," Lux answered. "It's the dry season, so we will need an extra rainfall each week. Sixteen for the month, four per week."

"Fantastic, can do," Kalline responded with a smile.

"Are we just going to pretend like yesterday never happened? Don't you want to know what the Ahi and Coralen had to say about your request?" Zyleh blurted out, making everyone uneasy.

"We already talked to the Coralen, so we know their response, but sure, what did the Ahi say?" Kalloe's dislike for Zyleh was worse than Darrow's today.

"They also thought it was selfish."

"We never intended it to be selfish," Darrow explained. "We thought it would be a good opportunity for the Earth to heal, once and for all, and for the Elements to reunite and bond. We want our relationships to be as strong as they were during the golden age. We want all the Elements to have genuine friendships."

"The only Element out of the friendship loop is you, and it's your own fault that you sit on the outside. Your pretentious attitudes and belief that you are somehow better than the rest of us put you there. It's amazing you think thousands among the other Elements should die in an unnecessary war to help fix problems that have nothing to do with us."

"We didn't see it that way, we imagined it being a clean and swift victory, but we understand your reservations," Kalline said, trying to calm Zyleh's rage, but he continued.

"Again, you think you're better than us, so our lives don't matter."

"Stop lumping all of the Ayrenese people together under the same elitist blanket," Jorban blurted in aggravation. "We aren't all as snobbish as the Heads."

"We understand that things are not run properly in Ayren," Kalline tried to explain without disclosing too much. She could not divulge the truth about the Law of Secrecy because it would only create additional tension between them and the other Elements. No one knew that the majority of Ayren were oblivious about the existence of the Debauched, so she danced around it. "We have been trying to mend the ways in which our territory is ruled for centuries. We know the plan was extreme but it was an attempt to fix everything without completely destroying the fine lining holding Ayren together. We thought a task as large as that would not only open the eyes of our people, but also help reestablish our relationships with you, the Ahi, and the Coralene. We understand your opposition, so we will keep trying. We will find another way to fix Ayren and reestablish our relationships."

"Our main motivation was to prevent the worst-case scenario: the Debauched attacking first. I can promise you, Ayren would not be ready to defend our skies, your land, or the ocean if things remain as they are within our society. Being on the offensive would force us to change how we operate, making us stronger as a whole on behalf of ourselves and all of you," Jorban added.

"If the leaders of your realm are so obstinate and foolish that they don't believe you when you tell them what you just told me, then maybe it's time to overthrow them. It was crazy to ask us to risk thousands of lives in order to help you clean up the dirty politics of Ayren." Zyleh said, deep concern in his eyes.

"We get it. It was just an idea. Sorry it bothered you so much." Kalloe rolled her eyes, uninterested in a second round of appalled attacks from Zyleh; they heard most of this rant the day before.

"I'm just so confused by your rationale. The Debauched should be extinct in less than a hundred years. Maybe two hundred. We've kept them unaware of our existence for two thousand years, I think we can keep them at bay for a few hundred more. Am I missing something?"

He was, but none of the gliders were going to fill in the missing piece to the puzzle.

"No, I just suspect you're trying to rub it in that we tried and failed," Darrow said in frustration. "Well, go on if you must, but you won't dampen our spirits. Our intentions were good, whether

29

you want to believe it or not, and you harping on the matter is a waste of everyone's time. The issue is dropped. We're over it, and you should get over it too."

Zyleh opened his mouth to retort, but Relina cut him off.

"Drop it. It's over." She redirected her attention to the gliders. She picked up the baskets filled with fresh fruit, vegetables, herbs, and spices, and handed one to each glider. "Is there anything else we should discuss today?"

"I think that covers it," Darrow answered.

Before they could part ways, a young Tierannite with blood smeared beneath each of his eyes emerged through the canopy, out of breath.

"Zyleh," he panted, then caught sight of the gliders. His eyes shifted with rage as he stormed toward the spot where they hovered. "What have you done?" he bellowed. The gliders answered with a look of confusion. "You'll kill us all!"

He lunged to attack but Relina seized him before he could grab one of the gliders by the ankle.

"Marlo, what's wrong with you?" she demanded.

"They went through with it anyway!"

"What are you talking about?" Zyleh stepped in.

"They initiated a war with the Debauched!"

Chapter 5

The Tierannites glared at the gliders in unison.

"No we didn't!" Jorban interjected.

"Yes, you did," Marlo spat back, sending a malicious glare his way, then returned to look at Relina and Zyleh. "A bright light fell from the sky last night and the Ahi are now trying to determine if the Debauched saw it." He returned his attention to the gliders, "I wonder what might have caused such a phenomenon? Since it came from the sky, I blame you."

"Is this true?" Eluno stepped forward and looked to the gliders with utter disappointment.

"No. Absolutely not," Darrow swore. "We did not send any kind of light into the night sky for the Debauched to see. We would never betray you like that."

"The Sovereigns saw the nighttime light show during their early morning mediation. They spoke with Juniper, who received confirmation from Gaia. She sees all." Marlo's expression was savage. He was ready to tear the gliders from the sky.

"What *exactly* did she see? Because we have no idea what you are talking about." Kalloe was having trouble masking her aggravation.

"That the light came from Ayren!" Marlo said, as if it were obvious.

"What caused the light?" Jorban asked.

"A girl," Marlo seethed. "Did you sacrifice one of your own for the 'greater good'? Gave her a little shove, and whoops, a falling star?"

Darrow did not hear the defamatory comment; all he heard was that Gaia saw a girl fall from the clouds of Ayren.

"Maila," he exhaled, so soft only the other gliders heard him.

Jorban's head snapped to look at his best friend, "Oh no."

"What did you say?" Lux asked, his face red with fury.

"It wasn't intentional," Jorban explained as Darrow began muttering to himself. "Our friend went missing and I think you just filled us in on her fate."

"No one has ever fallen out of the sky. How does such an accident occur?" Eluno asked in disbelief.

"We don't know," Kalline's eyes filled with tears. This development was new to her and Kalloe too.

"Is she dead?" Darrow asked the group. He looked down at Marlo and screamed, "Is she dead?"

Darrow's face was ghostly white, paler than the normal white pigment of Ayrenese skin, and his eyes had become bloodshot from the sudden burst of anxiety. He didn't know whether to cry or scream, and the internal battle was visible in his face. The Tierannites witnessed the gliders raw reaction to this news and couldn't deny its honesty.

"I don't know," Marlo answered, his previous vigor had softened.

"We were over water," Kalloe offered in a muffle, not wanting to send Darrow into a tailspin, but needing to offer the facts.

"Water," Darrow repeated. He handed the basket of herbs to Kalloe. "Coralen. I need to speak with the sea patrol." The monotony of his voice was unnerving and his friends looked at him with concern. He went from madman to robot in moments; his heart couldn't handle this news.

"Let us talk to them for you," Kalline suggested.

"No!" he hollered, then paused. "No." His tone was flat again.

"Sorry about this," Jorban addressed the Tierannites, who watched the unexpected breakdown in bewilderment. "We will get this sorted out and do what we can to rectify it."

"Sorry about your friend," Relina offered, then departed. Zyleh, Marlo, Lux, and Eluno followed suit, leaping away across the treetops and disappearing into the lush greenery below.

"Let's find Maila," Kalline said to Darrow with compassion, and they headed toward the open sea.

Chapter 6

Darrow and Kalline glided just above the ocean's surface, letting its mist spray their faces. The cold water helped calm Darrow's nerves. Jorban and Kalloe returned to Ayren to fill Maila's parents in on the news. The entire ordeal was shocking and terrifying, and Kalline kept a close eye on Darrow. His eyes were bloodshot and his face too pale. She worried he might get sick if he didn't get back to the clouds to rest.

He was determined to carry on. He wore a stained-glass pendant around his neck, which acted as a meeting initiator with the Coralene. He wiggled it around frantically in strategic patterns as daylight faded. Once he caught the setting sun's reflection, he shot it into the dark water. To his luck, the signal worked quickly.

"Kalline," he said, "look straight ahead, about fifty yards or so, do you see that?"

She did: It was a return signal. They redirected their glide by a few degrees and headed toward the sea glass response. When dealing with the Coralene, you could never be sure who would rise out of the water to greet you, so Darrow was relieved to see Clydde and Talley, the two sea patrollers he usually communicated with.

Clydde rose above the water on a sustained wave that held him up at his waist. It continually lapped from behind and cascaded in front of him, keeping him in one spot. The wave appeared as part of his body, though Darrow knew they had legs beneath the water propelling the wave into existence. Talley came from behind on her wave and settled next to her patrol partner. Talley had beautiful auburn hair that was wet and messy. Purple scales covered her curvy chest and ran down along her muscular arms. She was much younger than Clydde and probably only a few years older than Darrow. Her body fit into her wave perfectly as she flashed a smile at Darrow. Their skin was pale, almost translucent, with a dull, bluish-hue deep beneath the surface. They looked like they were drowned and brought back to life. Despite their ghoulish complexion, their faces remained ridiculously attractive. It was a strange paradox, that of a gorgeous dead person. Darrow imagined they looked much different while flourishing in their element, and that the light beneath the water cast them in a heavenly glow.

Clydde greeted them. "Hello, young riders of the wind." He inhaled the fresh air dramatically. "What a day to be alive."

Darrow's heart quickened in panic and Kalline stepped in to steer the conversation in the right direction.

"Clydde, we just received dire news. One of our friends fell from the sky two nights ago. We were over the Atlantic Ocean, between the North American Debauched territory and Tier. Please tell me one of your people were able to rescue her."

"Oh my seas, what a grave topic indeed." He said no more. Darrow waited, exercising his patience, but neither of the Coralene said anything else. They just stared with their big opal-colored eyes reflecting infinite shades of pastels. Their pale, dead-looking skin amplified the profoundness of their hollowed cheeks. Talley shook her head a few times, as if she answered something that was inaudible to Darrow.

"Okay," Kalline stepped in, hesitantly, "so did you see her?"

"Oh, barnacles," Clydde immediately apologized. Talley looked around confused for a moment before realizing their mistake as well. "My blunder," he continued, "for me to forget that you could not in fact hear us. My brain must be filled with bubbles."

"Our apologies, Darlo and Karline," Talley added, getting their names wrong, as they always did. Her pretty face was sincere as she explained the miscommunication. "We don't speak with our mouths under the water, as you know, so sometimes we forget that you cannot hear our mindspeak. We waded here, both thinking what we wanted you to know, having a conversation with what we thought was all four of us. Alas, we were mistaken." It sounded like she wanted to laugh, but she contained her snickers.

Clydde smiled apologetically, which changed his entire demeanor from grim to positively radiant.

"Neither of us have seen her," Clydde answered. Upon seeing Darrow's face shift with defeat he added, "Though, we will stop at nothing to find you an answer."

"Thank you," Kalline replied. Darrow remained silent. His face was blank and his eyes were empty. Kalline needed to get him home before he gave up entirely and plummeted into the ocean. "We will be back for an update soon."

"Wonderful. We are on the case of the missing sky girl," Clydde exclaimed, completely neglecting the serious nature in which he should have responded. "Many good tides to you."

He and Talley disappeared under the ocean's surface, leaving the gliders hanging over the water with no leads.

Darrow was numb. He watched as the Coralene dove out of their waves and into the water. As they swam away below the ocean's surface, he noticed how seamlessly they blended in with the water. He tried to follow them as they moved deeper beneath the surface and in the brief moment in which he could still see them, they appeared to turn into water as they swam. They submerged and disappeared so quickly he couldn't be sure. Perhaps it was his imagination. Or perhaps it was his grieving mind playing tricks.

"Are you with me?" Kalline asked, shaking Darrow out of his wandering thoughts.

"I think my insides are collapsing," Darrow said. His sight was blurry from grief and his energy was depleted.

"Let's get you home," Kalline said, grabbing his hand so he didn't dip any closer to the water. "There's still time for a miracle."

Darrow nodded, thankful she was remaining optimistic for them both. They made a slow trip back to Ayren and Darrow prayed to Gaia for that miracle.

Chapter 7

Zyleh headed toward the Northeast checkpoint to converse with the Ahi and fill them in on all that was revealed. There were five main checkpoints from Ahi that led into Tier. Four on each corner of the continent and one that was located at the center of Tier, near the Heart.

The tree branches became a blur as Zyleh bounded between them toward the Northeast checkpoint. When he reached it, Zyleh pushed aside the huge boulder that covered the opening. The tunnel below was pitch black but the movement of the rock let some sunlight sneak into its depths. Though it remained dark, he could see enough to know there was no one down there.

Thousands of Ahi spanned throughout the tunnels at all times. The underground empire of Ahi covered the entire globe and they could be anywhere at anytime, so unplanned meetings often required a wait. He went to the nearest tree and ripped off a medium-sized branch. He threw it down into the tunnel and moved the boulder back over the opening—an ancient rule created by Eshe, Champion of the Core; too much outside air contaminated the core's delicate ecosystem. If a meeting needed to be called in reverse, the Ahi would emerge from the tunnel and leave a few lava rocks next to the tunnel opening. Zyleh sat down on a bed of leaves and watched the moon as he waited.

An hour passed before the rock moved. There was barely a sliver of space when a tiny head popped out of the crevice and looked around. This particular Ahi was a child, and Zyleh groaned in frustration.

"Hello?" the child shouted. His tiny head was covered in thick black braids knotted tight to the top of his blood red scalp. The whites of the boy's eyes darted back and forth as he looked for the sender of the tree branch.

"Hello, young Ahi," Zyleh said as he stepped closer to the rock so the young boy could see him, "thank you for emerging. I assume you saw the tree branch?"

"Yes," the boy said with a mischievous grin. His red eyes gleamed. "My name is Tyoko Pyrrhus."

"I'm Zyleh, Leader of the Carriers. Is there an Ahi official I can speak to?"

The boy's smile disappeared. He wanted to act as receiver of the summons.

"There are tons of Ahi officials, but none are around right now."

Zyleh sighed, "Well, do you think you could try and get one of them to come and speak to me? It's really important."

Tyoko's black irises bore into Zyleh as he dipped back into the ground without saying another word. The rock slowly moved back into place to cover the tunnel's opening and Zyleh was alone again.

An hour passed without an Ahi official emerging from the tunnel. Zyleh was about to give up when a loud thud came from beneath the checkpoint. Just then, the rock flew to the side and the tree branch he previously dropped into the hole came flying out. It landed a foot away from where he sat.

Two enormous, dark red hands appeared on the ground at the outer edge of the opening. They grasped the earth and lifted a giant Ahi man to the surface. He pushed his body up with such force that he flew into the air and landed firmly on the jungle floor with both feet. The huge man jerked his head to the side once to crack it and then looked straight at Zyleh. The whites of his eyes contrasted drastically with the crimson hue of his skin. During their evolution, the people of Ahi turned a menacing shade of dark red.

"Young Tyoko said there was a Tierannite looking to speak with an official. I am Culane Naga, Leader of the Carvers. I am authorized to speak with the other Elements."

Zyleh never met Culane before, though he was just as physically imposing as the officials he spoke to on a regular basis. His muscles bulged from every angle and looked to be on the brink of combustion. But it was all a pretense. This was how Culane *chose* to be viewed. The Ahi never stayed the same height or width; they could change their size at will. They could shift from ten feet tall to a fifth of that size in a matter of seconds. It was an essential gift during the evolution process because the tunnels leading to the core of the earth varied greatly in size and they needed to fit through all of them. Whenever they met with the other Elements they transformed to their largest proportions, and even though the Ahi and Tierannites were on good terms, this was their attempt to instill a level of intimidation.

"Hello Culane. I am Zyleh León, Leader of the Carriers. We have not had the pleasure of meeting before." Zyleh gave him a pleasant grin, but the nicety was not returned, so he continued, "I requested this meeting because we spoke to the Ayrenese gliders this morning."

Culane snorted and spit on the ground at the mention of Ayren. The Ahi people had a strong distaste for the distance the Ayrenese had put between themselves and the rest of the world.

"I understand your people are not fond of the Ayrenese at this moment, but I came to update you on the matter of the falling star." Zyleh's composure was that of flawless confidence. Although the Ahi were bigger than him and came off as terrifying to some, Zyleh was unfazed.

"This should be good," Culane growled.

"They said it was an accident. That a girl fell from the clouds."

Culane let out a terrible laugh in response.

42

"Since when do they 'fall' off their clouds?"

"If I hadn't seen their reaction to our accusation first hand I would've thought it was a lie too, but the one in love with the girl who fell suffered a mental breakdown right before my eyes. If it was fake, then he is a brilliant actor because I've never felt so uncomfortable in my life." Zyleh shrugged. "I don't like them, or what happened, but I believe them."

Culane huffed, his agitation for the Ayrenese displayed plainly in his expression. "Even if I take your word and believe it was an accident, it doesn't change the fact that we are now in grave danger because of them. There are laws against them leaving the shelter of the clouds after dark for this exact reason."

"I know. I'm not justifying it, just giving you an update. Is there any word on the Debauched? Did they see her glowing free fall?"

"We have our spies roaming the sewers of the Debauched cities on a daily basis. There's no news yet but you'll be the first to know when there is. Let's hope it stays quiet. We want no part in the evilness that resides there."

"I can only imagine."

"Was there anything else you needed? Or may I return to Ahi?"

"That was it."

"Good," Culane said. "Also, let our sky friends know we'd appreciate a face-to-face apology. Their absence does not go unnoticed. I don't think a person of Ahi has seen an Ayrenese in centuries."

"I'll relay the message.

"It's a shame. It should not be this way. Our Champion ancestors were a family, yet we live in this world as strangers. Eshe is so disappointed."

Zyleh agreed. No words of defense could be offered on Ayren's behalf.

"I must be on my way," Culane said. "My wife is a spy and in a few hours she'll be home for the first time in a week. She was beneath North America staking out the president's quarters from the sewers near his home. It was a dangerous task and I will be extremely grateful to have her back in my arms." A glimpse of tenderness crossed Culane's face. It was the first time he appeared soft in nature.

"Go to her, friend."

Culane nodded and turned back toward the tunnel's opening. He jumped into the hole, with ease, and shifted the rock back over the opening.

Zyleh was alone again with minimal progress made on matters that could change all of their lives. He feared the worst, but hoped that Gaia would reward all their devoted work with a miracle.

Chapter 8

The filthy morning air choked Violet awake. Its thickness sat in the back of her throat and her body went into a series of aggressive coughs.

At some point in her sleep her thick wool scarf unwrapped from around her face, leaving her nose and mouth exposed to the toxic air that filled her home. Once her coughing fit ceased and her throat was cleared, she wrapped the dirty scarf back around the bottom half of her face and pulled her knit hat down so it covered her ears and eyebrows.

Her mother knitted the scarf and hat for her. It was the last gift she gave Violet before she died. They were dirty but she cherished them all the same.

The disease killed her parents when she was only ten. It was devastating, but she survived the sadness. Spending the last three years alone made her stronger than she ever imagined she could be.

She slept in the alley underneath President Lamorte's skyscraper. He owned the entire building—he owned everything in North America—and he lived in one of the top suites. It was a safe place for Violet because no other homeless people dare stay there; it was too close to their ruthless leader. It was also where she grew up. She lived in this alleyway her entire life with her parents and it was home to her happiest memories.

Whenever Mr. Lamorte left his building, which was rare, Violet hid behind trashcans to avoid being spotted. He didn't like the homeless and was known to tyrannize them for entertainment.

The sound of static blasted into the stale air, which meant Mr. Lamorte was about to give his weekly speech. Televisions in homes and businesses powered on by themselves and flickered with his broadcast. She didn't have a TV, but heard rumors that the channel couldn't be changed while he spoke. People who could not afford such luxuries, like her, and lived too far from Old New York to attend in person, heard him speak via the speakers and jumbo screens displayed on every street corner throughout the continent. During this time, they were turned up to deafening volumes so his voice echoed throughout all of North America. It was impossible to avoid.

Violet never had to leave the shadows of her alleyway to hear the nonsense. This week's speech echoed through the sky and she did her best to ignore the pointless propaganda and his feeble attempts to sound like he cared about the people living under his impoverished reign.

Mr. Lamorte droned on but she tuned him out with memories of her parents. Her love for them rang louder. She missed them terribly and her recurring daydream about them coming back was especially vivid today. When they got ill they did their best to teach her everything they knew so she was prepared to live on her own: the secrets of getting by in this decrepit world, simple life skills that would help her survive day to day, and stories to help her distinguish who was trustworthy from those who were not. But after they died, she made up her mind that she could trust no one except an old family friend named Pascal. Her parents had trusted him, so she could too. Pascal helped her through the initial grieving stages after they died. He helped her get food and told her wonderful stories about things he read on the Internet when he was young and wealthy.

A few months after her eleventh birthday, she went to visit Pascal at his makeshift home in an alley near the center of the city. When she got there, she found him lying on his cardboard mat, dead. His hand was cut off at the wrist and his watch was missing.

She stayed by his side that night and cried herself to sleep next to his corpse. She didn't want him to be alone and they kept each other company one last time.

The following day was a Wednesday, which was body pick-up day. She protected his body until the dump trucks came that evening. This reoccurring clean up was Mr. Lamorte's heartless way of dealing with the masses who died in bulk each week. If she could have given Pascal a respectful burial, she would have, but those traditions ceased when concrete replaced soil. Now the only option was cremation, and for the homeless, these burnings happened in bulk. She dragged his body to the curb and made sure the cadaver collectors retrieved him before any scoundrels could raid him for parts to sell.

In that moment, she decided he was the last friend she would ever have. If she stayed alone, this type of heartbreak could never happen again.

Two years passed since that day and she still could not forget the awful feeling of predators lurking in the shadows, waiting for her to leave his body so they could rob him further. When they stole pieces of a dead body for trade, such as hair, eyes, teeth, and limbs, they were also stealing the dignity of the person who used to live in that body. It was deplorable.

She was tired of the cruel world that surrounded her and wished to escape, but there was nowhere to go. There was no point in moving to another location on the continent because the entire landscape was exactly the same; a metal wasteland ruled by Mr. Lamorte. Leaving the smog was the only option, and that wasn't possible. Its border was rumored to be miles thick and swarming with fumes so toxic, any exposure would kill a person before they got to the other side. Still, she dreamed of trying. Whatever existed on the other side had to be better than the terror that thrived within.

Pascal told her that there was a time in history when things were better and Violet wanted to believe she could have a life similar to that of her distant ancestors if she got out of this place.

Four thousand years ago, the human race was thrust back into simple living when the planet crumbled under an onslaught of natural disasters. They were forced to start over and while some humans flourished in their new, modest lifestyle, others were discontent. Insurgent groups formed that lived to return the human race back to its former glory. Sergei Lamorte was elected leader of the rebels and that began their family reign. For the next four thousand years, all the way to the present day, the Lamorte family ruled. What was once called The United States of America was simplified to North America, as there were no longer divisions amongst the land, and all former state and country lines were abolished and turned into quadrants. Certain areas retained their old names, for convenience purposes, but most locations were defined by a letter and a number on a grid. Former Canada and Mexico were described as the northernmost and southernmost territories, respectively.

As the Lamorte's reign flourished, the human race devolved. Under their rule, the nation's agenda focused on land acquisition and nothing more. The economy tanked, leaving the majority of the population in poverty, and the educational systems were abandoned. Though the goal of the Rebel Party was to return to the success they'd achieved before the disasters, they failed. The human race looked nothing like it had in the previous century. All development ceased due to lack of education, and the extreme deprivation people were forced to live in made it impossible for anyone to thrive. No one had the means, financially or intellectually, to make the dire changes their society needed. While the population suffered, all that mattered to those in charge was the power and expansion of their empire. This continued on for thousands of years, with no one educated enough to dethrone the Lamortes.

Two thousand years after the Lamortes took control, the smog appeared. It only took a few days for it to materialize and trap all inhabitants within its confines.

For a short period of time, the Lamortes forced groups of innocent, destitute people into the smog to see what would happen and to determine if there was a way out. The bodies of these sacrifices always floated back into the barren harbors the following day, skin eaten alive by the poisonous smog.

The Lamortes refused to accept their role in creating this dark, new world, and dealt with it by blaming the impoverished populace they were supposed to serve and protect. This manipulation generated a population contaminated by fear. Their daily lives were riddled with desperation and their instinct to survive trumped basic ethics. All moral code and humanity disintegrated, turning humans into wild animals forced to fend for themselves.

Though Violet had not lived during these pivotal times, she found herself enraged at the injustice, disturbed that the Lamortes had ruined their second chance at a fulfilling life. Even those like Violet, who had minimal education but fire in their spirit, were unable to break free of the oppression. They were stuck with no place to run.

She hated feeling trapped, but knew she was strong enough to survive. She preserved the small education she was given and did her best to expand upon it whenever she could. One day it would be useful, one day it would help her escape.

Mr. Lamorte's speech was coming to an end.

To close, I have delightful news. His voice echoed across the entire continent. *I caught sight of activity beyond the smog. Two nights ago, I received the sign I've been waiting for. A falling star graced my vision. It called out to me, daring me to give chase. And so we shall. Prepare, my beloved citizens, for new horizons are upon us.*

Chapter 9

Maila opened her eyes for the first time in two days. Terrified, she assessed her surroundings without saying a word: a ground that felt coarse and moved in tiny pieces, the ocean she almost died in, and a giant woman with big opal eyes staring down at her.

It made no sense—the last thing she remembered was dying.

The lady's light skin had a blue undertone that made her look eerie and ghostlike. Purple scales were clustered around her chest and pelvic area, but also trickled in patches down her arms, legs, and torso. She had strategically-placed seaweed and ropes knotted around her lengthy limbs. It showed off her lean muscles, broad shoulders, and skinny legs. As the woman tilted her head to examine Maila more, the pastel colors in her eyes shimmered. Maila never saw a person like this before. She was equally as beautiful as she was haunting. The lady's skeletal face made her features appear larger than normal and her cold, watery skin made her look lifeless.

"Am I dead?" Maila whispered, afraid to hear the answer. The tall lady laughed in response.

"Of course not. You are quite alive!" A smile spread across the stranger's mouth, showing off large, perfect teeth.

Maila suspected this hero of hers was from Coralen. She never saw a sea person before, but it seemed more logical than an angel of death. She looked over the lady's foreign exterior and imagined if she spent her entire life submersed in water, she might turn a washed-out shade of blue, too. The woman spoke again.

"You've been in and out of sleep for two days now; your body needed time to heal. It's a relief to see you fully awake."

Maila looked around confused. *Two days?*

"Are you from the sea?" Maila asked, recalling her last memory of a stranger pulling her toward the ocean's surface.

"Yes, I am. My name is Kaam Brinicle. What is yours?"

"Maila Celesse. Thank you for saving me. I would have died if it wasn't for you."

"I am relived I found you in time. I thought you were already dead when you dropped into my sea garden, but then you opened your eyes. Blessings from Coral, indeed."

Maila tried to stand up, but her body still ached from the fall.

"This is a terrible mistake. I should not be here."

"Well of course you shouldn't," Kaam said with a laugh. "You belong among the clouds."

"I thought I could do it." Maila's head hung low, heavy with shame. "I thought I could glide, but I failed miserably. I almost killed myself and now I have no idea how I will return home. No one in Ayren knows I'm here."

"Don't you fret," Kaam said, eyes squinting with determination. "I will do all I can to help. I will tell my husband Clydde of this event and I am certain he can convey it to your gliders."

Maila's hopes returned.

"I would be forever grateful."

"Anything for a friend," Kaam's smile sparkled in the sunlight. "I've been out of the water for far too long now. We have a strict oxygen cycle to abide by and these past two days of being on land watching over you is sure to mess up my air allowance. I will return with an update as soon as I can. Stay exactly where you are. This is where help will come."

Without another word Kaam ran down the beach, dove back into the ocean, and disappeared beneath the crashing waves.

Two days passed without sight of her hero from Coralen or any gliders. It was disheartening, but Maila refused to lose hope. To pass the time, she strolled along the shoreline and used a tiny white tree with orange leaves as her landmark to return to the spot where her rescuers would be searching. Taking walks helped and acted as therapy for her injured body, but the days still felt long on this lonely beach.

In addition to the physical injuries, she also suffered from short-term amnesia. She was having trouble remembering the moments leading up to the fall. Her memory was bruised and she couldn't fit the pieces together. All she could recall was that her free fall was the result of her attempt to glide. Something in her gut told her she needed to remember more; that something monumental pushed her to such extremes, but her memory remained blank. She hoped there was a justifiable reason because she was feeling quite foolish and had no idea how she'd rationalize her choice to jump off a cloud when she returned to Ayren.

Maila looked down at her wrist, relieved that her father's sundial watch survived the fall. It no longer worked, but she kept it fastened tight. As she lifted her wrist and tilted it to the side, a few drops of water leaked out of its casing. She placed the watch against her heart and shut her eyes. She was happy to have a piece of him there with her.

She played with the textured ground as she admired the illusion of the setting sun falling into the ocean. She remembered learning that this type of soil was called sand. They didn't teach much at the Learning Center in Ayren, but they did give the children some names to basic components of each Element. Never having seen any photographs or drawings, she was proud to recall their names from the memory of her teacher's verbal descriptions. This beach she sat on, the ocean she fell into, and the jungle that began fifty feet behind her were spared from her short-term amnesia.

She let the sand sift through her fingers and longed for her harp. Playing it always made her feel better. With eyes closed and fingers plucking the salty air, Maila softly sang her father's lullaby:

> Skylight, oh why must night silence your daze?
> Through twilight a glow from the heavens remain.
> If I were the angels I'd sing out your name,
> and promise these eyes shut till you're mine again.
>
> As night comes, I fear you must fallaway, fallaway.
> Into your dream's embrace, fallaway, fallaway.
> Sunrise will find night's end;
> shadows aren't permanent.
> Night only makes sunlight fallaway, fallaway.
>
> So sleep through the stillness the night has devised,
> and by your choice, without force, just close your eyes.
> The dark cannot win if its game you refuse,
> and suddenly night is the darkness you choose.

The clouds beckoned her home. As she repeated the song once more, she watched them shift through the sky and wished she could find her way back to Ayren. She attempted to levitate, but could not find a way into the air from the ground. It didn't work at this altitude.

With each hour that passed, her body ached more ferociously. The fall, plus constant contact with solid ground, was wearing on her tiny, hollow bones. In the sky, taking breaks on their solid, glass-floored homes was always a great release. Down here, the longer she remained grounded the worse she hurt. She didn't know what the correlation was, but the sickness creeping through her spine was worrisome.

Maybe it was similar to how the Coralene had strict schedules for when they could be out of water. Maybe the Ayrenese could only spend small amounts of time out of the sky. She wasn't sure, no one ever tried it before, and being the first test subject was unnerving.

To ease her mind, she hummed the lullaby again. She hoped it would help pass the time, but it didn't. Instead, her thoughts were redirected to her stomach as it sang along in sporadic grumbles. She stopped the song and clutched her aching belly. The Ayrenese didn't eat a lot, just jungle fruit and nuts delivered by birds from Tier, but after spending two days on the beach without food, she could no longer deny her hunger.

Her body was still healing, so she stood up with care before walking along the tree line in search of food. She meandered for half an hour before spotting a bush full of ripe raspberries on the outskirts of the jungle. She fell to her knees in front of it and ate, picking a handful of berries and shoving five into her mouth at a time. She closed her eyes and savored the taste. The juicy sweetness rolled down her throat and settled the rumble in her stomach.

As she ate batch after batch, the sky shifted to a light shade of red. The dark of night approached and the change in atmosphere was tangible. Goosebumps rose on her arms at the sound of a low, rhythmic purr coming from deep in the jungle. The hum continued and additional melodies added on top of the first one in higher pitches.

Maila flew to her feet.

Her instinct was to run, but her body felt compelled to drift into the jungle. The build-up of the melody's trance was overwhelming and left her spellbound. She pinched her arm in order to regain focus and snap out of the jungle's captivating lure. It sent a jolt of pain that awoke her senses and freed her from the rhythm's grip. With her mind back under her own control, she tiptoed in reverse toward the ocean, afraid to take her eyes off the jungle for fear of what might come at her from behind. Before she was out of earshot, a whisper of words accompanied the last notes she heard.

You will be mine, love.

Chapter 10

Zyleh's fingertips were deep into the earth's soil. He did not feel guilty for what he was doing, but supposed he should. The girl from the stars would not appreciate his actions, but he did them with her best interests in mind.

Ayren was no longer safe, not after Maila's illuminated skydive. While she was unconscious, the Ahi learned that the Debauched saw her fall and were determined to leave the smog. They hadn't told the gliders yet, but the sighting was confirmed. Zyleh was positive she'd be safer with him in Tier, so he took matters into his own hands, moving the little white tree with orange leaves, her only landmark, a little further from where she started every time she went for a walk. When the war began, Zyleh was certain that the first attack would be directed toward the sky due to the nature of how their existence was revealed.

He wasn't sure why he took such an interest in the strange girl, he never cared much for the Ayrenese before, but he'd been watching her since he learned she was on their beach and noticed that her aura felt different than what he was used to feeling from the gliders. She was curious and daring, innocent yet brave. He took a step closer to the tree line and examined her from the shadows. He had been studying her and was growing steadily more fascinated. Listening to the songs she sang to herself, and singing his own melodies to help ease her worry. Though he was warned to keep his distance, he refused and found himself becoming enamored. Her long white hair, glowing skin, and bright lavender eyes were captivating, but his attraction was more than physical. He was most impressed by her courage. Not once had she given up hope during her extended solitude on the beach. Not once did she break down or surrender.

If his people were not so adamant about keeping her far away from the heart of Tier, he would have taken over the moment she arrived on the shore with the Coralene woman. But he had to bide his time, had to convince the Sovereigns it was their duty to take her in. Though she may have accidentally initiated the next planetary war, she was still a courageous soul who escaped the confines of a supercilious society.

Still, her choice to glide at night was perplexing—this oversight baffled him. Surely, she was aware of the potential repercussions of such actions. The Debauched were under the Elements control for years, and the fact that they might attack right before they died off naturally was a monumental disaster. This unthinkable turning point in history would be a result of Maila's fall. Though some Tierannites suspected it was an Ayrenese conspiracy to "accidentally" initiate the war they requested previous to her plummet, Zyleh could not agree. After seeing the gliders search frantically for their lost citizen, he knew this was Maila's idea and nobody else's.

Zyleh watched her intently through the trees. Her body glowed in the moonlight, making her shine like a star. Zyleh's heart beat faster; his feelings for her grew at a pace he had not anticipated. From afar, she had seized his heart.

Maila shifted around on the sand. Her dreams were causing discomfort. The moans and tears began slowly, increasing in volume as time passed.

"Darrow," she cried softly, "Darrow!"

Zyleh's heart contracted painfully within his chest. He watched her have this nightmare before, and it bothered him that he could not comfort her.

Maila's nightmares appeared to be increasing. She choked on a sob and abruptly sat upright. She looked around confused and then used her arm to wipe the tears from her face. Gently, she returned to the ground and surrendered back to sleep.

Zyleh would not let her desire for another deter him—they were only dreams after all. She was on his turf, she landed in his world, and his feelings were genuine. His heart could not be swayed and he trusted that Maila would one day come to feel the same.

A warm breeze filtered past her, accompanied by another loud crash. This time it sounded much closer to where she sat. She quickly got to her feet and tiptoed toward the ladder. She could not risk being found by a violent or delusional homeless person who might try to hurt her. Or worse, a member of Mr. Lamorte's police force that scanned the sewers.

Violet reached the ladder when a third enormous bang sounded. She swallowed the saliva gathered in the back of her throat with a gulp, then peered into the distance of the tunnel one last time. All she saw was darkness.

The strange, warm breeze returned, carrying a low growl.

Leave and never return.

Chapter 13

An entire week had passed with no sign of help. No search parties from Ayren, no return visits from the Coralene, and Maila was beginning to feel forgotten. She wondered if her choice to glide on her own made them so mad they decided to leave her grounded. She shook her head; her father and Darrow would never disown her, no matter how angry they were.

She tirelessly tried to recall the events leading up to the fall, but her brain remained blank. Each attempt left her mentally exhausted and she hoped the memories returned soon. She had to piece this puzzle together.

Another night arrived with no progress made. She nuzzled her small body into the sand and tinkered with her father's sundial watch until she slipped into a dream.

• • • • • •

She was hand in hand with Darrow atop a raincloud. The swirling cloud tickled the backs of her arms as it churned. She should have been frightened—the cloud could rip open at any moment, dropping her and Darrow to the earth below—but she felt inexplicably calm. Darrow was a brilliant glider and would never let her fall.

They lay side by side, letting the thunderstorm roar beneath their comfortable quiet. The fun they had together was effortless and she could lay in this spot forever with Darrow's hand in hers. The cloud beneath them trembled lightly and she shut her eyes to concentrate on the audible rainfall below.

Darrow rolled to face Maila and brushed her knotted mess of long white curls away from her face.

"Will you fly for me?"

"You know I can't fly," Maila said uncomfortably. The ease from a moment ago vanished and her guard returned. Years of practice went into suppressing her ability; it was the only way to protect herself from the scrutiny that came with her gift. He was requesting she do the one thing that embarrassed her most. She took a deep breath and reminded herself he wasn't asking out of malice.

"I know you can't *fly*, but you know what I mean. It's been forever since I've asked and you know how amazing I think it is."

Maila hesitated. Darrow wanted her to levitate. He wanted to see her rise into the air and defy the law of gravity. Maila hated doing it. All her life her mother told her she was a freak for having this ability. The Heads of Ayren treated her as an outcast, which caused the rest of the population to do the same. No one else was born with this skill; she was the only anomaly. She was seen as the mutant who could defy the rules of the sky.

"Aria could levitate," Darrow went on. "Her direct descendants could levitate. You should be proud of this gift."

No one, but Maila, could levitate now—after Aria's initial ascent into the sky, this evolutionary gift ceased once the Ayrenese were safely situated amongst the clouds—and the people remained air bound using a combination of air manipulation skills developed through eons of evolving into the element of air. The regular population stayed in the sky via formulated clouds and a strict control over their centers, while the gliders spent years learning how to soar through the winds using their core strength and special breathing techniques.

When Maila was younger, she could not control when she levitated. She would float at random times in random places, and the sight of a little girl levitating petrified the closed-minded individuals of Ayren. They lived in a utopia, a perfect little paradise, and the presence of someone who did not fit into their uniform image reflected poorly upon them all. To them, she was a stain on the pristine Ayrenese image, and that's what they tried to make her believe so she would repress her genetic gift. For a while it worked, she did everything in her power to hide her abilities. It took years of soul searching to finally accept who she was. Her dad, Philo, and eventually Darrow, reminded her daily that her ability was a gift, not a curse. They helped her overcome the debilitating rejection she felt from everyone else. Though she wasn't that scared little girl anymore, she still didn't like to levitate in front of others.

"Please," Darrow continued, "I really think you ought to hone in on your ability and stop treating it like a burden. Somehow, you were given the next evolutionary gene of Ayren. People may be scared of it now because they don't understand, but once their own children are born like this, they'll be running to you for advice. You are a miracle. You are special. You need to believe that too."

"I am an embarrassment. Ask my moma. I'm pretty sure it's the reason she can't love me like she's supposed to."

"She loves you just fine."

He was wrong, but she didn't want to talk about this deep insecurity, so she did not respond to his comment. Instead, she obliged his request.

Without much effort, Maila raised her body into the sky, did a barrel roll over where Darrow lay, lowered her body back onto the cloud, and landed on the other side of him. Darrow grinned ear to ear.

"My gliding would be significantly easier if I could do that."

"That's why I don't understand why you won't teach me how to glide. If I can levitate, doesn't it make sense for me to glide too?" Maila asked, eager to finally convince him.

"They are completely different skills. Gliding is all about controlling the winds with your breathing. You need unbreakable core strength to do it. It is not easy. The winds beneath Ayren are devilish to control, and as we've learned from your many reckless adventures that left you broken and bruised, your bones are more hollow than the rest of ours. As I see it, fragile bones are a small price to pay for the ability to levitate, but I'm afraid the winds we glide in would crack you in two."

"I can exercise to make myself stronger. I just need the gliding lessons."

He sighed and pulled her in closer.

"Just be patient, Maila. In time, it will all fall into place."

The dream shifted drastically and with a blunt transition, she was somewhere new.

Maila sat at the head of the table in the Regal Requirement Room. The Quarterly Head Meeting was about to take place and though she was uninvited, she was ready to speak her mind. As the Heads of Ayren arrived, they received her unwelcome presence with awkward glares and uncomfortable conversation. Years of growth and grace weren't enough to change the way they viewed her. They believed she was a humiliation, a stain on their pristine populace, and that her ability to levitate was unnatural.

Her parents were Head Climithes and controlled the weather—all the rain, lightning, wind, and cloud placement. Throughout Ayrenese history, this was always the most admired job. Being born into a climithe lineage, she found it hard to break free of the expectation that she would be a climithe too.

But she dreamed of being a glider. She wanted to communicate with the other Elements and act as a liaison between Ayren and the rest of the world. The gliders held everything together and made sure all inter-elemental functions were on schedule and working properly. The world would fall apart without them.

Darrow's parents, Drue and Celia Windell, were Head Gliders and sat to her left, and Madivel Marilys, Head of Architecture, and her husband Nolan, Head of the Cloud Solidifiers, sat to her right. The other Head Gliders, Willem and Fiola Havell, sat across from her. These were the only people in the room who valued her worth.

When her parents finally arrived, Philo entered first wearing an enormous smile that brightened his handsome face. He looked around the room at his comrades, but as soon as he saw Maila sitting in the head chair wearing a look of authority, his smile vanished. He stopped abruptly, causing Mira to slam into the back of him.

"What is wrong with you?" she demanded, wearing her usual scowl. She looked up and saw what Philo was staring at. Her face turned murderous as she saw her rebellious daughter sitting in her seat at the table.

The room hushed. Before she lost her nerve, Maila stood up and addressed the group.

"I am here to address an issue I feel is of the utmost importance. My parents continue to ignore my requests, so I have taken it upon myself to initiate a hearing of my own. I apologize for my abrupt style at gaining your attention, but you stopped accepting meeting requests from the public before I was born and I knew no other way." She took a deep breath before continuing, "The system in which you rule Ayren is corrupt."

An audible gasp of horror came from the majority of the group.

"Stop it right now," Mira demanded, but Maila continued.

"You expect the citizens of Ayren to live their lives in darkness, keeping them from knowing all the wonders of the world below. It's not fair and it's not practical. Imagine the increased productivity if we understood the complete purpose of our jobs and what they meant for the greater good of this planet. We deserve to know every factor that plays into the dynamics between us and the other Elements."

"What more do you need to know?" Charlette Kane, Head of Sky Patrol, inquired with a tone of disgust. "We send you all to the Learning Center. Every child is taught the essentials. Gaia, Mother Earth, is our creator and we are here as guardians of the air. Earth is comprised of four parts, four essential elements that keep the world spinning and the inhabitants on it living. Ayren controls the air, the Ahi are in charge of the fire deep within the earth, the Coralene command all bodies of water, and the Tierannites watch over the ground level of the earth where the forests produce oxygen. Together the four Elements work as one, and as long as they remain harmonious, Earth lives on."

"Oh yes, the same paragraph-long lesson that is taught year after year. We all have it memorized. Do you realize how loaded that brief history lesson is? There are thousands of questions that stem from that one lesson and no one is allowed to inquire about them."

"No one seems to care as much as you do," Sicilee Hemsbee, Head of the Solidifiers, stated simply. "We live in a peaceful culture. We have no worries, no strife. Everyone is happy with how we rule, except you." Her tone was condescending and fueled Maila's outrage.

"Say what you want, but you all know that what you are doing is wrong. It should be illegal. You are denying our people the right to their history, denying them their chance to learn about our brethren in the other Elements and form friendships with them. It is foul what you have done to this society and I don't understand how you are still getting away with it. No wonder Aria has abandoned us."

This was the most offensive insult she could deliver and its effect was visible through the outraged expressions the Heads now wore.

"How dare you," Mira's temper roared. "We are not to blame for Aria's absence. What a foul thing to accuse us of. And as I've already told you, once you accept your fate as a climithe, you will learn all the silly answers you seek when you become a Head."

Maila ignored her mother. "That is the crux of the problem; we should know all the information *before* choosing a profession. Imagine how excellently certain individuals might perform if they were given a role they were more suited for—one they got to choose instead of one that was forced upon them."

"Your radical thinking will destroy the harmony we have worked so hard to maintain," Harlin Swen, another male Head of Sky Patrol, shouted.

Mira had enough. She marched across the room, grabbed Maila's arm, and dragged her out of the Regal Requirement Room.

"All I ask is that you open your minds to this request," Maila continued to speak as her mother forced her out of the room. "Please consider it, for everyone's sake."

Mira shoved her through the tinted crystal doors, Philo following close behind, and slammed them shut behind them.

"What is wrong with you? You made us look like fools."

"I did no such thing. I only demanded the respect every citizen of Ayren deserves. If you won't let them have a voice, I will take it upon myself to have a voice for them."

"My dear, why have you done this?" Philo asked in a tender tone. "Now we must initiate damage control for your actions."

"They will question our power and control," Mira seethed. "If we cannot contain our own daughter's outbursts, how will they trust us to contain the entire population? It's bad enough that you're already considered an abomination to who we are as a race, but now you are threatening our lifestyle as well. This will cause mutiny amongst the other Heads." Mira's voice was frantic and cracked as she spoke.

"Calm down dear, they understand that Maila is at a fragile age. Many of them have children of their own."

"I am not a child," Maila demanded. "Stop talking about me like my opinions don't matter. As far as I can tell, I am wiser than the lot of you combined."

"Leave," Mira's voice shook. "Leave now before I disown you."

Maila's eyes grew wide in shock; this was a new threat.

"She does not mean that," Philo scrambled, trying to diffuse the tension. "This will all be settled in a few hours. Just head home, dear, and we can talk about this more rationally later."

"You know," Maila said calmly, "if you had just answered my questions at home this never would have happened."

Mira shot her a look of outrage. "Don't you dare blame your humiliating outbursts on us. I don't know who you think you are, but I have final say over your fate. If you ever dishonor me like this again, you will be sorry." Mira took a deep breath, miraculously regained her composure, and went back into the meeting room.

"Someone is hyper-sensitive today, huh?" Maila said, trying to mask the hurt she felt. Putting on a strong face was a skill she had mastered, but it didn't erase the pain. Feeling unloved by her mother stung deeply.

"What you did was wrong," Philo stated, "but I understand the message you are trying to convey. Unfortunately, that's just the way things are here. There is no changing it. I suggest you find a way to make peace with that." He cradled Maila's head and kissed her forehead. He gave her a reassuring smile and then walked back into the meeting.

Once the doors were shut, Maila crouched to the floor and listened through the cracks. The scene was unruly.

"Your daughter is going to make our job near to impossible," Fantaine Swen, Head of Regulations, shouted. Cavrel Bey nodded, his face lined with worry. They were in charge of population control. They maintained the social peace.

82

"If she only knew how disgusting the Tierannites are," Harlin said under his breath. The majority of the room mumbled in agreement.

"That's not fair," Celia tried to say in defense of the Tierannites, but the other Heads spoke over her. Willem and Fiola Havell shook their heads at the blatant disrespect their colleagues held for the other Elements.

"We are above this nonsense. We are the most important of all the Elements. We decide how we want to interact with those below us," Sicilee added.

"She's right, we cannot let one little girl change how we agreed to run our territory years ago," Lazro Kane, Head of the Solidifiers, interjected. "We've never had a problem before. I see no need to educate the rest of the population because one individual is unhappy with how we operate."

The overall consensus was overwhelmingly against Maila and those who liked her were either not speaking up or being talked over. Philo was angry; even he could only take so much of their arrogant chatter.

"Everyone, silence!" Philo said loudly, causing the boisterous group to quiet down. "There is no need for this to ruin our Quarterly Head meeting. Maila is a young woman with many questions, just as all of you were at that age."

"She is threatening our way of life," Gorlinda Ray, Head of the Lution Sifters insisted. "We have created a utopia in Ayren. We have worked very hard to keep it this way and we do not need an insolent child destroying all we have managed to maintain."

"She is right," Barle Hemsbee, Head of Sky Patrol, added. "The Law of Secrecy is imperative if we wish to keep the calm and serene nature of Ayren."

"No need to remind us of this," Mira said, her composure returned. "Maila will not ruin anything. I will see to it that she drops this quest for knowledge."

"I just hope you can all find empathy within your hearts to see the struggle Maila has been through," Philo said again, demanding authority. "She is my daughter and I will not have her name thrown about behind our backs. It was bad enough you made her feel unwelcome as a child because of something she could not control. I will not tolerate the discrimination any longer. She may be wrong in how she went about her actions today, but she still deserves our respect. It is not too hard to see why she has the questions she does."

The room was now silent. Mira gave Philo a disgusted look but the rest of the Heads made no noise. Philo was a man of great esteem and they did not want to risk their own reputations or standings within the community by tarnishing their relationship with him. In response to their clear understanding, Philo continued, "Fantastic. Now let's move on with our day then, shall we?"

Maila stormed away from the meeting room and exited the Grand Hall. Furious, she mounted her personal cloud and sped off in anger. From what she gathered, they were withholding dangerous information and what seemed logical to her was lost upon them: there was no room for secrets in a world that relied on honesty to survive. She arrived at Darrow's house and was greeted with a warm hug. Locked in his comforting embrace, the world dissolved around them.

• • • • • •

Maila awoke with abrupt clarity. It wasn't a dream, it was her subconscious reminding her of all she forgot. Moments prior to her fall were coming back. With a smile she fell back asleep, hoping to retrieve more memories in her dreams.

Chapter 14

The gliders weren't giving up. Zyleh couldn't believe they continued to look for Maila so tirelessly. Every morning and afternoon, there they were. Scouring the part of the beach where the Coralene said she would be waiting. He moved her landmark, so Maila was never there, but if he did not get her into the jungle soon, they would find her. He could not let her go back into the sky now, it was too dangerous. The attack on Ayren was imminent and he would never forgive himself if he put her in harm's way.

He needed to meet her. Perhaps convincing her to stay wouldn't be so hard if she felt for him what he felt for her. If their connection was true, she'd forget her quest to go home in order to be with him. He could not force her into the jungle, that would only anger her, but he certainly needed these searches to cease.

Right on time, Darrow and Fallon soared over the side of a distant cloud. Zyleh waited as they made their way toward him.

As they reached the beach, they did not notice Zyleh sitting on top of a nearby tree. He observed them comb the area frantically, including the shadows cast onto the sand near the tree line. As Darrow stayed within his course of manic tunnel vision, Fallon looked up and saw Zyleh watching them. Leaving his brother behind, he made his way over to the treetops.

"Zyleh," he said as he glided higher in order to converse at eye-level, "I'm sure you are already aware, but we are looking for the girl who fell from our sky. She is a dear family friend and we need to get her home. The Coralene said she'd be in this exact spot below, but we've come back multiple times with no luck. Are we looking in the wrong place?" Fallon's voice was tired but full of sincere distress.

"No, you are looking in the right place. This is where she was."

"Was?" Fallon's eyes grew wide, "What does that mean?"

Swallowing his guilt, Zyleh made the choice to lie.

"She died."

Fallon's eyes welled with tears. He looked back at his brother who still circled the beach, hopelessly looking for the girl he loved.

Fallon's voice was now a whisper, "How?"

"My guess is gravity. It dragged her thousands of feet into the ocean, then placed continued force upon her frail bones as she remained landlocked for days. I don't think her body could handle it."

"When did she die?"

"Last night," Zyleh said, reminding himself his intentions behind this lie were noble.

"But we've been to this exact spot numerous times before last night to retrieve her!" His frustration caused the tears he was

87

holding back to spill. "We were just here yesterday looking for her, but she was nowhere in sight. This makes no sense. If she was here, we should have seen her." Fallon buried his face in his hands, trying to determine what they did wrong.

Before Zyleh could make up another lie to keep the charade going, Darrow approached. He glided next to his brother, eyes wide with dread as he examined the state of Fallon's emotions.

"What's going on?" he asked, catching Fallon off guard. His older brother immediately collected himself and wiped the tears from his eyes. At the sight of Darrow, his demeanor transformed. He no longer showed any weakness and he reclaimed his strength, for Darrow's sake.

"She's dead," Fallon answered, trying to sound sturdy, but the strain in his voice revealed his pain.

The world fell away. Darrow was no longer with them. He slowly sank downward, eyes glazed over and expression blank. Fallon grabbed his arm and pulled him back up. Darrow shook his head as his brother's words repeated over in his head.

She's dead. She's dead. She's dead.

As their meaning sunk in, his face contorted with wretched suffering. Grief fell from his eyes.

"No." His body convulsed and he muttered the word repeatedly until he became so overwhelmed it came out as a shout. "NO!"

Fallon grabbed his brother and buried him in a tight embrace. He continued to shake in his arms as the sobs controlled his movements.

"It's all my fault," Darrow proclaimed into his brother's shoulder. Tears soaked Fallon's clothes.

Fallon flashed Zyleh a somber look, nostrils flared and lips pursed as he tried to hold back his own sorrow.

Immediately, Zyleh felt a surge of guilt and questioned if he had done the right thing. He had not expected his lie to cause such strife. Then he reminded himself that Ayren was doomed, that these two brothers could be dead in a few days, and that he did not want Maila there with them when it happened. He reminded himself that it was her best interest he had in mind, not theirs.

"I'm very sorry," Zyleh said, surprised that he felt bad about the pain he inflicted upon the gliders. It was raw and it was genuine. In their own, different ways, they both really loved her.

"I need to get him home," Fallon said to Zyleh as Darrow remained in the sky by his brother's secure hug. He took his hand and ascended, towing Darrow along.

Darrow's limp body trailed behind, no effort put forth toward gliding, and his tears fell like rain.

While Zyleh watched them depart, his conscience was conflicted about his actions. If everything went as he suspected it would, Maila would survive because of this lie. She would see the reasoning behind his actions and forgive him. At least he hoped she would.

Doubt filled his heart. Perhaps she'd never be able to forgive such a lie. Zyleh scrambled, unsure how to proceed. He was confident that his intentions were genuine and that there was no alternative course that would have achieved the same results. If he showed the gliders where she was, she would have returned home. If he talked it out with Maila and warned her that returning home might kill her, he suspected she would go back anyway. This was the only way. She might not like it, but it was for her benefit and one day she'd understand. He'd have to keep this interaction a secret until the consequences of her fall unraveled. When the Debauched came for them, she'd understand why he lied. Until then, he couldn't let her find out about this small deception that altered the course of her life.

Chapter 15

Maila contemplated her stranded predicament and decided she needed to prove from afar how eager she was to remedy her reckless mistake. It was time to take matters into her own hands.

Staring at the jungle's trees and the clouds that floated above them, she got an idea. Perhaps the beach was too large for the gliders to see her as they soared through the sky. Perhaps she was too small and they too high. If she could manage it, the treetops were the perfect meeting point between land and air. She needed to get on their level. After thinking it over many times, Maila decided her only option was to enter the jungle and climb a tree high enough for the gliders to see her.

She ignored the fear the jungle instilled in her over the past few days—her situation had grown dire and she needed to help the gliders find her. The spellbinding melodies were not enough to scare her away. She needed a climbable tree and she planned on finding one. Maila took a deep breath and entered the jungle.

One step at a time, she found herself traveling farther into this new scenery. Miles of lush forestry surrounded her and in every direction she looked, she was blinded by endless green foliage. As she moved further from the beach, the sound of crashing waves was replaced by the steady hum of insects and animals. The noise filled her entire awareness. It took everything in her power to stay focused.

She scanned the surrounding trees, looking for one that was tall and covered in thick branches. After venturing several feet away from the beach, she came across the perfect tree. Without hesitation, she ascended.

The first few branches were easy; they started low to the ground and gave her a safe trajectory upward. She made it halfway up the tree before she found that the branches at this height were scarce and her route more treacherous.

After a few rough jumps and painful body slams against thick tree branches, Maila found herself five branches higher than she had been. Her body ached ferociously but she couldn't give up. Once she got to the top she would allow herself time to rest and recuperate.

She cleared her mind and like the previous jumps, Maila whispered a countdown.

"Three... Two..."

"Where are you going?"

A man's voice came from a branch directly above Maila. It startled her so severely, she lost her balance and began to slip. The stranger jumped down to the branch she was falling from and caught her by her ankle.

"Who are you?" she screamed in shock as the stranger lifted her little body up by her ankle. The bottom of her white satin dress covered her face. Maila tried to fix it, but gravity won. Her mood instantly shifted from determined to furious.

"I am Zyleh, your savior," he stated cockily, watching her fight with her dress. "I already know who you are, Maila of Ayren."

She was incredibly confused and had an immediate distaste for this arrogant stranger.

"Put me down," she snapped at him while hanging upside-down in his grasp.

Zyleh's face flickered with a momentary twitch of annoyance before he gently placed her down.

"You should be kinder when someone saves your life."

"The only reason I fell was because you startled me. So if anything, you should be apologizing to me." Her cheeks were colored a menacing shade of red, a resulting combination of anger and embarrassment. Begrudgingly, he complied.

"I am sorry to have startled you. Let's start over. I am Zyleh León of Tier. Leader of the Carriers."

Still annoyed, Maila tried to readjust her first impression of him—he could be her ticket to the top of this tree.

He towered over her, just like Kaam of Coralen. The shadows of the falling day articulated his intense bone structure. He had high cheekbones covered in sun-kissed skin and a thin chin that amplified his youth. Most stunning were his eyes. Their intense green pigment glowed so bright, she felt the color must be a trick of the light; eyes weren't meant to shine like that. Maila silently accepted his apology and straightened her dress so it lay properly once more.

"I've been watching over you," he spoke again. "I saw your free fall. I saw Kaam save you and watch over you while you were unconscious. I looked after you as you waited for rescue from the gliders. I'm glad you're here now though. You will be safer with me in Tier. I can help you here."

"Great. Can you take me to the top of this tree? I believe the gliders will be able to find me there and I'll have a better chance to get home."

Zyleh's eyes flashed dark momentarily before he spoke again.

"No, you misunderstood me. You *can't* go home now. You are safer with me in *Tier*. You must stay here to remain safe.

"What are you talking about?" Her heartbeat quickened and she wondered if her negative first impression of him was correct.

"Ayren is no longer safe. I can only protect you if you stay here with me."

"Actually, I don't need your protection since there's nothing to protect me from," she scoffed. "I think I'll be on my way now."

"Do you really think your little skydive had no consequences? We are all in danger now." Zyleh was baffled, but Maila looked at him with outrage.

"I don't know what game you're playing but I don't appreciate it. I've been away from home for far too long and I don't like strangers threatening the safety of my loved ones. Or making up lies to convince me to stay with them. I've made enough of a mess and I don't intend to make it worse by getting lost in the jungle with *you*. I have to get home to Ayren and fix what I've done."

"First of all, I am not some creep trying to lure you into a trap. I do care about you, for some unknown reason I am drawn to protect you, but my intentions are not bad. I know you are safer in Tier than you could ever be in Ayren right now. And secondly, you cannot fix what you've done. Maybe you can apologize, but the damage is done. The outcome of your free fall is irreversible."

"You are infuriating. I have plenty of time to correct what I've done and when they see the efforts I've made to return, they'll understand it was all an accident. If you will not help me get up this tree then I do not need you."

Zyleh was confused, but his anger now surpassed his bewilderment over her nonsensical thought process.

"I understand that you must feel like the biggest idiot on the planet for falling off a cloud, at night no less, but don't take it out on me. I only came by to offer help."

"I didn't fall off a cloud," she retorted defiantly, "and if you were offering help then you'd be assisting me to the top of this tree."

"You're making a mistake," he warned.

Maila groaned with aggravation and chose to end their conversation. She turned around and continued her tedious climb up the tree.

Despite this terrible first encounter, Zyleh chose to follow Maila, branch by branch up the tree. It took her hours to overcome every minor obstacle, while Zyleh finished each in a matter of seconds. The ease with which he moved only fueled her frustration, but she didn't ask for help and he didn't offer it; he just stayed close behind.

Four branches and four exhausting jumps later, Maila's body finally started to give out. She looked up to see her destination still lay far out of reach and that the sky was beginning to darken. She turned her head to look at Zyleh who was leaning against the tree trunk picking at his fingernails. When he realized she wasn't getting up to struggle with the next jump, he snapped out of his boredom and gave her a cocky smile.

Maila snapped her head to look away, angry that her obvious surrender gave him pleasure.

"Can I count on you to pause your little quest for a bit?" he asked. She responded with an insolent glare, so he continued, "I

have some matters to attend to, but I'll be back before nightfall."
He gave her a curious look, one that was filled with intrigue, then
darted through the trees and disappeared.

Maila marveled at his speed and immediately felt conflicted
about this new acquaintance. He seemed to care about her well-
being, but how was she supposed to tolerate his company when
he had such an insufferable attitude? He was making up lies to get
her to stay with him, which was unsettling. Ayren was not in
danger because there was nothing to be in danger from. She did
not know Zyleh's motives for lying but it did not make her
inclined to trust him.

Maila tried not to worry too much about it. Soon she would be
home and this terrible mess she created would be resolved.

Chapter 16

Violet's food supplies were running low, which meant it was time for a trip to the market—her least favorite place.

She grabbed her satchel, pulled her blue knit hat over her knotty blonde hair, and began her trek. The market was five miles into the ghetto. It was a long walk, but it was better than living too close. The two places you never wanted to spend a lot of time were the market during the day and the city square at night; both were cesspools for disease and murder.

Violet kept her head down as she walked. Face scanners were placed everywhere—on door tops, windowsills, street lamps, trashcans—and she hated that someone in a room somewhere could track her walking down the street. She traced her hand over the metal sphere lodged beneath the scar on her forearm, wishing it wasn't there.

A gust of crude exhaust fumes smacked her in the face.

It must be Wednesday, she thought as a parade of huge, oil-black dump trucks drove by.

The only vehicles seen on a regular basis were the few lavish hover coupes of the wealthy, the armored tanks carrying Mr. Lamorte's militia, and the dump trucks that collected dead bodies off the sides of the roads once a week. Steel-rigged sky drones were a constant sight as they provided aerial surveillance of the population for Mr. Lamorte.

She walked close to the buildings while the large vehicles drove by, and as the last truck passed, it hit a puddle and splashed filthy sludge into her eyes.

Violet gasped in shocked disgust and tried to get the grime off her face with her sleeve. As she blindly walked forward, frantically rubbing her burning eyes, she tripped and fell over something sprawled across the sidewalk.

Vision blurry, but restored, Violet's heart dropped—it was a dead girl, just about her age. Repulsed and rattled, a surge of reality struck.

That could be me, she thought.

"Get out of the way!" one of the body collectors shouted as he jumped off the side of the truck and pushed the dead girl onto the truck's lowered platform. He pushed a red button, which raised the platform and launched the dead girl into the deep collection bed of the truck.

Violet shook her head, trying to get rid of the awful feeling that filled her heart. Dead bodies lined the street gutters every day; she tried to remind herself that this wasn't unusual. She just never saw one that looked so much like her.

The thought of dying terrified her. She feared strangers would trash her body once she was no longer alive to protect it. When people were really desperate, not only would they steal the clothes and belongings off the dead, but also parts of their body. They would cut the hair and pull out the teeth, then try to trade them for food at the market. Certain dark merchants would accept this type of payment and make wigs, dentures, or jewelry out of the pieces. The thought of it was enough to scare Violet into wishing for an immortal life of misery over a death riddled by disgrace.

The market came into sight. After tripping over the corpse, it was a relief to be surrounded by life, even if it was at her least favorite place.

"Little lady," a crackled voice called to Violet from a trinket stand to her left. It was Barnibus Blightly, a wrinkled old man who knew her parents. He always checked in on her when she made trips to the market.

"Hi, Barnibus." Violet walked over to him with confidence. She had to act tough in the market. If anyone thought she was vulnerable, they would try to rob her. "How's the trinket business treatin' ya?"

"Oh, you know, it's just trinkets," he smiled, "but people always find reasons to buy stupid junk they don't need, so I'm survivin'." His raspy voice sounded broken but he continued on. "I don't see ya much at the market, little lady, what've you been feeding yourself?"

"Regular food," she answered bluntly. "I just eat what I get sparingly. It saves me from having to make too many trips to this dump bucket."

He laughed. "You think this place is a dump? I'm sorry ya feel that way. I sell treasures and this place holds magic if you're lookin' in the right places."

"If by magic you mean murder and disease, then sure. This place is real magical."

Barnibus clicked his tongue behind his teeth and scrunched his face in annoyance.

"You're too cynical for someone your age. Live to be sixty and then come talk to me."

"I fear you'll be dead by then," she said with an honest edge. He laughed and tilted his head awkwardly to the side.

"You'd be right."

Violet smiled and picked up a flower made out of metal screws and flattened foil.

"You fancy that?" he asked.

"No, it's hideous."

"How's about you take it as a gift from me?" She looked at him with suspicion. "Don't look at me like I'm one of those murderers you was talkin' about. I've known ya since you was born. I don't get to help you much and you never come round anymore, so take it. Maybe you can trade it. Or maybe it'd just be nice to have a gift from a friend."

Violet considered this and looked up at him with a thankful smile. He nodded in acknowledgement.

"You should use that smile more often girl. Might get ya some more people who'd be inclined to offer ya kindness."

"Maybe." She shrugged her shoulders and started to walk away.

"You better be visiting me again soon, Miss," he called out after her. "You don't need to be goin' at life all alone."

She raised her right arm above her head with the ugly tin flower in hand and waved without looking back.

Violet continued walking through the market and pulled her scarf up to cover her mouth. She spotted the bread cart and walked toward it. To her dismay, Mrs. Yakley was running the cart this afternoon, which meant she'd probably be going home empty-handed.

"Hi, Mrs. Yakley," Violet said as sweetly as possible, "how are you today?"

"What can I help ya with, girl?"

"Well, I was wondering if I could have some bread. I don't have anything to trade at the moment but I could assist in some chores."

Mrs. Yakley shot her a suspicious look.

"Does Frank give you free bread when I'm not around?"

Violet adamantly shook her head no, even though it was a lie.

"He always makes me wash the cart or take the trash to the corner bins, or something."

Mrs. Yakley didn't believe her.

"If you're lyin' to me girl, I'll make sure you never get a loaf of bread from us again, you hear me?"

Violet silently nodded her head. It was a risk she didn't mind taking—she doubted Mr. Yakley had the guts to admit he'd been giving away free food.

"Alright, then. I have a chore I need done. I need this basket of bread delivered to the wig maker three blocks down that way. Make sure he gives you the package he owes me. He may be reluctant to hand it over, so be forceful." She thrust a heavy basket into Violet's arms. "If even one bite is missing out of this basket before Mr. Brand gets it, I will hunt you down and make you pay for it twice over, do you understand me?"

"Very much so," Violet answered. "How much bread will I be getting for this task?"

"Don't get sassy with me. Do what I've asked and that will be decided once you return."

Violet turned and began her trip to the wig maker's store. She hated being treated in such a demeaning manor, but if that's what it took to survive, then she had to swallow her pride.

She got to the wig maker's store relatively fast. His name was Carlstadt Brand and he was a sinister fellow. He took the bread without saying a word and then stared her down for a few unnerving moments.

Violet wasn't frightened, only uncomfortable. She wanted to get out of his malodorous store without delay. The stench of rotted flesh filled the entire space. She eyed him suspiciously, aware that he was one of the shifty merchants that made dirty trades with people who robbed the dead.

"Mrs. Yakley said there was something you were to give me in exchange for the bread."

Carlstadt grunted and slowly turned toward the dusty bookshelf he stood in front of. He took out a book, opened it, and removed a gun that was hidden in its cutout pages. Violet felt even more uneasy now. Carlstadt moved incredibly slow and took forever to wrap the pistol in a small cardboard box. Once finished, he handed it to Violet and stared at her with empty eyes.

Their fingers met as the box was transferred and Violet shivered at his touch. His skin was clammy and cold; similar to the skin of the dead girl she tripped over earlier that day. Violet quickly pulled the box from Carlstadt's grasp and left the store in a hurry.

She wanted to be done with this. She wanted to get this package to Mrs. Yakley, get her bread, and go back to her sewer where it was safe, where she would be left alone and far away from people like him.

She was two blocks from the bread cart when a group of young adults turned a corner and started heading toward her. The sight of them put a sinking feeling in her stomach.

Without looking up, she crossed the street, hoping she was far enough away that they would not notice. But as soon as she did, the tallest of the guys laughed, made a comment she couldn't hear, and then crossed the street as well.

Violet paused in her stride as the group continued to approach. They sneered at her, maintaining eye contact. She put her head down, pulled the package with the gun close to her chest, and began picking at the tape Carlstadt applied.

"Little pretty," the tall guy called out to her. They were on the same block now. In this moment, she found herself wishing to be back in the middle of the crowded market. "I see your purse, doll face. How about you lemme take a look inside?"

Violet hugged her satchel close to her body but the young man was already upon her. He had brownish red hair and freckles that blended in with small outbreaks of scabs across his face. He had the disease.

He slapped her hard across the face and she fell to her knees, dropping the package with the gun. The young man grabbed her satchel so hard it broke the shoulder strap.

"What's inside, Drake?" the girl of the group said, twitching with excitement. Violet didn't know much about drugs but the way her assailants moved and spoke, she assumed they were on some.

"Get off me, Trixie" Drake said, pushing the girl away from him by the face. Her makeup was smeared and she had ripped tights on underneath her plaid skirt. She backed away but didn't stop twitching and looking over his shoulder frantically. He opened Violet's satchel and snorted in disgust.

"An empty jar of jam?" He pulled it out of the bag and threw it at Violet's head. It hit her in the eye with force then shattered as it hit the sidewalk. He continued to look in the bag, but all it contained was the tin flower from Barnibus. The other young men chimed in.

"Drake, is there any money?"

"Any jewelry?"

They both had long, dirty brown hair and looked like they might be brothers.

"Not a goddamn thing." Drake spit on the ground then threw the satchel back at Violet, who was on her knees holding her bloody eye. "I guess you're only good for one thing then."

He put his hands on his belt buckle and slowly unfastened it as he walked toward her. The other two guys stood close behind him and Trixie giggled nervously.

Violet knew what this guy had in mind and couldn't believe a young woman stood by, cheering it on. It was a sad world they lived in and Violet was certain there'd be a special seat for this girl in Hell.

Violet scrambled for the package she had dropped and ripped it open. Drake had knocked her to the ground and hovered inches above her, but she grabbed the gun out of the box before he could react and placed the barrel directly between his eyes. He went cross-eyed for a moment in shock, trying to figure out what just happened.

"I will blow your brains out, you piece of scum," Violet spat in a low growl. She cocked the hammer and stared at Drake intensely. She had no idea if the gun was loaded but it didn't matter; she had the low-life quivering with fear.

Trixie collapsed to the ground, hugging her knees and trembling. She was saying inaudible things under her breath and tweaking out. The two guys shook off their initial confusion and started walking closer to Violet in Drake's defense.

"If you take another step I will kill him." Violet pushed the gun harder against Drake's forehead, pushing him upward and off her.

"Stop moving, you idiots," he screamed at his friends, his voice cracking under the stress. "What do you want?" he said to Violet. "You can have anything, just don't kill me."

Violet's nostrils flared as she considered how she should handle this. She never had the upper hand before; usually she just outran her aggressors.

"How about you tell me what you've got and then I'll decide if it's enough to save your life?" she said in a low voice. She was petrified and doing everything in her power to keep her hand from shaking.

"Give her what you got, boys. Do it now," Drake demanded.

"Why should we?" one of the brothers said defiantly.

"Are you kidding me? Everything you have is because of me, you idiot. Give it to her, or I'll beat you lifeless once this is over."

The brother didn't argue again. He placed his knapsack by Violet's feet and his brother did the same.

"The girl too," Violet demanded.

"Trixie, stop freaking out and give her your bag."

"But my inhaler –" Trixie whimpered, determined not to give her narcotics away. "I need it for the pain. It took me a whole year to get that supply of methadelic cartridges."

"Give it up. We'll find more." Drake demanded.

Trixie hesitated a moment before crawling on her hands and knees toward Violet and placing her small purse next to the two knapsacks. Drake took off his own backpack and dropped it next to the others.

"You've got ten seconds to get the hell away from me before I start shooting." Violet tapped the gun against Drake's forehead. "You better run."

He turned and sprinted with Trixie and the brothers following suit.

Once they were out of sight, Violet let go of the gun and dropped to her knees. She wanted nothing more than to hide in a corner and sob, but she took a deep breath and fought the feeling.

Violet contemplated the power of the gun. She wished she could throw it in the garbage so no one could have it, but she had to get it to Mrs. Yakley. Or maybe she could keep it. Part of her wanted to, even if it stayed unloaded, just so she could use it if she was ever put in a situation like that again.

A stream of blood trickled down her face from the corner of her right eye. She could feel its warmth roll down her cheek. The vision out of it blurred as it continued to swell. She shoved her satchel and the small purse into one of the bigger backpacks and found a way to get all the bags onto her back before heading to the alley she called home. She placed the gun back into the cardboard box and began walking. Maybe one day she would return the gun to Mrs. Yakley, but not now.

She took the long way and walked down and around a few buildings to avoid passing the bread cart. She emerged back into the market from behind Barnibus's cart. Violet hoped he wouldn't see her, but the moment she thought this was the exact moment he turned around and gasped at the sight of her.

"Holy cow. What in the hell happened to you?" he shouted in his hoarse voice.

Violet hushed him. "Stop drawing attention to me. I'm fine."

"You are *not* fine. Let me buy you some ointment," Barnibus demanded. Violet shook her head in refusal but he ignored her. "The right side of your face looks like someone took a meat cleaver to it."

He whistled at the lady who sold medicine two carts away, caught her attention, then waved her over. She rolled her eyes and reluctantly trudged through the crowd. She was probably only thirty years old but her face was worn, like she'd witnessed far too many tragedies in one short lifetime.

"What is it, Barney?" she scowled at him, but when she caught sight of Violet she gasped. "Oh my. What happened to this girl? Have you taken her to the Health Hub?"

"We both know how useless the Health Hubs are. How much you selling ointment and medicine for, Lucy?"

"Ointment is a dollar fifty. Medicine, for a wound like that, runs about five bucks." Lucy's tone softened considerably after realizing she was there to help a young girl and not to chat with Barnibus.

"Can you work me a deal?"

"You pay for the medicine and I'll give you the ointment free."

Without skipping a beat, he took a tin can off a shelf on his cart, pulled out a five-dollar bill, and gave it to her. Lucy left without saying a word.

"She's got a daughter who's a bit younger than you. I knew she'd help ya out."

Violet nodded, trying to ignore the ferocious sting resonating from her eye. When Lucy came back, her daughter was by her side.

"You see, Penny?" Lucy said fiercely to her daughter. "This is why you don't wander away from me. Do you want to end up like this?"

"No, mamma," Penny said. She was about seven or eight years old with long curly brown hair that fell in front of her face. She pushed it behind her ear with her tiny hand and looked at Violet's wound with sympathy.

"Okay then," Lucy said, happy she taught her daughter a valuable life lesson. She opened up the ointment, smeared it around Violet's swollen eye, and explained its usage. "You take the medicine once at night and once in the morning for two weeks. It should prevent infection. The ointment should ease the pain and help heal your wound with minimal scarring." Lucy shook her head as she held back tears. "Who did this to you?"

"I don't want to talk about it," Violet mumbled.

Lucy gave her a disapproving look but didn't push it any further. "Where are you living? You should stay with me until this is healed."

"Thank you, ma'am, but I have a home, outside the ghetto. I will be alright."

Again, Lucy looked down at Violet sternly. She did not believe her. "Well, if this isn't any better after the medicine runs out, you come to me and we will work a deal to get you more, you hear me?

"Yes, thank you." Violet very much appreciated Lucy's kindness. It was nice to be treated with a mother's care again.

"Alright." She closed the lid of the ointment and handed it to Violet, along with the medicine. "Take care of yourself and see me in two weeks if it's not healing." Lucy gave Violet one more serious look before grabbing Penny's hand and walking back toward her cart.

"Thanks, Barnibus," Violet patted him on the shoulder. "You're starting to put me in debt here. First the flower, now the medicine. Not sure when or if I'll ever be able to pay you back."

"Never said you had to."

She smiled and thanked him again, then continued walking toward her home, toward her alley where she could collect her thoughts and try not to think about how badly things would have gone without the gun.

After back-to-back encounters with devious individuals, it was a relief to leave the market with a reminder that there were still good people out there. Kindness was not dead, and neither was human decency.

Chapter 17

Relina approached Zyleh through the trees. Her footsteps made no sound as she ran along tree limbs to catch up to him.

She called out his name but he did not wait.

"Zyleh, don't be infantile," she said as she caught up to his slow and sluggish pace. "Let me walk with you."

Zyleh grunted loudly, uninterested in her company.

"What's wrong with you?" she asked, insulted. Zyleh was her cousin and closest friend. He could be trying at times, but she loved him dearly.

"I'm aggravated."

"Why? Are you still wasting hours every day watching that Ayrenese girl on the beach? Haven't they come to get her yet?"

"No, they haven't found her."

"How is that possible? Clydde of Coralen told them *exactly* where she was. There is no time for this. We need to get her home before the attacks begin." Relina shook her head, completely bewildered and annoyed, then she looked at him again because he continued to sulk. "I don't understand your fascination with her. You need to stop tormenting yourself. The Sovereigns are never going to give you authorization to bring her into Tier. She initiated a planetary war. Her actions are unforgivable." Relina huffed, "She can't enter Tier."

"She already has." Zyleh was monotone. He could not understand why Maila had been so cold to him. She should have felt their connection right away like he had.

"What do you mean she already has? She is in the jungle now?"

"I'm pretty sure that's what I meant."

Relina was annoyed, but ready to resolve this once and for all. "The gliders should be down for our meeting soon. We can deliver her to them." She looked at the sun to grasp the time. "Where is she?"

"No." Color rushed back into his face, shading his narrow cheeks bright red. "We cannot let her go back there. She will die in Ayren. That is where the Debauched will strike first."

"It is not our choice to make. I can't even imagine how sick she must be. The air in Tier isn't the same as what she's used to in Ayren."

"If she's sick, I will heal her."

"The problem lies in her genetic makeup and what her body needs to survive. There's nothing you can do to alter that. It's probably killing her."

"She isn't dying. She seemed perfectly fine when I was with her."

"*You* brought her into the jungle?"

"No," he insisted, angry with himself for this slight slip-up.

"Are you lying to me?"

"No. All I did was move the tree she was using as a landmark while she went on walks. I just kept her from being found. I never *made* her enter Tier."

"The gliders were looking for her," she groaned. "The Sovereigns denied your request to bring her to the Heart, despite your numerous petitions. They specifically told you not to meddle in this affair and to leave the girl alone." She examined Zyleh's indifferent expression. "It was a delicate situation and now you've made it worse."

"I am saving her life."

"I refuse to be involved. The Sovereigns are going to be furious with you. My advice is to own up at our meeting and let the gliders take her home." He remained expressionless. She shook her head, "Sometimes you're too stubborn for your own good. I hope you've thought this through." Relina walked ahead of him now.

Zyleh let the subject drop. She didn't need to know any more than he already gave away. They headed toward the treetops where they typically met with the gliders of Ayren.

"Will Lux or Eluno be there?" he asked.

"They can't. They are helping set up watch teams to secure the borders. Phelix should be joining us."

He groaned in response. Zyleh loved his younger brother, but his admiration and eagerness to please tended to grate on his nerves.

"Speak of the devil," he muttered under his breath as Phelix emerged from the trees with a huge smile on his skinny face. This was his first meeting with the gliders.

"Hello, brother," he said as he approached. "Hey, cuz," he said to Relina.

"Don't say anything during the meeting," Zyleh answered him back.

"Gee, that's real nice of you. I haven't seen you in days and that's the first thing you say to me?" Phelix said, looking up at his brother. He wasn't at his full height yet and was still too skinny. No amount of food could keep his bones cushioned at the rate his growth spurt accelerated.

"Stop."

Phelix directed his attention to Relina.

"Since Zyleh refuses to speak to me kindly, I will ask you instead. Has he stopped obsessing over the Ayrenese girl yet?"

"No, I don't believe he has," she laughed at Phelix's playfulness. "It's a disease, you know, to want what you can't have. For your sake, I hope it's not genetic."

"I hope so too. It seems quite miserable."

"Alright, enough," Zyleh interjected. He then pointed at the sky above the meeting place where four shapes hovered. "They are already here."

"What do I say?" Phelix asked, panicked that he had not been prepped.

"Nothing!" Zyleh repeated once more. His brother let out a small huff and resigned to silence.

The three Tierannites emerged from the depths of the trees and Relina raised her long thin arm in a wave to greet the gliders. Jorban and Kalline were there, along with two of the Ayrenese leaders they hadn't seen in a while, Willem and Fiola. They hovered above the treetops as Relina spoke.

"Welcome, friends," she began. "We already spoke with you about the incident from your sky. Today's meeting is to inform you of the repercussions of that night. We found out a few days ago that the illuminated free fall was seen by the Debauched. This will affect us all gravely. We still don't understand how or why this happened, but it is too late to fix the past. What we must deal with now is the future." Kalline sniffled back tears as Relina spoke and Fiola put an arm around her shoulder. Relina scanned their faces for the first time and noticed they all looked distraught.

"We do apologize," Willem said. "We don't know how or why it happened either, but we know how unacceptable the situation is."

"What she has done is unforgivable. Thousands will likely die because of her," Relina stated with conviction.

"It wasn't her fault," Kalline said with tears in her eyes. "The blame should be placed on me, my fellow gliders, and the Heads of Ayren. She begged us for the truth but the Heads refused her and we were too worried about breaking the law to oblige her request. She had no idea what her actions could cause. She just wanted knowledge and being a glider was the only way to get it, so she tried to teach herself." Kalline's face pleaded for forgiveness on Maila's behalf, "She didn't know the rules of the night."

"She doesn't know why no one glides at night?" Relina asked.

Willem took a long pause and a look of shame crossed his face.

"No one in Ayren, except the Heads and gliders, know about the Debauched," he responded.

"Why not? They are one of the reasons we exist!" Phelix blurted out.

Willem sighed, "It was why we came to you about eliminating the Debauched. Initiating a war was the only way to force the Heads in Ayren to abolish the Law of Secrecy. If all the other Elements had agreed with the gliders, Ayren would have needed to fall in line too. We couldn't have fought without our people knowing what they were up against." Willem shook his head, "It was a roundabout way, but it was our last plausible solution. The

Heads have been resolute on maintaining their carefully crafted utopia for centuries. The Law of Secrecy is what enabled our ignorant bliss all these years and no amount of reasoning by the gliders has been able to persuade them to abolish this unwise law. The threat of war destroying their perfect peace was the only sure way to get them to finally concede."

"She really has no idea," Zyleh mumbled to himself, but no one heard him.

"We've been trying to find a way to fix the current system in Ayren," Jorban explained, then thought of his best friend who was mourning back home. "Darrow was so hopeful. He was so determined to change everything for her. There was nothing he wanted more than to tell her the truth about everything. He waited years to share that moment with her."

Zyleh saw where this conversation was going and he needed it to stop before his deception was revealed.

"To this day, no one knows about the Debauched?"

"No," Fiola answered, "Once the dust of this latest tragedy settles, we will remind the Heads of the impending threat and why the law must be abolished."

"It has to happen today," Relina said appalled; they've had plenty of time to cope with the disaster of Maila's fall. She redirected everyone to the real problem at hand. "They are going to attack. There is no longer any speculation. The Ahi spies have confirmed that the President of Debauched North America, Mr. Lamorte, saw Maila fall and intends to do everything in his power to find the 'fallen star', as they describe her. They still don't know we exist, but they are going to try to leave their confines. The Ahi also stated that in the past few hundred years, while the Debauched have devolved intellectually, technologically, and medically, they've maintained their defenses. Even improved them in some cases. They have upgraded their fleets of boats and planes, making them strong enough to pass through the smog and wretched seas that kept them land-bound all this time. They haven't tried in over a thousand years, but after seeing Maila fall, it's inevitable their attempts will start again." Relina shook her head. "If your people don't know they exist, then it is time for you to return home and tell them the news. Ayren needs to be prepared to fight. Since the light they saw came from the sky, we assume you will be the first to have contact with them." She paused, looking at Fiola's horrified expression. "We wanted you to be warned."

Fiola was speechless, her eyes wide in fear. Willem put an arm around his wife and pulled her in close.

"We understand. Thank you for telling us. We have quite a lot of work ahead of us. I think we need to be on our way now."

121

"Yes, we don't know when they will strike, possibly a day or two from now. Maybe a week. But anything we can do to help, we will," Relina added, showing compassion for their dire situation.

The four gliders nodded in appreciation, then took off into the sunset toward the clouds of Ayren. They didn't have much time to educate the population, build up their borders, and learn how to protect themselves, so they needed to get to work right away.

"Go tell the Grand Paipa about the Ayrenese Law of Secrecy. Their ignorance impacts us as well." Relina instructed Phelix. He ran off without a word. Despite this shocking news, the meeting went as well as it could have, but she felt like there was something she forgot to do.

She looked at Zyleh and remembered what it was.

"Maila," she said aloud. She meant to offer her retrieval so they could take her home. While her forgetting was understandable, the fact that they never asked seemed odd.

"What about her?"

"They never even asked about her. You'd think they would realize with the beach being part of our land we would know where she was. They defended her thoroughly but never even asked for our help in retrieving her, whether it be from the beach or the jungle."

"She's safer here anyway."

Relina did not hear him. She thought back on the conversation with the gliders: their demeanor, their words, their implications.

"They spoke of her like she was already dead."

Zyleh sighed, too tired to lie again.

"That's because they think she is."

Chapter 18

Maila massaged her sore feet as the sky turned black. She had blisters forming and her tender skin threatened to rip open. The constant contact with the rough tree bark was proving too much. She hoped a good night's sleep would be enough time to heal the soles of her feet because she needed to continue her climb in the morning. Before she could fall asleep, Zyleh reappeared with three bananas and a huge grapefruit. Maila's stomach growled as he sat down across from her, straddling the tree branch so they faced each other. He placed the fruit between them.

"You looked hungry."

Despite her doubts about him, she could not resist an ample meal. It would replenish the energy she expended while climbing and give her the fuel she needed for tomorrow. She grabbed a banana and devoured it.

"Sorry if I was a jerk earlier. I'm known to have a quick temper," Zyleh said, scanning her expression to determine if she was angry with him. He hoped to ease the mood and gain her trust. He understood now why she thought she could still fix everything, why she thought she could remedy the outcome of her illuminated free fall. The ignorance the Heads of Ayren forced upon their people was unfair and dangerous, and Zyleh hoped that maybe he could shed some light on the situation for her.

"It's fine," she responded. "Thank you for bringing me food. This is a hearty meal." She mumbled through a mouthful of banana. "We don't eat a lot in Ayren, just small bits of whatever fruits and nuts you guys send to us."

"Wait until you try what we *really* eat. We can't send you sky dwellers the good stuff with those little birds."

"You need to stop implying that I am staying here with you. You will not deter me from getting home."

Zyleh sighed but said nothing. After she finished eating, he helped her get positioned on the tree to fall asleep. With her back against his chest, she was safe. He would not let her fall again.

The next morning, Maila woke at the first sign of dawn. Zyleh was still snoring, so instead of waking him up, she continued her climb without him. Two jumps in, Zyleh was up and following her. It wasn't long before he offered to carry her.

"It pains me to watch you leap and then body slam into each new branch. If you promise to give me a chance, I'll carry you to the top."

She looked at him through suspicious eyes.

"A chance at what?" She wasn't going to let him trick her with clever wording.

"To prove I'm not such a bad guy."

Maila let out a sigh. She never intended to make him feel like she was judging him, or unwilling to be friends. The whole point of learning to glide in the first place was to see the world and make genuine connections with the other Elements. The jarring reality of her free fall made her lose sight of the purpose behind its attempt. She wanted to get home but reminded herself that there was no need to be close-minded to the new experiences she encountered along the way.

"Okay, deal. Let's go."

Zyleh helped her onto his back, then raced up the tree with incredible velocity. Maila shut her eyes, afraid she might fall, and when she opened them again they were already above the canopy. He placed her down and they found a solid spot to sit. The view was amazing: endless ocean in front of her, green tree tops for miles all around, and Ayren above, glowing with sunlight.

"Thank you."

"Of course."

For the rest of the day, they sat atop the trees. Mostly remaining quiet, sometimes entertaining light chatter. Maila was too focused on watching the clouds to engage in any real conversation and Zyleh respected her silence.

At 2 p.m. he left to attend to Tier related business below. She sat alone with quiet hope for hours; the sky mimicked her stillness. There was no sign of glider activity. Not one of them came down from the clouds to look for her. As far as Maila could discern, the search for her never even began. She never saw them while she was on the beach, and now that she was high enough with a better view, she was certain they hadn't left the clouds once that day. She lost track of the amount of days that passed since she fell, but was certain it was over a week since she was home in Ayren. A whole week, and no one, not even Darrow, saw her mistake as the innocent blunder it was. Was life easier without her? For Mira it certainly was, but Darrow, Philo, Bellaine, and Madivel; those with whom the love and respect was reciprocal? If they weren't fighting for her retrieval, then no one was.

Zyleh returned at dusk. The sky was a shade of burnt orange and its reflection on the ocean's surface created the illusion it was engulfed in flames. Maila wished it was. She wanted any thing to feel as devastated as she did. As she let the imagery of the ocean being swallowed by an inferno take over, Zyleh sat down beside her.

"They aren't coming down for me, are they?"

"I am the wrong person to answer that question."

"I can't believe they just left me here. It's been over a week and they haven't come at all. The Coralene must have told them my location by now, it makes no sense."

"I don't know what to say."

"They are rightfully furious with me. I get that. But to leave me here, abandoned?" She shook her head, "They never even gave me a chance to apologize."

"I'm sure it's just a miscommunication," Zyleh said, feeling terrible that he was the true cause of her suffering. "One day it will be explained and it won't hurt so bad."

"I know I messed up. I know my actions probably hurt them more than they hurt me. It was selfish and stupid and I could have died, but they must know that becoming grounded was an accident."

"I'm sure they do." All Zyleh could do was appease her in an attempt to ease her distress.

"I just wanted the chance to make it right. I can fix what I've done." She swallowed a lump in her throat and held back tears. "They are going to forget about me."

"There is a lot I need to tell you." Maybe if he explained the war to Maila, she would stop beating herself up. She'd attribute their lack of a search with being preoccupied by an impending war.

This statement caught her attention, "Like what?"

"Let's head back beneath the safety of the treetops."

She obliged, letting him carry her to a thick branch below. He disappeared for a few minutes, then returned with an armful of fruit. She gladly took an orange and let the monotonous action of peeling the rind ease her worries. She had to get past this, she needed to cope. If she broke down now, she'd never get home. She needed to relocate her thoughts onto something less daunting than being abandoned.

"What does that marking on your leg mean?" she said, pointing to the tattoo on his left calf muscle

He looked down at his leg hanging over the tree branch, then swung it up so the sole of his foot rested upon the bark and the tattoo was more visible. He was happy to be off the previous topic and onto a safer one. He didn't want to tell her about the Debauched until she was settled at the Heart. There, he could control the situation better.

"Well, in Tier, we all do body markings. For males, the age of 13 marks the beginning of manhood. At this age, every boy gets their first marking. It is different for every family, but the boy will get the same marking his father got when he was 13." Zyleh pointed to the thick zigzag band wrapped around his calf muscle.

"How old are you now?" Maila asked

"23," he answered, still looking down at his tattoo, then continued explaining how the marking worked, "This is the same marking that my father, my younger brother Phelix, and all my male cousins and uncles have. It is the tattoo my own sons will get if I ever have any." Then Zyleh pointed to the two dashed lines wrapped around his calf above and below the zigzag band.

"These two lines indicate achievements I have made. The top one is for my discovery of a medicinal root when I was 16. It helped the Sovereigns create a medicine that cured a highly contagious virus that hit our people. The bottom one indicates my completion of our training and education groups, and my step into the role of teacher. It's not a daily thing, but after I completed my own education, they put me in charge of the martial arts and fight group."

Maila was fascinated. The questions she was asking were finally being answered. This new acquaintance was often disagreeable, but if he would engage her in meaningful conversation, then he might prove good company until she figured everything out.

"What types of lessons are each Tierannite given?"

"Well, there are groups for History, Current Affairs, Medicine, Battle Training, Herbal Chemistry, Music, Literature, Animal Communication, and the most important one is Earth Values. Every Tierannite is born with the ability to control the plants and the earth around us. That group helps our youth tune into their skills and perfect them. After each lesson is complete, they give you a bead." Zyleh pointed to a bead that was wrapped up in one of his braids. She then noticed all the other colorful beads hidden within his hair. "Some people make bracelets or necklaces. I put mine in my hair, as do some others. The only course you never really complete is Current Affairs, and that's because the information is constantly changing."

"That's amazing." Maila tried to hide her excitement, she did not want to seem ignorant, but she couldn't hide her thrill. "In Ayren, there is only one Learning Center, and Ayrenese children only go there from ages 10 to 13 before they start training in the field that eventually turns into their career. It's not nearly as interesting as your system."

"Sounds minimal."

"It is. What is literature?"

"Books, reading, and writing. We teach our youth to do it all in English and Spanish."

"And what about Animal Affairs?"

"That group teaches the youth how to speak with the animals. Again, that ability is in our blood, but it takes more effort and practice to awaken that skill. Kids also learn the anatomy and purpose for every animal in the jungle. It is important to understand the cycle of life and how every species is important to the balance."

"I think I'd love the Music group most."

"That is a fun one. Each child finds their musical calling in that class, whether it is a specific instrument or their singing voice. We have the gift of music in our genes. It is powerful within each of us. In many cases, it is how we summon our strength to communicate with the animals and move the earth beneath us. It is also how we express that which we cannot find words for, feelings that are too deep to surface verbally or hurt too much to say." Maila could understand this. It was often the way she felt when playing her harp. "We can also use our rhythms and melodies to evoke feelings or emotions in other people. I won't lie to you, I did it a few times when you were alone on the beach. You seemed scared, so I tried to help."

"Ah ha! So *that's* why I always got a creepy feeling from this jungle. Pretty weird, but thanks I guess."

"It was meant with good intentions," Zyleh said in defense.

"Was that your voice I heard among the hums and rhythms too?"

"You heard a voice?" Zyleh's eyes were wide in amazement.

"Yes." She wasn't sure why this was such a spectacular question. "Wasn't I supposed to?"

"No, I only sent you melodic rhythms, but anything is possible." Zyleh's heart jumped, but he hid his excitement. Hearing the words beneath a melody that is not intended to have lyrics can only happen between two kindred-souls, and it often only happened between soul mates. Knowing that the connection he felt with her was real validated everything he had done up to this point: all the doubt, the guilt, the lies. Eventually, once these days had passed, she'd feel and accept their bond too. He left this piece of the answer out. The timing was terrible and he did not want to scare her.

Maila moved on with their previous discussion.

"What does the top marking on your calf mean?"

She pointed and touched the band of small circles placed above the other three.

"I got this one when I became Leader of the Carriers. My job is to act as a liaison between all the Elements. Similar to the gliders."

"Do you have any other markings?" she asked with a mouth full of fruit.

"Nope, just these. Some Tierannites make markings on themselves as art in addition to achievements, but I think I'll only be adding more as I gain new milestones in my life."

This seemed logical to her. Then she wondered how long he would have to make these new milestones; he was only 23 and if the Tierannites lived as long as the Ayrenese, he could be covered head to toe in tattoos one day. "How long do people in Tier live?"

"Four hundred years, give or take."

"Us too."

"Yeah, all the Elements have evolved with lifespans that range that long."

Maila nodded, appreciating this small fact he gave her. She never knew that before.

"I am stuffed," she said as she finished the last bite of fruit.

"I'd imagine so, you barely even chewed," he mocked. "Don't worry, I'll get you more tomorrow."

"Okay, thanks," she said with hesitance. She didn't want to start depending on him for too much. One way or another, she'd find her way home.

"It's getting dark out. We should get some rest."

"Wait." Maila remembered what Zyleh said earlier, "What was it you had to tell me?"

"I'll tell you in the morning," he said, hoping he could stall until he brought her to the Heart. "For now we should sleep."

She didn't argue. She was willing to let him tell her as much as he wanted before she returned to Ayren where it was unlikely she'd ever get this kind of information again. She shuffled to turn her back toward Zyleh, then leaned onto him. He held her tight as he rested his bare back against the tree trunk.

"Sleep well, Maila," he whispered.

Maila stared at the moon through the trees as her drowsiness took over. She could feel his heart beating beneath her and after a few minutes, his heavy breathing added to it. She focused on the rhythm of his heart and soon, forgot about everything.

She could feel his body's tempo latch onto her mind and relax her into sleep. She momentarily wondered if this was one of the melodies he'd used to calm her down while she was alone on the beach, but then scoffed at the illogical thought. He was asleep and

Maila didn't know of any living being that could control the rate of its own heartbeat. It was irrational, so she let this thought slip out of her exhausted mind.

Just as she was about to ease into a dream, she heard him hum a soft melody, one she recognized.

If I were the angels I'd call out your name//and promise these eyes shut till you're mine again.

The words hidden beneath the notes were magically revealed, but before she could address what she just heard, her body surrendered to sleep.

Chapter 19

• • • • • •

"Maila," Darrow whispered into her ear as she slept atop her cloud. "Are you alright?"

"Yes," she mumbled in response, still half asleep. "I thought I fell asleep next to Madivel's cottage"

"You did. I passed Madivel's house on my way home and relieved her of her watch. She was keeping an eye on you, but I could tell she was tired. Why were you sleeping out in the open?"

"My parents are mad at me and I didn't feel like going home." She yawned and rolled over to face him. She opened her eyes halfway and was greeted with his silver-blue gaze shining back at her. His white, straight locks were tangled and dirty from a long day of gliding.

"You know," she said, realizing how exposed they were, "people may get the wrong idea." Her eyes widened and she gave him a little smirk.

"And what exactly is the wrong idea?" he asked playfully as he bear-hugged her and buried his face into her long, wavy hair. Her exhaustion was much stronger than her instinct to battle his affection, so she did not protest his playful embrace. She yawned again.

"Won't you sleep inside? Fallon's room is empty. He and Lillaine are living together now."

"No, no," she smiled, "I'm comfy here, but thank you." She stretched, casually easing out of his embrace. "Come find me in the morning when you wake."

"I don't like you sleeping out here alone."

"I do it all the time."

"I don't care that you do it all the time, I don't like it." His face was serious and protective. They weren't dating so it didn't feel right to let him sleep next to her. He was very clear that he wanted to be in a relationship with her, but she couldn't let it go there. They'd been friends forever and the suggestion of romance was uneasy territory. She had trouble believing someone could love her when her own mother struggled to do so. Though he tried to prove his affection was solid and sincere, she had trouble trusting that it wouldn't fade over time. Having it, then losing it, would hurt more than this temporary tension. Plus, experiencing love was at the bottom of her list of priorities; discovering the secrets of the world ranked at the top.

She stared back at him, trying to mimic his grave expression but failing miserably. A grin crept through her forced frown.

"This isn't funny," he insisted.

"Of course not." She tried to put on a stern face. "Sleeping alone on a cloud should never be taken lightly."

"You're mocking me."

"Maybe a little," she confessed with a smile.

"You're lucky, Mai Love," he retorted as she rolled her eyes, "that your stunning good looks hypnotize me into doing your bidding." Maila laughing at his goofy attempt to appease her.

"Dar, if that were true, we both know I'd be out gliding with you by now."

He sighed, then wrapped his arms around her again and was silent for a little.

"Could I at least stay with you until you fall asleep?" he asked, choosing not to acknowledge her comment about gliding. She conceded and nuzzled herself into his arms. She had no energy to start an argument they'd already had a million times before and his body warmth comforted her on this chilly night. Her head rested upon his chest and the calm rhythm of his heartbeat soothed her to sleep.

The scenery changed without warning.

Maila stood at the edge of her home cloud, staring up at the monstrous glass castle her parents built. It was far too big for four people; three, once Bellaine married Roxil and moved out.

The cool glass kissed her bare feet as she entered. The sound of her mother's shrill voice echoed down the stairs and sent chills down Maila's spine. She dragged her feet away from her mother's voice, turned the foyer corner, and was greeted unexpectedly by the sight of her twin sister, all alone, in her wedding dress. Utterly consumed with every angle of her image in the mirror, she didn't notice Maila standing there.

"You look beautiful, Bell."

Bellaine turned in surprise to see Maila, and a huge, radiant smile appeared on her face. It was the same enchanting smile their father wore.

"You think so?" she asked without expecting an answer. "I just worry that it's too flashy with so many beads and crystals." She turned back to the mirror.

"No, really," Maila insisted, "you look perfect."

Although she and her sister were twins, they were not identical. Bellaine was much daintier and delicate than Maila. She also had their mother's sharp chin, whereas Maila's face was more heart-shaped, like their father's. Unlike Maila's constant set of long knots, Bellaine always wore her long white curls pulled back into a neat bun or a long ponytail, and she carried herself with graceful rigidity.

When they were younger, Maila would get into trouble for catching birds and locking them in her room while Bellaine was winning awards at the Learning Center. But their uncanny differences didn't prevent them from having a close bond.

"Bellaine, are you coming? I have a few diamond hair clips for you to choose between." Mira shouted down the stairs.

"Yes, moma." She turned to her sister. "Let's go. We need to decide what you will be wearing too."

"No, I can't," Maila said, "Moma is probably still furious with me. I don't want to ruin your dress fitting with our tension."

"What happened now?"

"I invited myself into the Quarterly Head meeting. Moma and popa never give me any answers, so I thought if I pleaded my case, somebody else might."

Bellaine rolled her eyes. "You need to be patient and appreciate the fact that you live on Earth's first utopia."

"It's not a utopia if the happiness of the people is built on lies."

Bellaine huffed. "I'm sure whatever extra knowledge exists out there would play no part in fluctuating our happiness. I don't care what the Ahi do for fun, or how the Coralene sleep beneath the sea, or if the Tierannites eat dirt for dinner. That's the type of stuff you're fighting and making a scene in front of everyone to learn about. Is it really that important?"

"If that's all there was to it, they'd have told me by now. And besides, I *want* to know the small details. The little things are the most important."

"I think you're going to be terribly disappointed one day when you realize you made such a big stink over nothing." She paused, then shook her head with a smile. "But there's no denying your spirit. It's beautiful, and I love you for that."

"I wish moma saw it that way."

"I think you just confuse her. She doesn't understand you or why you feel the way you do."

"She wants me to be something I can't be," Maila said bleakly.

"She wants you to be a climithe."

"No." Maila turned and looked at her perfectly composed twin. "She wants me to be you."

"That isn't true," her sister rushed to her side and placed her arms around her. "It isn't."

"Tell me with a straight face that she doesn't favor you over me."

Bellaine's face went slack because Maila was right. Mira never tried to hide the favoritism.

"She doesn't want you to be me, she just wants you to be more like her." She brushed a few loose strands of hair out of Maila's face.

"It's because of my ability to levitate. She can't forgive me for the embarrassment I caused when I was young and couldn't control it."

Bellaine pulled her sister into a tight hug.

"I think you are perfect just the way you are. One day, everyone else will see that too."

Bellaine disappeared and Maila was transported to a memory she had with her father.

"I think it's time I told you the truth," Philo said to Maila as they sat on the front porch of their glass castle.

"The truth about what?"

"You."

Beads of sweat gathered on Philo's forehead as he struggled with the words he wanted to say. Maila was petrified and unsure what to expect.

"After your wild attempt to retrieve answers at our meeting yesterday, I realized that it was time to ease some of your curiosities. You are right, it isn't fair that you are kept in the dark about certain things and I hope what I am about to tell you will help ease your mind a little bit. It won't answer your questions about the world, but it will clarify the strained relationship you have with your mother." With his cotton sleeve he dabbed the sweat off his forehead. "This may not be the best timing, with Bellaine's wedding approaching, but I cannot continue to keep it from you. Seeing you suffer breaks my heart." He took a deep breath, "What I am about to tell you must remain a secret after you're told. Do you understand?" He looked at her with earnest concern, making sure she understood the importance of this agreement.

142

"I can keep a secret."

He swallowed hard and shifted his gaze to his fidgety, interlaced fingers.

"Mira is not your moma." Maila's vision splintered as she tried to grasp what he said. "I'm so sorry. I should have told you years ago, but Mira did not want the scrutiny of our society upon her shoulders. She wanted to pretend you were hers in order to maintain her reputation."

"Mira is not my moma? I have no relation to her?"

"No."

"Are you my popa?"

"Yes, yes, very much so." Philo gave her a comforting smile.

"How?"

Another deep breath and he dove into the details. "I was in love with someone else before I married Mira. Her name was Clara." He leaned back to look through a window and check that no one was listening. "But I was a climithe and she was a glider, so it could never work. Times were different then and arranged marriages were strictly enforced. I had no choice but to end things with Clara and marry Mira, who I grew to love as well. I was faced with difficult choices as a young man and I did the best I could. It was hard to abandon my love for Clara and enter into a marriage with someone I barely knew, but it was how things worked. I was expected to obey my parent's wishes and follow the rules of our culture. Perhaps, looking back on it now, I see things differently, but there is nothing I can do to change the past. I am grateful every day that I got two beautiful daughters out of it."

Maila looked at him skeptically. She didn't like the idea of Philo abandoning her real mother. He could see the internal struggle play out in her expression and continued.

"I can see that you think I should've chosen Clara, but at that time I did not believe I had any other choice. I also had no clue Clara was already pregnant with my child. I thought I was doing the right thing by everyone. I thought I was making my family happy and keeping Clara safe from a world where she would never be accepted. About six months into my marriage, when Mira was already pregnant with Bellaine, I learned Clara was also pregnant with my child. She was due any day when she finally told me. Mira was furious and demanded I not be part of this child's life. She insisted that Clara's unborn child would not be recognized as mine. She was petrified of the judgment that would be passed over her from the rest of our society if they learned of this scandalous situation we were in. By the time Clara swallowed her pride and told me of our child, I barely had time to process what was happening before she went into labor and had you."

Maila's eyes filled with tears: the shock, resentment, sorrow, and relief hit her all at once. She lived her whole life thinking her mother never loved her, when in fact her real mother was a complete stranger to her.

"I have never heard of a Clara," Maila said, holding back tears. "Where is she and why did I wind up with you instead of her? At least with her I would have been wanted."

A pained grimace crossed Philo's face at her harsh comment, but he accepted her anger and explained.

"Because she died giving birth to you." His tone was hushed and she saw now that he still grieved for her.

A lump caught in Maila's throat at this piece of the story. Her real mother was dead and a devastation she never knew she was capable of feeling for a total stranger coursed through her body. She never got to know her real mother and never would. She would never know what a mother's love felt like.

"I always intended to keep you in my life, even if Clara survived the childbirth. That was one thing I would not let Mira control. Every day I see you it keeps Clara alive in my heart." A tear rolled down his cheek. "You look just like her."

Maila nodded but her mind was elsewhere.

"So this is why Mira hates me?"

"She doesn't hate you, she hates everything you remind her of. I think when she sees you, she sees Clara and it reminds her that I loved another woman before her. It reminds her that another woman almost took her place. Every time she sees you, I think she wonders if I still love Clara more than I love her. It's a very unfair position I put Mira in and seeing you every day keeps that old pain alive."

"But none of that is my fault, or Clara's fault. The only person to blame is you. Her resentment about the situation should land on you, not me."

"I know, but if you put yourself in her shoes you may see why it's so hard for her. It was embarrassing and made her feel like a fool. Irrational behavior is the curse of love. As it was, this situation broke her heart, causing all rationality to shatter along with it."

"If she knew she could never love me properly then you should have let me live with Clara's family. I'm sure they would have been happy to have me."

"Yes, but I knew I would love you with all my heart too. And I have, every day since I first saw you. Although I understand why Mira feels how she does, I never imagined she would harbor such resentment against a child. I insisted we take you into our family and once Mira finally conceded, she laid out the conditions to ensure no one would know you weren't hers. The doctors told everyone you died along with Clara and we kept you hidden until Bellaine was born. We told all of Ayren that Mira had twins. This prevented anyone from questioning where you came from."

Another devastating blow. The bond she had with her twin sister was the only love she believed to be unbreakable, because by science, they were bound. It felt so authentic. What had she been feeling toward her half-sister all this time? All the love and connections in her life were based off a lie. She felt nauseous. She couldn't believe they went to such lengths to put on this charade. "Does Bellaine know about this? And what about Clara's parents? Didn't you think they would want to have their granddaughter in their lives?"

"I know. A day doesn't go by that I don't wish her family knew. I am sure one day they will, but at the time, keeping it a secret was the only way I could get Mira to agree to let me take you."

"How could you let her do this? This lie affects so many people more severely than the truth would have ever hurt her reputation. I think our hearts outrank her vanity."

"It broke her heart, too. I did not want to hurt her any further, so I tried to be as gentle with her during the situation as I could without letting you go." He paused, forming his thoughts. "I would not abandon you. Any compromises I had to make in order to keep you seemed reasonable at the time."

Maila shut her eyes and sighed. She was beyond overwhelmed; she felt dead inside. Different emotions tugged her in opposing directions: she wanted to scream, to cry, to disappear.

"My whole life is a lie," she confessed. "I feel so betrayed and unsettled about everything I have ever known."

"Please forgive me."

"Stop."

Every word he said hurt.

"I need to be alone for a while." She stood up and walked toward the edge of her home cloud.

It felt like she was walking to the edge of the world. Part of her wanted to fall right off, straight into the nothingness below. Every inch of her ached. Tears filled her eyes again as she walked away from her father. She still loved him, but felt wildly betrayed.

Once on her personal cloud, the only possible destination in her current state was Darrow's house. The day's wind whipped at her face and dried her tears as she sped forward. She promised her father she wouldn't tell anyone, but she needed help deciphering the overflow of emotions. Right now, she was submerged, and if someone didn't pull her to the surface she would drown.

Her memory skipped forward a few hours, landing her in Darrow's bedroom.

"It was a really bad day," Darrow explained with annoyance. He tried to mask his mood, but failed. She put her own worries aside to find out what was bothering him.

"Are you okay?"

He looked defeated, but didn't say anything. He plopped onto the floor next to her and maneuvered them to the ground.

The floor was cool on Maila's back. Darrow buried his face into the side of her neck, wishing he could hide from the world there. She stroked his arm softly.

"You're my everything," he confessed.

"Thanks," Maila responded awkwardly. The comment, and its sincerity, caught her off guard.

"Thanks?" He pulled away from her.

"I'm sorry, I wasn't expecting that."

"Well, a normal person would have said something nice back."

"I thought I did?"

He groaned. "I'm too tired to explain something so obvious."

"You do seem tired," she was desperate to change the topic, "were you up late last night?"

"No. Just a very, very bad afternoon," he replied with clipped curtness.

"You know you can talk to me about anything, right?"

At this, his eyes turned a shade of fatal blue and he took his arm off her.

"You know I can't." He stood up and moved away from her.

"What do you mean? Of course you can. You can always confide in me."

"Stop it! You always try to make me tell you things you know damn well I'd get in trouble for. I am working so hard to bring radical changes to Ayren and my main motivation is you. But I can't have you pestering me all the time for information or for gliding lessons. I know it's unfair that you are being kept in the dark, but it's also unfair that you keep putting me in this position."

"I can keep a secret," she began, but he ignored her.

"I am extremely tired, in more ways than one. I am swamped with the burden of these secrets and having to keep them from you. But I am also feeling torn that I am doing all this work for a girl who will never love me back. What we have is so obvious and so good, yet you fight it constantly. I have a hard time believing you are as oblivious as you act and it torments me because I cannot figure out how you feel. It doesn't make me very inclined to want to tell you all the things you beg of me every day." Maila was speechless, but Darrow continued on, "How can you not see what we have together? It's insulting Maila."

"I just don't want to ruin our friendship. You are my only friend and I can't lose you. In a few months, or maybe years from now, there's a good chance you won't love me anymore. I'd rather have you as my friend forever than as a significant other temporarily."

"That is a terribly negative way to think of it."

"Well, it's what I know. Unconditional love is rare. These things don't always last." She thought of her father and Clara. "And hearts get broken. I can't handle making my life any more complicated than it already is. I need to sort out the truth about the world before I can start figuring out the truth within my heart."

"So you don't feel the chemistry between us? Can you honestly say you don't feel what I feel?" His eyes searched for a sign of hope from Maila.

"I don't know, maybe," she stammered, afraid to admit she did. "I'm not sure I know what love feels like."

"Don't you want to find out?"

"I can't." The words escaped as a sob. The tears came out of nowhere as she imagined herself finally allowing the love she felt for Darrow to surface. Accompanying this was the fear that he would eventually realize he never loved her as much as he thought he did. An image of Mira popped into her head and the feeling of being unlovable returned. She tried to remind herself that Mira wasn't her real mother and that she couldn't count that love as something to put much stock in, but it was still too soon to put all these newly discovered pieces in their right places.

Darrow's face went slack. His heart contracted within his chest from Maila's continued lack of commitment.

"I guess I shouldn't have expected anything more from you. You were raised to be oblivious. Until things change, I can't tell you anything."

"You say you love me and that we should be together, but you can't even trust me with the truth. It's a glaring red flag that maybe you don't really care for me how you think you do. If you did, you would trust me enough to know me better. How can we be together if you can't even tell me about a simple glide you did this afternoon? That's all I was asking about in the first place. You just blew it out of proportion." Her fists became clenched. "I am sick and tired of everyone keeping secrets from me."

"I can't tell you what you want to know because of the way things are. That part is completely out of my hands. And I question whether I even want to confide in you because you refuse to acknowledge the feelings you have for me that you so adamantly suppress. If I knew how you felt about me and I felt more secure about where this friendship was heading, I'd feel more comfortable sharing more than I do. But you are not a glider and you insist we are just friends. So I'm sorry, but you don't fall into a category that entitles you to this knowledge from me. It doesn't work that way." He paused, noticing Maila's shocked expression, "I can't trust you because you don't trust me. If you did, you'd trust me with your heart, which you clearly don't."

He was hurt, but Maila didn't care because she was hurt too. And he was wrong. She didn't trust him with her emotions because of her own complicated family life, not because of anything he did. But she was feeling too fragile to go into that with him now. It was why she initially went to his house but she no longer felt comfortable confiding in him.

"And as for gliding, I flat out refuse to teach you that." Darrow's initial gusto returned and his eyes lit up with obstinate certainty. "You are a climithe, whether you want to accept it or not. You are genius at it. I never want to put you in danger, and teaching you how to glide would do just that."

"Well," Maila said quietly, her voice shook with aggravation, "maybe if someone, *anyone*, would tell me the simple answers to the simple questions I ask, which, by the way, I have every right to know, then maybe I wouldn't be so hell-bent on gliding."

"I'm not debating this with you any longer. All I do is try to protect you. I try to keep you safe and you fight me every inch of the way."

"I'm not a child. There is nothing to *protect* me from. They're just facts and I will find a way to get the answers I seek. I promise you that."

Her vague threat sent Darrow over the edge. His blue eyes flickered black for a second and a deep fury emerged that Maila had never seen in him before.

"I swear to the Heavens, Maila, I would never forgive you if you did something stupid because you haven't gotten your way. I have worked far too hard trying to make things right for you to go and ruin everything."

"I don't need your forgiveness. I am entitled to my history, all of it, and I'm not afraid to go it alone."

"You will have to go it alone because I am done with this same, strenuous argument we've had a hundred times before that neither of us will ever win." He threw his hands up into his hair and let out a loud, annoyed groan.

"Fine. I operate better alone anyhow," Maila said defiantly.

"I have never, in my entire life, had someone frustrate me as deeply as you do. I can't even stand to look at you right now."

"Then don't." Her face tightened. "Maybe you should just forget you ever knew me."

"I wish I could," he hollered. If his words could cut through skin, she'd be sliced in two. Realizing the harshness of his statement, Darrow clammed up, ashamed at the hurtful words that just came from his mouth. He remained silent as he looked at her. Neither of them could believe it went this far. His cold front quickly dissolved as the severity of his words replayed in his head. If he could rewind and take them back, he would, but the damage was done.

Maila could see nothing but blurred shapes through the tears that welled in her eyes, and she supposed it was fitting. She was now realizing that maybe she never saw anything clearly. And though Darrow's face showed remorse, there must have been some truth to his words. Rejection was nothing new, but feeling it from Darrow *was*, and it hurt deeper than any pain she ever experienced.

"It wasn't supposed to go this way," she stammered. She was lost in her mind and the words coming out now were mere reflections of the dark swirls that engulfed her heart. "I came to talk, to feel better. I needed you," she said as she blindly backed her way toward his open bedroom window, "but I see now you were the worst thing for me." And she left without looking back.

• • • • • •

The choking sensation of remembering this pain startled Maila awake. All her memories flooded back and she couldn't process the varying emotions all at once. She caught her breath and leaned back against Zyleh's chest with eyes wide open, afraid if she closed them, more horrific moments might return.

Chapter 20

Morning snuck up on Lillaine when the sound of birds chirping reverberated like an alarm through her window. They were always noisy, but on this morning their pretty songs had morphed into desperate cries. She rubbed her eyes and rolled over to face Fallon. His face was lined with worry as he slept.

Yesterday was the memorial for Maila. Regular Ayrenese funerals consisted of a ceremonial burning of the body and a final farewell where the ashes were released into the night wind. Since they had no body to burn, Maila's memorial was anything but regular.

It was chaos. The whole ordeal was encased in anger and fighting, which overshadowed the true purpose of the event. Philo wanted to wait until they could retrieve the body but Mira fought him, saying it was cruel to force the public into continued mourning. They had an epic quarrel on the steps of the Axis for all to see. Deplorable words littered with accusations were exchanged, leaving everyone in awkward shock.

Fallon and Celia glided down to the shore in hopes of retrieving the body, but the Tierannite who told them of her death also told them the body was gone and buried according to the Tierannite custom.

They returned with the tragic news, casting a greater shadow over the state of Ayren. Philo, Darrow, and Bellaine were devastated, inconsolable with grief. While a traditional Tierannite ceremony was respectable, it stole their moment to remember Maila in the fashion they were accustomed. Mira rushed the procession, unconcerned that others already buried the body. Some found her haste distasteful. Lillaine did not appreciate the way in which she rushed her own daughter's funeral, but she tried not to judge. Everyone was entitled to deal with grief in their own way.

The ceremony was glorious despite the shameful fighting and lack of a body. Beautiful words were spoken in her honor, they burned a portrait of her in lieu of her body, and the ashes danced through the starry sky. A shooting star passed by as the cinders floated away, which was a spectacular sight amidst the tension and discomfort that still plagued the crowd. The whole occasion was peculiar, but lovely. Lillaine thought it was fitting since those were the words she'd have used to describe Maila.

It was a new day and Lillaine hoped everyone could move forward and be happy while keeping Maila in their hearts. She rested her chin on her fiancé's shoulder, studying his handsome face. Eyes closed, he looked like an angel in slumber. Fallon felt her gaze on him and slowly awoke. Light blue radiance shone from his eyes as he looked over at her with a smile.

"You're up early," he said with a yawn. His eyes still bloodshot from the tears shed yesterday.

"Do you hear the birds?" she asked. Her steady sapphire gaze remained serious as he listened.

"Yes. I do hear them." He sat up and furrowed his brow. "It doesn't sound right." He turned his head toward the eastern wall to look out into the sky where the bird's cries came from. Through the tinted crystal wall he saw nothing. He got up and opened a window. The bird's sorrowful song instantly became louder as it rang through their room. Lillaine got out of bed and joined him at the window.

"The birds are in a state of terrible strife." She burrowed in closer to him as he wrapped an arm around her. A light breeze wafted through the window, carrying a terrible odor. Fallon became tense.

"Do you *smell* that?"

He received his answer from the horrified expression on Lillaine's face. He let her go and ran out the front door of their small house.

The bitter smell filled the entire sky and made his eyes tear up. Lillaine stood at the front door with her hands over her mouth and nose. She managed a muffled yell.

"Where is it coming from?"

Fallon shook his head in response. He didn't know what it was either.

She continued, "I'm going to the other side of the house to see if Madivel is awake. I'm pretty sure she and Nolan settled next door to us last night." Fallon nodded his head to acknowledge he heard her and she left.

He peered out into the distance but saw nothing to explain the revolting odor that wafted through the air. The bird's grief-stricken song was quickly turning into a long and distressed screech. He didn't know whether to cover his nose or his ears. Just then, he heard an even louder scream from the other side of his house. This one was human.

Lillaine, he thought and sprinted to where she was.

Upon his arrival, he saw her standing at the edge of their cloud, looking over it with her hands covering her mouth and tears streaming down her cheeks. As she heard him approach, she turned to face him.

"What is *that*?" Her voice cracked with fear as she asked him to explain something he had not seen yet. He stood next to her and gazed over the ledge of their home cloud. The second he saw what she was talking about, a wave of nausea cascaded through his stomach.

"Do you know what it is?" she asked. "It looks evil, like nothing I've ever seen."

He pulled her into his arms and stroked her hair as he tried to determine what to do next. Lillaine was not a glider or a Head, she was a regular citizen of Ayren with a profession as a beginner architect. The efforts of the gliders to grant the population an education were continually thwarted and she did not know the truth about the Debauched.

"We have failed," he muttered under his breath. "It's them."

"Who?" Lillaine exclaimed.

"Lilla, we need to get to the Axis. Immediately. There is no time to waste. I promise I will tell you everything after I speak to the other gliders." And he meant it; he was tired of keeping secrets from her.

She accepted his promise and he summoned his personal cloud. They both got on and sped toward the Axis.

Fallon looked over at Lillaine whose facial expression was fraught with worry and confusion. Even after the warning from the Tierannites, he was still forbidden to tell her the truth about everything. The other Heads refused to concede despite the dire circumstances. They did not believe the threat of an imminent attack and therefore did not see the urgent need to tell their people the truth.

They arrived at the Axis to a scene of complete chaos. The Heads of each department stood on the steps of the Grand Hall and hundreds of people gathered around shouting questions.

So many clouds lined the edge of the Grand Hall's cloud that they had to park three rows back and jump from cloud to cloud to get close. He held Lillaine's hand as they maneuvered their way through the crowd until they reached the steps where his parents and the rest of the Heads stood facing the masses.

Mira Celesse stood at the back of the crowd. She was scolding Charlette Kane, one of the four Heads of Sky Patrol, for this debacle.

"Why weren't you manning your post? You were assigned to watch over the smog," Mira said with hushed anger, only the other Heads surrounding them could hear.

"The area hasn't been active since I took that station a hundred years ago. I've never seen any movement or sign of trouble. Checking it once a week was always more than enough."

"After I told you what the Tierannites relayed to the gliders you should have paid more attention to the Debauched region. This is all your fault." Mira deflected the blame from herself. Charlette slunk further into the back of the group of Heads as Mira stepped forward.

The crowd was demanding answers. Instead of answering their queries, Mira shouted for them to calm down, sporting her usual arrogance.

"It's time you told them all the truth, Mira," Fallon shouted from the front row.

"Shut up, you fool," she growled under her breath, but the comment brought forth a new outburst of questions and demands from the crowd.

"Tell us the truth!" a man next to Fallon yelled.

"What have you been keeping from us?" asked another voice.

"I just want to know about that contraption in the sky," a worried mother shouted as she clung to her children.

"Are we safe in Ayren?"

"I say we fight it. Knock it down into the ocean," a brave old man called out.

"Enough!" Mira shouted until there was silence amongst the crowd. "We will hold a Head meeting and then convene back here before sundown. Nobody leave your clouds today and do not go anywhere near that flying abomination. We will take care of it and use the wind to remove it from our airspace. In the meantime, you all must remain hidden from its view. If it sees you, we will all be in danger. Until sundown." Mira turned and entered the Grand Hall.

Fantaine Swen and Cavrel Bey, Heads of Regulation and in charge of social order, stepped out of the group of Heads and ushered the crowd back toward the rows of parked clouds. People obeyed and began to disperse slowly, accepting the fact that no answers would come to them yet. A few straggled behind to ask others what they knew, but Fantaine and Cavrel put those

162

conversations to rest before they produced rumors crafted from fear. Quite a few people circled around Fallon to question him about what secrets he asked Mira to reveal, but Drue quickly pulled him out of the small mob that had formed around him, and the regulators got those dawdlers to leave as well.

Lillaine stood quietly as Fallon went up the stairs to gather with the other Heads.

"Go home, Lilla, I'll be there with you soon."

She nodded and trusted he would explain everything to her later.

"I love you," he added before entering the Grand Hall and disappearing out of sight.

Chapter 21

A gush of light hit Mr. Lamorte's face and a feeling of warmth rushed through him. It was something he never experienced before. Even through the windows of his indestructible hover-tech airship, he could feel the heat from the sun's rays.

It was true: there was a sun. He always assumed that if the sun's existence was proven accurate he would hate the luminous monstrosity. He did not like any source of power that threatened his own. But seeing it now and feeling its radiance, he couldn't help but feel intrigued. He wanted it all for himself. A surge of excitement gushed through his cold-blooded veins: *there was more of this world to possess.*

As his steel airship trudged along through the sky, leaving a trail of black smoke, his brain was overloaded with exquisite and foreign visions. They left the gray smog of North America behind and entered what felt like a brand new planet. He was witnessing things he only ever saw in pictures. The further they flew from the city skies, the more fascinating the world became.

"Donovan," the captain of the blimp shouted, "we made it out. I didn't think it was possible!"

This historic achievement would be added to his legacy and Mr. Lamorte was too elated to chastise his cynical captain's doubt. He had a star to find.

The black, steel airship drifted further into the open sky. The clouds around them were white, a color rarely seen in the city.

Looking down, Mr. Lamorte's breath halted at the sight of the ocean. It was crystal blue, unlike the murky gray waters that surrounded North America. He could not put boats into his bay to sail because the water was too thick with filth and the waves too violent. The water beneath him now was calm and pristine. It held an immense serenity that was alien to him. Acquiring the sun and ocean was now added to his to-do list.

"Donovan, look," his lawyer, Fronk Dredge, shouted, "Land!"

Mr. Lamorte's gaze shot up and looked in the direction Fronk pointed. Through the glass windows, far ahead in the distance, they could see a patch of green that grew larger as they approached.

"Tell me what I am looking at. Why is it green?" Mr. Lamorte demanded.

"I don't know," Fronk said. His beady eyes squinted as he adjusted his spectacles.

"Captain, go faster. Take us toward that green blur," Mr. Lamorte commanded.

The airship steadily approached the land in the distance. As they got closer, the shapes became clearer.

"Those are trees," shouted Eugene Pamaloge, Mr. Lamorte's doctor. "It's a forest of some kind, quite possibly a jungle. I have read about these archaic ecosystems on the Internet Archives. They still exist!"

Mr. Lamorte's eyes grew wide with greed as he approached the window and stared down into the forestry they floated over. All of this land could be his. To think he came out looking for a fallen star when there were much greater treasures to be found.

In a deep but quiet voice, his bodyguard Conrad Van Greigle spoke up. "We have just discovered a miracle. I say we go back and talk strategy on how to capitalize on these newfound resources."

"Yes. You are quite right, Conrad. I think it's time we took these lovely prizes as our own. After trapping us in the smog for eons, the earth owes us." He shouted back to the captain, "Turn this airship around!"

As the hover-tech airship began a slow rotation, a blinding light shot through the window.

"What was that?" he shouted, enraged at the pain the brightness caused.

"I don't know, sir," Eugene answered, also readjusting his sight, "Something caught the light of the sun and its reflection hit our line of vision as we turned."

Mr. Lamorte stormed to the window and looked up into the clouds. He was furious. He did not like surprises. His eyes scanned the sky for anything that could have produced the freakish flash of light.

"What in the hell?" Fronk muttered under his breath. "Donovan, look to your left, about fifty feet up."

Eugene, Conrad, and the others joined Mr. Lamorte and his lawyer at the far window. It was a diamond palace in the sky.

"There's a castle on that cloud," Conrad stated with wonder.

"*People* live out here? But how?" Eugene pondered.

Mr. Lamorte's nostrils flared and fury coursed through his veins, but he managed to maintain a calm and steady voice.

"I see only one solution if there are other people living in these parts of the world."

"What do you suggest?" Fronk asked eagerly, a crazed look in his eyes.

Mr. Lamorte glared at the shimmering palace that sat undisturbed and free from worry.

"We destroy them."

A hushed eagerness filled the airship.

"We will create an army," Mr. Lamorte continued. "We will infiltrate the seas and forest. We will knock whatever lives in these skies straight into the ocean below. There is room for only one power on this planet and the power to prevail will be mine. Captain," he turned back to the pilot of the airship, "capture the coordinates of that diamond castle."

The captain used his fingertips to extract a 3-D grid from his dashboard. The airship showed up on the hologram map and the captain tapped his finger twice upon the part of the grid where the castle's coordinates matched its location on the map. As he turned the ship around, a strong wind came from the aft, pushing them back toward the smog.

"Now take us back to the city," Mr. Lamorte demanded, "I have an army to build."

Chapter 22

Maila wasn't able to fall back asleep after the memories returned. She laid in the dark, eyes wide open, and heart pounding. Mira wasn't her mother and she'd never get the chance to meet the woman who was. Quiet tears fell, catching the moonlight as they rolled down her cheeks. It was a level of grief she never knew possible.

And Darrow's cruelty. A part of her wished she hadn't recalled that memory; it was a moment she wished to erase. She wasn't sure how he felt toward her now, nor was she certain how she felt toward him, but the sting of his words hurt worse the second time.

She now understood why she tried to fly away.

The sun had barely peeked over the horizon when they were bombarded by other Tierannites. Maila rubbed her eyes to adjust to the growing light and tried to focus on the unexpected chaos. Zyleh stood to talk to them. She couldn't catch what they were saying; their accents were thick like Zyleh's and they spoke rapidly.

"What is going on?" she asked, but the three boys ignored her and kept talking.

"We have to go now," the boy on the tree trunk said. Blood decorated his cheeks, underlining his intense green eyes.

"Yes, Zy, you can't stay here any longer," said the other boy standing on the tree branch with them. "It's happening."

"Marlo, have the hunters been gathered at the borders?" Zyleh directed this question toward the boy with blood on his face.

"Yes, but so far the Coralene haven't reported any action in their waters."

"We need you back at the Heart, Zyleh," the boy with dark green eyes said. He looked much younger than the other two, maybe only 15, and his antsy nature made her nervous. He was ready to bolt.

"Calm down, Phelix," Zyleh said, also noticing his unnerving jumpiness. "I'm coming with you."

Zyleh looked down at Maila with sympathetic eyes. Her once silky white hair was now knotted in long wild tangles and her pale skin glowed through the dirt collected on it. She stood there, her silvery, purple eyes darted back and forth between the three boys, unsure of what was happening or how it affected her. She looked up at Zyleh, waiting for an explanation, but he remained silent.

"Zyleh," Marlo insisted, "it has to be now." He shifted his glance to Maila, indicating she needed to come too.

"No," she said. "No, I have to get home. I need to stay here. They won't know to look for me in the jungle." Defiance radiated from her the moment she realized they intended to take her with them. The gliders may not have come for her yet, but she had unyielding hope that they still would. Zyleh said they'd talk, but instead she was being forced to abandon her post without any explanation why. She turned to Marlo and Phelix, but they returned her pleading look with remorse, understanding she had no idea what was going on.

"Maila, you have to trust me," Zyleh said.

"You told me you'd talk to me today, that you had a lot to tell me. I'm not going anywhere until you fulfill that promise." Maila was being stubborn but she didn't feel bad. She had to get home. There was more to fix than she realized, and so much left unsaid.

"There's no time right now. I will tell you once we get to the Heart."

"No."

"Maila—"

"Zyleh," Phelix interrupted their banter. He pointed at the sky, his arm shaking with fear. An enormous black object was hovering high above the treetops, as ugly as it was huge. Phelix ditched them with haste.

"Zyleh, now," Marlo screamed. Maila froze in terror upon seeing the flying contraption in the sky. Zyleh picked her up, threw her onto his back, and began soaring through the trees with Marlo close behind.

"Why haven't they shifted its course? We warned them this might happen," Zyleh yelled back as they dashed through the trees at incredible speeds.

"I don't know. They must not have been protecting the smog's borders like we warned them to," Marlo answered back.

Zyleh's face tightened with disappointment as he continued to run. Maila buried her face into his neck, trying to keep herself from getting sick.

She had to get back to Ayren. She needed to make sure her family and Darrow were okay. It didn't matter who was mad at who, or who was in the wrong; those issues could wait. Making sure her loved ones survived the peril they now faced was far more important. With no idea what was happening, she had no choice but to trust Zyleh.

Seeing the hideous black apparatus floating ominously in the sky changed her mind about her previous plan. Waiting above the trees was no longer safe and she prayed Darrow and the other gliders weren't out in the open sky with that thing nearby. She didn't know what it could do or if it might hurt them. Maila was scared, confused, and eager to get to the Heart so she could demand answers.

Keeping a tight grip around Zyleh's neck, she endured the remaining trek to the Heart. It was a long journey and the impact of his rough movements made it hard to hold on. The big, black flying machine continued on without following them, indicating their presence went unnoticed. Even though it seemed gone, Zyleh and Marlo stayed out of sight in the middle layers of the trees, just in case.

She kept her face buried against his neck. He smelled like the earth and it reassured Maila that she was in good hands. He hummed a soothing melody and she gratefully shut her eyes and listened.

Maila's thoughts drifted away with his song, so when they arrived at the Heart she couldn't recall how they got there. The sudden stop brought her back to reality.

Marlo was no longer beside them, but integrated somewhere below in the sea of green eyes that stared up in their direction. She stood next to Zyleh on a high branch in one of the fifty trees that formed a perfect circle around a shorter, fatter tree in the center of an open space. On top of this short, ancient oak stood thousands of Tierannites. They were scattered amongst its branches, glaring up at her. She couldn't tell if it was curiosity or resentment harbored behind their eyes. Zyleh walked to the edge of the branch and addressed the crowd.

"My people. The Debauched have taken to the sky after years of inactivity. Put your anger aside for we must band together to protect ourselves."

"The skies?" a lady's voice cried out, appalled. "How?"

"Zyleh, you are a fool," yelled a man.

"Tell your sky girl to fix this," cried another.

The shouts of the crowd continued and Maila tried to shrink as far back into the shadows as she could. Zyleh looked back at her sympathetically then readdressed his people.

"She is not in her Element. She couldn't redirect their airship any better than one of us right now."

"Then you should have left her."

"It's her fault."

"Why have the Ayrenese let this happen?"

The crowd erupted, proclaiming their various opinions.

"Let them have their star!"

"We can't be cruel. She is just a girl."

"Where is the Grand Paipa?"

"Yeah, he told you to leave this alone."

"It's not the girl's fault, she didn't know!"

"It's *completely* her fault."

"I think she's brave."

"Your father should have you banished for this burden!"

"Don't disrespect the Major like that."

Maila sank down to her knees, completely overwhelmed and unsure what any of this meant. For the first time, she truly felt the depth of her ignorance. Zyleh looked back at her again and, with a newfound gusto, took charge.

"Stop it, all of you! This is not our way. She is one of our allies, she is from Ayren. You were all advised to show patience and instead you attack us on our arrival with hostility. You are very aware of the situation. Hate me all you want, but I doubt any of you would have done much differently than I."

"Except none of us are infatuated with her like you are," cried an angry man. "If you were acting with your brain instead of your heart, you never would have brought her here. You would have helped her get back to Ayren."

"We can see reason, you cannot. Your priorities are disheveled," a calm lady added.

"I did try to help her get back to Ayren, but it was too late," he lied. "I wasn't going to leave her to die, and if you would have, then I am ashamed to call you my brethren." This silenced the majority and the mood shifted.

Zyleh regained control and commanded respect. For the first time, Maila noticed the level of authority he held.

"None of your approval is needed. What's done is done and I will handle it from here. All I ask is for your patience, respect, and open minds." He scanned the crowd with confidence, giving them a look that implied he wasn't asking, he was demanding.

"Grand Paipa!" he squinted his eyes down at the crowd as he shouted, "I seek your counsel."

"He is below, consulting the Ahi," a mild mannered man informed Zyleh.

"Thank you, brother."

He held his hand out to Maila and helped her onto his back. They soared through the trees again.

The congregation atop the center tree, the Heart, dispersed and went about their usual business, or so it appeared to Maila. Zyleh carried her down and around the circle of trees toward a place he knew they could have the uninterrupted conversation he promised.

Chapter 23

As they traveled, Maila noticed the hammocks and small huts built around each tree, covering them from top to bottom. She also realized not every Tierannite had gathered with the angry crowd atop the old oak tree in the center. Many had watched the showdown from the comfort of their own personal dwellings.

As Zyleh and Maila passed them, most gave nonchalant waves or grunted in greeting. They even got a few who said 'welcome back' and 'welcome to Tier'. It gave her some relief that every Tierannite didn't hate her for reasons unbeknownst to her.

After they rounded half the circle, Zyleh came to a stop at a tree Maila hadn't noticed before. All the other trees surrounding the Heart had multiple huts built on them, scaling from roots to top branches, but this tree supported only one tree house on its massive trunk. Maila figured an important family must reside there since they did not have to share.

"Is this the Grand Paipa's house?" she asked as Zyleh helped her onto one side of a swinging bench that hung twenty feet above the ground.

"Yes," he responded and sat down beside her.

"Are you sure it's okay that I be here?"

Zyleh laughed. "Oh, I think so. My father has always been fond of the Ayrenese."

Maila looked at him shocked, realizing he was a member of the highest-ranking family in Tier. Similar to her situation in Ayren.

"I like that clip in your hair. It shines in the sunlight," Zyleh commented casually, "just like you do." Maila smiled at the compliment.

"It was my grandmoma's, on my father's side. I guess I must have taken it from my moma's jewelry box before I fell."

"Funny that it happens to be a star. That's what everyone is calling you: a fallen star."

Maila sighed. "I guess it's better than being called an idiot."

Zyleh laughed. "Well, some of them are calling you that, too." She didn't find it nearly as comical as he did, so she changed the subject.

"Can you please explain what in the Heavens is happening? You told me you would last night."

"You're right, I did." His smooth accent was like soft silk wrapping itself around her ears. "Where would you like me to start, Miss Maila?"

There was so much to know. She could finally ask anything she wanted and get a truthful answer, but now that she had the opportunity, she couldn't think of a single question. Zyleh smiled at her, understanding the enormity of this moment.

"It's a long story, you tell me where to start," he coaxed. The inflection of his voice echoed inside Maila's head.

"Your voice. Why does it sound so different than mine?"

"*That's* what you want to know?" Zyleh let out another laugh.

"My mind is all over the place. It's all I could think of!" Maila tried to defend herself, but Zyleh chuckled and placed his hand on her knee. He lightly pumped his legs in a manner that caused the swing to sway back and forth.

"English is not my only language. The Champion of Fresh Water was from Brazil, and some of her followers returned to South America to be with Juniper. Long ago, half of us spoke English and the other half spoke Spanish. The group learned how to speak both languages fluently. When the followers of the Champion of Soil merged with Juniper, Ukrainian and Saudi Arabian were introduced to our culture as well, but English remained the common thread. It wasn't until we finally made contact with the other Elements that we realized all four Elements had to agree on a shared language in order to communicate cohesively. I guess the Latin accent stuck through the centuries." His eyes flickered with kindness as Maila soaked in every word he said.

"Do you know what my people spoke before we all learned English?"

"The Ayrenese spoke the most varieties: English, Icelandic, Hindi, German, French, Italian, Romansh, and Nepali. Your people were a blend of those who escaped into the mountains from Iceland, Canada, India, and Nepal. They used English to communicate with each other since their native tongues were so vastly different and not commonly known. Considering the fact that you did not know this, I think it's safe to assume those other vernaculars are now dead. But yeah, English was an easy choice for the Elements to agree on. It was the common denominator."

Maila was overwhelmed. The blood pounding inside her heart was becoming louder than the thoughts flooding her mind.

"I know of the Champions; they taught us about Aria, but I don't know much about the others. Everything else you said is completely foreign to me." She swallowed the nausea of her ignorance. "But please keep going."

Zyleh paused. He would be just as upset if the roles were reversed. Maila lived her entire life in a world she knew nothing about, and many of the words he used to describe things were unfamiliar. She had no definition or reference points to understand the context of his explanations. Darrow was right; this conversation was a turning point in Maila's life. Zyleh recognized the importance of this moment and how lucky he was to share it with her, so he continued on more slowly, explaining things as he went.

"All four Elements originated from the human race. Well, we are still human, but we are evolved. The places I mentioned before were the ancient countries your people came from." He noticed her sad expression at the idea of her lost heritage and quickly added, "But that was thousands of years ago, so no need to feel too sentimental toward any of it now. We all evolved from different locations on the globe. Your people found safety in the mountains of Nepal and Switzerland, my people began in the forests of Washington, USA, and the Ahi started off in caves on the outskirts of giant volcanoes in Hawaii and Africa. The Coralene, who were mostly Caribbean, Indonesian, and Australian, made the long journey across the oceans to the South Pole, which was called Antarctica. The earth was being destroyed, so our ancestors were instructed by Gaia to go into hiding."

"What were they hiding from?"

"The other humans."

Maila was taken aback. It didn't make sense to her.

"Why would they need to hide from other humans?"

"The human race was killing itself. They built cities that covered the entire landscape in metal and created nuclear weapons that contaminated the air and soil they needed to survive. They were destroying everything that they should have been protecting. They lost sight of the basic functionality of life on this planet and began constructing a world in which the natural resources of Earth could not survive."

"And Gaia handpicked a few humans to lead our evolution into the Elements?"

"Right. The Champions, our direct ancestors. Gaia was very fond of humans; they were one of her favorite creations. So when the time came to take back the planet and start over, she hoped the few humans she selected would appreciate nature and live happily in simplicity. With Gaia's help, we evolved into the Elements. We are her greatest hope for Earth and so far, we haven't let her down."

"What about our evolution? How does that story go?"

"It took thousands of years to get to where we are now. The Coralene began their aquatic evolution through Coral, Champion of the ocean. Antarctica is where they mastered their adaptation to freezing temperatures, grew gills, and developed mindspeak. Their transformation from human to Coralene still boggles my mind. Second in impressiveness would be the Ayrenese. Their bones became hollow and they honed in on their ability to manipulate air. When they ascended into the sky and began living among the clouds, we all were amazed. The powers of the Ahi are incredible, too. It is rumored that Eshe, Champion of the Core, is still alive and in hiding at the very center of the earth. I've heard stories that she lives on a throne made of hardened magma surrounded by pools of lava too extreme for even the Ahi to traverse, that she bathes beneath waterfalls of lava and feeds off the fire of the earth, but the Ahi refuse to confirm these rumors. Her survival would explain their strength, though, as well as their unwavering conviction. They can produce fire from their skin and change the sizes of their bodies at will. Tierannites never experienced such law-defying changes as the other Elements. Our evolutionary gifts all originated from the earth and keep us bound to soil. We received some miraculous powers too, though. Just none as mind-bending as those."

Maila held onto every word he said.

"What can the Tierannites do?"

"We received the gift of hypnosis through music, we have absolute control over all life that grows from our soil, and we are able to communicate with animals and trees."

"The trees?"

"Yes. Spirits are reborn as nature, if they so choose. When I die, I will live on through the trees. When you die, I suspect you'll choose air."

"What if I don't want to be anything?"

"Then you'll live in the infinite dark."

Maila was intrigued, though she'd certainly choose to live on as air.

Zyleh continued, "All Tierannites can talk to trees, but only our Sovereigns speak to Juniper, who lives on in the Juniper tree within the Heart."

"There's a tree within a tree?"

"Yes. She relays all of Gaia's advice, concerns, and love directly."

"I don't think anyone has talked to Aria in ages."

"Maybe she's just waiting to find someone who is worthy," Zyleh suggested.

Maila shrugged, but secretly hoped he was right. Aria's absence was a disgrace, one the Ayrenese deserved, and Maila hoped they'd find a way to make her return. She wished to make her Champion proud.

"Thank you," she said softly to him. Hearing everything he told her only validated her curiosity. This was her history and she had a right to know it.

Zyleh felt an overwhelming sense of accomplishment. She would forever correlate him with this milestone in her life. It was something that could never be taken away and he hoped it was a stepping-stone in earning her trust.

"I'm sorry you never knew any of this until now."

"This is all I've ever wanted."

"I'm surprised you haven't asked me about the hovercraft yet," he said.

Maila's eyebrows furrowed. "What is a hovercraft?"

"That atrocious black contraption we saw floating in the sky earlier today."

Maila's eyes shot wide open. The sun reflected off her lavender irises as her pupils dilated in horror.

"Oh my Heavens. Zyleh, how could I have forgotten that so easily? My people! My family! Is it dangerous?"

"Yes, very. That's why I have been so insistent about keeping you *out* of Ayren."

"You knew that thing was coming? Did you warn my people?"

"We didn't know it was coming, but we suspected. And yes, we warned the gliders, so what they did with the information is their business. The fact that they even let it get that far out of its confinement leads me to believe they either didn't take us seriously or they didn't have enough time to prepare *and* educate the entire population of Ayren."

Maila shook her head. "Where did it come from?"

"The Debauched." He saw that Maila didn't recognize that word. "They are the leftover humans."

"The Debauched," she whispered so softly Zyleh didn't hear her.

"Yeah, we are still waiting for them to die off naturally beneath the smog."

"Smog?"

"The Elements turned all their pollution and toxic waste into a dome that confines them. Outside of keeping the planet alive, our main function is to keep the Debauched from discovering our existence. We cannot let them find out there are still healthy, surviving areas on the planet because they would only seek to seize and destroy what we were created to protect. The Coralene keep their boats at bay by making the waters at their borders thick with waste, and filled with rough and un-navigable currents. The Ayrenese are in charge of keeping their planes grounded if they try to leave the smog via air. The Ahi spy on them through the underground Debauched sewers that connect to their tunnels beneath the earth. Up until today, it was believed impossible for them to leave via sky or water."

"But that thing, the hovercraft—" Maila stammered, trying to cohesively put together the infinite questions swirling inside her brain. "Are my people okay? Did the Debauched on that hovercraft hurt them?"

"No. Not yet, anyway. We believe they sent that hovercraft out on a scouting expedition. And unfortunately, since your people did not turn it around quickly enough, they got to see that clean skies, lush forestry, and unsullied oceans exist beyond the confinements of their poisonous, metal city."

"A scouting trip?" Maila hung onto this thought. "What were they looking for?"

Zyleh paused before uttering a single word.

"You."

Chapter 24

Violet's eye was still swollen and though she often felt drawn to touch it, she did her best to leave it alone. The medication Lucy and Barnibus gave her wasn't very potent and the wound was healing at a painful pace. Advanced ointments existed that could heal simple wounds in a matter of seconds, but she was given an old formula. Only people with wealth had access to the most updated forms of medicine and technology.

Her eye throbbed as she looked down at the three bags she took from her attackers. She hid the gun in one of the knapsack's pockets, but hadn't found the energy to see what new items waited for her in the dirty backpacks. Those slimy boys had the disease and Violet was unsure how long the virus could survive on non-living objects, so she waited.

She prayed there would be food or water in them. Ever since Mr. Lamorte returned on his airship, the entire city went into a panic and it was next to impossible to get food. Nobody knew why he left, what he found, or what was to come of it, but alarming rumors were circulating. Everyone was spending their entire savings to stock up on food and items they needed to survive in case things became worse than they already were.

There was a mandatory assembly at the town hall today, which only heightened everyone's nerves. Anyone within a 10-mile radius declared absent would be tracked down, imprisoned, and likely executed.

Violet did not want to be near the large hoard of people that would be at the town hall; it was a guaranteed way to catch the disease. But she also did not want to risk being found and shot for disobeying Mr. Lamorte's orders. His militia would be scouring the streets, using their scanners to make sure everyone in the city was in attendance. Violet placed her hand over the tracker in her forearm and wished it wasn't there.

The five-minute warning bells rang over the loud speakers on every street corner. Violet grabbed her scarf and knife, and then headed to the assembly. It was an unusually warm afternoon. Despite the balmy weather, she kept her scarf tightly wrapped around the bottom half of her face. Today would not be the day she caught the disease. She tucked the Swiss Army knife into her pocket and trudged slowly down the street toward the town hall. Once there, she hid in the shadows at the back of the massive crowd. At least two thousand people were in attendance, if not more, and they were gathered in front of the stage where Lamorte would speak. She tried to stay a safe distance from the bulk of the crowd and found a good spot right behind the last row of people. There was enough space around her to prevent strangers from breathing down her neck.

The family that stood a few feet to the left of Violet was terribly sick. Their youngest daughter coughed into her scabbed hands, covering them with blood from her lungs. The little girl cried and her mother pulled her in close, stroking the top of her dirty, brown hair. The girl's doe eyes peeked out from under her mother's arms and over at Violet. She gave her an empathetic wave and the girl smiled back before burying her face into her mother's side.

Violet looked far ahead of her, into the distance where the podium sat on the stage. Mr. Lamorte approached wearing a sapphire mask, which hid nothing from anyone. He was sick and all the medicinal mask did was increase the anger and resentment within the population. They were trapped in this disease-ridden hellhole because of him, and instead of sharing this temporary relief with his people, he flaunted it in front of them.

As soon as the TVs surrounding the town hall lit up with Mr. Lamorte's face, armed forces stepped out of the shadows and circled the perimeter of the crowd. The electric force field that connected the guardsmen trapped the citizens in place and prevented anyone from leaving. Violet became tense with fear.

"Hello, my people. Thank you for joining me. I called you here today to let you know I have made a glorious discovery. I traveled beyond the smog and found there is clean air and new land for us to acquire," he paused and his eyes flashed with an evil twinkle, "and I need your help. We suspect there may be unknown civilizations living out there and we need to form an army in order to conquer the land." A low murmur of disapproval traveled amongst the crowd, but Mr. Lamorte paid no mind. "I need you all to fight on behalf of this continent. I need everyone to unite so we can seize control of the world just outside our borders. The clean air will benefit us all, as will the extra land." He scanned over the crowd for a reaction, but they remained silent. A vein in Mr. Lamorte's neck spasmed before he continued.

"Your participation in this war is not optional. You *will* fight. I need every man, woman, and child contributing to the cause." This time, he got a reaction.

"What could you *possibly* use children for in battle?" a man yelled out from the middle of the crowd. Then another.

"Fighting *your* war is mandatory? This is your battle, not ours!"

If those men had not been deep into the middle of the crowd, they would have been shot dead for questioning Mr. Lamorte's demands.

"Yes, it is mandatory that every single one of you fight. Children will be trained to use weaponry and then sent out to fight alongside the adults once they are ready."

"If there really are other civilizations out there, they will fight back. None of us are trained for combat. This will be a great loss to our people," the first man shouted again.

Mr. Lamorte let a sinful smile creep across his face. He'd be happy if half the population of North America died fighting his battle, so long as he won in the end. It made Violet's insides boil. In the loudest voice she could muster, she yelled out over the crowd.

"It's not right to seize land that isn't yours! You may be able to force us to live in filth, but you can't force us to be evil." Her tiny voice projected loud enough for Mr. Lamorte to hear.

He squinted his eyes, trying to find the source that so foolishly called him out as the immoral manipulator that he was.

As hard as he tried, he could not see Violet. She was too short and too far back. The people standing directly around Violet shifted uncomfortably and avoided looking at her. Even if they agreed with her, they did not want to be mistakenly associated with such radical thoughts. The only person that made eye contact with Violet after her proclamation was the young brunette girl. Her big eyes peeked out from under her mother's arm and she stared at Violet in awe.

"How dare you utter such profanity against all I have done for you," Mr. Lamorte shouted, still struggling to find the tiny voice that shouted such large accusations. "Every single one of you ought to be grateful I even let you remain here. You are all in my debt and it's time I collect. Training begins now."

The guardsmen stationed around the crowd closed in. The electric force field between each soldier was four feet long and sizzled ferociously.

They were being herded like farm animals. Pascal told her ancient stories about the slaughterhouses that used to exist and how the dogs would round up the cattle when it was their time to die. The dogs herded the animals into a close, compact group and then led them to be butchered. Fear engulfed her heart as she realized she was one of the cattle.

She had to get back to her alley. She needed to hide in the sewer. She didn't care what voices echoed through the darkness, it was the only place she would be safe. She looked for a way out but there was no escape in sight. Time was running out as the troops continued to close in tighter around the people gathered in the concrete yard. If she did not escape now, she would be forced onto the next boat headed toward imminent death.

To her right, a hysterical woman clawed at the armor of the guardsman she was closest to, begging him to let her go. He ignored her. Then in a moment of madness, she attempted to run through the electric force field.

Upon contact with the electric gate, her body rose into the air, shook violently, then fell lifelessly to the ground. The guardsmen callously stepped on her as they continued herding the crowd in the direction of the "training" camps.

The father of the family next to her during the speech was furious. He started pushing one of the guardsmen, telling him to let his family go. He tried to talk reason, but the guardsman maintained his stoic expression and ignored the desperate pleas.

The father, an enormous man with great strength, threw a punch at the guardsman. It hit him hard in the face and knocked him to the ground. The electric force field was momentarily broken, leaving a wide enough gap to escape through.

This was her chance. Violet ran toward freedom, along with a few dozen other people, and managed to make it out before the guardsman recovered and resealed the electric gate. Gunshots fired at her and the other escapees, so she ran faster. Faster than she ever knew she could.

She needed to get as far away as possible. There was no time to look back or wonder how many others escaped, she had to save herself. She needed to make it back to the sewer. Her mind went blank but her feet carried her there. She didn't stop running until she was standing over the sewer grate.

She lifted it, threw her bags into the sewer, got onto the ladder, replaced the grate overhead, and climbed down.

She had to get the tracker out of her arm before they started roaming the streets to find the escapees. They would discover her in hiding if she didn't. Without fear, she tore off her top layer, long-sleeve shirt, opened her Swiss Army knife, and pressed the blade into her scar. Blood spilled over the sides of her forearm but she didn't stop. The only way to be safe now was to remove the tracker. She grimaced as she moved the knife around beneath her skin. When she felt the tip of the blade hit metal, she took the knife out of her skin and stuck her fingers into the wound to feel around. Once she touched it, she slowly coaxed it out of her body. It was a circular piece of metal with a faint glowing light inside. She placed it on the floor and smashed it with her foot. The blue light in the tracker went out, indicating it was destroyed. Only then did she notice how fast her heart was racing and the intensity of the pain in her arm.

She tied the sleeve of her shirt around her bleeding forearm, applied the ointment she had been using on her eye, then sat against the wall and hugged her knees close to her chest. Her breathing was heavy and slow. A few moments passed before she even realized silent tears dripped down her cheeks and onto the sewer floor. It was the first time in years she couldn't control the urge to cry.

It felt foreign to her. She hadn't allowed herself to break down since Pascal died. She let the moment linger a few seconds before hastily wiping the tears off her face, smearing the dirt that collected on her cheeks over the years. With a shiver she grabbed her coat and hid beneath its warmth.

The warm and unwelcoming breeze returned from the depths of the sewer tunnel, but Violet refused to move. There wasn't anything that could scare her more than what just happened at the town hall, and there was no way she was going back into the city. Hiding in the sewer was her only option. If she wanted to survive, this was where she had to stay.

She heard the noisy sirens searching the streets above for anyone who got away. The entire world was changing. Everything that was bad before was now significantly worse. She wished to help more people by letting them hide in the sewer with her, but she could not risk surfacing to see who else needed shelter. Not now at least.

The warm breeze had not stopped and as time passed, it grew stronger and more forceful.

"I am not going to leave," she shouted into the empty space, "I have nowhere else to go." She took a deep breath. "I mean you no harm. If you leave me alone, I promise I will leave you alone in return." She waited for a response but was answered with stillness. A metal door slammed in the distance and the warm breeze abruptly stopped. Violet took this as a sign of truce.

A grin crossed her face and she felt a little better about her situation. All she could do now was sleep and pray that tomorrow she'd find hope hidden somewhere in the darkness.

Chapter 25

"You need to steady your stance. If you keep skipping around so much, you'll never get a solid swing at me," Zyleh said while blocking Maila's feeble attempt to strike him with her wooden sword.

She ignored him and tried again. She did a spin then crouched down low and managed to jab him in the gut. Her quick movements distracted him, leaving her room to strike.

"Got you!" she exclaimed, happy that after two weeks of practicing basic combat with Zyleh, she finally broke his defense.

"Took you long enough," he responded, teasing her.

During the past two weeks, Maila had come to terms with what her fall had caused. She unintentionally initiated a planetary war and the weight of this burden plagued her every second of every day. In order to stay distracted and feel productive, Maila insisted Zyleh teach her how to fight. Relina and Phelix took turns giving her combat lessons as well since Zyleh was busy preparing for battle. He was the Major, next in line to become the Grand Paipa, so he was often unavailable.

Maila's body was weak, but she saved her energy for these lessons. She couldn't sit back and let the war she caused unravel without trying to help. If she got the chance to fight, she would.

"You know, if I could *glide* while fighting, I bet I'd be much better," Maila said, thinking out loud.

"Have you tried to glide since you fell?" Zyleh asked, walking over to her.

Maila hesitated. She had not told him about her ability to levitate. Being in Tier with no one realizing she was abnormal was nice. The feeling of being constantly judged for something she could not control was the only thing she did not miss about Ayren, so she continued to keep her secret.

"Yeah, I tried once on the beach," she twisted the truth, "but it didn't work. The gravity down here is too heavy and makes it difficult to catch a current."

Zyleh nodded thoughtfully and then placed his hands on Maila's waist. She flinched, but had no time to ask what he was doing before he tossed her high into the air.

A scream escaped Maila's mouth as she was launched fifteen feet high. She quickly fell back into his arms.

"What is wrong with you?" she screeched.

"Try to glide," he said casually, then threw her into the air again without warning. This time she hit twenty feet before plummeting downward and landing in his grasp.

"I don't think this is going to work—" she tried to explain but he threw her into the air a third time without listening.

She hit twenty-five feet and her stomach turned, anticipating yet another free fall, but when a light breeze crossed her path she realized this was her chance. Maila seized the gentle wind and wrapped the current around her body. It worked. She was now floating high in the sky above Zyleh, who looked much smaller from this height. Being back in the air, defying gravity, Maila felt great delight. It eased the ache in her bones and provided a moment of much needed relief. Since it was such a fragile current it only lasted a few seconds, but she used the remainder of the breeze to ease herself gracefully back to earth, letting the air circulate around her body as she descended. She couldn't tell if she levitated or glided, the sensation was entirely foreign at this altitude, but it felt fantastic.

"I did it!" Maila exclaimed, landing lightly on her toes.

"I knew you could."

She was thrilled to discover she could manipulate the air in the jungle if she was high enough and had an adequate current. She was slightly out of breath from the training she'd done before being tossed into the air three times, but her gut told her this was a good avenue to pursue in addition to combat.

"Once I get some energy back, we need to practice this more."

"Of course," Zyleh smiled. Relina walked over, impressed by what she just witnessed. Relina was always kind to Maila, but if Zyleh was around, her demeanor became toxic. She was extremely hostile toward him. Maila did not know why, but decided not to ask. She wanted no part of their family drama; she had enough of her own.

"Did you just glide for a moment?" Relina spoke to Maila, avoiding eye contact with Zyleh.

"Yes!" Maila was grinning ear to ear. "If I keep practicing, I might be able to stay afloat for a decent amount of time on a day that is windy enough."

"That's really innovative," Relina commented. She admired Maila's determination to stay active. Despite her body being fragile, she never missed a day of training.

"Can you help her get back up to the tree swing? My father needs me to attend a meeting with the Ahi." Zyleh was looking toward the sun for an indication of the time. "I should probably be there already." Relina nodded without a word and Zyleh sped off, running so fast he blurred out of sight.

Maila climbed onto Relina's back and was carried to the tree swing near Zyleh's home. Staying high up and suspended in the trees helped ease the pain gravity caused. The further she was from the ground, the better she felt. They fed her well, so she had some energy and strength, but the weight of the air in Tier still pressed upon her lungs every day, making it hard to breathe. She didn't complain though.

Relina sat next to her and together they watched the scene below. In the open space around the Heart, the older Tierannites trained the younger ones in combat. They practiced every day from sunrise to sunset. Maila wondered if her people were preparing as thoroughly as the Tierannites. If the Heads finally told the people of Ayren the truth about what was happening, then maybe they'd be ready to defend the sky in time.

Maila stared up at the clouds. She missed her home terribly and wished she could see her father, Darrow, Bellaine, and Madivel again before the Debauched attacked. With everything put into perspective her father's betrayal and the fight with Darrow seemed trivial. Their love was stronger than their quarrels and they'd overcome their issues in time. The impending war forced her to imagine a life without either of them and the idea of losing them tore her apart. They meant too much to her to harbor resentment, and if anything happened to them before she got the chance to return home, resolve their issues, and tell them how much they meant to her, she would be heartbroken. She still struggled with the idea that they abandoned her, but knowing the other components taking place during the time she expected them to come gave her hope that they were just busy preparing for war. Through the tree branches, she watched the clouds. A smile crossed her face as she imagined the day she would get to go home.

"Staring at the clouds again?" Relina asked, noticing she was no longer watching the Tierannites train below.

"Staring at my *home* again. I hope they know what's coming."

"I can't imagine they wouldn't. The hovercraft must have forced the truth out of those who knew. They need to be prepared to fight."

Maila looked down at her knees. She was covered in dirt from her time spent in the jungle. Her white dress made of satin, feathers, and lace was covered in dust and grime. Mysterious cuts and bruises, with no determinable origin, covered her body.

Her dirty long curls of white hair fell in front of her face as she thought about the Debauched and how they took to the skies because of her; that they only left their confines because they saw her illuminated free fall. The guilt she wrestled with for the past two weeks was returning.

"The responsibility I feel for all of this still plagues me." She looked up at Relina through a few strands of her fallen hair, then back down at her knees. "If I hadn't tried to glide, none of this would be happening. People are going to die because of me."

"Stop it," Relina said gently. "Yes, the Debauched saw you fall and that is what gave them the determination to escape their confines, but the blame is not yours to carry alone. The leaders of Ayren must take some responsibility as well. You didn't know you weren't allowed below the clouds at night. You didn't even know the Debauched existed. The fault also belongs to those who chose to keep the people of Ayren uneducated. When I learned none of your people knew one of our main purposes for existing, I was surprised something like your free fall hadn't happened sooner. You are brave and we will get out of this okay." She smiled and her eyes became a paler shade of green.

"I know they probably blame me for all of this, but I hope they can forgive me." Her thoughts circled around her insecurities. She feared she wasn't loved enough to be worth a second chance. "I hope that's not why they left me on that beach."

Relina's shoulders slumped with misplaced guilt. She felt terrible about the secret she held for Zyleh. He made her swear to keep his little lie private, and out of family loyalty, she obliged. But the more she got to know Maila, and the more she grew to like her, the harder it became.

"I doubt it. I bet they just looked in the wrong place." Her conscience clawed at her insides as she told Maila the truth, but left out the details.

"I climbed to the top of a tree, I sat there from sunrise to sunset, and they never came down once."

Relina shook her head. "I don't know. Maybe it was an off day. Don't assume the worst."

"This is all my fault. I can't blame anyone but myself for being left behind. How could I have expected them to save me after I put them in grave danger?" The feeling of unworthiness that she conquered as a child was beginning to resurface. "I don't deserve their loyalty after what my actions caused."

"Stop it. The laws in Ayren are detrimental to the safety of the whole planet. If they aren't blaming themselves for your fall, they should be. You had good intentions, they just didn't go as planned." Relina no longer blamed Maila for the war. If *she* was trapped in Ayren under a regime of forced ignorance, she'd have tried to glide too. "It will all be okay."

"I hope so." Having a friend remind her of the truth surrounding her fall and what caused her to take such drastic measures made her feel better. She'd get past this.

"There will be loss, but if nothing else, this will bring the four Elements back together. Maybe it will even end the problem of the Debauched sooner than we expected." Relina smiled again, "You may have changed the world for the better. Just give it time."

"Do you think all the Debauched are bad?" Maila asked. This had been on her mind the past few weeks as well. She knew the main powers of the Debauched were evil, but what about the people born into that life with no other choice? She thought of herself in Ayren. The Heads of Ayren held a tight rule over the Ayrenese people and acted like they did not care about the rest of the world, but that didn't mean the people of Ayren didn't care. If they knew the truth, Maila was certain they would take an interest and step up to the challenge of defending this planet.

"I don't know if they are all bad," Relina answered, thinking about this for the first time. "But there would be no way for us to pick the good ones out of the bunch. Definitely not before this battle begins. Even if there are 'good' Debauched people, we can't save them."

"Maybe we could."

Relina tilted her head and pursed her lips in disapproval.

"Kudos to you if you can think of a way, but it seems like a lot of work to me. There are thousands of them. Where would you even begin the process of weeding out the good ones from the bad? Honestly, protecting ourselves and keeping them off our land is a bigger priority."

Maila did not argue with her, but her mind continued to spin around the idea. She looked over at Relina, who was focused on the progress of the combat lessons below and appeared to be calculating their odds inside her head. When Relina let out a defeated sigh, Maila couldn't help but gather that her calculations were grim.

Chapter 26

It was nice to spend the afternoon with Relina. She was a good friend to Maila. They watched the Tierannites train below and while Relina thought about tactics, Maila studied her friend's appearance. Ever since arriving in Tier she took it upon herself to study and take note of all its fascinating details: the environment, customs, beliefs, abilities, and people. The female Tierannites were a fierce group that exuded strength and femininity in graceful unison. While all Tierannites had markings, theirs differed from that of the males because not only did they indicate achievements, but they were also intended to showcase how pretty each girl was in their own distinct way. Their markings were placed around the features that made them stand out from the crowd. Although Relina's face was exquisitely stunning, her arms were her most unique feature, so her beauty marking was on her left arm. It was a vine that twisted around her bicep, augmenting the appearance of her strength. Some girls had the tattoos around their eyes, others their abdomens, some were on their feet. It always varied, but it was a nice way for each girl to feel beautiful and valued for what made her different from everybody else. In Ayren, Maila was shunned for her differences and it was nice to see a society that celebrated the things that made each individual unique.

A squeak came from above the tree swing. Maila looked up and saw the monkey that befriended her upon her arrival at the Heart. She gave it a smile and the monkey jumped from its tree limb onto Maila's lap. She gently rubbed the back of the monkey's ears while it played with the woven lace of her dress.

"He is going to dirty your clothes–"

"I doubt he could make it any worse."

"Say the word and I'll get him to stop bothering you."

"No, it's okay. I like his company. I've named him Bazoo."

Relina laughed; she had never heard of someone naming an animal before. Some animals would tell you their chosen name, but most did not bother with titling themselves. They existed in simplicity, living out their purpose in the ecosystem without rules or formalities. Creatures of the jungle were respected just as much as humans and no one took them on as pets. Doing so would be a terrible insult to the animal's worth. The Tierannites did not value mankind over the varying creatures they cohabitated with. Each life form served an important purpose in their cohesive circle of life.

"We don't claim animals as pets."

"He's not my pet, he's my companion," Maila said defensively.

Bazoo then wrapped his furry arms around Maila's waist and pressed his face into her belly. Relina dropped her argument after seeing this exchange of affection.

On the ground below, the training went on. Some Tierannites practiced with sticks and others stayed to the side crafting additional weapons. It was very basic artillery: branches with pointed ends and sticks with sharp rocks fastened to them. These types of defenses would not do much damage against the weapons Zyleh explained the Debauched used. He said they had metal hand machines that shot steel shells at speeds fast enough to travel straight through a person's heart. They also had firebombs, which were deployed from far away. When they landed, they exploded, causing devastation for miles around the point of impact.

If the Tierannites were going to fight against this kind of weaponry, their sticks and stones weren't going to cut it. They were counting on hand-to-hand combat, in which the Tierannites would dominate. They were huge, and from what she learned, the Debauched men only averaged about six feet tall, same as the Ayrenese. The Elements would win if the fight involved individual combat, but if the Debauched used manmade explosives, the fight would be much harder.

"Hello, Relina, I'm glad to see you're keeping our guest company," a deep voice emerged from behind. It was the Grand Paipa, Zyleh's father and Relina's uncle. Maila had not met him yet. She had been in Tier for almost three weeks, but he was so busy they never formally met. He rounded the tree and came to sit on a branch a few feet above the tree swing. "Do you mind if I have a minute alone with her?"

"Of course." Relina smiled at him, then swiftly descended the tree to resume her part in the training below.

Maila was now alone with the Grand Paipa. His long brown hair was sprinkled with gray and tied into knots. Vines, sticks, and leaves interlaced between his braided locks. He carried a walking stick that was covered with inlaid stones and carvings. The cane was so beautifully crafted she imagined it held magic within.

When she examined his face she saw the family resemblance. Like Zyleh, he had a sharp jaw and high cheekbones. Maila looked down at his right calf muscle and saw he had the same zigzag tattoo as Zyleh.

He looked at Maila kindly and smile lines surrounded his glowing green eyes. He meant her no harm, so she could not determine why his presence was so intimidating. Maila never met anyone like him before. The powers of Ayren had the same confidence but theirs was lined with arrogance, whereas the Grand Paipa's was lined with kindness.

"I meant to speak to you sooner, young Maila, but with all that has been going on the time just did not exist. I am sure Zyleh filled you in on all that is happening." She nodded. "I must admit, I was furious when I first heard of your fall through the night sky.

The lack of discretion was appalling. I was horrified that you put the entire planet in jeopardy with such disregard. Then we later learned of the ignorance forced upon the Ayrenese people. That the powers in Ayren kept our history and the existence of the Debauched a secret. Again, I was appalled. Both at the stupidity of keeping such a secret and for the fact that I assumed you to be a menace to our way of life. I was ashamed to have jumped to such conclusions. When I learned you had not known of all the wonders and dangers the world beneath you held, my horror turned into admiration. It was dangerous what you did, you could have died, but your bravery and determination to learn about the world you live in made me proud. It gives me hope for your people and I commend your valor."

"Thank you," she responded, grateful that he saw her as brave, "though I am still very sorry for the trouble it caused everyone. It was not my intention to start a war. I never wanted others to die because of my actions. If I had known the consequences, my choices would have been different."

"I know. You are a good soul. Your heart beats a fragile rhythm, similar to another I've known." The Grand Paipa scanned Maila's face. "You do in fact remind me of her. Are you related to any gliders?"

Maila's mind raced. At first she thought to say no, but then her heart fluttered as she remembered her one direct connection to the gliders.

"Yes. My moma, actually."

"Ah," he said with a smile. "Clara?"

Maila's heart swelled. "Did you know her?"

"I did. She was lovely. I used to be a carrier, like Zyleh. I spoke to all the other Elements and Clara was always my favorite. She was smart and brave and filled me with hope for the future, the same way you have. You are much like her, though I am sure you hear this often."

This was the first time Maila was presented with the chance to speak to someone about her mother. Tears filled her eyes but she did not let them fall.

"I never knew her. She died when I was born. I didn't even know she was my moma until the day I fell. That was another secret they kept from me." There was no bitterness in her tone, just deep sadness.

A look of true sorrow flashed in the Grand Paipa's eyes as he found out about the death of someone he once held very dear to his heart.

"You are strong and I sense there is more greatness to come from you." He smiled at her. "I must be going now. I have a speech to make to the people of Tier. I am glad to have spoken to you and to have been reminded of a time when I was filled with hope. Those years when your mother was part of my life were very special to me." His voice trailed off a bit as he remembered something he did not say aloud. Then he caught himself and continued, "Having you enter into my part of the world is a good sign." He nodded his head with certainty. "I do believe it is a good sign." He gave Maila one last smile before departing swiftly down the branches of the tree.

"That was nice," she said to herself.

Bazoo squeaked. He remained on her lap and fidgeted with the broken sundial watch she wore, which was still waterlogged.

"If you can get it to magically work again I would be eternally grateful."

Maila looked down and saw the Grand Paipa standing atop the Heart. As he spoke, the entire jungle became quiet. Even the insects seemed to stop their buzzing as the leader of their land commanded full attention.

"My brothers. My sisters. First of all, I want to let you all know how proud I am. You have trained and prepared diligently for whatever may come. It fills me with pride to know all of my people are so dedicated to protecting our way of life. Because of this, I want to honor every single one of you before the time comes that we need to fight. Since we do not know what will happen or what casualties will come of this, I want to honor life tonight. I want everyone to revel in the company of their brethren and use this time to become stronger with the love we have for one another. Finish what you are doing. At sundown, we celebrate."

With that, cheers came from every direction. From the Tierannites training in the open space below, all the way through the depths of the trees that formed a circle around the heart. Tierannites shouted and rejoiced, and Maila could feel the outpour of love that lived within Tier.

Chapter 27

Mr. Lamorte was ready for war. It had been two weeks since his expedition through the smog. Two weeks since he herded his first group of soldiers into his military boot camp. During this time, his militia scoured the streets within a three hundred mile radius of Mr. Lamorte's home base in quadrant B4, "recruiting" more people from nearby districts to join his army. Their guns were quite convincing.

Mr. Lamorte planned to send his soldiers through the smog in rotations. As the first round of troops died and he needed to replenish his ranks, he would move further west and create more boot camps to train new soldiers. There were plenty of people living on his continent and he planned to utilize all of them. For now, the twenty thousand soldiers in his first camp were shaping up nicely.

All the planes and battleships were ready. They hadn't been used in ages, but a crew of mechanics restored and updated them with the latest advances in technology. There weren't many enhancements to be made since most development ceased along with the use of these vessels, but they needed refurbishing regardless due to extensive lack of use. The few, new additions included 3-D mapping grids and improved turbo engines.

The military's arsenal of guns, bombs, and missiles were continually updated and redeveloped, so no work was needed there. Each soldier would receive a weapon as they were shipped through the smog, and every boat and plane was armed with countless bombs. He also had home-based missiles ready to launch. All that was left to do was prepare his soldiers.

The recruits in the Northeast boot camp had been in training for two full weeks. The facility itself was a former prison turned into conditioning grounds for his soldiers and it was four square miles that contained half a dozen brick buildings.

Building 1 imprisoned all those resistant to the training. These people were tortured until they were in compliance to fight.

Building 2 housed the cooperating soldiers. This unit was surrounded by the blacktop they trained on.

Building 3 boarded the children. Each child was put through rigorous psychotherapy to wipe their minds clean of all they learned in their short lives. This enabled Mr. Lamorte to take their empty brains and mold them as he wished. The children were never allowed outside, even if their brainwashing was complete. It wasn't safe for them to be around the adults who could easily influence them and reverse the progress made.

Building 4 and 5 were additional housing units for the large quantity of soldiers being kept within the confines of the boot camp.

Building 6 was the medical and prison ward. This was where medical tests were performed on unwilling participants, where specialized torture proceedings took place, and where certain individuals who misbehaved were locked up.

His militia guarded the boot camp with violent force. They were very aware that their positions as guardsmen kept them safe from being shipped into battle, so they obeyed Lamorte's commands without question.

More than three quarters of the people in the camp were still unwilling participants. While it frustrated Mr. Lamorte, he had a plan to overcome this obstacle. His chemists were working on a steroid-like mind control pill that would turn his soldiers into monsters. He wanted soldiers without a conscience and this pill was the ticket. It was a drug that would make them physically strong and mentally numb, which would make his army indestructible and compliant.

Today marked the end of the final trial of the pill. There were many deaths and horrifying side effects in the first few trials of this pill, but the chemists promised Mr. Lamorte that they finally got it right. If all the test subjects were still alive at 5 p.m., Mr. Lamorte planned to administer a dosage to the entire army.

His black luxury sedan rolled through the front gate and pulled up to Building 6. His driver exited the vehicle and walked around to open the back door for Mr. Lamorte. The driver also

215

opened a large black umbrella for him to walk beneath until he got into the building. It was not sunny and it had not rained in eons, but Mr. Lamorte liked to feel shielded from the sky and the air around him.

After seeing the clean world on the other side of the smog, he became fixated with his health. He did not want to get any sicker before being able to live outside of their toxic confinements. Perhaps the air out there would cure him; the possibility that it *might* became his new obsession. His eagerness to get to the other side was becoming unbearable and the importance of beginning this war pressed upon him every time the wound beneath his mask throbbed. Walking under an umbrella would not protect him from the disease, but this new habit of staying shielded comforted him. Winning this war was his chance to make history. It was his chance to make sure his name meant something after he died. He could not fail. He could not let the disease consume him before he made his mark on the world.

Mr. Lamorte walked directly to the room where the latest test subjects were being held. There was a one-way mirror, which allowed him to see the patients strapped tightly to beds while maintaining a safe distance. A guard stood in each corner of the room with tranquilizer guns pointed at the unconscious patients. The doctor was already waiting for him in the front half of the room.

"The drug is ready, sir," Dr. Pamaloge said, an uneasy smile on his face, "and as the week went on, they actually stopped being resistant. The combination of chemicals is proving to invoke dependence among the test subjects. This morning, three of them actually *asked* for the pill. They wanted more. This is great news. If force was needed to make the soldiers take the pill every day, it would be impossible to regulate their intake once you shipped them through the smog, but now that the drug has an addictive quality, those issues will never arise. It seems we've finally created the perfect pill."

A slimy smile slithered across Mr. Lamorte's face, and his dry skin cracked at the corners of his mouth. The doctor continued.

"Also, the delicate balance of opiates versus steroids versus sedatives created your desired effect. All ten of them are full of energy, have grown at least ten times as strong as they were at the start of the dosage, and are too numb in the brain to question any task we ask them to perform."

"Wake one of them up. I want to see the effects myself." Mr. Lamorte stared at his monsters through the one-way mirror. They all slept peacefully under the effects of sedatives.

Dr. Pamaloge looked nervous as he walked through the door connecting the two rooms. He locked it behind him before heading toward the largest test subject. Once at the side of the bed, he reached into his lab coat pocket and pulled out a small metal bottle with a spray top. He held it in front of the man's face and spritzed it directly into his nose. The man's eyes shot open, then darted around the room frantically. His breathing was furious as he tried to move his arms but couldn't. A low growl emitted deep from the depths of his gut as he attempted to break free from the leather straps that contained him. The veins in his neck bulged as he let out a roar and broke free from his bed. Like a wild animal, the man sniffed the air, looking for a scent he could not place. His large body, covered in newly formed muscles, walked toward the doctor. The guards lifted their rifles, ready to tranquilize the man but Mr. Lamorte hit the speaker button allowing him to communicate into the room.

"Do not shoot."

At the sound of his voice, the savage man snapped his head toward the mirror Mr. Lamorte hid behind. Though it looked like a mirror from his side, he walked toward it anyway, continuing to sniff the air with intention. Upon reaching it, he scowled at his reflection with anger. His eyes narrowed as he took a few steps backward.

Without warning, the man launched his body through the mirror and into the part of the room where Mr. Lamorte stood. The glass cut his face and pieces stuck out of his arms and legs, but this did not stop the man from standing up quickly and grabbing Mr. Lamorte by the neck. He slammed the president's lanky body against the wall and held him up so high his feet dangled by the man's stomach.

"I could smell your rotten blood through the wall," he whispered into Mr. Lamorte's ear while choking him. "It will be an honor to deliver your death."

"Put me down," he said calmly as the oxygen in his lungs drained. He refused to die today. This monster belonged to him and he would make it obey.

The man licked his lips and smiled. "No."

"Shoot him!" Dr. Pamaloge shouted but Mr. Lamorte held up his hand indicating for the guards to hold their fire.

He stared the monster down as the oxygen left his lungs. When only a few breaths remained, Mr. Lamorte tapped the heel of his shoe against the wall, ejecting a blade from the front, and then kicked the man in the stomach, plunging the blade deep into his abdomen. The man groaned in pain and dropped Mr. Lamorte. The guards then shot the man in the back twice with tranquilizer darts, dragged him back to his bed, and refastened his constraints.

Mr. Lamorte should have been scared, but he wasn't. He rubbed his neck where the man's hand had been and relished how good the threat of death felt.

"I am so sorry, Mr. Lamorte. My apologies."

"What are you sorry for? They are perfect. Their hatred for me has not been muted, but that is a small matter. I won't be training

219

them and I will not be with them as they fight. With enough time, the drug might even erase their hostile memories of me."

"Yes, it's very possible," Dr. Pamaloge stuttered, a bit confused but relieved as well. "Clearly, the drugs have worked. As you can see, whoever they will be battling is in for the fight of their lives. On this drug your soldiers will be monsters. I wouldn't want to be on the other end of their guns."

"Wonderful. Have the chemists deliver the full batch of pills to us immediately. Every soldier is to have one with their dinner tonight."

Dr. Pamaloge nodded and entered the data into his touch-screen table. Mr. Lamorte exited the room. He twisted the dial on his wristwatch and paged the guard who was watching over the warships, fighter jets, and missiles. The first strike was coming and his insides churned with excitement.

Chapter 28

Celebrations were rarely thrown in Ayren. In fact, Maila could not recall one party she ever went to besides the few Mira threw at their home for the Heads. Gatherings took place at the Axis, but those were usually for informational purposes, never to celebrate.

Marlo was on top of the Heart, standing on its highest branch. As always, his face was covered with blood, which Maila learned marked a Tierannite as a hunter. After taking a deep breath, he placed a wooden horn to his lips and sent a roaring noise through the jungle that echoed for miles. With excitement, she watched the commencement of the celebration.

Crowds surfaced from the shadows of the trees surrounding the Heart. Everyone traveled in groups with arms around each other and smiles on their faces. Some Tierannites were running and playfully pushing each other, while others held hands and walked slowly.

"I hope you didn't think I forgot about you." Zyleh jumped across a few tree branches before landing next to Maila on the tree swing.

"I can't wait to see what a Tierannite celebration is like."

"Let's go. You'll be celebrating too," Zyleh said, grabbing her hand and helping her climb down the tree. The jungle floor was covered in lush leaves and moss that felt soft beneath Maila's bare feet. They were still in the shadows of the jungle and had to travel between a few trees before they entered into the open circle around the Heart. As they approached, the noise of the crowd grew louder.

Zyleh stepped out of the shadows and into the circular dirt space. He held out his hand for Maila to join him. She took it and stepped into the light. Sunrays beat down on her face and filled her body with warmth. After leaving the damp, shadowed moss, the dry dirt surrounding the Heart stuck to the dew on the soles of her feet. It was probably the only spot in the jungle that wasn't entirely green.

"You are going to love this," he said with a mischievous grin.

He pulled her through the crowd that had already multiplied in size. Maila tried to take everything in as Zyleh tugged her forward. A group to the left of her chanted something in another language:

Como el río, fluimos juntos. Hacia la oscuridad a través de lo desconocido. Un corazón, muchas vidas. Juntos vivimos, juntos morimos.

The group was huddled together with their arms in the air, jumping up and down. More Tierannites came from every direction, making the small group larger. The chant continued.

Un corazón, muchas vidas. Juntos vivimos, juntos morimos. Un corazón, muchas vidas. Juntos vivimos, juntos morimos.

Soon it appeared that every Tierannite was part of this group, shouting out with forceful passion. Smiles on some faces, intense expressions on others.

"Zyleh, what are they saying?"

"Like the river, together we flow. Into the darkness, through the Unknown. One heart, many lives. Together we live, together we die."

Maila tried to walk slower so she could watch the herd of people moving as one, yelling out this proclamation, but Zyleh kept pulling her along.

"Don't you want to be a part of this?"

"What I am taking you to will start as soon as they settle down. I don't want you to miss it."

Reluctantly, Maila let him yank her onward while keeping her attention on the pack of Tierannites who cheerfully repeated their mantra. She was so fascinated with watching them that she walked right into Zyleh once they reached their destination. He muffled a small laugh then banged his fist four times against the trunk of the Heart.

Maila was aghast at how large the Heart was at this proximity. From the tree swing, the Heart seemed tiny compared to the trees that surrounded it. Up close, it was enormous. Its trunk was massive and its roots came out from under the ground in all directions, creating a beautiful mess of the earth. Maila looked up and noticed the intricate branches that lay hidden beneath the thick layer of leaves covering them.

Zyleh slammed his fist against the trunk of the Heart again, in the same rhythm as before. This time, the large root next to them slithered through the dirt like a snake and retracted back up into the tree. The soil and dirt around this root shifted like water, conforming to its movement. As soon as the root disappeared, a golden light emanated from the large hole it created at the base of the tree.

Maila's eyes grew wide and Zyleh looked over at her with a confident grin.

"We need to hurry, the opening ritual is almost complete."

Zyleh stepped into the tree, his silhouette vanished into the golden glow, and Maila followed behind him. She blinked her eyes a few times, trying to adjust her vision to the blinding light. Eventually, her sight became better than ever.

"I can see."

"What do you mean?"

Maila was at a loss for words as she tried to understand the phenomenon happening. "I'm not sure, but the way I see things in here, it's so crisp. Everything is so clear."

"I always wondered if that silver sheen over your eyes impaired your vision. Seems it does."

The silver sheen over all Ayrenese eyes was to protect them from their proximity to the sun, but maybe it also hindered their vision; she never saw the world with such clarity before.

Zyleh continued explaining, "This tree, the Heart, holds an immense amount of power. Generally, when a person enters into it, its magic enters into them."

"Will it last?"

"Temporarily. With time, its effects will fade. Your vision will go back to how it was. It can only permanently fix things that take one time to heal, not conditions that are recurring or genetic. A deep cut, this magic will heal forever. A disease or chromosomal impairment, it cannot."

Maila nodded, disappointed, but still thrilled that she would get to see the world through her improved vision for a few more days. She took the time to look around. The inside of the tree trunk was filled with gold light. The entrance they came through closed behind them and the blinding light settled. It was then that Maila noticed the tree within the tree.

Her eyebrows furrowed and she looked at Zyleh.

"That's Juniper. Well, it's her tree. Her spirit lives inside."

Maila was in awe. She was in the presence of a Champion and she felt incredibly humbled.

"I wonder where Aria's spirit lives."

"I'll ask Juniper for you."

Zyleh crouched and placed his fingertips in the dirt. He closed his eyes and was silent for a few moments. When he stood back up, he smiled at Maila.

"She travels the world as a breeze. According to Juniper, Aria was the current that cushioned your fall into the ocean."

"She was with me?" Her eyes welled with tears.

"Yes. You weren't alone."

A smile emerged on her face and she made quiet plans to seek out that breeze when she returned to Ayren. Maybe Aria would talk to her; maybe she'd be the one to restore her faith in her descendants.

"I thought only the Sovereigns could talk to Juniper?"

"And her distant progenies."

"You're a direct descendant of a Champion?"

"I am."

Maila was impressed. She wondered who in Ayren, if anyone, were direct descendants of Aria.

Before she could inquire anymore about the history of the Champions, a spiral staircase made of vines and tree bark materialized. The staircase went up along the walls of the tree trunk, as high as Maila could see.

"Where now?" she asked, excited for what was next.

"Up," Zyleh answered with a smile as he scaled the spiral staircase.

Maila's initial thought was that the climb would take a toll on her achy body but instead, ascending the steps felt like floating. Maila closed her eyes, took her hand off the vine railing, and imagined she was in the sky. She pretended she was home on her cloud, floating through the air. Riding her cloud next to Darrow's or heading home to see her father and Bellaine. She missed them so much. Darrow most of all. Her heart ached as she saw his face again in her memory. She shifted the eye of her imagination and saw the face of a woman she did not recognize, but in her heart, she knew it was Clara. Maila imagined her to be beautiful, with a kind face and a brave soul. They rode clouds next to each other in Maila's musing and a warm sensation filled her heart.

She knew it was the Heart's magic making her feel this way, but it was intoxicating. She kept her eyes shut with her arms out and continued to climb the stairs, pretending she was home, floating through the sky with her loved ones.

The force of walking into Zyleh again broke her daydream. He had stopped on the steps and was watching her.

"You could've told me that you stopped."

"I was too busy enjoying how happy you looked."

"That's the first time I ever saw my moma's face. I look just like her. Do you think I made up her image?"

"No, the Heart only shows the truth." Zyleh smiled. "If you stay here with me, we could come here often and you'd see more of her."

"I can't base my life around illusions."

He nodded in understanding, but his face was lined with sadness.

Maila knew he wanted her to stay with him in Tier and he knew she couldn't. Zyleh had become Maila's friend over the past few weeks, but she would never feel for him how he felt for her. He did his best to keep his feelings for her unspoken, but his desires were certainly not unknown. She could see the love in his eyes every time he looked at her.

Her near-death free fall made it clearer than ever that her love belonged to Darrow. She missed him every moment of every day and hoped her failed attempt to glide hadn't ruined everything between them. It was a chore not to mention him to Zyleh in conversation. She knew expressing her feelings for Darrow would hurt his feelings and as his friend, she did not want to do that.

"This is it." Zyleh's confident smile returned and with his left pointer finger, he traced an elaborate pattern onto the wall of the trunk. As soon as he finished, the invisible pattern exploded with gold light and the tree trunk began to disappear, disintegrating until it became an open doorway.

Zyleh took Maila's hand again, his large palm dwarfed hers, and led her out onto the tree branch. They were high up in the branches of the Heart. Five female Tierannites sat side by side at the end of the branch to their right, waiting as the crowd below settled.

Zyleh sat, straddling the tree branch, and leaned back against the side of the tree where the door had been. After exiting, it morphed back into solid bark.

Maila sat down, too. The sun began to set and the sunshine that previously filled the celebration was gone. The sky was now a hazy shade of pink, leaving the open space around the Heart a little darker.

"I heard you singing on the beach," Zyleh explained. "Your voice is beautiful and I thought you would especially like this part of our celebration. I wanted you to hear it without the distraction of the crowd."

The smallest of the five ladies started singing. She hit a high note, held it, then let her voice trickle down into a melodic rhythm. Then the largest of the five ladies came in at a lower octave, creating a bass line for the song.

Soon enough, all five Tierannite women sang in a strange and enchanting combination of *oohs* and *aahs*. Their layered harmonies sounded otherworldly, like its creation was not possible by living, breathing beings.

Maila noticed they each had the same marking down the rims of their right ears and again along their left ankles. It was a marking of tiny stars and dots, which appeared as delicate on their skin as a silver chain of jewelry. All five of them had long hair in shades of dirty blonde to brown, which they wore slicked back against their scalps in braided ponytails. This made their cheekbones appear sharper and their large green eyes the focal point. The emotion of the song played out in the twinkle of their eyes.

Unlike the typical dark brown wardrobe every Tierannite made for themselves using leaves, hemp, and other materials they found in the jungle, these singers wore long flowing dresses made of a silver material that danced in the wind as their feet hung off the side of the tree branch. The five ladies gracefully moved their feet so their dresses moved to the rhythm of the song, creating an abstract and hypnotizing picture in the movement of their skirts. The entire production was mesmerizing and Maila was engrossed.

Zyleh reached out to squeeze her shoulder lightly and she looked over at him in appreciation. She was happy he was there with her and felt touched that he knew this was something she would enjoy. It was the prettiest sound she ever heard.

The crowd below was silent. Some Tierannites shut their eyes and others listened while holding someone they loved in a tight embrace. The rowdiness from earlier vanished and all that remained was a solemn stillness. Thousands of Tierannites gathered beneath the branches of the Heart but not one of them made a sound.

Halfway through, a band of instruments joined the song. They slowly entwined their notes between the voices of the women. Maila looked for the source of these new sounds and noticed a few Tierannites perched among the higher branches, playing their instruments softly.

Darrow and her father taught her about the instruments that still existed in the world and Maila looked to see if she recognized any being played now.

In a tree branch to the left she saw two old men playing violins, and then further away she saw a younger fellow with an instrument that sounded like soft bells. On a tree branch to her right was a lady playing a small harp and Maila's heart filled with excitement. Seeing the harp and hearing its music filled her with warm memories.

The Tierannites playing instruments stayed hidden in the shadows of the tree branches. They were hard to locate and the music sounded like it was magically born from nothing.

She focused back on the singers. After about five minutes, the song ended with the ladies hitting an eerie note in five-part harmony. They never said a word the entire song. It concluded as an instrumental, their voices being the primary source of music.

Though the song sounded sad, it felt optimistic. After it finished, the crowd below burst into a roar of applause and cheers. The five ladies stood up, bowed silently, and then leaped through branches in different directions. They moved so fast, Maila did not know which lady to watch depart or where any of them went.

Zyleh gave Maila a hug and she shifted to face him.

"Who were they?"

"Daughters of the Sovereigns. You won't see them again. They, along with all Sovereigns and those lined up to take that role, live in solitude. They stay removed from the rest of the world in order to maintain pure serenity and transparent judgment. It's why they're so good at what they do. Their inner peace is nonreplicable and it makes their decisions on matters the best for all parties involved. It's impartial and untainted. They are the trusted advisors to the Grand Paipa."

"We need Sovereigns in Ayren," Maila muttered, imagining her home having wise counselors talking sense to the Heads, but Zyleh did not want to talk about politics or her troubles at home.

"Did you enjoy that performance?" he asked eagerly.

"Very much so. I have never heard anything like that in my life. What was the song about?"

"It's a love song. A tragic love song actually. It is about love that doesn't come easily, or that faces many obstacles. But it is also

232

about love that has hope despite the hardship and despite the hurdles thrown in its way. A love that fights to see each new day." Zyleh paused for a moment, and then continued, "Right now this song is perfect. Every single one of us can relate. We all will be fighting when the time arrives and we cannot determine who will live to see the other side of this battle. Whether it is a friend, a family member, or our beloved that we lose, we all face the burden of tragic love in this moment. It is why we celebrate tonight. So we can have this joyful memory with our loved ones, in case it's our last."

Maila could feel the heartbreak in his voice. For himself and for all the people he loved and considered family below. Though the crowd was loud once again, Maila realized now why they had fallen so somber during that song. It wasn't only because of the beauty the song held or the impressiveness of the voices and instruments, but because they all felt the heartbreak and hope the song portrayed. It was something everyone, including Maila, could relate to.

"I am happy you enjoyed it," Zyleh said, trying to lighten the mood. "Your voice is elegant and quite charming. When I heard you singing on the beach it reminded me of the Sovereigns' daughters." Maila blushed.

"I didn't realize anyone was listening."

"It was beautiful."

"Thanks," Maila responded, embarrassed. She liked to sing, but only when no one was listening. The harp on the other hand, she did not mind who heard. "I actually play a harp in Ayren. It's much bigger than the one the lady was playing during that song, but very similar."

"Is that so?" A mischievous smirk appeared on Zyleh's handsome face. "Then I think we ought to find you a harp to play."

He jumped to his feet, picked Maila up without any warning, tossed her over his shoulder, and descended the side of the Heart. Maila barely had time to blink before she was back on the ground and Zyleh was towing her toward a group of individuals sitting in a circle playing instruments.

While being pulled forward, she continued to observe everything. She saw one group of kids tossing around a sandbag and another group of adolescents, running around, chasing each other. There were some older ladies chatting and braiding hemp, though the majority of adults were organizing the next big event. They were gathering dead wood and piling it into a pit. It was beginning to get dark, so she assumed this was a fire pit that would begin once the sun had set.

Upon reaching the large group of people playing music, Maila's nerves surfaced. They were mid-song when Zyleh walked directly into the middle of the circle, dragging Maila alongside.

"Hello, my friends," he said with a little too much arrogance. The music stopped awkwardly, instrument by instrument, before a guy playing guitar said something.

"We were in the middle of a song." He had a tribal tattoo that circled his neck, traveled down his back and stomach, and ended at the top of his left thigh. It was made of thick black lines and was filled in with elaborate markings that made the whole tattoo move across his body like a gust of wind.

"I noticed. I would've waited until the song was over, but we all know how your songs never end. You guys will jam until you're so tired you fall asleep with your piccolos in your mouths."

"What do you want?" The guy playing the piccolo asked angrily. Zyleh's comment brought back embarrassing memories.

"My friend here plays the harp. I was hoping you guys would let her play a song with you."

The man on guitar looked over at the lady playing the harp, who stood up and waved for Maila to take her spot. It was much bigger than the one the lady in the tree played during the haunting love song and was more like the one she played in Ayren. The body and column of her harp were made of blown glass while this one was made of beautifully carved wood. Flowers and small forest creatures were carved into the wooden head and foot of the instrument. The design was a work of art and Maila hoped her playing matched up.

"Lead us off, sky girl," said the man on guitar. He gave her a reassuring smile and Maila took a deep breath. She closed her eyes and placed her fingers on the strings.

Without too much thought, her fingers began to move. They chose the strings whose notes would mirror her current sentiment. Her plucking created a quick tempo filled with warmth and mystery. Slowly, others joined in, adding depth and interesting layers to the song. She opened her eyes and smiled as she saw everyone around her enjoying themselves.

The song took shape into a peculiar, smooth-moving jig, and the Tierannites who stood around the group began to dance with one another. Laughter and music filled the air. Maila never knew music could bring such joy to anyone but herself, and she was thrilled to be part of the creation of the happiness that now surrounded her.

Out of the corner of her eye, she saw Zyleh at the edge of the crowd. Not dancing, just smiling with genuine delight as he watched Maila play. She smiled back at him and continued to feel euphoric as more and more people came over to dance.

The music grew louder, as did the laughter. The old lady next to Maila played the bongos and her skinny, wrinkly arms flew all over the place. She created a fantastic rhythm that partnered with the beat created by the young man playing five different-sized drums.

The tempo was building and its crescendo filled the sky with noise. Excitement coursed through Maila's veins. It was a collective excitement, one everyone around her felt. It fed off each person until it became so big, it felt like it might explode.

And then it did. A huge blast ripped through the air and Maila was shaken; a feeling could not explode. The music very slowly dwindled down to nothing and devolved into furious chatter and questions.

Maila looked around, still unsure what just happened. She looked at the drummer to her right, thinking he might have produced the sound, but he was confused too. She looked to her left to see a few Tierannites with their eyes fixed toward the sky.

Someone let out an agonized scream. Maila whipped around and saw a woman standing behind her, blood streaming down the side of her face. A few men rushed over to help. Then another scream came from the opposite direction.

Ten feet away, a young boy had fallen to the ground. His arm was sliced from shoulder to elbow. The woman next to him picked something up off the ground and shouted.

"It's raining glass!"

"Take cover," shouted a man who had another injured woman in his arms.

Maila's head spun. Everyone was in a panic, racing to and from, trying to save themselves and others. In between those dashing about were those falling down, injured by the hurtling chunks of sharp glass that rained from the sky.

A thud landed next to where Maila sat frozen. She looked down and saw an old man was dead beside her. The piece of glass that hit him fell so fast it passed through his skull like a bullet. Blood trickled out the sides of his mouth.

Zyleh raced toward Maila through the chaos of people. She sat there, numb, trying to make sense of what was happening. Without stopping, he scooped her up and ran into the jungle, finding them shelter beneath the treetops.

Maila was frantic. "Glass? Do the Debauched attack with glass?"

"I don't know. We don't know all their weapons." He looked worried. His mind was racing just as fast as Maila's. "I'll be right back."

Maila shouted, trying to grab his arm, but he was already back in the open space, dodging the deadly downpour and carrying the injured under cover.

Standing under a thick set of tree branches, she watched as glass fell like bombs into the Heart, shattering in every direction. Smaller fragments fell to the earth like daggers, piercing through anything in its way.

A huge piece of glass plummeted to the ground, right in front of where she stood. It did not shatter like the rest; it only cracked in half. Maila took a step closer to look at it and was horrified at what she saw.

It was the head of the owl sculpture that sat on the Axis. Her heart contracted as she noticed the bloody feathers stuck to it. This was not the Debauched attacking Tier, it was the remnants of their attack on Ayren.

To her dismay, the deadly downpour was only a prelude to the horrific finale. As the last few pieces of crystal fell, a moment of silence passed before the true climax of aftermath began. White feathers and fabric stained with blood started to drift into Tier from the sky. Slowly and methodically, swaying in the evening air as they fell toward their final resting place. Traumatized, Maila froze as death rained over her. They fluttered toward the jungle floor: some still stitched together, others torn apart, all covered with red stains. Her heart broke apart as she realized what was happening.

"Ayren," she cried. She stepped back into the open space, stood next to the broken owl, and stared at the sky. "The Axis. They've hit the Axis!"

She could not control her rage. She picked up a patch of bloody feathers that looked to have been the sleeve of someone's shirt. Her entire body trembled.

"My people," she muttered to herself, then called out to the frenzied Tierannites, "The Debauched are not attacking you, they attacked Ayren!" Maila fell to her knees and placed her hand on the diamond owl. A stray hunk of glass fell and shattered five feet to the left of her. Debris hit the left side of her body, leaving small bloody cuts all over her arms, legs, and face. She didn't care. Who died? Which of her people were at the Axis? How could they have prepared or protected themselves from something that caused this much devastation? Glass and blood-stained feathers covered the ground around her. Maila's world froze as she sat amidst the rubble of her home.

The Grand Paipa reemerged through the branches of the Heart. He stood atop the tree with tears in his aged eyes. "It's begun," he shouted, "The war has begun!"

Chapter 29

Blood was everywhere. Broken glass, broken people. Darrow could not escape the remnants of the blast. The horror of the explosion persisted as an incessant ringing in his ears. He squeezed the sides of his head, hoping to stop the noise, hoping to end the misery.

When the strike hit, he was heading to the Axis. The missile flew by, ten feet to his left, buzzing with so much electricity the hair on his arms rose. He watched as it crashed straight into the Axis.

He now stood in the ruins, trying to think of a way to help. People were scattered everywhere, crying and attempting to identify the mangled bodies of those who died. From every direction he saw hundreds of clouds speeding toward the debris. Soon, this scene would be even more chaotic. The addition of scared people looking for their loved ones would make the task of recovery even harder. He took a deep breath.

He and the other gliders went above the law and told everyone the truth about the Debauched. Despite the sighting of the hovercraft and their recent inquiry for answers, people were still reluctant to believe them. By the time they finally got most of Ayren to take the impending attacks seriously and accept the danger they were in, it was too late. The strike was upon them before they could prepare.

He began to count the casualties he could see without having to dig beneath the rubble. Once he got to twenty, he stopped. He couldn't go on, there were too many and each extra tally was an additional knife to the gut.

The ringing in his ears continued. He shook his head violently, trying to stop the noise, but only managed to make himself dizzy. He dropped down to one knee and shut his eyes, trying to regain focus.

As he steadied himself with his eyes closed, a new sound accompanied the terrible ringing. A baby's cry. He opened his eyes and went toward the noise.

Under a large sheet of glass was a woman, lifeless, and beneath her arm was an infant. Darrow carefully lifted the child and cradled it with tenderness. The mother's blood covered the infant from head to toe. Darrow held the baby close, trying to soothe its pain.

As the loud buzz in his head started to grow dimmer, the cries of torment around him became more prominent. The initial shock of what happened was fading and everyone was beginning to comprehend the horror.

A woman with disheveled white curls and her husband's blood all over her hands called out to Darrow.

"What happened?" she cried, getting off her knees and walking toward him with a faint limp. "You have been spouting horrible premonitions like this for weeks. What is this?" She shook her hands toward the sky.

"This is war," he answered calmly. "We tried to warn you. We desperately tried to make everyone see reason, but no one wanted to believe us. No one wanted to listen to the gliders. You were all much happier eating up the falsities the Heads continued to feed you. It was easier to accept their pretty lies than our ugly truth." Darrow was angry but he tried to keep his temper in control. "I hope you believe us now."

The woman said nothing because he was right. With the back of her hand, she wiped the tears from her face, leaving a trail of her husband's blood across her porcelain skin. Without a word, she bowed her head and walked back toward her loved one's lifeless body.

If the people of Ayren were educated from the start, Maila would have never fallen. If Maila hadn't fallen, she'd still be alive and the Elements existence would have remained a secret from the Debauched. And even if the Debauched somehow discovered them on their own, the Ayrenese would have been prepared enough to redirect the missile and fight back. He hoped that after this, he and the other gliders would have sufficient time to train enough people on how to use the element of air to fight the Debauched when they attacked again.

Maila slipped into his stream of consciousness and his overwhelming heartache returned to the forefront. He could feel the uncontrollable surge of sorrow rising through his chest.

He needed to calm down and focus on the people around him now. Though he tried, he wasn't confident that he could handle this new heartbreak on top of the one already living inside him. He rocked the baby gently in his arms. Drue was now at the Axis too and stood next to his son. Together they observed the devastation that surrounded them.

"I miss her so much."

"I know," Drue responded, "I miss her too. She was a brave girl."

"Once everyone settles down from the shock of this attack, they are going to blame her. They are going to say it was her fault the Debauched found us. The Heads haven't taken any heat whatsoever for what they've done. The people are not correlating this attack and our unpreparedness with the forced ignorance they placed upon us as a society." Darrow's breathing was heavy, "It's not her fault. We can't let them think that."

"We won't. The Ayrenese are naturally logical. We look at things from both sides to rationalize our opinions on matters. With a proper and truthful explanation, our people will see this whole ordeal for what it really is. While she must take some of the blame, it does not fall on her alone."

"I should have told her what she wanted to know. My reasons for keeping the truth from her were childish and selfish."

"We all had an opportunity to ease her curiosity. Her fateful actions were foreshadowed and could have been prevented with the truth. Her outburst at our Quarterly Head meeting should have been an indicator that she had reached her breaking point. We should have seen it as a warning sign. We could have prevented all of this if we only listened to her instead of dismissing her."

"Is it wrong that I am also angry with her?"

"Not at all, that's natural. You loved her, and even if it's through death, she left you."

"It's that, and the fact that her actions were very selfish, too. I know I was stubborn, but I would have eventually answered every question she could think of. She took my maps and tried to teach herself to glide, knowing it might not work. She was willing to risk her life and leave me behind. Didn't she realize that if her self-taught gliding lessons didn't work out and she failed, which was always in the realm of possibilities, she'd break the hearts of everyone who loved her?"

"Probably not until it happened. I don't think the possibility of dying ever crossed her mind before she fell," Drue answered honestly. "I bet she realized a lot of things after surviving the fall, though."

"I love her too much and it is making it hard for me to see any of this clearly. My whole life was dedicated to fixing our culture so we could have a relationship that wasn't cursed with secrets, and now she's gone forever. I feel helpless and angry. I feel like I failed her." Drue put his arm around his son.

"Keep her in your heart, but let the rest go. We cannot change the past, we can only accept how things have unraveled and do our best to adjust our actions in the future. You did not fail Maila. We all did."

"If only our plan worked. Everything would be different. Maila would be alive and this war would be in our control. The Elements would be on the offensive, shaping the war and taking it to Debauched land, instead of being at our opponent's mercy and defending our home territory."

"Stop beating yourself up. You'll make yourself sick if you keep trying to fix the past. Focus on the future."

With that, Drue gave his shoulder a supportive squeeze and departed to continue taking care of the injured. Darrow took a deep breath.

Over the side of the cloud the broken Axis sat on, a flock of birds appeared, each carrying small packages made of leaves.

Darrow's eyes welled with tears. They were not alone or forgotten.

The birds landed amongst the rubble, dropping their packages and flying back over the side of the cloud. Darrow gently placed the baby down in a safe spot and chased one of the birds, catching it before it took off. He held it in his left hand and with his right, unwrapped one of the leaf packages. It held vials of medicine. On the leaf wrapper, he crudely carved out the words *"thank you"*.

Darrow barely knew how to read, let alone write, but the gliders kept the basics of this art form alive within their group. Darrow hoped he spelled it correctly, or that it was close enough that the Tierannites would understand the message.

He then placed the leaf into the bird's skinny talons and held it aloft with both hands.

"Deliver this back with our thanks," he whispered, then opened his palms and the bird flew off toward the sun. He watched it until it disappeared in the distance.

Darrow bent to pick up the baby, but when he turned around he was greeted with a shocking sight. The baby was levitating, floating two feet above the spot where he placed it a moment ago. The child cried incessantly and as soon as Darrow shook away the astonishment, he plucked the child out of the air and cradled it close to his chest.

This was the first time Darrow ever saw or heard of another Ayrenese person who could levitate. For an entire generation, Maila had been the only one who could do it. Eighteen years later, another child was born with the same evolutionary gift. This meant it was finally happening. The change would slowly transform all of Ayren with the gift of levitation. If other children were being born with this trait, people would be forced to accept it. They would be forced to learn how to cope with the inevitable change. They would see it in an entirely different light now that it was affecting their own babies and grandchildren. Darrow's delight crumbled as soon as he imagined Maila's smiling face. She would never learn of this.

Darrow held the baby close, protecting it from the mayhem that consumed their world. The baby looked up at him with fearful innocence and in that moment, he made a promise to himself that he'd assume Maila's role in championing the acceptance of this new change in the Ayrenese people. She would have been thrilled to be the advocate that ensured these young children did not suffer the same cruelties she had. Now, he would do it for her.

Those who raced to the Axis from afar had arrived and the calm chaos following the explosion erupted into a frenzied one. Everyone was screaming, crying, and scavenging around the debris, looking for loved ones and trying to help the injured.

"Use the medicine in the leaf packages. It was sent to us from the Tierannites," Darrow instructed people as they passed, and then watched them work with optimism. They wasted no time and did everything they could to save those still clinging to life. Their passion for survival proved that after this tragic wakeup call settled, they would be ready to fight back.

Chapter 30

Zyleh raced to where Maila sat and carried her back under the shelter of the trees. She was shaking. He sat on the jungle floor and held her close. He whispered into her ear and rocked her gently, trying to calm her down.

"There is nothing we can do yet, you have to stay strong."

"They could all be dead," she said with heavy sorrow, thinking of her loved ones in Ayren. Terrible anxiety filled her heart for the only place she called home.

"I know. I am so sorry." For the first time since they met, he looked scared.

Together, they stared into the open space. It was filled with the aftermath of the attack on Ayren. Nothing but bloody feathers fell from the sky now, and the amount cascading down seemed never-ending. She could only imagine the devastation unfolding above them.

For Tier, five Tierannites died from the fallen debris and forty were injured.

Maila stopped trembling and slowly calmed down. Zyleh stood up with Maila in his arms and carried her to his tree home.

"I have to find my father," he said after helping her into her hammock. "He is probably assigning tasks. Are you okay up here until I get back?"

"Yeah," Maila answered, trying to shake the horror out of her system. "I think a nap would do me good. I feel useless. I should be in Ayren helping my people fix what I caused."

"Don't be hard on yourself. We are going to help them the best we can. We are all going to beat the Debauched together. You should rest so you are prepared for whatever tomorrow brings."

Zyleh began to climb down the tree.

"Try to talk to a glider. Find out every detail you can," she called down to him.

"I will do my best."

At that, Maila rested her head and shut her eyes. Bazoo swung down from a higher tree and landed next to her. She put her arm around him and he snuggled into the crease of her body.

Zyleh slid down the tree in record time and saw his father standing under the Heart with a score of Tierannites surrounding him. He ran over to find out who was doing what and how he could help.

"Relina, I need you to tell the Coralene that the war has begun, though I am sure they already know. I can't imagine the glass of Ayren did not fall into their waters as well, but make sure they are aware. Find out what their plan of action is and if there is anything they need from us. Bring Marlo and Brenna with you."

"Yes, Grand Paipa," Relina bowed her head and ran off with Marlo and Brenna.

"Lux and Eluno, head to the treetops. See if there are any gliders around to talk to. If you can make contact with them, find out their damage and if there is any way we can help. Ask them what they need us to send them. The Sovereigns have already sent up a flock of birds to deliver small vials of healing lotions and syrups. Ask them if they need more, or anything else. Make sure they are prepared in case another attack comes soon."

Lux and Eluno both nodded, and Zyleh interrupted. "Grand Paipa, can I go with them? I'd like to be on that mission."

"No, I need you to go and see the Ahi."

"But–"

"No. It is done. Lux and Eluno, please go." The two older men darted swiftly into the jungle.

"Zyleh, you communicate best with the Ahi. You and Phelix will go to the Northeast checkpoint and tell the Ahi what has happened. It is possible they are unaware that the first attack has been made. Make sure they have all their tunnel exits into Debauched territory sealed and that they are ready to fight alongside us. If the Debauched manage to pass through the seas and reach Tier, we will need their numbers in order to win a ground attack."

"Understood," Zyleh replied, angry he was not able to go with Lux and Eluno, but very aware of the importance of his own mission. He waved Phelix toward him and they sped off into the trees.

Side by side, the brothers ran so fast their shapes became distorted. Upon their arrival at the Northeast checkpoint, Zyleh immediately pushed away the rock to reveal the tunnel below. He did not see any Ahi, but there was no time to waste on a tree branch summon. They needed to speak with someone immediately. He got down on his knees and shouted into the darkness.

"Is anybody down there? This is Zyleh, Major and Lead Carrier of the Tierannites. It is extremely urgent."

There was no response. Phelix stood behind his brother, looking around nervously.

"What if the Debauched have already reached the jungle? We are alone; we have no one to fight with."

"You need to stay confident, brother. We would know if they entered our land. We would feel it all around us: in the trees, in the soil. They are not here."

Phelix nodded, still looking unsure. Zyleh shouted back down into the tunnel.

"Hello?" He waited for his words to echo softly back. "We need to speak to a member of the Ahi authority immediately."

Just then, a pair of glowing red eyes appeared in the darkness. He backed away from the tunnel and an enormous blur of scarlet shot out of the ground and landed on its feet. It was Culane again. He immediately covered the entrance to the tunnel.

"You know we do not like to leave our tunnels exposed to outside air for long periods of time," Culane said sternly.

"Yeah, well I think that will be the least of your worries when you realize why we are here. The Debauched have attacked Ayren. They hit what the Ayrenese call their Axis and it rained glass all over Tier. Five of our people died, forty are injured, and we are still trying to find out the damage caused in Ayren. We are unsure if any glass fell into Coralen, but that information is being sought out as well."

"Have the Debauched struck again since?" Culane's tone changed from annoyed to concerned. He was focused on the severity of what was to come. His massive hand stroked the top of his head, moving smoothly across the black braids knotted tightly to his scalp.

"No, just the one strike on Ayren. Did the Ahi spies not hear anything about the preparations for this attack?"

Culane's chest muscles flexed, twitching slightly at Zyleh's question.

"We did not. And I hope that is not an accusation that we would withhold such critical information."

"Of course it wasn't," Zyleh said, annoyed that Culane took his comment as an accusation. "I only asked out of curiosity, in hopes that your spies have found the location where they would overhear Debauched war plans."

"We did not hear anything about the attack on the sky. Nor have we heard any murmurs about what is to come," Culane paused, looking concerned. "We have not been able to locate the president and our spies assigned to the northeast region of North America say the streets are barren. Something suspicious has happened and we haven't been able to find out what they are doing or where their planning is taking place."

Zyleh sighed but contained his frustration.

"Alright, well we wanted to let you know the war has begun. They made the first strike and it's time for all of us to get ready for battle. The Ahi will be fighting alongside the Tierannites if a battle occurs on our grounds, correct?"

"We wouldn't miss it." Culane's eyes flashed with blood thirst.

"Wonderful. The skies are extremely vulnerable at this time so let's hope they do not attack Ayren again. Hopefully the Ayrenese are taking this time to train."

"I am going to tell our spies the urgency of finding where they can get inside information on these attacks. We have to know what is coming." Culane gave him a solid nod. "In addition, I will have someone assigned to stay beneath this tunnel entrance from now until you summon us to fight. We do not want to miss any communication." Culane began to move the boulder from over the tunnel entrance.

"Greatly appreciated, my friend. Take care and keep hope."

"My sentiments exactly." He gave Zyleh a final nod, shot a look of acknowledgment to Phelix, and jumped back into the tunnel. The rock slid over the entrance and the brothers were alone again.

"I hope their spies can find out where the Debauched are doing all their planning," Phelix said.

"Yes, but we can't rely on that. We have to be ready for anything. Let's get back to the Heart and find out what additional information was gathered from the other Elements."

Without a word, the brothers took off, making a quick trip back to the Heart.

Chapter 31

Lucy was all alone in the boot camp. She had been with her daughter and Barnibus during Mr. Lamorte's speech, but as soon as the guards closed in and began herding the crowd, Barnibus was separated from them. Upon entering the boot camp, the militia split up the men from the women and the children from the adults. She and Penny were put into separate housing units and two weeks had passed without any contact with her daughter. While she knew many people in the boot camp from the long days she spent working at the market, she still felt wildly alone. The only person she wanted to be with was her daughter. She hoped Penny had some friends with her in her ward. Maybe some of the kids from their neighborhood, or the strong young lady named Violet they met through Barnibus. The thought of an older girl protecting Penny set Lucy's nerves to rest.

Each day held new horrors and Lucy barely had the strength to wake up anymore. When the militia burst into her ward to force them out of bed at 5 a.m., she could not find the will to rise and face another day.

"Up and out," one of the men yelled. "Conditioning on the blacktop in ten."

Lucy remained in bed, numb from the abuse she faced during the past two weeks. The left side of her face was swollen beyond recognition from a beating she received earlier that week. In an attempt to persuade a strong young man to fight willingly, they ordered her to torture his elderly mother. She refused and received the beating instead.

The guard shouted for everyone to get out of their beds once more but Lucy continued to lay there, motionless.

"If you aren't out of bed in thirty seconds I will cut off your ear." His spit landed on her face as he shouted.

"One less ear would be nice," she replied monotonously, "less of your screaming I'd have to hear."

The man slammed the side of her head with the backside of his rifle. He then leaned in close and whispered menacingly in her ear.

"I said get up, Lucy. I know your weakness. Either you oblige willingly, or I'll be forced to use Penny as motivation."

Lucy looked at the man's face for the first time. It was the same guard that had separated them when they arrived in the camp. His name was Grimson. He was reassigned to Lucy's bunk recently and was now the head guard for her ward. He had a thick moustache that swirled at its ends and eyes dark as night.

"Penny is a pretty little girl, isn't she?" He licked his lips. "She's shaping up quite nicely over in the children's ward, too. It'd be a shame to have to lose her."

Lucy sat up and spat in his face. Disgusted, Grimson slapped her hard, knocking her to the floor.

"If you ever do that again, I will shoot you on the spot." He kicked her once in the ribs with his steel-toed boot. "Get downstairs with the rest of them." He made his exit, leaving her on the floor in pain.

The room reeked of sweat, blood, and rot. Lucy would never get used to the potent odor that filled the camp. There were no showers and dead bodies fermented in the open air for days before being taken away. She hoped Penny wasn't witnessing these things while locked away in the children's ward.

On the blacktop, the conditioning was always the same. Five hours of intense exercises that built up their endurance, strength, and speed. They ate lunch then trudged back out to the blacktop to do another round of pushups, squats, jumping jacks, and quick sprints. Occasionally, they spent the last two hours of the afternoon learning how to fight each other, but everyone always participated halfheartedly. No one wanted to be part of this. Mr. Lamorte thought he was training his "soldiers" so they'd be stronger, but these exercises were pointless. He could make them physically powerful but it wouldn't change their lack of passion. As far as she was concerned, she planned to leave the smog and beg whoever they were attacking to let her make a home with them. She'd offer to fight alongside them in exchange for refuge in their land. She had a feeling many others planned to do this, too. Mr. Lamorte was so self-absorbed he did not even contemplate this possibility. If it worked, his entire war plan would backfire.

They served dinner in rotations. A few thousand people were crammed into a small cafeteria at a time and forced to eat everything put on their tray. Every night, Lucy hopelessly searched the room for Penny, wishing to see her tiny, beautiful face again. After the first few nights, she realized the children were never in the cafeteria with the adults, but Lucy always scanned the room. It was all she hoped for.

On this night, Lucy was greeted with a plate full of gray mashed potatoes, processed meatloaf, wilted greens of unknown origin, a protein bar that tasted like chalk, and a glass of whole milk. All the food was crafted in factories since there was no natural vegetation anymore. Farming now happened within large, steel warehouses where the animals were kept in dark corners, fed minimal amounts of man-made nutrients, and killed as young creatures. Any food product from an animal came from creatures so frail and chemically intoxicated it might as well have been fake. Most species were already extinct due to the extreme conditions of these slaughterhouses and Lucy could still recall when the last goat died three years ago. It was a sad day. While goat tasted foul, it was a solid source of food. When they went extinct, not only did they lose a valuable protein, but also a source of milk and cheese.

She looked down at her meatloaf. Her stomach protested each bite as she wondered how many different animals and body parts were mixed into it. No one was allowed to leave the cafeteria until his or her plate was clean, so she dug in.

The potatoes tasted like cardboard but she forced them down with a sip of sour milk after every mouthful. The green leaves were rotten and smelled spoiled, but she held her nose and swallowed them whole. The meatloaf was worst of all. Lucy chewed each bite slowly, holding her breath to avoid the taste. She was halfway through the mystery meat when she bit down and something crunched between her back molars. Bitter dust exploded in her mouth causing her to cringe in disgust. She tried to wash the taste away with milk, but it lingered. Paranoia hit her like a train: she was either being poisoned or drugged.

She sat there, motionless, waiting to see what effect it was going to have on her, but she felt nothing. She looked around the crowded cafeteria and saw no commotion or concern from anyone else. No one seemed to notice the foreign substance in the meatloaf. Perhaps hers was supposed to disintegrate into the food but hadn't. Or maybe it was only meant for her to receive.

Lucy finished the meat and ate her protein bar quickly. She had to escape the cafeteria. She was afraid her body might betray her in the next few minutes, or possibly hours, and she wanted to be in her bed when it happened. Her bed was the safest place if this unfamiliar ingredient caused her body to behave unpredictably. Once in bed, she hugged her knees to her chest and tried to fill her mind with beautiful memories of Penny as she drifted to sleep.

The next morning, Lucy felt agitated and swollen. She was very uncomfortable, but okay otherwise. The chemical in her food hadn't affected her as intensely as she feared. While that should have been good news, it only caused her paranoia to grow. If it had no effect, what was its purpose? She made her way down to the blacktop for training. Today, they only kept them there for an hour before giving them an unexpected meal for breakfast.

There was sour fruit, dry oatmeal, and a glass of grapefruit juice. Lucy did not want to eat a bite of it; the whole thing felt suspicious. Everyone around her rejoiced at the extra food, but she had a creeping suspicion something was amiss. She stared at the bowl of oatmeal in front of her.

"Eat it," a sadistic voice hissed from behind. It was Grimson.

"What's in it?"

"What do you mean? Don't you know what oatmeal is? It's food, you ungrateful rat. Now eat before I smash the other side of your face in."

Lucy kept her lips pursed together. Her nose crinkled in refusal but Grimson grabbed the back of her neck and forced a spoonful of oatmeal into her mouth. As soon as it hit her tongue, she could taste the same bitterness that had been in her meatloaf the night before. It was faint, but it was there. Her eyes grew wide and she tried to shut her mouth in protest, but Grimson was too strong. He shoved another spoonful into her mouth and she almost choked on it as it slid down her throat.

"Are you poisoning us?" she asked as loud as she could before Grimson had a chance to force a third spoonful into her mouth. "Have you been drugging us?" She hoped she was loud enough to cause others to raise questions too.

Lucy could see the people within close proximity take a second look at their plates but since they could not taste it, they did not protest. The cafeteria remained loud and her words were lost. Grimson pulled her in close.

"Eat your food like a good girl. You won't remember any of this in a few days." Then he force-fed Lucy the rest of her oatmeal before walking away.

Lucy saw the day go by in a haze. Or maybe it had been two days. She lost track. The world around her became a fog and she tried desperately not to lose herself. Her clothes no longer fit and were ripping in awkward places at their seams. She was given replacements: a short-sleeved shirt and pants, both poorly made and colored gray. Sores formed in random places along her body, the skin on them raw from their rapid growth.

She was in the cafeteria but forgot how she got there. She looked around, trying to remember the events that led to this moment, but couldn't recall anything. Anger overtook her and she threw an apple from her tray with force across the room. She wasn't sure why she did it, but it hit a man sitting a few rows in front of her. He stood up and screamed. He looked around frantically, then pinned the blame on another man who sat unaware at the table behind him. The man who Lucy hit grabbed the other man around his neck with both hands. He held him in the air and shook him until he passed out. Guards rushed over to the scene. The fog was beginning to settle around Lucy's mind again as she ate her soup calmly. That man was dying because of her outburst, but the soup tasted too delicious to care. Lucy slipped into a daze, leaving the rest of the world behind.

"You can run faster than that. Go again," the man yelled at her. Sweat dripped down Lucy's face. How had she gotten here? What day was it? They were on the blacktop and lined up to race. A starting gun fired.

Lucy ran toward a line on the blacktop that marked the finish. How many times had she done this already? Her feet moved like the steps were memorized but she did not remember running this particular race before. Adrenaline rushed through her body as she looked over at her opponent. Suddenly, all that mattered was winning.

The woman beat her by a second and Lucy went ballistic. Rage consumed her and she went after the woman, grabbing her hair and slamming her face into the cement. Lucy laughed; the noise that came from her sounded foreign, but felt familiar. As she went after the woman again, Grimson came out of nowhere, pointed a gun at her head, and demanded she stop. Lucy threw her arms up in playful surrender and walked back toward the group, chuckling as she joined the other soldiers who stood there with apathetic stares. The woman Lucy attacked did not take it in stride. She stood up and pounced on Lucy while her back was turned. Lucy's animalistic instinct to fight returned and the women scratched at each other's eyes, trying to claw through their opponent's skull. Death was the only way to end this quarrel. Lucy jabbed the woman in a raw sore on her arm causing her to howl in pain; in retaliation, the woman punched Lucy hard in the jaw. The fight continued until the guards broke it up. Lucy let out a scream as a guard held her arms securely behind her back. She screamed so loud the skin on the inside of her throat ripped.

As the noise echoed out of her mouth, her mind went blank. She forgot what she was screaming about. She looked around confused, wondering what had been so bad she felt the need to shout like that, but she could no longer remember.

It was nighttime and Lucy was standing in a long line. It was a slow progression toward a large vehicle wrapped in electrified chains. Militiamen surrounded the line making sure no one tried to escape. Everything was blurry. She shut one eye, trying to focus on the guard standing closest to her. This threw off her balance but let her see more clearly. Instead of focusing on the guard, she saw past him and noticed the faraway electric fence with high voltage spikes that glowed blue at the top. It was entrancing.

Then, a little shadow entered into the glow and disappeared beyond the fence. Lucy scrunched her nose as she became filled with conflicting emotions. An escape? She wanted to escape, too. What little shadow was that? There was a vague memory buried somewhere in her mind of a little shadow she once knew. She searched her memories, trying to remember more, but she could not find its face. Tears of fury filled Lucy's eyes. She couldn't decipher the feelings crisscrossing through her. She pushed past the two people standing next to her and broke free from the line. She had to make it over to the fence where the little shadow disappeared, she had to decipher this strange and overpowering emotion.

"Get back in line!" It was Grimson again. Lucy growled back, though her growl held no words and sounded like it belonged to a wild beast. She lunged at Grimson, knocking the gun out of his hand. She took her fist and plunged it straight into his chest. Blood poured out of his body. Her fingers twisted his insides around before she removed her hand and he fell dead to the floor. She was no longer in control of her mind or body. Pure adrenaline fueled her actions and she howled at the sky. Grimson's blood dripped off her fingertips as she took big, uneven steps toward the distant fence. The muscles that formed awkwardly all over her body caused her strides to be stilted, but that didn't stop her. One goal consumed her mind now: the little shadow.

A gun fired from behind, grazing the side of her face. Lucy's head snapped around, looking for the culprit. She quickly forgot about getting to the fence and now focused on finding out who tried to shoot her. Her nostrils flared as she began to sprint toward the culprit. Her strides were low to the ground and she raced toward him like an attack dog. Another gunshot sounded. This time, it hit Lucy directly in the forehead and she dropped dead. A stream of blood trickled down her face, drawing a neat line between her vacant eyes. It was over. And though her body lay lifeless on the concrete, not even two feet from the crowd, the guards resumed loading the long line of soldiers onto the trucks, as if nothing happened.

Chapter 32

Zyleh needed to find Lux and Eluno so he could get an update on the Ayrenese. He needed to fill Maila in on the status of her people.

"Relina," Zyleh shouted across the Heart, "Has Lux or Eluno returned yet?"

She was tired and had no energy to be harsh with her cousin right now. She gave him hell every day for the lie he told the gliders and let him know his actions were heartless. She warned him to come clean because they'd inevitably find out and Maila would never forgive him, nor would the people of Ayren, but he chose to ignore her. This only intensified her anger. He put her in a position that tested her ethics, jeopardized the harmony of her conscience, and ruined her integrity. She didn't appreciate it and was beginning to resent him.

Today, she needed a break from their personal warfare. Her eyelids threatened to close over her bright green eyes as she answered.

"No. Not yet, but the Coralene were a mess. Glass fell into their water, too. Debris from the explosion was littered throughout our jungle all the way to the beach. I can't even imagine what it looks like in the sky right now." She shook her head, "It's bad. My guess is the gliders haven't left the clouds yet and Lux and Eluno are still waiting to make contact."

Zyleh's head throbbed.

"Were any of the Coralene hurt?"

"No, they said the glass fell through the water slowly. They had plenty of time to dodge. They seemed ready to fight though, which was encouraging. If the Debauched attack by sea, they have to keep the ships off our shores."

"I hope they can. It is the only sure way to prevent our people and the Ahi from having to fight." Zyleh was exhausted. "I am going to find Lux and Eluno. I can't check on Maila again until I have some sort of update."

Relina nodded, not caring what he did. She gave him an emotionless wave as he darted back toward the jungle.

As he ran, he quickly scanned the surrounding trees to determine which one he would climb to reach the treetops. As soon as he picked one, he rounded a corner and bounded straight into Eluno, knocking them both to the ground.

"What the hell?" Eluno shouted.

"So glad I ran into you," Zyleh said, smirking at his own joke. He stood up and offered a hand to Eluno as Lux caught up with them.

"Well I'm not. What are you doing out here?"

"Looking for you two. Did you speak to any of the gliders?"

"We couldn't make contact. No one came down from the clouds," Lux answered. The sun tattoo on his chest changed size as he breathed heavily. He and Eluno were brothers and were much older than Zyleh. Lux's eyes flashed green beneath the small wrinkles around his eyes. "But we will be returning later tonight to try again. We suspect they may glide down at night, after they clean up, since it no longer matters if the Debauched see them."

"Wonderful," Zyleh said, pulling Eluno, who finally accepted his outstretched hand, to his feet. "I will be joining you."

"If you must." Eluno was tired and not in the mood for Zyleh's antics. "Can we please get back to the Heart now?"

The three ran back to the Heart where people were still cleaning up the mess made from the explosion. Between the disorder that remained and every person trying to make themselves useful, the Heart had regressed into a harried and unruly scene. Zyleh weaved through the people in his way and went directly to Maila in her hammock.

Her sleep had not been peaceful. She couldn't stop worrying about the attack on Ayren. She needed to know who was hurt and how bad the damage was. Zyleh appeared and she hoped he would have the answers she sought.

"Have you heard any news about my people?"

Zyleh sat in the tree swing next to Maila's hammock.

"No, not yet. The gliders did not come down from the clouds."
Panic raced through Maila's heart and Zyleh could see the fear in
her eyes. "But don't worry just yet," Zyleh continued, "I am going
back with Lux and Eluno in a little bit to try again. I won't leave
until I talk to someone."

"Make sure to ask them about Darrow, Philo, Bellaine, and
Madivel."

"I will," Zyleh reassured her. "Did you get some rest while I
was gone?"

"No, not really. I couldn't stop my mind from spinning. I am so
worried about them."

He nodded quietly. There was no good response, as he did not
want to give her false hope. The explosion was massive and there
was no way for him to know the casualties of the Ayrenese
people.

"I am so happy I've been training in combat. I am ready to
fight," she continued eagerly. "What can I do to help?"

"Honestly," he responded, "the best way you can help is to
stay here."

Blood flushed into Maila's cheeks. She didn't think anything
could make her angrier than the attack on Ayren, but his
implication was just enough to push her over the edge.

"The best thing I can do is nothing?" she said incredulously. "Are you kidding? Why don't you just come out and say that I'm useless?" She balled her hands into fists at her sides.

"No, you're misunderstanding me—"

"I don't think I am. This is *exactly* why I belong in Ayren. At least I would be of some use there."

"If you had found a way back to Ayren you could be dead right now. This," he threw his arms out to emphasize the destruction that originated from the sky, "was why I was so hell-bent on keeping you *here*. I knew the Debauched would attack there first and that your people would not be prepared in time. I would not have been able to live with myself if I exposed you to that kind of danger."

"While I appreciate the sentiment, it isn't your choice to decide my fate. If I was there right now I could help take care of the wounded and teach people the skills I know that would help them fight and defend our skies. I am inadequate here: I don't fit, I don't belong, and I can't do any of the things I could do back home. I want to be where I can help."

Zyleh's expression was stone cold. He was becoming angry too, but tried to contain it.

"Well, I'm sorry to break it to you but you're stuck here. These people you care so much about left you for dead. I picked up the pieces in an attempt to make you feel better about being deserted.

272

I'm sorry it has been so miserable for you in Tier, despite all my efforts to make you feel welcome and happy. I have gone above and beyond for you and you still choose the people who don't care about you over me."

Maila's eyes filled with angry tears, "They didn't come because of the impending war. I know they still love me." She wasn't even sure if she believed the words she was saying, but he was using her insecurities against her and she refused to grant him that power. He wanted her to stay with him, he wanted her to reciprocate his love, but she wouldn't let him bully her into submission. So she spoke with certainty, feigning strength and hoping the words she said were still true.

"Believe what you want," he retorted. "That's not the point of this discussion. I have been nothing but kind to you, yet you continually dismiss me. Your heart has been closed to me since the moment we met." Zyleh's defense softened, "I just want you to stop caring about the life you left in Ayren so you can start caring about me."

"I do care about you. You're my friend."

"I want a chance to be more than that." Maila wished she could have stopped this conversation before it started, but Zyleh kept talking, "I want you to love me back." Maila felt sick. "I want you to build a life with me in Tier."

Her nerves eased a bit. He handed her the perfect segue to divert the conversation from feelings into logistics. She could keep his feelings spared from the truth about her love for Darrow.

"I don't belong here and never will. I'm sorry if that hurts your feelings, but it's the truth. My body rejects the gravity, which leaves me feeling nauseous and achy all the time. My lungs constantly feel like they are collapsing beneath my chest. My bones were already hollow and fragile to begin with, and being down here has decreased their density even more. I will die if I stay here much longer."

"I can heal you. You felt the magic the Heart held."

"The root of the problem lies in my genes. That magic is only temporary for a condition like mine. You told me that yourself."

"You're right, but I can find the right combination of herbs, roots, and magic. I will make you a remedy. I've done it before, I helped stop that plague. I can do it again."

"Please stop. You aren't getting it. This isn't about you or my feelings for you. This is about my well-being. Tier isn't my natural habitat. I can't stay here."

"It's because you don't love me." Zyleh clenched his teeth and moved the muscles in his jaw. "After all this time and everything I've done to prove our connection is real and worthwhile, you still won't let me into your heart. My feelings for you are unreturned.

I've tried to keep them to myself, waiting for the day you felt the same way I do, but I am seeing now that day may never come."

Maila buried her face into her hands. "This is the most pointless conversation we could possibly be having right now."

"To *you*, maybe, but not to me. I have loved you since the day I first saw you. We are connected, whether you want to admit it to yourself or not. I know you are fighting it, or ignoring it, and I can't even express how hurtful that is."

"My feelings are at the very bottom of my list of things to be worried about right now."

A shout came up from the ground. "Zyleh? Are you ready to go?"

It was Lux. Zyleh looked over at Maila, his eyes vivid green with pain.

"I get it," he said angrily, but he didn't get it at all. "I can't help how I feel for you. I have to go now. Enjoy your space." And he was off.

Maila threw her body back against the hammock, aggravated that this was now another thing she had to deal with. It was the same argument Darrow always presented to her, but now with everything in perspective, she was positive she loved Darrow. But how could she ever tell Zyleh that without seeming cold-hearted? He was so thoughtful and attentive during her time in the jungle and breaking his heart would be an awful way to repay his kindness.

Through the tree branches, Maila could see the stars twinkling above her. The moon was bright and cast a glow onto the world beneath. The adult Tierannites left the Heart and traveled into the jungle, making preparations Maila physically could not be part of. This frustrated her beyond belief. She wanted to help but was so out of place that she would only get in the way. Refusing to feel defeated, emotionally or physically, Maila brainstormed new ways to be productive.

Chapter 33

Relina appeared out of nowhere, leaping from tree to tree toward Maila. She landed next to her on the tree swing and took a deep breath.

"What a night," Relina said, exasperated.

"I can only imagine. I wish I could be of more help."

"We will get you back to Ayren soon." She gave Maila a smile. "I can't stay long but I wanted to check on you. Wasn't sure if anybody came by recently. I know Zyleh is all over the place right now."

Maila grunted. "He found time to come by. He is incredibly hard-headed." Relina nodded in agreement and Maila continued, "He insists that I should love him, that I am unaware of my feelings for him, but I am positive I know what my heart wants. I left someone back home who I need to return to. I'm not really ready for love because there is still too much to be done, but when I am, I am sure it will be with him. But how can I possibly tell that to Zyleh after all he has done for me? He has been so kind and truthful. He taught me everything I always wanted to learn about the world. He actually answered the questions I had and gave me the long overdue gift of my history. He's taken care of me in Tier and has been such a thoughtful friend. I don't want to break his heart."

Relina was done. The lie Zyleh crafted had gone too far. Maila was her friend and she couldn't cover up her cousin's actions any longer.

"You don't owe your love to anyone but yourself. And if I were you, I wouldn't worry so much about Zyleh's feelings. Sure, he has been there for you and has helped you, but he doesn't deserve the consideration you are trying to give to him."

"Why not?" Maila insisted.

"This is terrible timing with the war approaching." Relina shook her head but could not deny Maila the truth. She deserved to know. "Between you and me, Zyleh is the only reason you're stuck down here at all. He moved that little white tree while you walked up and down the beach, which essentially moved you very far from where the Coralene told the gliders to look for you. They came many times but never found you because Zyleh moved your landmark. Then, when the gliders persistence to find you continued, he told them you died so they would stop looking."

"They think I'm dead?" Anger swept over her like a tidal wave and she could hear her heart pounding inside her head.

Relina nodded, "I told him to come clean. I told him what he did was unforgivable, but he swore he did it with good intentions."

"Good intentions? Where in the Heavens do his 'good intentions' fit in amongst the hurt he caused? Not only did he make me feel like I was inconsequential to the people I love most, but he also made my loved ones suffer terrible grief."

"I don't know why he thought it was a good idea. I guess he thought he was keeping you safe. It was only a matter of time before Ayren was attacked and maybe he thought you'd see his side of it once you saw the devastation first hand and realized you survived because he kept you far away from it." Relina shrugged. "Maybe he saw it as the only sure way to keep you alive."

"I don't care!" Maila shouted, "What he did was selfish and cruel. I spent hours beating myself up over why they left me here, to the point where I started to believe I never deserved to be saved at all. I felt unworthy of their love and understood why they might not care about me anymore after I put them in such danger."

"Oh, they still cared. The gliders came down each morning and afternoon after receiving your location from the Coralene. They searched tirelessly, spending hours trying to find you."

Maila's eyes filled with tears. "I thought they left me here by choice. I thought they were so mad at me they couldn't forgive me. I started to believe I wasn't worth a second chance."

"They never stopped loving you."

"Zyleh is a monster. How could he do this to me?"

"I'm not going to defend his actions, but I know he believes his intentions were honorable. Hopefully you guys can hash it out and come to a peaceful resolution before this war picks up momentum. I think he's wrong, but I know he genuinely loves you. Maybe he'll give you an explanation you could accept enough to move past this. It would be terrible if he went into battle with your hatred aimed his way."

"Are you kidding me?" Maila's fury was unbreakable. "I thought he was my friend! Friends don't deceive friends. He destroyed my trust for him with utter completeness."

Relina understood. "I don't expect you to forgive him. I wouldn't."

"And he claims to love me? How could he ever expect me to forgive him for this atrocious crime he's committed against me and all my loved ones? Whether I found out today or in ten years from now, the amount of hurt I'd feel would be the same. He tried to destroy everything I've ever loved."

"I'm sorry I didn't tell you sooner. At first, I didn't know you. Then once I got to like you and we became friends, I was torn between family loyalties and doing what was right."

"Did he act alone?"

"Absolutely. I'm the only other person that knows and he told me by accident. He's been threatening me to keep my mouth shut every day since."

"Then the blame is solely his." Maila couldn't believe it. She never even loved Zyleh, but in his own twisted way, he still managed to break her heart. As her friend, he betrayed her on the deepest level. "I'm sorry he put you in a miserable position as well."

"I'm just glad you know now. I'll help you get home to Ayren once things settle." Relina was glad to have the weight of this lie off her back.

"Thank you."

"I have to go prepare for battle. I'll see you again soon." She gave Maila a hug and then sped down the tree.

Maila rubbed the back of Bazoo's neck as he lay sleeping by her side. She was livid to learn that her friendship with Zyleh was based off a lie. He deceived her, he tried to manipulate her, and she was unknowingly kept prisoner in his egocentric world. Every nice moment she ever had with him was now tarnished by deceit. The outrage she felt threatened to take over her mind and soul, but she could not let that happen. She would not let him get the best of her anymore. Now that she knew the truth he could no longer control her fate. She had to calm down and sleep it off. It was the only way to recollect her composure and move forward.

Her mind ran wild with anger, sadness, and confusion as she tried to fall asleep. To center herself, she shut her eyes and focused on the calming buzz of insects that came from deep in the jungle. There was no room for more negativity in her shattered world. All that mattered now was Ayren and the fate of her loved ones. The sooner she could get back, the better.

Chapter 34

"Heyya, little chickidee."

Maila's sleepy eyes popped open at the sound of a tiny voice calling to her from below.

"Little chickidee, wake up," the tiny voice whispered again. Maila looked over the side of her hammock and saw a body, but could not tell who it was. The clear vision the magic of the Heart gave her was wearing off.

"Who's there?" she called down in a half-whisper, aware that Tierannite children were trying to sleep all around her.

"Be quiet and come down," the tiny voice implored, somehow managing to be quiet and loud all at the same time. "I am from Ahi and your people need you."

Maila's heart beat fast with renewed hope and the idea of seeing Darrow again filled her mind. After all this time, she never imagined the Ahi would be the ones to help her get home.

Without a second thought, Maila began her climb down. Bazoo tried to follow her but she stopped him.

"You are a wonderful friend, Bazoo, but you must stay here."

The monkey whimpered, letting out a squeal of protest.

"If there is a way to get back, I must take it." She scratched him beneath his chin and then gave him a kiss on the nose. "I will miss you, my friend." She smiled and continued to climb down the tree.

She got to the ground floor and the source of the little voice was already upon her.

"Shh," he whispered. It was a little boy with blood-red skin. The whites of his eyes were prominent around their dark red irises, and his jet-black hair was braided tightly in many rows against his scalp. His eyes held a secret.

"What is your name?"

"Tyoko."

"I'm Maila."

"I already know that."

"The gliders have contacted you?"

Tyoko's eyes darted around suspiciously as he ignored her question.

"Shh," he insisted again. "You must be quiet. The people of Tier cannot know you are coming with me."

"Why not?" she asked, confused.

"We have no time for questions. The gliders have come, do you want to go with them or not? I can show you the way."

Of course she wanted to go home with them—she wanted that more than anything—but how could she leave here without saying goodbye? Zyleh didn't deserve her farewell, but the rest of the Tierannites did. Despite their initial prejudices, they opened their minds, homes, and hearts to her, and eventually accepted her as one of them. Just then, she heard Bazoo behind her and an idea emerged. She turned to her monkey friend and spoke.

"Let all the Tierannites know that I am sorry I did not get the chance to say goodbye or properly thank them for their hospitality. Their acceptance means more than they realize and the warmth with which they treated me will live in my heart forever. Tell them I wish I could have waited, but there was no time to spare." She stared intently into Bazoo's eyes. "Be sure to let Zyleh know he is not a recipient of that group message."

Bazoo grabbed her arm and shrieked in objection, but Maila shook free from his grip and went back to where Tyoko stood.

"I'll miss you, Bazoo."

Tyoko started to run and with a deep breath, Maila ran after him. She heard Bazoo wail with protest, his cries fading as they traveled further away.

Once they were a decent distance from the Heart, Tyoko paused for Maila to catch up.

"You are moving too slow. Get on my back," he ordered.

Maila was about to protest that she was too big when the little boy grew larger right in front of her eyes. His muscles elongated, his bones appeared to stretch, and he magically transformed into a tall boy. Her jaw dropped. Was it magic? Did his bones really grow and shrink at will? Zyleh mentioned this skill, but seeing it happen in real life raised a whole new set of questions.

"Get on," he insisted. She climbed onto his back and he carried her at high speeds through the forest.

They were now many miles away from the Heart and Maila could not wait to see the faces of whichever gliders had come for her. She had an uncontrollable hope that Darrow would be one of them.

After a few miles, Tyoko stopped and put Maila down.

"We're almost there. Follow me." He set off into a sprint again and she chased after him. She was having trouble following the boy, who was weaving in and out of trees. His coloring was so dark it was hard to keep track of him in the moonlight.

"Stop running so fast," she called out, but he did not hear her.

The hard ground hurt the soles of Maila's bare feet with each step she took. Her body felt heavy and her head throbbed.

As Tyoko passed through a small clearing, he vanished back into the trees on the other side. She ran a little faster, using all the energy in her body to catch up.

As she was passed a large rock, the ground disappeared from beneath her feet. Her body hit the side of the hole before plummeting downward. She let out a small scream as the familiar feeling of falling took hold of her stomach. This time, she couldn't even try to control the fall with levitation.

This fall was much shorter than the one from the sky. As she hit the ground she transitioned into a smooth roll the best she could, but her joints still jammed and her knees and palms cut open.

She looked up and saw that the opening to the world above was seven or eight feet high. Furious, she called out to the boy.

"Tyoko," she screamed, "I've fallen. I need you to help me get out."

No response.

After a moment, she heard a small laugh and saw the light of the moon begin to disappear.

"Help!" She clawed at the walls in an attempt to climb back up to Tier, but her nails merely scratched the dirt and her feet could not find any solid nooks to step on. She continued to cry out for help, hoping a Tierannite might hear her, but the opening to the hole above her was almost completely covered. From above, she heard the small Ahi boy singing. His voice was distant but the words were clear.

"Catch a falling star and play a little trick.

Baddest of them all is trapped inside a pit."

He laughed with self-amusement, then carried on with his improvised song.

There was barely a slice of moonlight left before Maila stopped her feeble attempt to climb and fell to the ground. She watched the last sliver of freedom disappear before the feeling of complete terror washed over her.

She had fallen into Ahi. Tyoko fooled her and led her into this trap. She didn't like that his song implied she was the bad guy, but assumed the Ahi still held a grudge against her for her accident. Tyoko must have overheard gossip, rumors, and hatred spoken by the adults he looked up to. Maybe he misinterpreted what they said, or maybe the Ahi really did view her as a villain.

But she wasn't a villain, nor was she a victim—there had to be another way out. Everything was pitch black, so she focused on what she heard.

The sound of running water echoed in the distance. It was a soft, steady murmur, so she placed her right hand against the wall of the tunnel and began to walk, feeling her way toward the only sound she heard.

Chapter 35

Violet had not left the sewer since Mr. Lamorte herded the other citizens into his personalized nightmare. Her swollen eye was healing on its own, which was essential since the remaining medicine was used on the wound she created during the removal of her tracker. She had no clue where Lucy was and there were no other merchants to get medicine from. The market and all its inhabitants were gone.

The sewer was her new home. It was as cozy as she could make it, and if she rationed her portions carefully, there was enough food and water in her assailant's backpacks to survive in the sewer for a few months. She assembled the contents of the bags to resemble what she imagined a kitchen would look like. One of the bags had a rolled up sleeping bag attached to the bottom of it, so she laid it out as her bed and used her oversized jacket as a pillow. There was also a flashlight with extra batteries, a portable radio, bandages, a notebook, pens, rubber bands, rope, and a deck of playing cards.

The days were long and dull and Violet spent her time making up card games, drawing pictures in the notebook, spying out of the sewer grate, and rationing her meals.

Repeating this routine in isolation day after day was beginning to feel selfish and the time to leave the sewer and help others was approaching. If she managed to escape, then others must have too, she just hoped they managed to survive all this time.

She sat on the cold floor, listening to a faint stream of water trickle in the distance. The suspicious warm breezes had ceased, as did the whispers telling her to leave. She hoped this welcomed silence continued.

On this day, she planned to eat half a can of vegetables and two pieces of beef jerky. She also had half a bottle of water left over from yesterday, but that needed to last another day.
Violet pulled back her messy blonde hair with a rubber band and opened a can of vegetables with her Swiss Army knife. After finishing her meal, she looked at the portable radio next to all her stuff. She hadn't found the courage to turn it on yet.

She craved to hear another human voice, but her nerves always got the best of her. If anyone above heard the noise, her hiding spot would be ruined. She picked up the radio and held it in her small hands. Without turning the power on she played with the knobs and sighed heavily. Her heart ached to know what people outside this area of North America were broadcasting.

Over the centuries, the government focused so much of their energy on the Internet that the radio became a lost form of communication. So much so, the radio started being used as an underground method of communication. It was the only safe place for individuals to express themselves outside the government's control. It took some finagling to find the wavelengths unmonitored by the government, but it was possible. People were always more courageous when speaking on the radio. Violet thought if she turned it on, she might hear people talking freely about what Mr. Lamorte was doing.

She looked into the light coming in from the grate above and made a deal with herself: if she did not see anyone in the streets for the next ten minutes, she would turn the radio on at a very low volume for a minute.

Once she reached the top of the ladder, she very carefully lifted the grate just enough so her eyes were above ground level. Her gaze focused on the small stretch of street she could see at the end of her alley. Deserted, as it had been for the last week.

She waited a while to be sure, then climbed back down, settled onto her sleeping bag, and turned the radio on. Static noise blasted from the speakers and her heart pounded with fear as she tried to locate the volume knob. When she finally did, she lowered the volume all the way to mute.

Furious with herself, she listened to the silence around her to determine if she had foolishly revealed her hiding location. There were no sounds other than the trickling of sewer water. After a few minutes, Violet very cautiously turned the volume up until it was barely a whisper. White noise was all she heard, so with her ear to the speaker and a hand on the dial, she slowly searched through the stations until she found one that came in clear.

A few stations broadcasted pre-recorded propaganda announcements for Mr. Lamorte's war initiative. The sound of his voice made Violet's blood boil. She continued scrolling through the stations until she came across one that was distinctly clear.

"—this is not the end. Follow me and be set free."

She was intrigued, but skeptical.

"If you've tuned into this station it means you're off the government's frequency. Our wavelength is untraceable. Here, we talk as freely as we please. If you're listening in from the East Coast, congrats on surviving." As the man continued to speak, his voice sounded familiar. "For our veteran listeners, hello again. To those who are new, welcome. This station is dedicated to the resistance, to those of us in hiding and waiting for the opportunity to fight back. This is a secret frequency, only capable of being heard on the underground wavelengths. If you're out of bounds of the government's frequency, in possession of a radio they didn't plant their chips into, or were smart enough to find a way to remove the microchips, then we've got your ear."

Violet couldn't believe this radio station existed. She assumed she'd hear people speaking out against Mr. Lamorte, but not a secret station dedicated to resistance.

There was a tinkering of bells and whistles, then the man's deep and altered voice came back.

"Today's news: Lamorte's militia has been prepping a large fleet of battleships in quadrant D4, off the coast of Old Florida. Reports came in today that a caravan of trucks was seen traveling down the East Coast Highway toward the southern region. It's rumored they began their drive last night at the Northeast boot camp in B4. And what's even weirder? The backs of the trucks were covered in black tarp and wrapped securely with thick metal chains glowing bright blue with electricity. What does this mean, you ask? Well, I'll tell ya. Lamorte is sending off his first batch of soldiers. They will be the first round of cattle prodded onto the restored battleships. If you live in the western quadrants, watch out! My guess is once these soldiers crash and burn, he'll be moving on to recruit you next."

Another, meeker robotic voice chimed in.

"Nobody wants to fight, so how is Lamorte forcing them to? Is he just hoping they will turn into well-behaved soldiers once they get there? I sure as hell know I'd show up on our opponent's land, drop my weapon, and beg for them to take me in: as a soldier, as a slave. *Anything* to save me from Lamorte's rule. And why were there chains around the trucks? Any regular person couldn't break free from a normal truck's locks, so why the extra security?"

"Good points, Rufus. These questions are still mysteries. If anyone has any tidbits on this, you know the number. 91-000-BRAVERY. This station is just the beginning. Together, we can stay informed, and together, we can find a way to fight back. We're going off air now, but tune in tonight at 8 p.m. Eastern Standard Time for more updates. You know how it goes: *Be brave, we are not Lamorte's slaves.* This is Barnibus, signing off." Static.

Barnibus? Violet thought the voice sounded familiar but it was hard to decipher who it was through the voice disguiser. She prayed it was the Barnibus she knew.

If she could get to him, maybe together they could work out a plan. She hastily grabbed the notebook, knocking down a stack of cans in the process, and scribbled down the phone number. Finding a way to call in would be her next adventure.

Violet smiled for the first time in weeks. She never stopped hoping, but now, she finally had something concrete to believe in.

She leaned her head back against the brick wall of the sewer and shut her eyes. Before she could relax, a rustle came from above. She jumped out of the light cast down from the grate, dragging her sleeping bag, jacket, and satchel along with her. All her other belongings were already out of sight.

Her heart pounded. She prayed it was a rat or a crow and not one of Mr. Lamorte's militiamen, but her hopes were squashed when a human voice echoed through the grate.

Chapter 36

"Hello?" a tiny voice called down.

Her mind raced. It wasn't a policeman; it sounded like a small child. Or was it a trap? Did Mr. Lamorte have kids working for him now? Paranoia commandeered her thought process. Perhaps Mr. Lamorte created a child army that was sent out to trick the escapees.

"Hello?" the tiny boy whispered again. "I'm all alone. If somebody's down there, can I stay with you?" he asked timidly, his voice shaking.

Furious with herself for even considering to ignore the boy, she stepped into the light and climbed up the ladder. She could finally help someone other than herself.

"What's your name?" she asked through the grate.

"Colin Roe," he said through sniffles. Her heart tightened, he looked to be only six or seven years old.

"My name is Violet," she paused. It hurt to say her last name out loud. It reminded her of a time when she had a family. "Violet Linvale. I'm going to let you stay with me, but first, did anyone see you come here?"

"No, I don't think so. The streets are abandoned. I'm sure they know I escaped by now, I've been gone since last night. But even if they are looking for me, they don't know where I went."

"What about your tracker?"

Colin immediately held out his left forearm nervously.

"My mom took them out of me and my brother once she heard Mr. Lamorte made it through the smog. The day he came back, she did this. I guess she knew bad things were about to happen." His eyes grew wide as he remembered the pain of having his tracker removed. "It hurt really bad."

Violet sighed in relief.

"Okay, good. Now look me in the eyes and don't you dare lie to me," she said sternly. He looked right at her, his big brown eyes wet with tears. "Do you have the disease?"

"No. I don't have it. And no one in my family had it either. We knew the remedy."

A remedy? Without another moment's hesitation, she opened the sewer grate enough to let him slip through the crack and climb down the ladder. Once inside, she moved the grate back in place.

On the sewer floor, Colin sat against the far wall, opposite of where her stuff was set up. He looked at the loot in amazement.

"How did you find this place?" he asked.

"Some dumb rat," Violet said. "The real question is how did *you* find me here?" She needed to know what gave her away. Whatever it was, it would never happen again. She had her fingers crossed it had not been the radio.

"I was hiding out behind a dumpster in the alley above and I heard a crash come from this direction."

It was the cans that fell when she grabbed her notebook to write down the phone number. She grunted in frustration at her own carelessness, and Colin's face shifted with disappointment.

"Don't look sad, I'm not mad that *you* heard me. But if you were a militiaman, I'd be furious." She gave him a smile and Colin let out a tiny laugh. "I'm glad you found me actually."

Colin nodded, accepting what she said as the truth.

"Where did you get all this stuff?" he asked as his eyes scanned the wall lined with candies, bread, jelly, water, and many other supplies. Violet thought carefully before answering.

"I won it." She left it at that. He did not need to know the gruesome details. "Are you hungry? I'll make you a deal. You get this one time to take anything you want, and then you go onto the same rationing plan as me. We need this food to last. Deal?"

His eyes grew wide with delight as he looked over his options. He picked up a package of chocolate chip cookies then looked at Violet, waiting for her approval. She gave him a smile and he ripped into the wrapper.

He devoured the cookies like a starving, wild animal, and she was grateful she could feed him. He took off his tiny jacket and his arms revealed the scar where his mom removed his tracker. It was a much neater scar than the one forming on her arm. Hers was long and raised, still sore to the touch. The leftover eye medicine that Lucy and Barnibus gave her only did so much for a lesion as deep as this one, but she hoped to at least prevent infection. It seemed to be working. All that remained from the wound was a fresh scab covering what would soon be a large scar.

She pushed her bottle of water toward Colin.

"Don't drink it all. Filtered water is one thing we cannot waste."

Colin nodded and took a few tiny sips. He put the bottle back down and continued eating his cookies.

"How old are you?"

"Seven," he said with his mouth full.

"Where did you escape from?"

"The boot camp." He swallowed a mouthful of cookie. "It was awful."

"You escaped after you were already inside?" she asked, impressed.

"Yeah, it wasn't easy. I had to wait until all the focus was on shipping the adults to battle. That was when I snuck out of our building and explored. I found a broken spot in the electric fence that circles the property. That's how I got out. I escaped last night and have been walking around since. I didn't know where to go."

Colin ate another cookie. She was fascinated and wanted to know more.

"Did anyone else escape with you?"

"No," he shook his head sadly, "just me. My little brother, Dax, was already brainwashed and I knew if I told him what I was gonna do he would snitch on me. It was hard to tell who had turned, so I figured it was safer to go alone."

Violet nodded in understanding.

"Well, you can count on me. We are a team now."

The boy's eyes lit up, thrilled that he wasn't alone anymore. He smiled.

"You can count on me, too."

"Do you think there is any way we could sneak back to the boot camp and save others?"

"I don't know," he hesitated with fear in his eyes. "I guess so. But with the kids, it's hard to tell who is okay and who is brainwashed. And Mr. Lamorte already gave the drug to all the adults. The few left behind are too scary to save. They'd probably kill us if we tried."

"The drug?" she asked, confused.

"Yeah," he explained, "Our guards talked about it all the time. Mr. Lamorte forced all the adults to take a drug he made. They told us to stay far away from the adults because they were stronger than superheroes and meaner than monsters. It was really scary the way they changed so fast. I saw them get put into trucks from a window in the children's dormitory. I couldn't even tell who was a girl or who was a boy anymore. They all had big muscles and walked with their heads down. They didn't seem scared and they didn't fight the guards. They just obeyed. It wasn't like that the first week. All the adults fought back. If I saw my mom or dad now, I bet they wouldn't even know who I was."

Violet was at a loss for words. She knew Mr. Lamorte was forcing people to fight, but she had no idea he was using drugs to turn them into obedient war machines. She then thought back to the radio show she heard earlier. That was why they wrapped the trucks in chains. These soldiers are so strong they could break through the truck's locks and the guards weren't taking any chances. They couldn't risk these monsters escaping before they were put onto the ships and deployed through the smog.

"We need to find Barnibus," she blurted out.

"Barnibus?"

"My friend. He has an underground radio show dedicated to the resistance, and they need to know about the drug. People from different areas of North America need to know what to expect once they are captured and put into a boot camp."

"Okay, how do we find him?"

"I'm not sure. I only have a phone number."

"Do you have any coins? There is a screenphone around the block."

She grabbed the closest backpack, remembering that dozens of coins were at the bottom of the bag. She thought they would be useless now that the market was gone but never considered she'd need to make a call. She grabbed a handful of coins and couldn't believe how much money she held in her hand. It was the most she'd ever seen in her life.

Colin must have felt the same way because his eyes grew wide when he saw her fistful of change.

"Yup, that looks like enough," he said animatedly.

"Colin, before we go, tell me more about your family's remedy for the disease."

"My mom was a chemist for the government until they fired her. But she kept working at home and eventually figured it out. My whole family had a spoonful of it every day."

"Do you have any of it with you?"

"No, but I know where my mom kept it hidden in our apartment. We lived in the ghetto on South Street 9."

"Okay, that will be a journey for another day. I'm not ready to venture that far. Do you know the ingredients?"

"Yeah, my mom made us memorize the different parts. It is bloodroot and lomatium," he stumbled over the pronunciation of this word as he sang the ingredients to the tune of an ancient nursery rhyme. "Water, oatmeal, lemon balm, and sodium." The song ended and he explained the rest from memory. "It makes a paste. It tastes horrible but it works. And you have to grow the bloodroot on your own, so we need to go and get the plants my mom was harvesting before they die. My mom hid backup seeds throughout the house, but it would be easier if we started with the ones that are already grown."

"I agree. We will try to go soon. And you are positive it works?"

"Yup. One time, a few years ago, an old man covered in the disease sneezed right into my face. His spit got into my eyes and mouth, but I took the remedy my mom made and I never got sick."

"Gross."

"Yeah."

"I'm glad you remembered the ingredients." Violet marveled at this little boy's intelligence and his mother's wise foresight, then continued her thought, "If we can get through to Barnibus on the radio, maybe we can let him know the remedy, too. He can share it with other survivors like us. He has a much bigger reach than we do."

"Okay, that's a great idea."

Violet placed the coins into her pocket.

"Ready to go?"

Colin nodded and they both headed up the ladder and out the sewer grate.

Chapter 37

The city felt muggy and thick compared to the air Violet was used to breathing in the sewer. She immediately regretted not wearing her scarf.

The street outside the alley was abandoned. Everything was deserted, which made the city creepier than usual. The only noise she heard came from the crows overhead. Thousands of them sat on the building tops and power lines. Their black, beady eyes watched her and Colin as they walked. Only the vilest of animals thrived in Mr. Lamorte's kingdom: crows, rats, and cockroaches were most commonly sighted.

Mr. Lamorte had a fleet of drone crows that provided surveillance of the streets, but those mechanical crows had glowing red eyes and all the birds Violet saw now did not. She assumed they were put to use somewhere else now that this part of North America was vacant, but she kept an eye out for the red-eyed drones just in case.

They turned the corner and were greeted with more stillness. The air around them was dense and Violet took long, slow breaths in order to inhale as little air as possible. They walked to the end of the sidewalk and made another right turn. As soon as they did, she saw the screenphone. In ancient years, an archaic version of the screenphone was used. It was abolished once individual, handheld devices were adopted as commonplace. As North America tried to rebuild after the purge, they did not have the means to restore the cell towers, so landlines were reestablished.

This screenphone was on their side of the street, only a few feet ahead of them. The sign on the phone read 48¢. Violet looked down at her hand, unsure which coins made up the amount she needed.

She looked over to Colin, embarrassed that she wasn't more familiar with the denominations of money. She understood numbers and their value, but her parents never had enough money to teach her the numeric worth of monetary artifacts. Just like she did while surviving on her own, her parents made all purchases through the bartering of alternate goods or services.

"Do you know how to count change?"

"Yeah, my parents taught me," he answered, excited to help. He grabbed Violet's hand, lowered it to his eye level, and sorted through the coins with his tiny, dirty fingers. All the coins had various faces from the Lamorte dynasty on them. Violet did her best not to look at their sinister smiles as she took the counted amount from Colin.

"Thanks," she said. "You're going to have to teach me how to count money that fast when we get back to the sewer."

Since she did not want the noise of the call to be released into the quiet city air, she picked up the receiver, which made the audio of the phone call private. She put the sleek handset to her ear and dropped the coins into the slot on the side.

As soon as she dropped the last penny into the phone, a dial tone appeared.

"It's working," she said breathlessly as she used the touch screen to dial the number. The phone rang three times into Violet's ear before a patchy clicking noise took over.

It clicked five times then beeped twice. Normally the face of the person on the other end would pop up on the screen, but all Violet saw were an assortment of colorful, wavy lines.

"Is your line secure?" a deep voice said. It sounded disguised, just like the voice of the man on the radio show.

"Uh, I'm not sure. I'm at a screenphone on the corner of –"

"Please hold."

She was cut off and the clicking and beeping noises started up again. She looked down at Colin and shrugged her shoulders.

A minute went by, though it felt much longer. Violet's eyes darted around, looking in every direction as she waited. She cautiously watched the crows, checking their eyes as they sat on the rooftops.

Then the voice returned. The man's voice was raspy and no longer disguised by a machine.

"You're supposed to say 'Sorry, wrong number' as soon as the clicking starts if you are calling from an unsafe location. Then we'd know to switch you over to a secure line."

"Oh, okay, I'm sorry. I heard the radio show for the first time this afternoon. I didn't know."

"No worries. If you don't say the password after I answer, I usually just disconnect the call. But you sounded young, so I cut the line and reconnected on a different frequency. Just listen for the password during each show and say it next time you call in."

"Okay," she answered, "sorry about that."

"Don't fret it."

"Why can't I see you?"

"We disable the camera function for all calls. You can't see us, we can't see you. Safest that way."

"Makes sense."

"So what is your situation?"

"Are you Barnibus Blightly?"

"That's what they call me."

"Barnibus. It's me, Violet. I've been in hiding. When you said your name, I thought it must be you, so I had to call in." The screen of colored lines cut out and was replaced by Barnibus's old, but happy face.

"Little lady, you survived! How'd ya manage?"

"A fight broke out at the back of the crowd where I was standing and the electric fence went down long enough for me to run through and hide."

"Something similar happened in my section. You remember Lucy who gave you those meds? I tried to help her escape with me, but she and Penny didn't move fast enough. You haven't seen them by any chance, have ya?"

"No, this is the first time I've left the sewer since that day."

Barnibus groaned and his voice was distraught. "I keep seeing her scared face in my dreams. I didn't mean to leave her behind. If I could've done more, I would've, but those damn guards recovered mighty fast. I never would've made it out if I waited."

"Don't beat yourself up. Maybe they made it out too. You never know."

"I hope so. That was a nasty afternoon. I'm glad you're alright. Are you survivin' okay? Got enough food and water?"

"Yeah, I'm set up for a while," she answered confidently before looking around again to double-check their surroundings for other people. The coast was still clear. "Barnibus, I am calling in with very crucial information."

"Okay, what is it?"

"A boy escaped from the boot camp. He found me and said that Mr. Lamorte is using a drug to turn people into uncontrollable monsters. I think that is why they chained those trucks you were talking about. Colin said these people on the drugs had grown to be enormous. Huge, muscled-up, emotionless wrecking machines."

"You've got to be kidding me."

"I'm not."

"Did he say if everyone was on the drug already?"

"The children aren't, but Mr. Lamorte is brainwashing them. He didn't know how many kids were effectively molded when he left because it's hard to tell. As for the adults, he's nodding his head at me that all the adults in the camp were forced to take the drug already."

"Dammit."

"Yeah, I know. But Colin also said that only a small fraction were shipped out in the first round. The rest are still hoarded and confined at the camp. Maybe they can be rescued? If not, at least you can warn everyone about what he is doing. That way when he moves west to recruit and capture others they'll know what to expect. Might even be the motivation people need to rally and fight back."

"Don't you worry, we will broadcast this information on our 8 p.m. show. Everyone needs to be aware."

"Another crucial bit of information," Violet continued. "Colin's mom used to be a chemist for the government. She got fired but continued working on a cure for the disease at home and came up with a remedy that kept Colin and his family healthy."

"A remedy? That's ridiculous, girl. If there was a remedy, Lamorte would have it figured out by now."

"Well, it seems he was dumb enough to fire the one chemist who was onto something. Colin knows the ingredients and says there are batches of it hidden where he used to live with his family."

"Well," Barnibus didn't sound convinced, "what are the ingredients then?"

Violet handed the phone to Colin and he moved to stand in front of the screen. He sang the ingredients into the receiver, even spelling out some of the words for Barnibus, then handed the receiver back.

"You get that, Barnibus?"

"Yeah, I wrote it down. Don't know if it's legit, but I'll broadcast it anyhow and let people figure it out for themselves. We ain't got no high society or government folks listening in, so we don't have to worry 'bout them getting this gem if it turns out to be true." He stopped to cough. "Sounds like you got a little genius over there, huh?"

Violet looked over at Colin proudly. "Yeah, it sure seems so."

"Good find. Keep him around. Are you gonna be able to stay in touch via the phone? Or do I gotta come find you if I need to talk to ya?"

"I've got enough coins for a few more phone calls. If not, I'm by Mr. Lamorte's skyscraper. Call out into the alley and I'll find you."

"You got it. Why is your eye still bruised?"

Violet had forgotten about that. She touched her eye, which was still sore.

"It'll be fine. Least of my worries at the moment."

"You got that right. Okay, take care, little lady. And thanks for the information."

"Yup. Talk to you soon."

"Ta-Ta." And he hung up.

Violet grabbed Colin's hand, eager to get back into hiding, and pulled him along as she ran.

They turned both corners and she could see the opening to the small alley next to Mr. Lamorte's building. She stopped running as soon as she got to the front door of his skyscraper. Violet peeked through the glass window to make sure no one would see them run by. The lobby was empty, so she continued pulling Colin behind her and they rounded into the alley. They descended into the sewer and she felt safe again.

"Do you feel that?" Colin asked. His eyes were wide with worry.

"Feel what?" Violet asked. But all too soon after asking, she felt the warm breeze filter through the sewer. An uneasy feeling entered her gut.

The breeze flowed past them continuously. Violet's heart fluttered, scared of what might emerge from the shadows of the tunnel. Then, as swiftly as it appeared, it ceased.

"That was weird," Colin said.

"It's happened before," she answered, still trying to see into the darkness of the tunnel. Colin's eyebrows raised in fear. "But it's nothing to worry about. Just a warm breeze that comes from time to time." Violet changed topics. "Now, you need to teach me how to count coins."

Colin smiled, excited to teach his new hero something. While they went through the lesson, Violet maintained a strong facade, but in the back of her mind she could not shake her doubts about what mysteries the breeze held. It wasn't only her well-being at stake, but Colin's too. His protection was her responsibility and she'd stop at nothing to keep him safe.

Chapter 38

"They've breached the smog!" Relina shouted as she ran through the shadow of the trees toward the Heart. She was out of breath, which was unusual. "I was just with the Coralene and they told me the Debauched are exiting the smog via sea. They sent out their ships this morning, at least a hundred or so." Her green eyes were wild with panic as she announced this message to everyone within earshot. Lux, Eluno, and Zyleh ran out of the jungle behind her. The Grand Paipa pushed through the small crowd toward her.

"Did they say whether or not they would be able to stop them before they reached Tier?" His voice was solemn.

"It was a brief meeting. Clydde said they've already shifted the currents around the smog. That should delay their exit, but it won't stop them forever. The Coralene cannot get too close to their polluted border, it's too dangerous and the chemicals could kill them. They can only use their greater defenses once the Debauched have cleared their confinements and are on open water."

"Are their defenses strong enough to stop them?"

"Clydde isn't sure. The Debauched sent a large fleet out to sea. The Coralene sensed the presence of at least one hundred huge battleships in their water, possibly more. He said they are coming from the north. He also said his people were preparing for this, but had not anticipated such a large number of boats." Relina was speaking fast and her sentences overlapped as her mind raced. "But he said they were going to do their best. He wanted to tell us to get ready in case their best wasn't good enough."

The Grand Paipa held his head high, though his face was lined with worry.

"And the Ayrenese? Any word from them yet?" He held up a leaf. "I received this note from one of our carrier birds. It had words of gratitude carved onto it."

"No word yet. None of the gliders came down," Eluno answered.

The Grand Paipa sighed.

"We need them. They could be helping the Coralene keep these ships at bay. I'm aware they just suffered a great blow, and I can't imagine we would be ready to fight so soon after losing half the people we knew and loved, but it doesn't change the fact that we need them. They are a key factor in helping the Coralene stop the Debauched from reaching Tier."

The Grand Paipa shifted his focus and addressed the entire crowd.

"Attention! The time has come to take your places for battle. Every citizen received previously assigned areas of the jungle to protect, but now that we know they are coming from the north, I want every man and woman capable of fighting to hide out along the northern borders. Put your children to bed and head out immediately."

Relina cut in again, addressing the concerned faces of those who stood around her.

"The Ahi will be there already. We told them to take their places among the forest as soon as we got word from the Coralene, and they filtered into Tier through the Northshore checkpoint. Don't be alarmed when you see them hiding throughout our jungle."

"Fight valiantly, my people. Protect each other the best you can. I pray that when a new day arrives, we will share it with each other." And with that, everyone scattered.

Some darted immediately toward the north shore, while others tended to their children and the elderly before heading to battle. Zyleh raced toward Maila. Despite their fight earlier, he had to see her again before he went into war.

He got to the tree and climbed with haste. When he got to the top, Maila wasn't in the hammock. His heart began to pound. He looked in every direction but did not see her.

Then Bazoo climbed up the tree, squeaking furiously. Zyleh sat on the tree swing and the monkey jumped next to him.

::Go slower, what is it?:: Zyleh asked the monkey telepathically.

::*Maila,*:: the monkey answered. ::*Boy from Ahi came. Tricked her to go with him. Big hole Maila fell into. Boy trapped her inside.*::

Zyleh let out an audible groan.

::*Can you lead me to her?*::

Bazoo nodded and then darted down the tree. Zyleh followed, frustrated that this was happening at such a critical moment. He needed to be out along the north shore, helping his people protect their land in case the Debauched ships reached their sands. He didn't have time to run through the jungle, letting a monkey lead him to Maila's latest disaster.

Ten minutes into the run the monkey stopped at a huge rock that Zyleh recognized as the Northeast checkpoint.

"Here?" Zyleh said, not wanting to believe she had fallen into Ahi. Best-case scenario would have been a normal hole or pit, not a tunnel with thousands of causeways branching off it, each with more potential trouble for her to get into. But Bazoo nodded his head and Zyleh got to work pushing the rock away from the tunnel's entrance.

He shouted her name into the darkness but got no response. Worried the fall caused her harm, he got down on his knees and stuck his head into the hole.

"Maila? Are you here? Are you hurt?"

::*Maila okay,*:: Bazoo answered, squeaking while he communicated. ::*Yelled and screamed after fall. Not dead.*::

315

If she wasn't unconscious, Zyleh didn't know why she wasn't answering him. His concern for her well-being slowly shifted into anger. He shut his eyes and opened them again in night vision. He could see the floor of the tunnel and Maila was not there. He looked left, then right, but still did not see her. His suspicions led him to believe she wandered, in the dark, to who-knows-where in Ahi. Zyleh let out an aggravated growl.

"I don't have time for this!" he cried out, irritated that his home was going to be attacked and he wasn't on the frontlines to protect it. He got back to his feet then jumped through the hole and into the tunnel. It was an 8-foot drop but Zyleh landed effortlessly.

He shouted up to Bazoo.

"Keep a look out and make sure nobody moves that rock. If they do, go back to the Heart and let a Tierannite know."

Bazoo squeaked in understanding and Zyleh took a guess at which way Maila went. A soft humming noise was audible in the distance, so he headed toward it.

He tried to memorize every step he took: the smells, the way the air felt, and the direction he was going. He absorbed every detail because once he found Maila, he had to remember how to get back. If he didn't, they could be lost in Ahi for days.

Chapter 39

This was Zyleh's first time in Ahi. Now that he was
experiencing the habitat he could say with certainty that he did
not like it. The air was thick and hot, making him sweat, and the
darkness was perpetual. Night vision helped, but using it beneath
the earth gave him a headache. Zyleh wondered if this was how
Maila felt being out of the sky and grounded in Tier. If so, he was
beginning to understand her discomfort a little better.

He shouted her name as he crept along. He hoped he'd run into
her soon because the path he traveled felt endless. He wasn't sure
how many more turns he'd be able to remember before he got lost.

He tried to stick with making right turns only, but at certain
points, he encountered three-pronged paths. As he walked down
the dark tunnel, he noticed a faint light at the end of it. He ran
straight ahead, hoping this was what Maila saw too.

As he crossed into the light, his eyes shut out of instinct. He
had to switch out of night vision so the brightness did not blind
him.

When he opened them again, the sight was overwhelming. He
stood in the middle of a circular room with hundreds of archways
that served as entrances to paths leading in numerous directions.
Zyleh looked behind him to determine which path he came from,
but the sudden light disoriented him long enough that he could

not tell the three paths behind him apart. He did not know which one led back to the Northeast checkpoint.

A ringing sound entered Zyleh's head as he tried not to panic. He screamed out Maila's name, but got no response.

Zyleh walked toward the closest rock wall and drew an X on the ground in the loose dirt in front of the three tunnels he thought might be the way back. There were at least fifty passageways leading off of this room and he did not want to forget the three that were his best bet. The Ahi underground tunnels spanned across the entire globe and one incorrect turn, and enough time traveling in the wrong direction, could land him on the other side of the planet. No time to stress about that yet. He still had to find Maila.

He placed his right hand on the wall and walked along the perimeter of the circular room. As he passed each tunnel opening, he called her name and waited a few seconds for a response. He did this twenty times before he realized he was already on the other side of the massive room and across from where he entered. The air was dense beneath the earth and the humidity was crushing.

Growing tired and frustrated, he called out her name into the next tunnel. He waited a few seconds, heard nothing, and continued to walk. As he moved onto the next archway, a noise emerged. Zyleh leaned backward and stuck his head into the previous tunnel.

"Maila?" he called out again.

"Zyleh?" he heard a small voice ask from the distance. Without hesitation he ran straight into the darkness of that tunnel. He shifted back into night vision and before he knew it, he saw her, blindly wandering through the tunnel.

"Bazoo followed you and told me what happened," Zyleh said immediately. "After you fell into Ahi you should have stayed put. You've made it incredibly hard for me to find you and getting back to that specific checkpoint in Tier is going to be impossible. What could the Ahi boy have possibly said that would have convinced you to chase after him into the jungle?" he asked, trying to control his anger. Despite being grateful to have help getting out of Ahi, she was still furious with Zyleh.

"You have a lot of nerve."

"What is that supposed to mean?" Zyleh was taken aback, unsure where Maila's anger stemmed from.

"Relina told me everything. She told me what you did to get me lost on the beach and to prevent the gliders from finding me. And how you told the people I love most in this world that I died so they would stop looking for me. Do you understand how selfish and sadistic that is?" Zyleh ignored the accusations and tried to explain himself.

319

"I did it for your well-being. I did it to keep you safe. Ayren got hit first, just like I suspected it would, and in good conscious I could not allow you to return there while a strike was imminent."

"You told everyone I love that I died. Don't you see how horrible that is? You let me believe they stopped looking for me, or possibly never even tried at all. In fact, you endorsed that lie to my face earlier this evening when we fought! Your actions made me feel dismissed and unloved. It was horrible that you told the damn lie in the first place, but what's worse is that you let it go on while being fully aware that I was devastated by its affects." She was exasperated and just wanted to get out of the muggy, humid world of Ahi. She examined Zyleh's stubborn expression. "You don't even feel bad about it."

"You're right, I don't. Moments arose when I questioned if what I did was the right thing: when I saw how sad your friends were, when I felt guilty for causing you pain, every time Relina laid into me about the moral implications of my actions. But then I remembered it wasn't about any of us; it was about you. I don't care if your friends are grieving, because you're still alive. It doesn't matter if your sorrow fills me with guilt, because you're still alive. Relina can think whatever awful things she wants about me, because guess what, you're still alive. Why are you alive? Because I kept you in Tier. There's a good chance you'd be dead up there if I hadn't, and if I had to do it all over again I would tell that lie again. You can hate me forever but I know what I did was right." He ended his rant out of breath. Maila was fuming.

"My fate is mine to determine, not yours."

"I only did it to save you."

"You're missing the point. What you did is unforgivable. I'm done with this conversation," she paused, "and I'm done with you."

"I guess that means you don't want my help getting back to Tier?" Zyleh's arrogance was back in full force.

"Of course I do, you owe me that much."

"I don't owe you anything." He was done being nice, done trying to explain his reasonable motives to a person who refused to see the good in him. "There is a war going on above and you are preventing me from taking part in protecting my home and loved ones."

"Now you know how *I* feel." Maila gave him a furious stare.

He couldn't argue.

"Whatever. Jump on my back. I can at least get us back to the circular room. From there, I'm not so sure."

Maila let Zyleh carry her through the darkness. Once they reached the room of countless passageways, Zyleh put her down and walked toward the tunnels he marked with an 'X'. He took long strides with his muscular legs and Maila followed in a brisk jog to keep up.

"It's one of these. When I ran into the room, the light blinded me for a minute and disoriented me. When I looked back I couldn't tell which tunnel I came out of, but I am positive it was one of these three."

"How are you so sure?" she asked skeptically.

"I just am." His patience was wavering.

He motioned for her to jump on his back again. She did so and they took a step closer to the tunnels.

"So, little fallen star," Zyleh said playfully, trying to lighten the mood, "which of the three tunnels will we be taking?"

She rolled her eyes and as a wild guess, chose the middle one. Without a word, he ran into the dark tunnel ahead.

The hot air of Ahi made them both sweat. The further they ran the more slippery Zyleh became. Maila used every muscle in her body to hold on.

After an hour of running, she whispered into his ear.

"Are you okay?" She didn't like being kind to him right now, but the situation seemed dire and her resentment could wait until they resurfaced in Tier.

"Yeah," he answered between two heavy breaths. "I thought I remembered the way back after that circular room, but we should've been there by now."

Maila didn't know what to say so she stayed quiet, and Zyleh kept running without questioning her silence. He did not expect her to know the way either.

The time that passed beneath the earth was indeterminable, but it felt like another hour went by. The heat of Ahi was getting to Maila and her grip was loosening from around Zyleh's neck. As she began to slip, she snapped out of her daze and readjusted herself. Everything was still pitch black and she was beginning to wish she had night vision, too. The constant darkness was starting to make her feel anxious and the longer they remained lost, the guiltier she felt for making him trek down there to find her when he should be above ground, protecting his land. He did not deserve her sympathy but she found herself giving it anyhow. Perhaps this was karma paying him back for keeping her out of Ayren when she needed to be there to help the injured and defend her home. Maila tried not to dwell on it. Instead, she focused her energy on staying positive. Nothing worse could happen now.

They turned a corner and the air in the tunnel suddenly cooled. Alarmed, Maila picked up her head and opened her eyes.

"Do you feel that?" she whispered into his ear. "The air has changed."

Zyleh ran a few more feet before he felt it too.

"Yeah. What is it?" He slowed his pace.

"I'm not sure, but the air has gotten cooler. It even feels fresher, more pure."

Zyleh turned around in a slow circle, looking up and down, trying to determine an explanation for the change in air quality.

"Either we are closer to the surface or deeper beneath it. I don't know how the air works beneath the earth." Maila said, trying to make sense of it.

"I don't know either," he sighed and began to jog again. "Keep your gaze up, look toward the sky. If you see any cracks of light, tell me. Sometimes I can't see the light when my vision has adapted to the dark."

She focused ahead and upward as Zyleh continued to run.

Time was moving slowly, so she wasn't sure how long they continued onward, but Maila finally saw light.

"Look up." Zyleh stopped running. "All the way out there, right at eye level, do you see it?"

He shifted out of night vision. When he spoke, his voice was overcome with relief.

"The light, I see it." Then he ran, faster than he had the entire time they were lost in Ahi, and Maila held on tight.

The light illuminated their faces as they ran toward it and in a matter of seconds they reached its source.

"This doesn't look familiar," Maila said, worried. Zyleh helped her off his back.

"It's not the Northeast checkpoint, it's a different location. It's probably one of the others in Tier. There are five of them total. As long as it's not the Northshore checkpoint where everyone has congregated for battle, we can exit here."

Hope filled her once again. It was a large circular cutout in the ceiling of the tunnel and the light shone through the cracks of the closed exit.

With all his force, he slowly pushed upward on the opening, raised the circular door, and pushed it to the side. As he did so, gray light poured in. It wasn't bright, but certainly was not as dark as Ahi. The stark contrast was drastic; it was two very different kinds of darkness. Zyleh jumped up through the hole and landed on his feet. He then reached down through the opening and took her hand, pulling her out of Ahi and into the dim light.

Chapter 40

During Violet's travels she came across an ancient book. It was called *Humans of New York* by a man named Brandon Stanton and the stories were rumored to be true. Every page had pictures of different people with their real-life achievements and struggles documented beneath. Life wasn't perfect thousands of years ago, but there was a beautiful undercurrent of love, hope, and decency. She decided to share a few of the stories with Colin before they went to sleep.

"Do you think those things really happened?" he asked.

"I like to think so. If the people in this book are our ancestors, then it's nice to know there was a time that good triumphed over evil and that the noble humans outnumbered the bad ones."

"We aren't all bad. You're good," he smiled, "and I like to think I'm alright."

"Of course you're alright," Violet laughed. "You're one of the few good ones left."

"I bet if the others were given the chance, most of them would surprise you," he said, very seriously.

Violet wanted to disagree with him. She wanted to tell him that it was his innocence speaking and that she had seen the evilness others were capable of, but she kept her thoughts to herself. There was no need for him to be jaded too.

She looked at him and shrugged her shoulders. "Maybe we can change things, you never know."

"You're going to have to start trusting other people if that's your plan. There's no way we can do it alone."

Violet took a moment to digest this and realized he was right. She didn't like the idea of letting others get too close, but it was the only way they'd ever make a sizeable difference.

"Do you really think there is a way out without Mr. Lamorte?" Colin continued.

"This war is proof that this sick and twisted life beneath the smog doesn't have to be our final fate. I know a greater power exists somewhere out there, a power stronger than the evil we know. That something, or someone, is watching over us. I don't know if it's a God, or spirits, or something else. I just know there's something better out there and that I'll find it one day."

"I hope you're right," Colin said with a sad smile.

She pulled him into a hug and read a few more pages until he fell asleep on her lap. Though they hadn't been together long, their bond was strong. Violet had no siblings but her feelings toward him shifted seamlessly into that of a protective older sister. He was so little, yet so brave, and Violet wanted to keep him safe. The longer they were together, the more she felt the need to protect him, to keep him innocent. He was a pure soul in a tainted world and she wanted to spare him from the heartbreak she grew to expect from life.

She ran her skinny fingers through his messy brown hair and gently moved him onto the sleeping bag. She turned the flashlight off and rested on her large jacket next to Colin.

Sleep eluded her and she counted the seconds as they passed. After a few hours, the warm breeze returned. Normally, she only felt it for a minute or two, but this time was different. The warmth that came from the darkness lingered, as if to taunt her. Its looming presence made her paranoid.

After fifteen minutes, Violet had enough. She couldn't take it anymore: the wondering, the fear, the curiosity. Without waking Colin, she grabbed the flashlight and walked into the breeze.

The warm air blew her knotty blonde hair behind her as she tiptoed slowly through the shadows. Her pupils dilated as she strained to see past the light of her flashlight, but yielded nothing.

Though she was walking very slowly, the pace at which she moved the flashlight was dizzying. She couldn't stop the panic that rattled her bones.

As she tried to calm her nerves and focus the flashlight more steadily, a weird smell filtered through the breeze. It wasn't bad, just foreign; a scent she never experienced before. She didn't know how to describe it. It smelled dirty, but fresh at the same time. The smell wafted past her and as she tried to determine its source, the sound of footsteps materialized. Her heart palpitated with such vigor she feared she might lose her breath.

Frozen in place, she waited. Her flashlight focused straight ahead, concentrated on the ground. Whoever moved toward her made minimal noise.

When the footsteps were upon her, it sounded like two people instead of one. She swallowed hard as she anticipated the moment of contact.

Violet screamed when the pale white feet entered into the beam of her flashlight. She tried to back up but tripped over herself and her flashlight shone on the rest of the stranger as she fell.

It was a ghostly girl with bright, wide eyes. She was dressed in a beat-up white dress that fell right above her cut up, knobby knees. She was so dirty that it looked as if she dug herself out of a grave. Her long white hair fell all the way to her waist and hung in loose, messy curls. Violet moved the flashlight so she could see the girl's face. It was heart-shaped and pretty despite the hollowness beneath her cheekbones. A living doll. Beautiful, like the porcelain dolls the rich girls carried around the city. She looked about as delicate as one of those dolls, too.

The girl's skin was so pale that it appeared to glow in the beam. She looked otherworldly. Violet wracked her brain for any explanation, but kept landing on the notion of ghosts. The girl appeared to be illuminated. She was so white beneath the dirt that she looked like she might be dead. Violet could not control her nerves any longer.

She screamed again and tried to stand up and run, but her fear kept her from finding her balance and she fell back down. The glowing girl took a step closer and when the flashlight hit her eyes, a blast of lavender illuminated from them. Horror coursed through Violet. What *was* this person?

"Get away from me, ghost!" Violet shrieked with panic as she used her hands and feet to scoot backward.

The strange girl's eyes grew even larger with a look of confusion. She stopped walking toward Violet and stood still in the light. She tilted her head and squinted curiously before turning and shouting into the shadows behind her.

"Zyleh, it is official: we are *not* in Tier."

A man's voice came out from the darkness.

"Yeah, I kind of realized that as soon as we left Ahi and there wasn't a tree in sight, but thank you for your wise observation. I don't know what I would do without you." His voice had a thick, smooth accent; very different from the girl's, which was choppy but soft.

The man entered the light and stood next to the girl. Violet's breath was taken from her once more. She expected him to look similar to the pale girl who glowed, but as she moved the flashlight up and down the man who stood there, she saw they were complete opposites. The stark contrast in his appearance from the girl's was incredible.

He was enormous and his skin looked healthy and tan. She circled the light around his feet then moved it up his body. He wore a pair of loose shorts made out of a foreign fabric that was tied together with ropes and green stitching. The rest of his healthy, browned flesh was exposed, all of which covered pure muscle. She scanned the light over his face and shaggy brown hair, which had beads tied into the tiny braids scattered throughout. Even in the dim light, the man's bright green eyes stared down at her with intensity. His sharp jaw twitched.

"Turn off your hand light. It's blinding me."

"No," Violet replied, her confidence returning. "Then we will all be in the dark."

"I have night vision and that light is messing it up," he answered back with anger. His attitude toward her was foul.

Violet stood up, refusing to let this stranger boss her around.

"Well, I don't have night vision and I can't see in the dark. This is my home, so the flashlight stays on." She stood there, flashlight pointed at his face.

"I like her," the pale girl said with a smirk. Zyleh scoffed at the pleasure she received from Violet's resolve against him.

Violet's wits were returning and she was beginning to comprehend how abnormal this entire situation was. The terror she felt previously was gone. These weren't Mr. Lamorte's militiamen, they were foreigners. People from someplace else, somewhere outside North America. All the fear she had was replaced by curiosity. She had to be strong if she wanted these outsiders to take her seriously.

The man's nostrils flared in aggravation but the ghostly girl stepped forward and spoke before he could make any more rude demands.

"I'm Maila," she said with a smile. "Sorry if we scared you. We got lost and did not intend to wind up here."

"What *are* you guys?"

"We cannot tell you that," the man answered. His accent was laced with disdain for Violet, who did not understand what she had done to deserve such contempt.

"I don't know why you are being so mean to me. I haven't done anything to you."

"Stop being a jerk, Zyleh," Maila said to the man, then turned back to Violet. "We are going to leave you alone. We aren't going to hurt you. It might be best if you just forgot about us."

"How could I possibly forget this? You look like you're from another world!" Violet paused to think about what she just said. "And if you are, then I'd like you to take me with you when you leave."

Despite the uncomfortable vibe she received from them, any place had to be better than here. Hiding in this sewer forever wasn't her fate. They came from someplace else, somewhere she wanted to go, and maybe they were the answer to her prayers.

"That's ridiculous," Zyleh snorted with laughter at Violet's suggestion.

"Why?" Violet demanded. She puffed up her chest in an attempt to appear larger than she was. "What's so wrong with me that I can't go with you?"

"Everything."

"You don't know anything about me." Violet was offended.

Strong resentment, the cause of it unknown to Violet, poured out of Zyleh.

"You are what is wrong with this world and you belong here, in this grimy city, with your repulsive and depraved people."

A surge of heat rushed to Violet's cheeks. His assumptions were infuriating. She did not belong here and she wasn't going to let some ill-mannered stranger tell her otherwise.

"You are wrong. Believe what you want about this city and the people in it, but just because some are bad doesn't mean we all are. I don't know where you're from, though I can take a guess, and if I'm right, you're from beyond the smog and there's no way you could *possibly* know a damn thing about this place."

"Trust me, we know enough. You're all the same."

"Has it ever crossed your mind that maybe some of us have no choice but to live here? We were born into this. If I could change it, I would, so don't tell me what you think you know about me because you don't know anything." Tears of anger filled her eyes as she once again realized how little control she had. She had been the victim of circumstance her entire life and she was tired of it. "I'm done. Feel free to leave my sewer now."

With that, she turned to walk away. She wanted more than anything to escape but not at the price of her dignity. And not with people who would be just as cruel as those who surrounded her in North America. If they wouldn't tell her where they were from, then she didn't care. She survived for thirteen years in this brutal city and she had no doubt she could endure more.

As she walked away, she could hear their continued conversation. She slowed her pace to listen.

"Let's go," he demanded but Maila did not obey.

"No. What if we can save her?"

"Are you out of your mind?" he shouted back at her. Violet stopped to listen. She was only a few feet away and they seemed to have forgotten she was still within earshot. "No more of your horrific ideas. All they cause is trouble."

"She's a little girl. I don't believe that *all* of them are evil. We could save her and some of the other good ones."

"I am going to leave you here in this sewer with the Debauched girl if you don't stop your nonsense. You've wasted enough of my time," he said stubbornly.

"You know you're wrong. You thought all the Ayrenese people were arrogant and heartless until you met me. I was trapped in a society I couldn't control either. Of course, Ayren doesn't even compare to the Debauched, but my situation is very similar to that girl's. You gave me a chance, why won't you give her one too?"

"I am beginning to wonder *why* I ever gave you a chance."

Maila became silent and the tension that filled the space between the two strangers was potent.

This was Violet's opportunity to try again. They were her ticket out of the smog and she would do whatever it took to make sure they didn't leave her behind. Their appearance was a sign from above, or beyond, or wherever her prayers were sent after she said them. This was the answer she sought; she could feel it in her soul. She swallowed her pride.

"I have a proposition for you," she called out from the darkness. "I know things. Information you couldn't possibly be privy to. I can help you if you help me." The strange man looked intrigued.

"Go on, little girl."

"My name is Violet," she snapped back at him, then continued, looking only at Maila. "I assume your land is what Mr. Lamorte is after and I know what is coming your way."

"We already know they are preparing battleships," he interjected, trying to belittle Violet's offer.

"Well, did you know that the soldiers on those ships aren't normal humans? They were drugged with some concoction and turned into monsters. Half of those people used to be normal like me but now they are killing machines."

For the first time, Zyleh looked at Violet without disdain.

"Drugged? Like medicine?"

"No. Like narcotics. I don't know the exact formula but I do know that whatever was in those pills made them apathetic and numb to normal human emotions. They don't feel *anything*. They don't care if they live or die, so they fight recklessly. It has erased their consciences, and some other component in the drug made them bulk up. They are ten times as strong as they ever were. When you fight them, you'll see. Mr. Lamorte turned them into freaks." Violet took a deep breath before speaking again. "If you want to end this war, you have to kill Mr. Lamorte. He is the only one who wants to seize your land. None of his soldiers want to fight. He had to drug them into compliance. If you stop him, the rest will follow."

"That's awful," Maila commented.

"We all hate him."

"Then why haven't you stopped him before now?" Zyleh asked, still skeptical.

"Our society is crafted in a way that everyone stays penniless and uneducated. We don't have time to work up elaborate plans to overthrow him—we're too busy trying to survive."

"So, kill him. Not much educated planning needed there."

"He never leaves his building without security. It would be impossible to kill him without being killed in return. His guards would shoot anyone who tried on the spot. Trust me, if there was a way, it would have been done by now."

"If you want to prove your worth, then find a way to get rid of him. There is no way for us to eliminate him if he never leaves his confines. This job falls on you."

"I know you are young," Maila cut in, "but I am sure you can rally others to help. You just need to be prepared to strike when the moment presents itself."

Violet wondered if she was capable—if she could rally the resistance to take down Mr. Lamorte, then she could end the war and free the people from oppression.

"Promise you will take me away from here," she finally agreed, "and my little brother, and I'll find a way to complete this task." She knew she could recruit others. Barnibus and his crew would be excited to take part in this revolution.

"Fine, but don't you dare tell a soul about us. Just because you think you can trust people, doesn't mean you can. You need to keep this meeting a secret, otherwise all deals are off."

"I won't tell a soul." She had no trouble keeping secrets.

"Don't worry, Violet. You can do it," Maila's eyes twinkled at her. They had an instant bond that Violet couldn't explain.

"Thanks. I'm gonna do my best if it means Colin and I will be free."

"I trust you and you can trust me. I won't forget our end of this deal." Maila said, giving Violet a hug. Violet froze—she hadn't felt this type of affection since her parents died.

Before Maila let go, she whispered into her ear, "If I can think of a way to help you complete this task from afar, I will. Just be ready at all times."

"Okay," Violet whispered back.

Maila let go, stepped into the darkness to follow Zyleh, and disappeared.

"Aren't you guys going to tell me where you're from?" Violet called out after them.

"In time, little girl," Zyleh shouted. Then they were gone, right along with the warm breeze.

Chapter 41

Right outside the smog and beyond the murky waters of Debauched North America, the Coralene waited. The perfect moment to attack was growing near as the battleships steadily approached their defensive line. They held hands and formed a line beneath the ocean right under where the battleships would cross. In a united force, they used their powers to shift the tides away from Tier. A strong undertow formed at the water's surface and the Coralene hoped that once the ships crossed it, they would either sink or be pushed back through the smog.

Throughout the centuries, the Coralene helped the Tierannites detach their half of the land mass from the Debauched half. South America, now Tier, resided a safe distance below the Debauched continent of North America and was separated by a massive ocean. While creating this distance proved to be a wise choice over the years, the space between the two opposing forces was now being tested. Coralen was the only hope Tier had in keeping their beaches battle free.

Clydde stood next to Kaam, their fingers interlaced. They remained intently focused on keeping the tides turned. In the back of his mind, he was prepared to take action and execute an alternative plan if any of the ships made it past their line of defense.

The light from the sun hit the battleships as they approached, casting shadows on the sandy ocean floor. The Coralene watched as the shadows of the ships advanced slowly. They held hands, waiting for the moment the ships would make impact against their reverse current.

An eerie silence lingered around the Coralene as they anticipated the collision and a tense hope filled the quiet ocean. They prayed to Coral, their Champion, for blessings, and felt her divine presence in the currents that coursed around them. Together they waited, but no one said a word. Every person of Coralen remained focused on the job at hand. Too nervous to speak for fear that any distraction might break the steady stream that was shifting the water's flow.

The first person to communicate was Glynn, the man in charge of this defensive attack.

"Brace yourselves, swarmy. The impact is upon us," he called out through mindspeak to the entire population of Coralen.

The force of the large battleships hit the Coralene defense. Everyone held on, keeping the undertow strong. As the first three ships hit the point where the water changed, they immediately screeched to a halt, causing the ships behind to crash into their sterns.

Two of the boats began to sink immediately and the ocean became littered with flailing bodies and metal debris. The

Debauched couldn't swim. As they fell into the ocean they swallowed mouthfuls of saltwater and drowned. The boats were crashing into each other and it seemed as though the plan was working.

A feeling of elation reverberated through the line of Coralene as they stood strong. Ten boats were sinking and it looked as though another fifteen were caught up in the mess. Clydde looked past the scene of madness and toward the rear of the fleet. Some of the distant shadows began to reroute their course and maneuver around the wreck now blocking their path.

Clydde panicked. *"Look ahead,"* he shouted through mindspeak. *"The boats at the back of the pack are redirecting their course."*

"Ends of the line, hold your ground," Glynn commanded. But as he did so, one of the first boats that sank started to fall faster through the water directly above where they stood. The boat's rapid spiral forced those near Glynn to break the line. The battleship hit the ocean floor with a deep thud, sending a wall of sand into the space around them. They all moved fluidly away from the wreckage, avoiding any injuries, but the sand scattered through the water in every direction and temporarily blanketed their visibility.

"Quickly now. Reform the line behind the boat," Glynn shouted, but the momentary break in the current had already allowed some of the other Debauched boats to push through.

Glynn rethought his orders.

"Half of you hold the line, and the rest, form your groups of three," he commanded. *"It's time for Plan B!"*

Kaam remained in line with the majority of the Coralene population and Clydde met up with his group.

There were twenty sets of three assigned to Plan B. Clydde was teamed up with his sea patrol partner, Talley, and Mellvin, a fellow normally in charge of a school in the Deep Pacific.

They joined together and prepared to create an underwater cyclone meant to sink the ships, one boat at a time.

Clydde looked up and saw that only twenty-five ships actually sank from the first undertow. He could see the shadows of the remaining boats sailing around the rubble in an attempt to continue toward Tier.

"Talley, Mellvin, most of the groups are following Glynn east, so we should cover the west." Clydde looked behind him and saw Kaam holding a strong line of defense with the others, and though they fought hard, it would only hold off a few more ships.

"Let's get that one," Talley said, pointing toward the battleship that had traveled the furthest.

They swam with speed to the belly of the boat. The pace at which they accelerated caused them to blend into the shifting waters even more so than usual, making them appear to dematerialize as they moved seamlessly to their destination. Upon arriving directly beneath the ship, they got to work. Clydde, Talley, and Mellvin swam in a clockwise motion, swirling the water between them. As soon as they gathered enough speed, the cyclone took shape. They stopped swimming and harnessed the fast moving water between them. The quicker the whirlpool moved, the further they spread out from each other, making the cyclone larger.

"Upwards now," Clydde instructed, and they continued to spin the water between them while swimming up and elongating the cyclone funnel. They swam toward the shadow of the boat until they were ten feet below the water's surface. Treading in place, they pushed the cyclone into the boat and darted away from the oncoming destruction. The force of the cyclone ripped apart the boat's metal casing. Shards of steel flew in every direction as the whirlpool dragged the enormous battleship to its demise.

Clydde looked around and saw the other groups were having the same success with their underwater cyclones. Twenty more ships were being pulled toward the ocean floor. The brief hope he began to feel vanished as fast as it came when he looked to the ocean's surface and saw there was still a large fleet of battleships sailing freely above. He had no idea how they would stop them all before they reached land. The distance between these boats and Tier was rapidly shrinking.

Underwater cyclones were a devil to control and relocating one was too dangerous, so Clydde, Talley, and Mellvin disassembled the cyclone as swiftly as possible. They surrounded its base and dug their toes into the sand. They held strong stances and spun the water counter-clockwise.

It decelerated gradually, taking all the strength they had to decrease its momentum, but eventually they slowed the cyclone until it came to a complete stop and vanished.

Clydde looked around again. Half the groups were waiting for their boats to sink and the other half were disarming their cyclones.

Fear coursed through his veins. *"Quick,"* he said, *"there is no time to waste. We need to move onto the next boat. Let's get whichever boat has gotten closest to Tier."* The three of them swam so fast they disappeared for a moment.

They reappeared beneath another battleship. This one was at the head of the pack, though Clydde could see the shadows of all the other boats coming in close behind. They took their stance and prepared their second cyclone, but Mellvin stopped suddenly in his tracks.

"What is it?" Clydde asked, a bit tense, as he did not want to waste another second.

"Do you hear that?" Mellvin asked quietly.

The three paused to listen. Clydde tried to hear past the loud murmur from the battleship engines above and after a moment, he heard it too. There was a steady pitter-patter landing on the ocean's surface. Then, a loud shot of thunder.

"The Ayrenese," Talley exclaimed, elated, *"they've cast a storm upon the Debauched."*

A sense of relief poured over Clydde, not only because they now had assistance from above, but also because this meant the Ayrenese were going to be okay. He was sure they took a huge hit, but the fact that they rallied themselves together and were strong enough to help in this particular battle meant they weren't defeated.

Thunder crashed again and they got back to work making their next cyclone. Glynn's group and others were nearby doing the same.

They worked fast. As they did, Clydde looked above and saw that the Ayrenese storm created waves big enough to capsize three of the battleships. The boats were on their sides taking in water and the Debauched flailed at the surface as their ships sank.

Without stopping progress on the cyclone, he continued to observe the people that had fallen out of the ship. Like before, some thrashed around helplessly while others drowned in seconds. What he noticed this time was how big the Debauched were. Even from a distance, they had a very frightening appearance. Reports from the Ahi always described them as weak and sickly versions of what the Elements evolved from, but the people he was seeing now looked like grotesque, monstrous versions of what he imagined.

"Praise Coral, what have they become?"

He knew they were sick with some disease, but they looked more disfigured than ill. Seeing their physical strength made Clydde more determined than ever to stop as many boats as he could from reaching Tier. Their second cyclone reached the surface and dragged a new battleship into the water.

Once this ship was far enough below the ocean's surface, they disarmed their weapon with speed.

Despite their best efforts, their line of defense was pushed toward Tier's shore. They were now only seventy-five miles away from Tier with more than half the Debauched fleet still afloat. There was no way they could stop them all. And although the Ayrenese produced a storm, it wasn't making much of a dent in their progress. It was clear they were still recovering. If the Ayrenese were operating at full capacity they would have set the boats on fire with a lighting storm.

"We won't be able to stop them all," Talley said to Clydde and Mellvin.

"I know. We are just going to have to stop as many as we can and then the Tierannites and Ahi will have to take care of the rest."

Glynn chimed in through an open connection with all the Coralene.

"Everyone. We aren't far from Tier. We may not be able to stop them all but we aren't giving up yet. Stop what you're doing and meet me a few miles offshore. Prepare to craft waves."

Without hesitation, every Coralene swam toward the shore of Tier. They lined up next to one another and placed their open palms in front of them.

"On each count of three, push," Glynn shouted. *"One-two-three. One-two-three."*

Each time Glynn got to three, the Coralene pushed in unison out from their chests and upwards, creating waves in the water above. The Debauched moved fast overhead and the waves were not big enough to cause damage yet. The first battleship to cross made it over the waves and landed on the shore.

Glynn counted faster and the waves grew bigger and more frequent. It pushed a few of the boats back, but one by one they still crossed over the line of defense.

"We need the waves to be bigger. Push harder everyone," Glynn commanded urgently.

The waves above were now huge and the boats struggled to land ashore. Two of the boats at the back of the pack drifted into each other, puncturing holes in their sides. They began to sink, but not before the Debauched started jumping overboard and landing on the decks of the other ships nearby.

Even with two more ships down, it wasn't enough, but the Coralene did not quit. They continued to make the waves, hoping they could prevent a few more ships from reaching the shore. There was an unspoken agreement among the Coralene that they would stay there, doing their best, until there was nothing left they could do. They would not give up or surrender, even if the outcome looked bleak.

Dirty oil leaked from the battleships as they crossed over the Coralene, leaving trails of grease on the ocean's surface. The oil leaked down and filled the water surrounding them, making many cough and gag as the polluted substance entered their gills.

It wasn't long before all the remaining Debauched ships reached the shore. Kaam swam over to Clydde once the effort to stop the ships finally ceased and he held her tightly. They watched as the boats made it to land and wondered what would happen next.

"There has to be more we can do," he thought earnestly.

A sense of deep empathy filled the Coralene people. The battle in Tier would be much worse than theirs. Their defense was indirect and combat free. There was no immediate threat to any of their lives and they never had to make contact with the Debauched. On land, the battle would be face-to-face and bloody.

"I hope we stopped enough. The Tierannites and the Ahi have to win," Kaam thought, sadness ringing through her mind's voice.

"Me too, my darling," Clydde responded. *"I pray to Coral that they come out of this alright."*

One by one, the Coralene began to clean up the aftermath of the fight, and those in charge of managing pollution led the initiative. They did their best to collect the dirty water the Debauched brought with them through the smog and push it back across the ocean into the smog dome. Others headed to clean up the debris of the sunken battleships and the dead bodies of the Debauched. It was a gruesome task, but necessary.

The day was grave. Clydde wished he and his people could leave the ocean and help the Tierannites and Ahi fight, but they couldn't. They could not stay out of the water long enough to take part in a battle on land. When he heard the rain from Ayren cease, he understood their role in this fight was temporarily halted too.

Clydde squeezed Kaam's hand. *"I truly wish there was more we could do."*

Talley swam up, wading in the water next to her older counter parts as they observed the blurry silhouettes of the Debauched. Through the surface of the water they could see them standing aboard their ships and preparing to fight. Talley's pretty opal eyes furrowed in concentration as a thought came to her.

"They aren't out of our waters quite yet," her mind's voice was devious. *"Perhaps there's still more we can do."*

Kaam squeezed Clydde's hand and they looked from Talley's focused expression toward a rope ladder that flew over one of the ship's decks and into the water. One by one, all the boats lowered ladders into the ocean.

"Everyone, wait," Talley called out to the entire population of Coralen, *"come back toward the shore. Our fight isn't over yet."*

The submerged ladders began to shake and it wasn't long before the boots of the Debauched stepped into the shallow waters of Coralen. At this sight, Talley gave them a mischievous grin and everyone understood what needed to be done.

Chapter 42

"It's refreshing to see your true nature instead of that kind-hearted masquerade you feigned for so long." Maila said with spite as Zyleh closed the door above them. They were back in Ahi, just as lost as before. "Why were you so nasty to her?"

Zyleh rolled his eyes, not caring if she thought he was cruel. She already hated him and he no longer felt the need to parade around like the nice guy.

"She is a Debauched, Maila. She is part of the people who are attacking us, killing us, and trying to take our land."

"But she's not responsible for causing the war."

"Yeah, *you* are." Zyleh quipped back. Maila took a deep breath and purposefully ignored his hurtful remark.

"Violet can't control what the people around her do. The fact that she was hiding out in a sewer leads me to believe she wants no part of whatever plans her people are scheming. She sold them out without hesitation."

"Maybe, but I'm not going to put my faith in her just yet. I don't understand how you can trust her so easily."

"I don't necessarily trust her, but I have put some of my hope into her," she said. "If she can prove she's decent and committed, then it means there is some good buried beneath the evil of that city. Maybe all she needs is someone to believe in her. I like to think if we gave some of the Debauched a second chance they could change their ways and live in this world without destroying it."

"History has proven that they can't. Humans don't change. They are prone to destruction, greed, and self-absorption. Your hopes are wildly naive."

"What you see as naive, I see as optimism."

"You realize they've littered this planet with violence and war since the beginning of time, right?"

"We came from them and we aren't prone to such atrocities."

"We are human, but an evolved version of the species. We don't have the same genetic wiring as them anymore. They don't think like us and never will." His tone was condescending.

"Our ancestors were regular humans and they never reverted back to greed and violence. We evolved from them, why can't future generations of Debauched evolve from who they are now?"

"I wish you the best of luck, but it will take a lot of work to convince all the leaders of each Element to support a mission to save some of the Debauched, especially after they attacked us."

"I don't think you give our people enough credit. With reasonable explanation and proof, they might see what I see. Even if Violet fails but genuinely tries, they will see she can be redeemed."

"No. If she fails, we will make her forget she ever saw us."

"What?" she asked, puzzled.

"With a song. I'll make her forget everything."

Maila was taken aback that he was capable of doing something so powerful. She knew the Tierannites songs and rhythms could evoke strong feelings out of the person listening, but she had no idea they could change a person's memory.

"You can do that?"

"Yes, and honestly, we will probably have to make her forget regardless if she succeeds or not because she'll never be allowed out of the smog. I suspect if we don't give her what she wants she will tell the world what she knows out of spite and we can't have her blabbing to the other Debauched people about us entering through the sewer. With enough detective work, they'd find the entrance to Ahi. She knows too much."

"If the time comes and that is necessary, then fine, but I doubt it will be," she said, hoping Violet found a way to stop Mr. Lamorte for good. She didn't want to steal away the one sliver of hope they had given her. "If she succeeds, the forgiveness shown by the leaders of each Element might surprise you. Don't count her out yet." Looking toward the future, she wondered how they would ever manage to get back to this location. "We are going to have to remember how to get back here if we ever want to get more inside information from Violet."

"Priority number one is getting back to Tier. If I don't get back in time to help with the fight I will never forgive myself." He squinted while in night vision and looked into the distance of the tunnel, tensing up as he did so. "Who's down there?" he shouted unexpectedly.

There was no response and Maila did not know what he saw that made him think someone was there, but through night vision, Zyleh could see a small body skipping carelessly toward them.

"Who are you?"

"Who are *you*?" the tiny voice replied to Zyleh from out of the darkness.

Maila recognized the voice.

"Tyoko? If that's you, I've got some serious words for you."

"Words mean nothing," the boy said as he reached them. "They are only sounds that come from our mouths."

Maila wanted to scold him on the importance of words with some choice verbiage of her own, but Zyleh cut in.

"You're the little Ahi boy I met before I spoke to Culane."

"Yup," Tyoko said bored. "You two should not be here. Eshe is mad." His voice was small but menacing, and the whites of his eyes gleamed in the darkness.

"It's your fault we are," she retorted. "You trapped me in that tunnel."

"You weren't supposed to wander," Tyoko said, unfazed that he just admitted his role in the mean trick. "You really don't belong all the way out here. I'm not sure how you made it this far, but if any of the tunnel marshals found out you were here, you would be in serious trouble."

"I think you mean that *you* would be in serious trouble. We are only out here because you thought it was funny to be cruel." Maila quipped back confidently.

Tyoko's face scrunched up in annoyance.

"Follow me. I'll take you back."

"Actually," she said, thinking ahead, "you are now our personal tour guide of Ahi. If you don't want your marshals to find out what you have done, then your services will be at our disposal. We will need to get back here a few more times and you will be the one to lead us."

"No," Tyoko refused, "you can't make me do that."

"Oh, yes we can," Zyleh said, jumping in on the blackmail. "You started this mess and now you are stuck in it. I have no problem telling Culane what you did to Maila."

"They won't care about that; they will be proud of me for teaching her a lesson."

"You need to stop eavesdropping on conversations you cannot fully comprehend. Just because the Ahi adults say one thing in anger, does not mean they believe it when push comes to shove.

The relationship between Ahi and Ayren may be strained, but it is not broken. They would not like to know their youth is treating another Element so poorly. That is not who you are as a species."

"Perhaps, but I still did nothing they would not forgive me for."

"Is that so? You mean to tell me they wouldn't be furious with you for allowing us to wander *here*. I know where we are," he looked at Tyoko whose smug expression shifted to fear. "This exit leads to the Debauched. You let us wander to the one section your people take great pride in calling their own. The leaders of Ahi do not want *any* of the other Elements impeding upon their territory. They've worked hard for centuries to build a proper system of surveillance and one wrong move could ruin the whole thing. What if we entered the Debauched city, revealing ourselves to the wrong person? All could be ruined. I'm sure the punishment for your actions would be much worse than helping us out in the future."

"You winding up here was an accident. She wasn't supposed to wander. Bringing you back here intentionally would be an even worse crime."

"I have a feeling that Culane would be mad you even *let* another Element into the Ahi tunnels in the first place. But that's just my guess."

It wasn't a guess, Zyleh knew it to be a fact. The Ahi people were very protective and possessive over their land and only the Grand Paipa was allowed to enter. There was a fear in Tyoko now that had not been there before. He did not want to incur the wrath of Culane and the other marshals if they found out about his trickery.

"You're a sneaky little fellow," Zyleh continued, "I'm sure you can get us through these tunnels without anyone else knowing."

"Eshe always knows."

"Then she will also know that our intentions are noble."

"Fine, but don't expect this blackmail to last forever. There are certain lines I won't cross," Tyoko said, angrily. "And if Eshe ever demands that I stop, it's over."

"Deal." Zyleh's smile turned mischievous. "Is she still alive?"

Tyoko's eyes narrowed. "I hear her through the fiery bursts of air that emanate from the core. Just like you hear Juniper through the trees."

Tyoko turned and walked away from them with great haste.

"Good thinking," Zyleh whispered. "I'll remember how to get back this time and we may only need him once more to get here."

She jumped onto Zyleh's back and they followed their new Ahi guide. Tyoko could run just as fast as Zyleh, so getting back to the entrance of Tier's Northeast checkpoint took no time at all. At the room with a hundred openings, Zyleh paused as Tyoko kept running forward. He took a sharp rock and carved a small "x" in the wall next to the entrance that led to Tier. Amidst the many jagged edges of the rock wall, it went unnoticed, but Zyleh and Maila would know where to look next time.

The Northeast checkpoint was sealed.

"Who closed this?"

"I did." Tyoko answered boldly. "You left it wide open. You know how seriously we take the preservation of our air quality."

Tyoko scaled the wall with his hands and feet, then moved the rock from overhead. Maila was amazed at how easily he climbed the wall. Looking closer, she saw his toenails and fingernails were sharp little spikes that made small indents into the rock as he climbed. As Maila scanned the entire wall surrounding the entrance above, she saw thousands of these markings, small and large.

Tyoko climbed back down. Before letting Zyleh jump through the exit into Tier, he grabbed his arm.

"Be ready."

"What does that mean?"

"The Coralene could not stop all the ships from reaching your shores. The battle is approaching Tier."

"When?"

"Now. Their ships reached your shore about 15 minutes ago and they've been filtering onto the beach and through the trees ever since."

"Thanks."

With a small running start, Zyleh placed a foot against the side of the wall and launched himself to the ground above. His arms were long enough to grab Maila's hands and pull her up into Tier. She landed next to him and brushed the dust of Ahi off her filthy dress.

"Until next time," Zyleh said, pushing the rock back over the tunnel of Ahi. Tyoko gave him one last begrudging look before disappearing into Ahi's darkness.

"Get on my back. I need to return you to the Heart so I can go fight." She didn't oblige. "Hurry up! You've already wasted enough of my time."

"I don't need your help. I can find my own way back." Zyleh didn't know how to handle this continued rejection, so he reacted the only way he knew how.

"I hope you get lost!" He didn't mean it.

"I hope I never see you again."

She meant it. He could taste the venom in her voice.

"You might not have to," he muttered, but she didn't hear him. She was already gone, leaving him alone with the burn of her fiery words. He turned and headed toward the battle, very aware that her last wish might be granted.

Chapter 43

Darrow could see the Debauched unloading onto Tier soil. The bulking soldiers disembarked their ships and made their way to the beach. The first few made the shallow water walk with no problem, but the trip became deadly once the Coralene started grabbing ankles and dragging the Debauched out to drown. Though the attack was sneaky and effective, it didn't last long. The blue water was clean and clear, and the Debauched could see the Coralene as they approached. They began shooting from the safety of their boats and the Coralene had to retreat. In the moment of chaos before the Debauched caught on to what was happening they managed to eliminate another fifty soldiers, which was fifty less the Tierannites and Ahi would have to face.

Despite their recent tragedy, the general population of Ayren was beginning to thrive. With the help of their recently acquired knowledge and the glider's lessons on how to defend Ayren, it wouldn't be long before they were stronger than ever. Darrow just hoped their full recovery came in time to help the Ahi and Tierannites fight.

After the attack on the Axis, the Ayrenese people finally accepted the truth. The secrets kept from them were finally exposed and everyone was outraged. They recognized their forced ignorance as the main cause of this war and their resultant anger was powerful.

When it looked as though the people of Ayren were correctly directing their anger toward the Heads and not Maila or anyone else, Drue stepped in and redirected it toward the Debauched. It was more important they fight their immediate threat than to fight amongst themselves. The Heads of Ayren would face retribution when the time was right, and they would deal with appointing a new system of order in Ayren after the war was over.

Darrow was ready to fight. Since the attack on the Axis, training groups were formed to prepare each citizen for combat. No longer would they keep their talents confined to small, specific groups, and every Ayrenese skill was taught to the masses. Whether it was the responsibilities of the climithes, the lution sifters, cloud solidifiers, or the architects, the gliders tasked the population to learn every Ayrenese talent. They would be of no use in the war against the Debauched if they did not have a full arsenal of powers.

When the battleships entered the seas of Coralen, the people of Ayren could do no more than send down a heavy thunderstorm with hopes it helped the Coralene win the fight. It did not, but Darrow was confident that soon his people would be trained enough to make a bigger dent in the battle.

For the first time in history, they were attempting to teach all of Ayren how to glide. It was nerve-wracking because gliding was not easy and they needed to be careful that no one fell during the lessons. Despite the risks, Darrow was excited to share his skill with the rest of his people.

It made him think of Maila and how excited she would have been to learn how to glide. Pain seared his heart as he imagined sharing this special moment with her after waiting so long for the right moment to teach her.

Darrow shifted his grief into determination. He'd fight in Maila's honor. His continued devotion to their love was his driving force and he would not quit until they were victorious.

Chapter 44

Zyleh ran through the jungle, trying to forget that Maila sent him off to war with the most hurtful goodbye imaginable. It stung, but he deserved it. He just wished his fib hadn't unraveled right before he had to fight. It was a terrible way to be sent off toward possible death. Instead of dwelling on the pain, he used her anger as motivation to survive this battle so he could get back and mend her opinion of him.

He zipped through the trees at high speeds and headed for the north shore, completely unsure what he was running into.

A few miles from the shore the rumbles of war became audible. He darted forward and his heart rate quickened at the anticipation of intense combat. Once the first wave of battle was visible, he stopped and assessed where to enter the fray. A whizzing buzz flew past his left ear and pierced an unsuspecting Debauched target five hundred feet away, killing them instantly. Zyleh looked up and saw Marlo perched in the branches using his high-tension slingshot to pelt sharpened rocks at the Debauched. He had the best shot in Tier.

"There are thousands more still filtering into the jungle from their ships," Marlo shouted while readjusting the sack of earth-made bullets that hung over his shoulder. "The Coralene were drowning them as they got off their boats, but the Debauched

364

caught on and started shooting into the water. It was bad and they got a few; there's still blood washing ashore with the waves." Marlo shook his head. "The Debauched are stronger than we thought. Be careful."

"I will," Zyleh responded and Marlo disappeared into the camouflage of the treetops.

Zyleh took in the information and focused on the fight in front of him. No one saw him yet, so he observed. The Debauched were pushing the Ahi and Tierannites back with ease and entering further into the jungle. They had smooth metal tanks with spiked wheels that shot glowing ammunition. A thick, black smoke came out the back of these war vehicles as they plowed their way through the trees. One tank was already much further than the others. A loud, continuous growl came from its engine as it trudged through the jungle and demolished everything in its path.

Zyleh ran closer to it without letting the Debauched driver see him. Once close enough, he got down onto his knees, dug his fingers into the soil, and chanted beneath his breath. A series of thick roots sprouted from the ground and wrapped around the tank's tread, slowing its progress. He tightened the root's grip on the gears and heard a loud crack as the earth broke the slick metal molding that allowed the wheels to turn.

The tank stopped and its engine made one final cough of exhaust before going silent.

The top of the tank flew open and Zyleh ducked behind a nearby tree, ready to pounce.

A large, swollen head peeked out from the top of the tank. The man's crazy eyes darted in every direction before he dipped below to communicate with others.

The man with the large head eventually climbed out of the tank with a glossy automatic rifle slung across his back. He was fat and had bulges protruding from his skin in abnormal places. A raw lump on his hip peeked out from under the bottom of his shirt. These peculiar growths appeared on every man that climbed out.

In total, there were four men in the tank, and the fat man seemed to be in charge. The other three were sickly skinny. Their bones showed in the spots the bulging muscles did not cover. It looked as though the muscles formed so fast they ripped apart the skin and left it covered in scabbed splits and gashes. Their bodies were misshapen and their vacant eyes looked hungry for destruction.

"God, Chuck, ya moron. Get out of the way," the fat man said as he pushed one of the malnourished soldiers to the side. Zyleh expected that to be the end of it, but Chuck let out a high-pitched screech and wailed the fat man in the back of his head with the butt of his rifle. The fat man started bleeding from his ear and Chuck punched him. The former vacancy in his eyes was replaced with intense rage, the origin of which Zyleh could not define. All four men got involved, fighting just for the thrill of hurting each other. Zyleh watched in alarm at the ruthlessness with which the men brawled. They were scrappy, fighting with no rules or concern for their own safety. They took advantage of every miscalculation made by their counterpart and seized every kill shot presented, even if it might hurt them too. Zyleh was unnerved; they were supposed to be fighting on the same side yet they stopped to fight each other.

Their infighting worked to his advantage and he made his move while they were distracted. He quietly climbed a tree further along in the trail to its lowest branch. Once the men stopped squabbling, they continued forward on the preexisting path and Zyleh waited for them to pass beneath him. As soon as they did he pounced on the fat man and knocked him to the ground. He wailed him once on the side of the head, leaving him unconscious. He then stomped on the fat man's neck, breaking it, and ripped the gun off the strap on his back. He cracked the gun in two over his knee and it fired a glowing bullet that hit Chuck directly in the forehead. Chuck died instantly but his body shook violently from the electrified bullet still pulsating inside his skull.

The remaining two soldiers dove at Zyleh simultaneously. To escape, he did a back flip and managed to kick one beneath the chin. It knocked him to the ground but didn't stop the other, so he redirected his focus and charged at the man still standing.

He punched him in the eye then grabbed him by the arm, which was covered in bumps of raw skin. The man howled in pain as Zyleh swung him in one full circle and let go, flinging him directly into the side of a tree. He died on impact. The second man recovered and was crouched, waiting to make his next move. A rock flew out of the sky, hitting the Debauched man directly between the eyes. It hit him so hard, a small trickle of blood dripped from his nose before he fell lifeless to the ground.

He looked up to see Marlo perched on a low-hanging branch with his slingshot. He winked and pointed at Zyleh, then disappeared back into the trees.

Zyleh recovered his composure, then sprinted toward the bigger battle. As he ran through the herd of separate fights, he tried to evaluate where he was needed most.

He saw an Ahi man fighting four Debauched men on his own, so Zyleh jumped in to help. He grabbed one of their opponent's arms from behind, broke it, then took a knife from the man's grip and finished him off with a swift slice to the throat.

The Ahi man grabbed a fistful of leaves and dirt, heated them in the palm of his hand, and then threw the newly formed fireball at an oncoming Debauched. It hit the Debauched man in the chest, igniting his clothes, and sending him running toward the ocean. There, a Coralene was sure to finish him as he extinguished the flames in their water.

"Nice one," Zyleh said.

"Thank you, brother," the Ahi man replied as he choked one Debauched man and fought another with his fast fist. "I can finish these last two on my own. Go help my wife. She shouldn't be far from here."

Zyleh nodded without a word and made small dents in other fights as he ran along, trying to find the Ahi man's wife. The jungle was full of noise: people screaming, guns being fired, and agonized cries of the dying. Zyleh did not know what casualties were occurring, but the Elements appeared to be winning.

Zyleh was happy to see the animals making dents in this battle as well. He ran past an elephant crushing a small Debauched man with its hind legs and a cougar clawing the face off another. Tiny poison dart frogs hopped along the ground, rubbing their toxic secretions along the ankles and raw sores of the Debauched. The poison killed its victims in a matter of minutes. A swarm of killer bees moved from fight to fight, surrounding the Debauched and stinging their target a thousand times before moving on to the next. Each of their prey was left to endure a slow and laborious death.

Every living creature was fighting in this battle, protecting the place they called home. Things were looking optimistic until Zyleh got closer to the shore. The scene was portentous and seeing this new leg of the battle made him question his previous thought.

He was no longer sure if the Elements were winning. He was not sure where the Ahi man's wife was, so he jumped into a fight between a Debauched woman and a young Tierannite boy named Drey. The woman was prevailing, toying with Drey as he tried to hit her with a kill strike but couldn't. She was letting him live so she could laugh at his feeble attempts to beat her. She grabbed him and held him close, securing him against her chest. He squirmed, trying to get away, but she pressed her knife slowly into the side of his face.

"What a little angel face you have," she cackled. "Let me draw a pretty picture on your pretty baby face." She plunged the knife into Drey's cheek and he howled in pain. The woman's laugh echoed as blood flowed down his face.

"What's so funny?" Zyleh demanded, stepping toward the woman, deciding how best to attack her without causing more harm to Drey.

Her eyes lit up as he presented himself as a challenge; a real fight. She dropped the boy with the knife still stuck in his face, then skipped toward Zyleh while licking Drey's blood off her fingers.

Disgusted, he wasted no time. He lunged at her, clubbing her on the side of the head with his arm. She staggered only for a second before shrieking and jumping onto Zyleh's back. She wailed her fists into the sides of his head while he used his elbows to pry her off his back.

Drey stood back up and grimaced as he pulled the blade out of the side of his face. Vengeance emanated from his green eyes. He caught Zyleh's attention and tossed him the dagger. Zyleh caught it by the handle and thrust it upwards, stabbing the woman through her ear. She fell off his back and bled out on the jungle floor. Zyleh twisted the knife once before pulling it out of the woman's head and handing it back to Drey.

"Now you have a weapon."

"Thanks, Zyleh," Drey muttered through the pain. He made his best attempt at a smile, then ran back to the shore to find another fight. Zyleh looked around again to assess the pandemonium.

The battle was wild. The air reeked of blood and sweat, and the sounds of yelling reverberated around him. He had to determine his next move. Then he saw Relina fighting two enormous men who were better trained in combat than any other Debauched person there.

"Hit them in their sores, it slows them down," he shouted to her as he pounced on the back of the larger man.

"Zyleh, stop!" Relina tried to warn him, but it was too late. He felt the piercing stab of cold steel enter his side and the world around him slowed.

There is no time to feel pain, he told himself as he shook his head and stopped the Debauched man from stabbing him a second time. He twisted the knife out of his hand and turned it back on its owner, directing the sharp blade through the man's cheek and up into his brain. The man crumbled to the ground with Zyleh still on his back. He rolled off the lifeless heap of a man and onto the ground. Now that the fight was over, he finally allowed the pain to take hold of him.

Once Relina finished off the remaining Debauched man, she ran to her cousin's side. She picked him up by his shoulders and dragged him far away from the heat of battle.

"How bad is it?" she asked with deep concern in her eyes as she knelt beside him.

"Bad."

She lifted his hand from the stab wound and his entire palm was covered in blood. Relina bent down further so she was eye level with the gory opening beneath his ribcage.

"This is going to hurt," she said, then stuck her finger into the gash. He let out a howl.

"Oh man, this is deep," she determined. "We need to get you to the Heart now or you are going to bleed to death."

"I'll take myself, you need to keep fighting." He looked between the trees and toward the shore. Hordes of Debauched soldiers were still getting off the boats and filtering into the jungle to fight. Their numbers were greater than the Ahi and Tierannites combined, and even with the animals on their side, they weren't slowing them down. This was only the first round of troops the Debauched would send to Tier, so if they lost this leg of the war, they were sure to lose the rest as well.

"You are one of our best fighters, Relina," he continued. "Look at how many more are about to enter the jungle. You need to stay here and hold them off."

"You will never make it back to the Heart in time. This wound needs to be healed immediately or you will die."

Zyleh tried to stand up on his own to prove her wrong, but as soon as he did, the blood from his wound poured out faster, cascading from his abdomen down his thigh. He immediately got lightheaded and fell onto his knees.

An earsplitting whistle came out of the sky and Zyleh thought he might be slipping into unconsciousness, but then Relina covered her ears indicating she heard it too.

They both looked to the sky to see what new weapon the Debauched were attacking with. Zyleh scanned the treetops, looking for any sign of a plane or missile, but saw nothing.

"What is making that noise?" he asked.

"I don't know. I don't see anything." Relina stood up and walked to the tree line to investigate.

With a large gasp, she called back to Zyleh.

"It's the Ayrenese! I don't know how they managed, but they've come down to help."

"They've come *down*?" he asked, compressing his wound tightly and attempting to stand again. He limped, lightheaded, over to where Relina stood. His face went slack with awe as he saw the start of an aerial defense forming before him.

"I think they've got this. We need to fix you. Let me take you to the Heart." Her tone was calm and sure.

Zyleh conceded. The sight of the Ayrenese showed him they weren't as outnumbered as he thought. He would not let this wound be the end of him. There were still battles to be fought and forgiveness to be won.

Chapter 45

"Carry me steady," Darrow shouted through the whistle of the wind up to the newly formed group of climithes on a cloud above. They provided a strong airstream that allowed the gliders to create havoc near the beach. It was determined that if enough climithes worked together to fill the shore and jungle below with a constant wind current, the gliders would be able to soar closer to the ground and participate in the battle. Although there were new climithes working above, only experienced gliders rode these new winds in an attempt to fight alongside the Ahi and Tierannites.

Darrow held Kalloe's hand. Together they rode the winds at extremely high speeds, very close to the ocean. They, along with two other sets of gliders, circled the Debauched ships. Drue and Kalline rode the wind behind them, and Fallon and Jorban were paired up in front. The six gliders circled the shore in pairs, staying a consistent distance from each other.

Drue circled his fist in the air, instructing the climithes above to send faster winds, then he shouted out to his fellow gliders. "I see no Ahi or Tierannites on the shore. This is our target. Prepare to harness the tornado."

The gliders realized if they combined their skills with the skills of the climithes, they could create a devastating tornado *and* control its path. Though this was a first attempt, they had faith it would succeed.

The gliders carried the wind with them as they glided in a tight circle. Once the winds were fast enough, the six gliders joined hands and enclosed the wind in the middle. A vicious tornado materialized and they kept their hands clasped together tightly. They remained stationed toward the bottom of the tornado where its girth was skinnier and their circle could remain enclosed. Above them, the massive tornado roared violently.

"Clear out the Debauched along the shore first, then we will destroy the boats," Fallon shouted over the screeching wind. "And don't let the winds rip up the tree line. We can't risk injuring any Ahi or Tierannites."

Together, the six guided the tornado to hit their mark. The tornado was formidable and threw bodies in every direction. It sucked in the Debauched and spit them out, launching them against trees and hurling them into the ocean. The gliders remained afloat in the wind surrounding the tornado. Slowly, they cleared the entire beach of the Debauched and then honed in on wrecking the ships.

"Hit the boats lightly, we don't want to fling the debris into the jungle or hurt any unseen Coralene," Darrow instructed.

As a team, they made the tornado's outer winds hit the boats. The ships split apart, breaking beneath the pressure.

The gliders could see the Coralene coming to the surface and capturing the Debauched who had fallen off the boats. Some of the Coralene came straight out of the water to fight off the Debauched, while others snuck beneath them and dragged them into the depths of the sea.

All the ships were destroyed, as were thousands of Debauched soldiers.

"There's nothing more we can do. We have to dismantle the tornado," Drue called out. The gliders slowed the pace with which they let the wind circle between them, then eventually let go of each other's hands and pushed the volatile wind back toward the sky. They paired back up and continued to ride the winds that the climithes sent down. The loud whistle was gone but the steady rustle remained.

"Let's go back up," Kalloe suggested.

"There has to be more we can do to help. Look into the trees, there is still a battle going on," Jorban said, distressed.

"But what else can we do?"

"Let's fight," Darrow said. "I'm tired of feeling like I'm doing nothing. I'm ready to rip the Debauched apart."

"I'm in," Jorban and Fallon said simultaneously.

"Do you mean for us to kill them? With our hands?" Kalline asked, unsure.

"Whatever it takes." Jorban's eyes were wide with savagery.

377

"I am going to head up to Ayren to let them know your plan," Drue spoke. "They will need to give you stronger currents if you will be that close to the ground. Kalline, come with me. Are the rest of you okay with this?" They all nodded. "Okay, then wait here until I give you a push."

Drue and Kalline left and the other four gliders waited, their nerves electrified.

It wasn't long before they got the push from Drue. The current came from the east and pushed them westward.

"Alright, stay with your partner and always be aware of the other pair's location," Fallon instructed. "Let's go."

The four swooped down over the sandy beach, manipulating the wind provided.

"There's an opening right there," Fallon shouted, pointing toward a set of trees spaced far enough apart for the four gliders to fit through.

"Get ready to dodge," Jorban yelled as they entered the jungle. In a matter of seconds, the pairs were separated. The dense maze of trees prevented them from gliding next to each other and the pairs went in opposite directions in search of a fight to join.

"*Tree*," Kalloe warned as she yanked Darrow's arm, pulling him closer to her and preventing him from gliding face first into the thick trunk.

"Thanks," he said, out of breath as they continued to evade branches and tree trunks. They had to let go of each other's hands in order to do so, but they stayed as close as they could. They soared at high speeds, zigzagging above the chaotic fight that raged on between the Ahi, Tierannites, and Debauched.

"Let's circle around once. Get a feel for the size of the battle and where we can dip in to help," Darrow decided.

They made a large circle around a section of the battle to size up the situation. The large Tierannites used a combination of acrobatics and karate to take on the Debauched. The Ahi implemented different tactics. Their fighting style consisted of carefully aimed fireballs and brute force.

Darrow also noticed the animals of the jungle taking part in this fight. In the distance, he saw a giant feline rip out the throat of a Debauched man. Its sharp teeth sunk into the flesh with ease, killing its malformed prey without much effort. Right below them, a group of baboons beat a smaller Debauched woman senseless. Hairy arms flew in all directions, landing hard and crushing the bones and organs of the victim beneath. Darrow looked behind him as he heard loud thuds.

Three large, gray animals with horns protruding from their faces emerged from the dense forestry. Their massive feet pounded the ground as they bowled into a Debauched tank. They cracked the front of the vehicle in half, stopping it in its tracks, and continued charging forward unfazed. Darrow racked his memory for this animal's name: Rhinoceros.

Before the purge, Gaia relocated all the animals of the world to South America. Once Juniper started to evolve, she was tasked to create livable habitats throughout the Amazon for all the creatures of the planet. Gaia saved them from nature's purge and Juniper kept them sheltered during the aftermath. They opted to stay with Juniper instead of returning to their former corners of the world because life beyond the safe haven remained unstable. The choice was wise and spared them from inevitable extinction at the hand of the Debauched. The entire continent teemed with life and protected countless living species. Though it was impressive and mesmerizing from afar, this was the first time Darrow ever witnessed its glory in close proximity. Seeing all the animals up close was magical. He had never experienced a beauty as magnificent as nature's wildlife.

Then he took a closer look at the faces of the Debauched. Their expressions were full of defeated rage, not because they were losing this battle, but because they had lost a battle long before this one.

"The Debauched look like monsters. Besides their weaponry, weren't they supposed to be weak and easy to beat?" Kalloe asked, looking down at them with contempt.

"Yeah," Darrow said hesitantly, "they look deformed, like they've mutated or something." His heart beat a little faster.

"Are those women?" Kalloe asked, shielding her eyes from the sun so she could see better. Three Debauched women fought one Ahi man and managed to overtake him. The women attacked him barbarically, pounding their fists and grunting. Veins bulged out of their necks as they laughed and took turns beating the Ahi man, who lay on the ground with his arms protecting his skull.

Darrow nodded, appalled. It was against his moral code to lay a hand on a female, but he supposed the current circumstances called for different standards. "We need to help him."

"Okay, what do we do?"

Darrow wasn't exactly sure. He knew how to fight in the sky, on a cloud, against opponents that weren't really trying to hurt him. His mind froze on how to get closer to the ground to fight these mutant humans. He was holding Kalloe's hand again, trying to determine how they could possibly do this together amidst the tight arrangement of trees.

In the distance, they saw Fallon and Jorban swooping down to fight the Debauched. Their fellow gliders picked up speed then darted toward the ground. Darrow could see Fallon throw a powerful punch into the face of a grotesque Debauched man and then Jorban circled in from behind, kicking the man so hard in the spine that the guy folded backward in half.

"They aren't holding hands," Darrow said aloud. "Let go, Kalloe, I'm going down. Filter some of your wind into mine to give me extra speed."

She did so and Darrow felt his pace pick up. He pinched his shoulders back, kept his arms straight behind him, and let the wind carry him toward one of the Debauched women. They hadn't seen him yet.

The eyes of these three women were vacant with only a flicker of merciless anger hidden in their depths. They took turns pummeling the Ahi man's face, enjoying their role in the bloodshed.

Darrow came in from behind and swung his elbow around, striking the first Debauched woman in the temple. Her head twisted around, making a loud snap before her body crumpled to the ground. The other two women were startled and confused, completely caught off guard by their new opponent. Then he circled to the second woman. For a moment, the stream he rode faltered, becoming too weak to hold onto. As he feared he might fall, Kalloe gave him an extra blast and he regained control of his movement. He used the wind to flip his body and strike the woman, feet first. He crashed into her, his heel hitting her hard in the eye socket. She collapsed to the ground lifeless.

The third woman stopped beating the Ahi man and turned to face Darrow. As he glided directly toward her, she laughed.

"Flying monkeys? Come closer, funny monkey, so I can taste your flesh," she taunted, a crooked smile of rotted teeth crossed her face. Beneath her left eye was a large, raw sore protruding unnaturally from her skin. She licked her lips as she braced herself to fight Darrow.

He looked down at the Ahi man as he continued to glide in circles above the woman.

"Get up. I've bought you some time."

The Ahi man peeked out from under one of his arms, realizing that another hard blow from the Debauched wasn't being delivered. He stood up with newfound assertiveness.

"Not so strong now, are you?" the Ahi man said in a low roar as he took slow steps toward the last standing Debauched woman.

With a manic laugh she looked down at the other two women dead on the floor. Her eyes darted back and forth between the Ahi man and Darrow, and her face contorted into a look of distorted pleasure. She laughed aloud again as the fear of dying and the desire to fight battled each other in her expression.

Darrow flipped his body in the wind and kicked her into the arms of the Ahi man. He secured her in his grip by placing both of his hands around her neck. His palms heated up and glowed fiery red as they scorched the woman's skin. Her loose hair caught on fire, igniting her scalp in a bright blaze. As she screamed in pain, the Ahi man snapped her neck and she collapsed into his arms.

He pushed her away, letting her fall with disgrace to the ground. The fire in her hair spread and her corpse became engulfed in flames. One less body to clean up later.

"Good to see you've come down from the sky," the Ahi man said as he kicked the few flammable pieces of forestry away from the burning corpse. He gave Darrow a quick nod of gratitude before running off in the opposite direction to continue fighting elsewhere.

Using the strong wind current, Darrow carried himself back to where Kalloe was waiting.

"You almost lost your grip after the second one," she said with concern in her voice.

"I know. Thanks for the extra boost."

She nodded and they circled the battlefield again. It was a bloodbath: dead bodies lay scattered everywhere. While the sight of so many deceased members of the Debauched and Elements was overwhelming, Darrow's overhead view looked optimistic. If the Elements stayed strong, they could win. With the help of the Coralene, the Ayrenese tornado, and the animals, the Tierannites and Ahi survived long enough to outnumber the Debauched.

"Over there," Darrow said to Kalloe, pointing at a smaller Tierannite boy. "We need to help him."

They sped toward the outer perimeter of the battle where the young boy attempted to fight off a Debauched man alone. The boy had blood dripping down his face from a gash under his eye, but it didn't slow him down. He ran circles around the large Debauched man, kicking him in the ribs and jabbing him in the throat whenever he got a clear shot. The Debauched man had a small pistol with a sharp blade attached, so the boy was being fired and stabbed at while he did flips around the man.

In the blink of an eye, the boy did a somersault in the air and landed himself on a tree branch above the Debauched man's head. Right after landing he jumped back down, attempting to body slam the man into submission. It half-worked: he knocked the man to the ground but the man grabbed the boy's ankle during the ordeal, leaving him trapped in his grip. The man raised the dagger end of his pistol and prepared to stab the boy.

Darrow took this as his cue to swoop down and help.

"Give me some of your wind, like last time," he said to Kalloe and then took off toward the fight.

Darrow planned to dive down, feet-first into the side of the man's head. The force of impact applied like that had proved to be lethal previously, so he hoped it worked again. As he came down, the Debauched man looked up and saw Darrow swooping in for the kill. Without hesitation, he redirected his bladed pistol straight at Darrow's heart.

Kalloe screamed, but Darrow could not slow down, he was already going too fast. He could feel Kalloe trying to shift his wind current to the left, but it wasn't enough. The blast from the gun sounded and the bullet hit Darrow. He immediately lost hold of the wind and fell to the jungle floor with a thud. Kalloe shrieked in horror.

"Help him," her voice cracked with despair. She could not get close enough to assist.

The Tierannite boy used this diversion to break free from the Debauched man's grasp. He quickly flipped over the man, who was still knocked to the ground, and stomped on the hand holding the gun. The man groaned in agony as his wrist broke. The boy picked up the gun and pointed it straight into the man's face. His hand shook.

"May Gaia have mercy on the broken," he said. A tear rolled down his cheek as he shot the man between the eyes. He then flung the gun as far as he could throw it.

"You had to do it," Kalloe said to him, as kindly as she could.

The boy looked up at her with wet eyes.

"That man was ruined. They broke him somehow. They have done something terrible to these people."

"What happened to them before they were sent here is out of our control." Kalloe tried to calm the boy down. She needed him to have a level head to help Darrow.

The boy used his arm to wipe the tears from his eyes, and dirt and blood smeared across his face. The gash under his eye was swelling. He walked over to where his Ayrenese savior lay and rolled him over. Darrow moaned in agony.

"The bullet missed his heart by an inch."

Tears fell from Kalloe's bright orange eyes.

"Is he going to die?"

"Can you heal him in Ayren?"

"Heal him? No, we don't perform magic in Ayren," she answered harshly between sniffles. "Even if we could heal him, I can't get him back to Ayren in this condition. He can't glide with a hole in his chest."

"Alright, we can fix him here. We have injuries down here all the time. Since it didn't hit any of his organs, it should be an easy fix. I just need to get him to the Heart."

"Go then!" Kalloe's brash attitude was unbecoming. The boy's bright green eyes grew wide with shock at her continued abrasiveness.

"I'm Phelix," he said, ignoring her rudeness. "In case you wanted to know who was saving your friend."

"Sorry, I'm Kalloe. And that's Darrow." She said, a bit abashed for not controlling her temper.

He stood up and walked to a nearby tree. He took a moment to look around, then pulled a plant out of the ground. Its long exposed root was thick and white.

He knelt back down next to Darrow.

"Chew on this while I carry you, it will numb some of the pain until I can get you the good stuff."

Phelix picked up Darrow like a baby, cradling him in his arms.

"I'll be back with help." She gave him a smile and then took off toward Ayren.

Phelix ran toward the Heart as gently as he could with Darrow in his arms. Darrow chewed on the root while Phelix hummed a soft melody meant to ease his mind from the discomfort. Darrow slipped into a painless dream as he let the song take over his mind. It was a long journey back to the Heart but Phelix had faith they would make it in time.

Chapter 46

Maila waited in the tree swing for an indication of how things were going. She didn't know what was happening, who was hurt, or where the battle was taking place. The steady hum of insects and rustling of animals was missing, which frustrated her further; even the bugs were of more use than her down here.

Despite her anger toward Zyleh, she still hoped he was okay. As he left to fight, she gave him a sendoff that was cruel and unnecessary. She might not be able to forgive him yet, but she certainly didn't wish him dead.

The jungle remained quiet and this time alone proved perfect for reflection. She finally had every truth she could possibly desire and the time needed to make sense of it all.

Darrow filled her every waking thought. She was ashamed that it took such extremes for her to understand how she felt for him, but maybe that was what she needed. She was angry with him for not telling her the truth, so she suppressed her feelings for him. He wouldn't tell her the truth because she refused to admit she felt the same way he did. Seeing it in hindsight the vicious circle in which they spun was obvious. If they both were less stubborn, things would have turned out differently. Even so, she decided weeks ago to take full responsibility for all she had caused. While the truth would have prevented all of this, she would not use that as an excuse. All she could do now was move forward and fix her mistake the best she could.

There was a lot to figure out once she got back to Ayren. The revelation about her real origin still felt like a dream. She had much to learn, and accept, about her mother, Clara. Though a lot of time had passed since she learned the truth, she still needed to sort out her feelings about that situation. It felt surreal and relearning eighteen years of her life was a daunting task. Perhaps once she finally let this truth settle into her heart, her difficult childhood spent trying to earn Mira's love would make more sense. Maybe the unreturned love wouldn't haunt her anymore. That relationship was always toxic and Maila finally understood why. Mira couldn't love her, but Clara would have. As mad as she was at her father for withholding the truth, she was happy to know it now. It cleared up many doubts she once had about herself as a person.

With those self-doubts erased, her heart felt wide open and ready to be filled with worthy endeavors. Instead of proving her worth to others or trying desperately to earn the affection of those who did not deserve her love, Maila could focus on the people who mattered. The new love she had for herself could turn outward and radiate upon those who valued her, flaws and all. Before her fall from the sky there was no room in her heart to love another, which was why it was so hard to accept Darrow's affection. But now, she could love herself *and* let others love her back. Better yet, she had room in her heart to take on loving the entire world.

There were many amends to be made among the Elements, and even some promising hopes for the Debauched. Maila wanted to be on the frontline for every future milestone to come. With her new outlook and education about the world, she felt unstoppable. She had many ideas to put in motion once she was back where she belonged and she was excited to get home and begin this crusade.

This made her think of Violet. The little girl was still hiding beneath the cement streets of that foul city. Alone and waiting for her and Zyleh to come back and rescue her from the terrible world she was born into.

A rush of worry engulfed Maila as she remembered Zyleh saying he would erase her memory if Violet could not complete her task. The task was a tall order for a young child to complete and Maila could not let her fail. She would not let Violet live the rest of her days believing there was no hope. Like Maila, Violet spent her entire life living in a world of secrets. It wasn't fair or productive. Maila shook her head, remembering how easy Zyleh made the task of erasing a memory seem. Just sing a song and it's all over, she'd forget.

Then, like a strike of lightning, it hit her. Maila knew how to fix everything. She had an idea that could save all the Elements without any more bloodshed. Her heart began to pulse harder beneath her skinny rib cage. She placed a hand over her heart and tried to slow her breathing.

She had to find someone. She had to tell Relina or the Grand Paipa.

Before she could make her descent to the jungle floor, a rush of air encircled her and she found herself levitating a few inches off the tree swing. The breeze was a cool embrace and suddenly, she wasn't alone.

My dearest, Maila. The woman's voice came from the air and was audible only to Maila.

"Who is this?" Maila whispered, afraid others in the vicinity might think she was talking to herself.

Aria, Champion of the Air. I have been watching you.

"Aria?" Maila asked in shock. "We've missed you, and oh, how we've needed your return."

I've seen the social decline of the Ayrenese; I've observed with great disappointment from afar. Ayren's detachment from the other Elements became such a letdown that I had to distance myself. That's not how it was supposed to be. My Champion sisters and I suffered through immense tragedy, and persevered through humanity's darkest days in order to build a world where nature's elements were in control and securely bonded. To see my descendants carelessly tarnish all that I built, all that I lived for, was too much to bear. *But you,* Maila could feel Aria's beaming smile inside her mind, *You've changed everything.*

"While I'm honored, I cannot pretend that I've done any of this on purpose."

It's not about your fall or this war, but about your bravery. The gliders gave me hope, but they were never courageous enough to make a bold move that would shake up the ignorant leadership in Ayren and force the culture to make drastic changes. They were too afraid of the backlash. You never cared if your questions offended your suppressors or threatened the sanctity of the sheltered community they so foolishly devised. You believed beyond what they offered and were smart enough to realize you deserved more. Your methods were unconventional but bold, and I am so delighted my lineage finally produced a heroine. I'll admit, when I saw you were the first to be granted the next evolutionary gift, I suspected you'd do spectacular things, I just worried the culture in which you were born might snuff out your glow. I am thrilled that you didn't let them.

"It wasn't easy, but every time I almost gave up it felt like a betrayal to myself. Though it would have made my life easier, it never felt right to give in. There was a fire burning inside me that I couldn't ignore. I had to seek the truth."

And I am so grateful you did. You've restored my faith in the Ayrenese and I am ready to return to your aid. I see your greatness and I believe you can bring out the best in the others.

393

"Thank you for choosing me. I am humbled and promise to make you proud."

You already have. Let me take you home. I would've offered sooner, but I thought it wise to let you have this time in Tier to reflect upon all that led you to this point and to give you a chance to interact with your brethren of the ground. To my delight, you experienced a bit of Coralen and Ahi too. I hope you don't mind that I came to your aid a little late, but I thought it prudent.

"I needed this time, so thank you, but I have one more order of business to attend to before I'm ready to go back to Ayren."

The moment you are ready, I'll come for you. Just call out to me in your thoughts.

"I will. And thank you for easing my plunge into the ocean. Juniper relayed that message. I would've died without you cushioning my fall."

Like I said, I've been watching over you. You are my greatest hope for the future of the air. I'll never let harm find you.

"Thank you."

Take care, Maila.

Aria disappeared along with the current.

Maila felt invincible. Her smile beamed from ear to ear and every weight she had carried to this point in her life felt lifted. Aria was on her side and nothing was better than that.

Chapter 47

As her bare feet landed in the soft grass she heard hurried voices approaching the dusty dirt area surrounding the Heart. She turned and saw Relina carrying Zyleh over her shoulder. Though his large body covered hers, she was still strong enough to run with him.

He was limp and not moving at all. Maila's stomach turned and she was afraid to ask what happened. She pushed through the fear and ran toward them. She called out, trying to contain the emotion building up inside her but unable to stop her voice from cracking. Despite his deception, she still saw him as her friend and it hurt to see him injured.

Relina put Zyleh down next to the tree trunk of the Heart.

"He was coming to help me fight but did not realize the Debauched he was attacking had a knife. The man stabbed him in the side. It's deep, but if we fix him fast enough he will heal."

Relina banged her fist four times against the trunk of the Heart. The exposed roots slithered through the earth, retracting into the ground as the trunk of the Heart opened. The dazzling glow from the tree illuminated Maila's face and she watched Relina carry Zyleh into the blaze of gold. It closed behind them, leaving her standing alone in the comparably dull sunlight, waiting for them to reemerge.

From behind, she heard more hurried feet running toward the Heart and she turned to see Phelix running toward her with a boy in his arms. The boy wasn't a Tierannite, though. As she refocused on Phelix and the body he carried, she noticed the injured boy was luminous like her. His bright blue eyes radiated as he dipped in and out of consciousness. Her heart stopped. It was Darrow.

"A few of the gliders came down to help in the battle," Phelix explained in response to Maila's devastated expression of paralyzed horror. "He was trying to help me but the man I was fighting had a gun and shot him in the chest, right next to his heart."

Maila shook with terror as she saw Phelix covered in Darrow's blood. Phelix knocked four times on the side of the Heart but it did not open. A look of puzzlement crossed his face; he looked back at Maila.

"Who's in there? The Heart won't open if its magic is being used on someone else."

Maila took a moment before answering. The silent onslaught of tears blinded her from the present moment.

"Relina and Zyleh," she managed to mutter through the blur of terrible thoughts consuming her entire being. "He was stabbed in the stomach."

Phelix nodded, taking in the information and digesting it without freaking out.

"As long as he is in the Heart, he will be fine. But I hope they hurry, Darrow here needs to begin healing immediately before we lose him."

Maila choked on the breath leaving her lips. Her entire world was on hold and Darrow's recovery was all that mattered now. Though she was unharmed, her well being relied greatly on his. She had to remind herself to breath; passing out from fear wouldn't help anyone. She stared at the trunk of the Heart, willing Zyleh's healing to be finished. Within a minute, the side of the Heart opened again and Relina emerged, followed closely by Zyleh.

As Phelix walked past Maila, Darrow's eyes grew wide at the sight of her. He opened his mouth to speak but nothing came out. Only a hoarse gasp. Her heart became heavy with anticipation as they disappeared into the golden glow. The Heart closed and Relina walked over.

"Who was Phelix carrying?"

Maila finally let the tears fall.

"That was Darrow," she explained between sobs. "He was shot in battle."

Zyleh was still dazed from the healing process, but the sound of Darrow's name caught his attention.

"The gliders fought in one-on-one combat?" he asked, knowing they came down but surprised they did more than a few acts from the safety of the sky.

"Yes," Maila confirmed while trying to compose herself.

"Don't worry, he will be healed," Relina said, understanding the tears flowing down Maila's porcelain cheeks.

Zyleh looked at Maila crying over Darrow and a flicker of pain crossed his face. The level of affection they shared for each other was undeniable. Part of him wondered if she reacted this way when she learned of his injury, while the other half confidently knew she didn't. The raw emotion Maila wore for Darrow was impassioned and he was amazed he ever believed he stood a chance.

By this time, the Heart was filled with more of the wounded. A long line formed with people waiting to be healed. Bazoo swooped down from the tree, climbed into Maila's arms, and wiped the tears off her cheeks. She smiled at him as he hugged her neck. His presence helped her recollect herself as she waited for Darrow to recover.

With a focused mind she remembered why she came down from the tree in the first place: her idea on how to stop the war. Just as she began composing herself to tell them her plan, a loud swooshing noise came from above.

She saw Drue first, followed by Celia, Fallon, Kalloe, Kalline, and Jorban. Her heart dropped again; it was overwhelming to see so many familiar faces after being stranded away from home for so long. Their expressions shifted to that of complete disbelief as they saw her standing there, alive and relatively healthy.

"Maila?" Celia cried out. The tears falling down her cheeks doubled.

Maila nodded her head, understanding their confusion. Bazoo climbed off and stood on the ground, still holding her hand.

"We were told you were dead," Drue said, his anger rising.

"It was a lie." Tears of joy filled her eyes as her fears were proven invalid. They did care, and they were just as furious as she was.

Fallon shot a glare at Zyleh, "How could you?"

"I thought she was safer with me in Tier."

"You let us believe she was dead! We held a funeral and mourned her death!" Jorban exclaimed.

"Our people were devastated," Kalline added, her face contorted with rage, "You broke our hearts."

"You'd rather her be dead up in Ayren?" Zyleh said in defense of his actions.

"We all survived it. You can't pretend to know she'd have died in that explosion." Kalloe spoke up on behalf of Maila for the first time ever.

"It's a foul thing that you've done," Celia spat at him, disgusted, "You should be ashamed of yourself and the pain you've caused."

"Your lie was extreme," Drue addressed Zyleh with ruthless conviction, "and it affected more than just you and Maila; it hurt all of us. I don't care why you did it. I don't want to hear your reasons. You aren't worth another second of my time." Drue redirected his attention to Maila, his whole demeanor softening as he did so. "I am so sorry you endured this heartache all alone. While we all grieved your supposed death together, you had to brave it out on your own. I can only imagine the ways our abandoned search made you feel."

"It's okay. I'm okay. It all makes sense now and any fears it caused are gone." Drue nodded, proud of Maila's strength.

The hate Zyleh felt radiating from the group of gliders was immeasurable. He slipped into the shadows of the trees, wanting to be as far away from these people as possible. He listened to the content of the meeting, but retained very little. His heart was racing too fast to notice anything other than its painful thuds.

"Where is Darrow?" Celia chimed in. For now, the previous issue was as resolved as it could be and it was time to switch the subject back to her son.

"He is being healed as we speak," Relina said.

"Will he be alright?" Drue asked.

"Yes," Relina said, "he should be. He may be drowsy and out of it for a while, but he will survive."

"Thank you so much. As soon as he is able, we will take them both home," Drue said with a smile at Maila.

"Before I leave, I have an idea," she shouted, her excitement barely containable. "I think I may have come up with a solution to end the war."

"What is it?" Relina asked with interest.

"Zyleh mentioned once that you guys have a song that makes people forget things. I figured maybe we could make the Debauched forget they ever left the smog and that this side of the world exists. Then the problem would be solved and nobody else would get hurt."

"Okay," Relina started hesitantly, "but there is no way we can hypnotize every Debauched person. We can't enter the cities to do this."

"I know," Maila smiled and then looked up at the gliders, "that's where we come in. We will carry the song into the city via the wind." She addressed Relina again, "You would need to get all the Tierannites to gather on the shore closest to the Debauched city. You would sing together loudly, then we would direct the winds to pick up your song and carry it through every inch of the city."

All the gliders looked at each other in question, curious to whether something like this would work. Relina looked over at Zyleh, who remained far off from the rest of them.

"It can't hurt to try," he said with a shrug.

"He's right, it's worth a shot," Relina agreed.

"Okay," Fallon cut in. "I like it, but how will we know if it worked?"

"Can the Ahi spies determine something like that? They weren't very good at predicting when the first attack would be," Kalloe said with accusation.

"No, they can only see so much," Relina agreed. "I'm not sure how we would be able to tell."

"Violet," Maila said under her breath. Zyleh heard her and stepped back into the mix before she said too much. They couldn't know about Violet. Not only would they be appalled that he and Maila let a Debauched person see them, but to know they made a deal with one? That they befriended one? The Debauched *just* attacked them and their level of acceptance was at an all-time low. Maila was still less aware of the workings of the world than he was, so he stepped in to prevent any scrutiny.

"I have a solid connection that can help us determine whether it worked or not." He saw their suspicious looks.

"Who is it?" Relina demanded first.

Neither group would agree to let one Debauched person go untouched by the forgetting spell, no matter how hard Maila tried to convince them the girl was innocent. The trust wasn't there yet. Violet had to prove herself first.

"I'd rather not disclose their identity. The relationship is sensitive and if anyone interfered, specifically you Relina, the whole thing could be ruined." Relina shot him a nasty look. "I know you all hate me right now, but you're going to have to trust me. This connection is our only way to be sure the hypnosis worked. Consider this my attempt to earn back your trust after my poor judgment with that lie."

Everyone looked around at each other with hesitance. No one wanted to put the fate of this new mission in his hands.

"I know the connection, too," Maila spoke up, seeing the dissention amongst her people. "And I am confident that they are reliable. If you can't trust Zyleh, then trust me. The source is legitimate."

A long pause passed before the group conceded.

"I trust Maila, and that's good enough for me," Fallon said.

"Agreed." Drue gave his stamp of approval. "As soon as we get Darrow back, we will return to the skies and prepare to carry your song toward the Debauched city. Do you think we can arrange this all to happen today before sundown?" Drue asked.

"Did you notice the state of the battle on your glide in?" Relina asked.

"It appeared over, with the Elements victorious," Fallon answered.

"Okay, great. Then sundown should work just fine," Relina concluded.

The group started talking amongst one another and Zyleh pulled Maila off to the side to talk to her alone. Regret finally surpassed his wrongful resolve.

"I'm sorry."

"That's the first time you've apologized."

"I know. It shouldn't have taken me so long but I was positive my reasons were gallant. Your ferocity after learning what I did and the gliders reaction to seeing you alive really put it into perspective. I see how deeply my lie hurt you and everyone you love. While I am sorry, I still believe it was the right move and I don't take it back. I hope you can understand my reasoning. I truly did it to protect you."

"I have no doubt that you believe that." Maila thought of her life back in Ayren and how often she sat beneath the shade of the diamond owl sculpture at the Axis. If she was being honest with herself, it's quite possible he *did* save her life.

"I'm still mad," she continued, "but I think with time to reflect I'll see things differently. This hardship has made us all better."

The potential for forgiveness was there, and it was all Zyleh had hoped for.

"I hope we can be friends again someday."

"I'm still angry, don't rush it."

"I know. If there's anything I can do to prove how sorry I am, I'll do it."

"Take care of Violet. Learn to see her the way I do." It was a challenge, but Zyleh would do anything for Maila. "Check on her whenever you can and no matter the outcome of this war, don't let anything bad happen to her. She doesn't deserve to suffer. She isn't evil."

"I'll do my best."

"I hope so. Make sure the forgetting chant doesn't affect her, too."

"I know. Let's just hope she follows through on getting rid of Mr. Lamorte. This little magic trick is useless if that bastard is still around. He found us once, he'll find us again. He needs to be eliminated."

Maila nodded, but said nothing. She already had a plan to help Violet with that task, but she was keeping it to herself for now.

"I'm glad you're okay." She motioned toward his healing wound.

It was a simple comment, but it held great weight for both of them. Zyleh stepped in and gave her a hug.

405

A rustle came from behind them and Maila's attention shifted to the source of the noise. It was Darrow walking through the golden glow of the Heart with Phelix.

Darrow's silvery blue eyes were half shut as he swayed in place with Phelix keeping him upright. He was still out of it and unaware of what was going on. Maila wanted to run to him, but Drue had already begun doling out instructions.

"Okay, Fallon and Jorban, pick Darrow up from under his arms and place him on my back. Then Celia, latch over top of him and onto my back to keep him steadily in place. I'll hold your legs tight so he doesn't slip out."

Once Darrow was in place, Drue focused on getting Maila into the air. He smiled down at her.

"I think it's time we taught you how to glide."

Maila's eyes lit up. She was going to need to learn how to glide properly in order to execute her plan to help Violet, so this was perfect. Maila bent down to give Bazoo a farewell kiss on the cheek, then said goodbye to the surrounding Tierannites, thanking them for all their kindness.

Fallon and Kalline took her hands and pulled her into the airstream.

"There's no better terrain to learn on than a current as strong as this one. If you can glide through this, you can glide through anything," Fallon told her.

"I am holding you both responsible for her. Do not let her fall again," Drue instructed. Fallon nodded as he and Kalline held her in the current between them. Maila's body immediately felt much better as she found her center and let the lightness of the air caress her hollow bones.

"It's nice to have you back," Kalline whispered into her ear. Maila smiled. She knew how terribly she missed all of them and it felt good to have that feeling returned.

"Which direction will we send the winds?" Celia asked the Tierannites over Drue's shoulder.

"Toward the northeast corner of the dome," Zyleh answered. "Where light can be seen through the smog."

"How will we know when to begin?"

"If your clouds are nearby in the sky, you will hear us," Relina answered with a smile. "But don't listen too closely or you will fall under the magic of the chant as well. Once you hear it, redirect it."

"Wonderful. Until then," Drue said with excitement. The worry that plagued his expression earlier was slowly beginning to fade. He quickly took off to the sky with Celia and Darrow attached to his back. Fallon and Kalline followed him with Maila in tow, and Kalloe and Jorban trailed behind as spotters in case Maila fell.

As soon as they were out of earshot, Relina turned to Zyleh.

"I'm sorry, cousin, but you know it is right for her to return home."

"If you had kept your mouth shut she never would have gotten so furious with me. You snitched so quick, I barely had a chance to see if she'd ever love me back." He still felt bad about the lie but needed a chance to release the anger he had toward Relina.

"You ruined your chances the moment you told that lie. Not to mention, she would have died if she stayed here," Relina tried to reason with Zyleh.

"I could have fixed her."

"Even if you made up some herbal remedy that eased the pain she experienced while living down here, it wouldn't have mattered. She loves Darrow and I don't think you would have ever changed that. What you did to all of them was terrible."

"Whatever, Relina. You've never been in love and I doubt you ever will be, so there's no use trying to get you to understand."

"You're an ass," she scowled.

"It's not my fault there isn't a man on Earth who is saintly enough to love a woman as difficult as you."

He was syphoning for blood, but she was the wrong person to challenge.

"You have it backwards, dear cousin. The only person here who is impossible to love is you. Maila is proof of that."

This statement hit him in the gut. Battle over.

Without giving him a chance to respond, she walked away, leaving him where he stood. He was ashamed of himself for taking his pain out on her and the guilt Maila had eased returned in a new form.

"I'm sorry," he called out to his cousin, but she ignored him. Phelix gave Zyleh a pat on the back.

"I'm going to miss Maila, too. You were a hell of a lot nicer while she was around," Phelix sighed. He felt bad for Relina. She always got the worst of Zyleh's temper.

"I know it's all my fault. I already feel remorse for what I did to Maila, so I'm not sure why I felt the need to add more to my list of things to feel sorry for."

"The gliders just ripped you apart and your emotions are shot. You made a mistake and are paying the cost. I know you're not a bad guy, and in time, so will everyone else. Just own what you've done and lay low for a while, and definitely stop taking your anger out on other people. You won't win anyone's sympathy if you keep that up."

"Thanks," Zyleh replied, unsure when his little brother became so confident and wise. "I have a favor to ask you."

"What is it?"

"I have to go and tell father about the plan we just made with the gliders, then I will meet you at the Northeast checkpoint to tell you what I need you to do."

"Why can't you just tell me here?"

"Just go and I'll meet you there," he insisted.

Phelix ran off and Zyleh looked up to the sky. The gliders were still visible as they soared toward Ayren and he watched them become tiny dots in the afternoon sky. His heart felt conflicted knowing that Maila was one of them. His intentions were good, whether any one else agreed with him or not, and he wished she hadn't left. The gliders could believe he was the bad guy for as long as they wanted, but it didn't mean it was true. Zyleh knew he wasn't a terrible person and he hoped Maila believed that, too.

His chest grew heavy as he watched the girl he would have given the world to fly away.

Chapter 48

"You need to breathe the current. If you let it flow through you it will be easier to maneuver," Fallon instructed Maila.

The air was strong but she was doing well. Fallon and Kalline stayed on both sides of her as she glided on her own toward Ayren. In addition to taking their advice as gliders, she applied her climithe skills to manipulate the air and make it easier to manage. With her wind harnessing skills she shifted the current to stop it from fighting against her, then she noticed the wind was causing the gliders trouble, too.

"I'm not sure if you know anything about the skills of the climithes, but if you snare the current, you can control it while you glide and it won't feel as tough to move through," Maila shouted through the rush of air. Combining her new gliding knowledge with her own expert climithe skills proved invaluable. Because of it, she now moved more fluidly than Fallon and Kalline.

"You are going to have to teach me that," Kalline yelled over the whistling airstream. Both gliders were impressed there was another way to do it and Maila couldn't believe it was coming to her so naturally now. With Fallon's pointers, she was gliding effortlessly.

Once they arrived on the cloud the climithes operated from, Drue began running around telling everyone the plan, as did Jorban and Kalloe. Maila hovered next to the cloud, pausing before stepping onto it.

"I am afraid I'm going to fall through," she said.

"Take my hand," Kalline said with a smile, her fiery orange eyes were full of compassion. "Fallon will take the other. We won't let you fall again."

As soon as her tiny bare feet touched the cloud, she could feel her whole body realign.

"Do you have your footing?" Fallon asked, curious to see what side effects came from being on the ground for so long.

"Yes," Maila exclaimed. "I was afraid I was broken and that I would never be able to live here again." Her eyes shimmered with joy and she let go of their hands to stand on her own. A squeal of excitement came out of her as she spun around with her arms in the air.

"Excellent," Fallon said. "I hate to leave so quickly, but I must help my popa spread the word about what we need to do. Every citizen of Ayren will need to take part in order to make an air current strong enough to carry the Tierannite song through every crack of the Debauched continent." Fallon gave them both one last smile before departing.

"Where is Darrow?" Maila asked Kalline as she turned, looking for him.

"I think Celia took him back to their home cloud to rest."

"I have to go see him. I've missed him so much."

"There is no time for that now," Jorban said, overhearing their conversation as he returned. "He won't be lucid for a while and it's best that we stay productive. The solidifiers are building a special cloud for what we are about to do. We should watch how they do it; observe how they move and the techniques they use."

Maila furrowed her brow; nobody ever cared to learn how others did their jobs. Kalline saw her confused expression and explained.

"Since the attack on the Axis, the Law of Secrecy has been abolished and everyone knows the truth," she said proudly, "As a community, we decided it was best that everyone learned how to execute every job in Ayren. It's the only way to make us stronger as a whole."

"That is wonderful," Maila said, a huge grin crossed her face at this news.

"Yeah, apparently they are going to make a huge, sturdy cloud with a hole in the middle of it," Jorban added. "That way, people can line the outer edges of the cloud as well as the hole in the middle. It will allow more people to take part in making the wind strong so we can carry the Tierannites song through the smog."

"That's brilliant," Kalline said.

"Yeah. They are working fast so it can be finished by sundown and from the looks of the sun, they've got about two hours."

They walked toward the edge of the cloud and Maila was ecstatic that she could finally glide alongside them instead of having to ride her personal cloud. She was aware of the time ticking away and that she didn't have much left to complete her solo mission, but she wanted to observe the solidifiers in action for a moment before embarking upon her next big feat.

"I am so happy I can glide," she said.

"Yeah, so far we've taught the basics to most people. Almost everyone can glide enough to get themselves from cloud to cloud," Jorban responded.

"Are you kidding me?" Maila said, "I fell all the way into the ocean and *then* you guys decide to teach everyone how to glide?"

"Sorry!" Jorban offered sheepishly, sensing Maila's playfulness behind her vexed proclamation.

"You're the reason all of this is happening," Kalline said. "You should be proud. Your bravery changed everything for the better."

"It's true," Jorban agreed. "It may have been crazy how you did it, but it worked."

An emotion Maila couldn't explain swelled inside her. They were putting great value on what she had done, when all this time she was worried everyone in Ayren might hate her because of it. Though she still regretted the turmoil it caused, she was relieved to know it brought about some good. Not only did it fix things in Ayren, but it also brought Aria back. She wasn't sure when she'd tell the others, but now wasn't appropriate. They had a mission to focus on.

They got to the area where the solidifiers were constructing their masterpiece and sat cross-legged on a nearby cloud to watch them work.

They used blown-glass horns to disperse the shaved crystal into the cloud's atmosphere. This solidified the cloud so the people of Ayren could safely stay upon it. Half of the solidifiers worked on the torus cloud from their personal clouds, while the other half used their new gliding skills to do their work. Those gliding were significantly more productive. They were able to hang upside down and swivel around freely while working, allowing them to get to places they may not have been able to reach if they were solidifying from another cloud.

"Gliding helps a lot. Look how fast they are moving," Kalline commented.

Maila looked over the cloud and saw the beach of Tier below. She remembered the days she spent there alone, wondering if she'd ever get home.

Kalline caught her staring down and put a hand on Maila's shoulder.

"We looked for you. Multiple times."

"I know. Once Relina finally filled me in on Zyleh's lie she told me. For a long time I thought you never came at all." Maila did not want to focus on the misplaced distress anymore. "I wish it hadn't happened how it did, but I guess if nothing else, at least I got to see everything I always wanted to see."

Kalline nodded, "You got to see more than any of us ever have."

Maila nodded, thinking of how she not only saw Tier, but parts of Coralen and Ahi, too. Though it was laced with sadness and hardship, it truly was a marvelous adventure.

"One day you'll have to tell us all about it," Kalline added.

"I will," She smiled at her, but Jorban reserved his curiosity to address another issue.

"You had us terribly worried, especially Darrow. I've never seen him so distraught. He made himself sick over your disappearance, and then supposed death."

Maila's heart contracted. She was happy to hear he missed her with such ferocity, but broken up to know his pain was preventable. He never needed to feel any of those things.

"I can't even express my fury when I heard about the lie. It wasn't fair to anyone," her voice quivered as the memory of her

416

heartache returned, "I missed him most of all. Every day I worried he would hate me for what happened. While I was alone down there, I realized how much he means to me."

"Well, we are all glad you're back," Kalline concluded.

The sky turned a shade darker and Maila remembered she still had another task to complete. It needed to be done before the Tierannites began their song.

"Can you go with me to the northeast section of the dome? Above where Mr. Lamorte resides?"

"Why?" Kalline asked.

"There is something I need to do."

Kalline looked worried.

"Can we help?"

"No, I have to do it alone. I just need backup."

Nolan, Head Cloud Solidifier, called out into the sky.

"The cloud is ready. Everyone come aboard."

The people of Ayren headed toward the new cloud, taking their places along its outer and inner edges. Inexperienced climithes were assigned to the outer edges and experienced climithes took reign over the inner circle. Drue glided above the scene, directing people to their spots and explaining how it would work. It was a chaotic scene as everyone got situated and Maila's time was running out.

"It needs to happen now," Maila insisted.

"I'll take you," Jorban offered.

"Okay, but I will need some climithes, too. I need a strong current. Kalline, tell Drue to hold off moving the cloud as long as possible. Try to wait until I get back. Everything needs to happen in that order."

"I'll try. But if the Tierannites start singing, we can't wait." She looked toward the sky. "You have a little over an hour until sunset. Hurry so you can make it in time. I'll be close behind with a few climithes."

Jorban grabbed Maila's hand and led her north. It was a quick journey and Jorban stopped once they were directly above Mr. Lamorte's dwelling. Faint light pulsated beneath the gray dome. In the past, this area of the sky was off limits; no one was supposed to travel here. Maila had disobeyed many times and though she knew the smog existed, she just thought she was looking down on earth's dead spots. She never imagined humans lived under the darkness.

The world was murkier here and the dim light was exactly what she needed in order for her plan to work. Kalline got there a few minutes after with Mira, Philo, and Windee and Huck Bay, who were another experienced climithe couple.

"I hope I've brought enough climithes," Kalline said.

"You're alive?" Mira mumbled, astonished.

"Maila!" Philo shouted, overwhelmed with joy. He went right to his daughter and buried her in a tight, tearful embrace.

"I missed you, popa." Her words were muffled by his embrace.

He kissed her forehead. "I most certainly missed you more."

"What are you doing out here, girl?" Mira demanded, disrupting their joyous reunion. Maila stepped away from her father and got back on track. She looked at everyone but her stepmother as she spoke.

"I need the four of you to give me a strong and steady current."

"What for?" Philo asked with concern.

"There's no time to explain. You just need to trust me." Her confidence radiated—there would be no arguing with her—so they obliged.

Windee and Huck nodded in understanding, Philo pushed back his sleeves, and Mira rolled her eyes. Maila then glided to where Jorban hovered a few feet away from the cloud the climithes and Kalline stood upon.

"What is your plan?" Jorban asked in a low, alarmed voice.

"Just wait for me here. I'll be back soon."

Jorban looked outraged as he realized what she was about to do.

"No. I'm not letting you go down there. We already thought you died once. I can't give you a second chance to make that a reality." He huffed. "I won't mourn you all over again. I can't.

None of us can. It was devastating. Not only would I hate myself if this resulted in your actual death, but so would Darrow. He'd never forgive me."

"I am confident in my abilities. I know this will work."

"Please don't."

"I am going whether you want me to or not." She placed her hand on his shoulder. "I have to. It's the only way to end this war forever."

"Then let me go with you, let me help you."

"No. I am not dragging anyone else into harm's way. Too many people already died because of me. I have to do this alone."

Jorban shook his head incredulously.

"What are you trying to accomplish here?"

"Mr. Lamorte needs to be killed. And if he left his dwelling once to try and get me, he'll do it again." She gave him one last look of certainty. "Make sure they give me a strong current."

With that, Maila swooped down and left them all stunned as she did a perfect nosedive into the smog.

Chapter 49

Mr. Lamorte woke in his chambers from a restless sleep. The time eluded him and his head throbbed too ferociously to look at the glowing clock. Camille slept next to him, her stomach swollen with his heir. He did not intend to impregnate her but as long as she gave him a son, it could prove worthwhile.

Too many things pressed upon his mind. He walked to his balcony, pushed open the glass doors, and stepped out onto the ledge to breathe in the grimy air. Its thickness filled his throat, causing him to cough. In the past he reveled in the awful suffocation the air brought, but now, he wondered what it would be like to breathe the clean air outside the smog. He had to know. He needed to seize that land. The gray sky above him remained stagnant, unmoving and lifeless. He stared up into it, as he always did whenever his insatiable hunger for power kept him awake at night.

Out of nowhere, a steady gush of air brushed against his face. Mr. Lamorte tilted his head as he experienced this peculiarity. The only breeze he ever felt came from man-made machines, not the sky. In the distance, a tiny orb blazed against the dark gray backdrop and it grew larger as it floated closer. He shook his head to snap out of his sleepy daze, not wanting to react in case his mind was playing tricks, but there it was: the falling star. Its glow was hazy as it traveled to him through the smog. The moment felt enchanted, like everything was falling into place.

He had to have it. This time, he would capture the star and put it on display in the city square. For miles in every direction, people would be reminded of his unyielding power.

He put on his medicinal mask and grabbed his robe. He made his way down the elevator and out the large glass doors of his skyscraper. The street was cold and abandoned. Almost everyone from this part of the continent was in the boot camp or shipped off to battle.

The star glowed much brighter than the first time and was steadily approaching. He could already taste the power it would give him. He reached his arms toward the sky, anticipating the moment the star was close enough to seize. An eerie melody entered his head as the joy of what was happening settled into his tiny heart.

Mr. Lamorte's eyes grew wide with greed as the star's shape took on a different form. The blurry, bright dot now appeared as a female silhouette. The blood flowed from his heart into his groin as the human sensation of desire that once was foreign to him reappeared. The urge to have her in every way flooded his senses, leaving him drunk with primitive needs. His fingertips stretched toward her as he waited for the moment he could grab her. Take her by the throat, strip her of her dignity, and then put her on display for the world to see. But as these new cravings materialized, they were simultaneously shattered. The girl changed her path and was now moving away from him, her image growing smaller as she departed.

"No!" His shout echoed through the deserted street. "You have to be mine!"

What a terrible tease. Fury engulfed him. His rage was so strong that it smothered any rational thoughts trying to enter his brain. The pounding of his heart was violent and loud, causing him to stumble in the street. His world spun as he tried to figure out how to stop her departure and finish this new quest.

The rustle of tin garbage cans against gravel came from the shadows. Goose bumps tingled into existence, covering his body at the sudden notion that he might not be alone. He had no militia to protect him, they were all waiting for the battleships to return to Old Florida, and even if he summoned them, they were hours away and wouldn't arrive in time for an ambush. His temper subsided momentarily and his fear shifted from losing the star to what lurked in the darkness.

Chapter 50

Maila did it—she lured Mr. Lamorte out of his building, leaving him as easy prey to those hiding in the sewers. Before she left, she could see people creeping in the shadows, watching and waiting for the right opportunity to attack. She was sure Violet was one of them and that their common enemy would finally meet his end.

She soared through the smog, which was thick and hard to navigate, but the climithes above gave her a decent current. She coughed into her hands as she accidentally breathed in too much of the polluted air.

The journey back toward Ayren was slow moving, but she accomplished what she set out to do. Mr. Lamorte would be killed and once they moved the forgetting chant through the city, the war would be over.

She was only a few miles from the edge of the smog when the sound of air being chopped rapidly approached her from behind. Maila spun around in the current to see what was making the noise and to her horror, a metal machine hovered in the sky and raced toward her. Its body was round with a long tail and it had sharp metal blades on top that spun in vicious circles, keeping it afloat.

Terror coursed through Maila's heart: it was Mr. Lamorte. He followed her. He had taken out one of his hovercopters to chase after her.

"Twinkle twinkle, little Star," his hoarse voice projected through a speaker.

Maila took the air she was gliding through and pushed it at the hovercopter. The force caused it to spin around once, but Mr. Lamorte regained control and continued toward her.

She refused to back down. She gathered more of the current into her possession and threw it toward him again, hitting the windshield of the hovercopter so hard it splintered down the middle.

"Tsk tsk, that wasn't very nice," his voice came through the speaker as he pushed the throttle down hard and sped toward Maila with the blades of the hovercopter aimed straight at her. She picked up her speed and continued throwing bursts of air at Mr. Lamorte while gliding backward.

I cannot enter the smog, but I'm here, Aria chimed telepathically. She then provided Maila with a surplus of wind to work with. While holding onto her own current, she grabbed a piece of Aria's stream and lassoed the air around the tail of the hovercopter, causing it to spin violently through the air twice before Mr. Lamorte was able to regain control.

It wasn't working. Throwing strong currents at him wasn't enough to knock him out of the sky. She needed something more powerful. Something that would stop him for good.

You are more powerful than you realize, Aria encouraged. *The glory of nature lives within you. Dig deeper.*

She trusted Aria and obeyed, digging deep and reaching into her soul, searching for the strength to end this chase. Mr. Lamorte was a parasite on Earth. He thrived off destroying innocent creatures and organisms. He tried to ruin her home. He threatened everything she held dear. She let her unending love for this planet fill her entire being. As the love overflowing her soul felt like it might burst, so did her hate for Mr. Lamorte, and a rolling crack of thunder exploded throughout the sky. A surge of power she never felt before rushed through her body and exploded out of her fingertips. A cage of lightning formed around her, flickering and causing static as it waited for her command to strike. She let the electricity filter through her, collecting it in her force field encasement. Once it became too powerful to contain, she began hurling bolts of lightning at the hovercopter. The toxicity in the air caused her lightning to glow in brilliant shades of neon. A phosphorescent bolt of purple hit the hovercopter blades, breaking one of them off.

This new development in her defense fueled Mr. Lamorte's anger and his refusal to back down intensified hers.

The electric neon lightning show grew bigger as she got angrier. She grabbed another current of electricity and flung it toward Mr. Lamorte. The lustrous green bolt broke the windshield, shattering glass onto the world below.

"What a pretty light spectacle." His voice crackled through the sky. He pulled out a pistol and aimed it at Maila. "I wanted to catch you alive, but it seems I'll have to take you any way I can get you." He shut one eye and aimed at her head.

Maila swerved through the air backward, refusing to give him an easy shot, all while tossing bolts of electricity at him.

An illuminated bullet fired from his gun and narrowly missed her head. He fired again, this time she swiped her hand causing a gust of wind to knock the bullet off course.

He screamed and aimed at Maila one more time.

"I don't think so," she whispered beneath her breath, then aimed an incandescent bolt of blue lightning at him. This one was a direct hit, slamming him hard in the chest, and his body convulsed inside the hovercopter. Maila took a gust of wind and pulled him out through the broken windshield. She wrapped the air tightly around his body, dragging him so he dangled in the sky before her. The hovercopter plummeted to the ground, whistling an eerie cry as it fell. They were face to face and the sight of him was repulsing. Even through all of this, even as she held his life in her hands, he wore a smug smile.

"Are you going to kill me?" he asked as Maila tightened the current that imprisoned him. It was cutting off his circulation and seeing the blood rush to his face enticed her to constrict him further.

"Yes, I am," she answered confidently.

Maila let go and as he fell to his death, he laughed. His deranged reaction sent chills down her spine. The sound of his manic cackle became muffled as he fell, and then disappeared as swiftly as he did. The cage of lightning she created faded as she let her body relax. She finally let herself feel the exhaustion that creating those powers took out of her and without further delay she turned and refocused all her energy on returning to Ayren.

When she entered the atmosphere of Ayren she was greeted by shocked faces.

"What in the world did you do down there?" Kalline shouted out as soon as Maila reemerged.

"You were streaming so much air from us. I was petrified we were going to lose you again," Philo said, his face wet with tears.

"What were all those colorful lights?" Jorban asked.

"I made lightning. I guess all the chemicals that fill the air down there made each bolt crazy shades of neon."

"You made lightning? Without the friction of cold and warm air? You don't even have a thermostatic modulator, how could you have possibly made lightning?" Mira asked, outraged.

"That's amazing," Jorban spoke before Maila could answer. No one questioned her story except Mira. There wasn't a doubt in any of their minds that her capabilities were endless. She was the start of Ayren's next generation of evolution.

"But why did you need to go down there in the first place?" Kalline asked again, eager to know what she just witnessed.

"To kill Mr. Lamorte," Maila said with a huge grin, "and I did it."

All their faces went slack with astonishment.

"You killed Mr. Lamorte? Little you?" Jorban asked, completely awed.

"Yup. Now, once we get the rest of the city to forget they ever heard of life beyond the smog, the war will *really* be over. We won't have to worry about Mr. Lamorte figuring it out again."

"I am so proud of you," Philo said, still unable to control his emotions. Maila smiled and glided over to him, letting her body rest against his in an embrace. There was no time to enjoy it, though. They needed to move onto the next step of the mission.

"Okay, we need to get back and help carry the Tierannite song through the city." Everyone agreed and headed back to the specially solidified cloud. A smile of victory remained glued to Maila's face.

Chapter 51

The hovercopter crashed close to Violet's hiding spot. One of the blades from the chopper catapulted over her head and hit the back wall of the alley causing sparks to fly everywhere.

Mr. Lamorte failed and Violet was relieved. When he took to the sky to chase the light, she couldn't believe they missed their opportunity. They took too long to strike and Maila became easy prey to his destruction. Violet's heart sank when she thought she not only failed her mission, but also got Maila killed. The moment Violet prayed for a miracle the sky blazed with explosions. Maila's neon blasts of fire lit up the smog and in a matter of minutes, the hovercopter came crashing down to earth. Mr. Lamorte finally picked a battle he could not win.

As requested, she didn't tell anyone about Zyleh or Maila while she rallied Barnibus and his people to help her kill Mr. Lamorte. That would remain her secret for now. Her loyalty to that promise of confidentiality would be dependent on their next move now that the task was complete. She may not have killed Mr. Lamorte herself, but Maila did. He was dead and she hoped her valiant attempt was enough.

She glanced toward her sewer grate where Colin still hid. His little head popped above the metal grate as he tried to see what was going on. She hastily waved at him to go back under and once he obeyed, she returned her focus to the crashed hovercopter. She tiptoed toward it, in case he was still in it and had managed to survive. When she peeked around the side and into the broken windshield, he wasn't there. Dead *or* alive. She waved Barnibus over.

"He's not in here. Where did his body go?"

"Probably got snatched out by the wind as it fell. No way he coulda survived," he said confidently.

Violet hoped he was right, but soon after he made that prediction, an image appeared that made them both gasp.

A white blur floated above them and drifted slowly toward the street.

"No," Barnibus said in disbelief. "You've got to be kidding me."

"What?"

"He had a parachute."

Violet looked toward the falling body. It was limp as it hung from the backpack harness.

The rest of her rebellion remained hidden in the shadows, as she walked out into the open. When Mr. Lamorte hit the ground, she callously ripped the fabric of the chute off his body and threw it to the side. He was still alive.

"How?" she whispered under her breath.

Mr. Lamorte was scorched. His body was burnt from the lightning attack and the disease on his face was exposed. Violet took the toe of her boot and lightly tapped it against the raw flesh near his eye. He flinched in pain.

"You are one of us," she said, loud enough so he could hear.

His eyes circled inside his head, looking for the source of these words. He was still disoriented, but he found her. The little girl who just paid him the greatest insult fathomable. She stood above him, looking down with disdain.

"I am nothing like you, little girl," he gasped through the pain. "and one day, I will succeed in ridding the world of your kind." He spit on her shoe, but he was helpless, and she took pleasure in cleaning his spit off her shoe on the shoulder of his jacket.

She knelt down next to him, careful not to get too close to his infection, and whispered, "You created us. We are all that you've allowed us to be—our pitiful existence is *your* design." She stood up again and towered over his damaged body. She placed the sole of her boot upon the flesh of his neck. "You hate us, so you let us rot with disease and starve to death. You sent us into war to die. Your neglect will be your greatest downfall." She pressed harder and he gasped for air.

For the first time in his life, he felt fear. Nothing mattered more to him than his legacy and she demolished it in the simplest of terms. Was this how he would be remembered? Was this the stain he'd leave on his family name? Donovan Lamorte, the man who created an entire populace in his polluted image. Donovan Lamorte, the man who hindered his empire's success by suppressing the growth of his people. His heart pounded beneath his broken ribs. Donovan Lamorte, the man who was beat by a little girl. His eyes grew wide as her boot cut off his oxygen.

Keeping a firm stance on his neck, she took the toe of her boot and forced his chin to point toward her. She shook her head. He was a disgrace and she was better than this. She lifted her foot, releasing him. He gasped for air and shouted profanities at her as she walked away.

"He's all yours."

At this, her fellow survivors crept out of the shadows. The streetlights reflected off their eyes, revealing the hate that flickered within. Some cracked their fingers as they approached Mr. Lamorte's damaged body, others sported sinister smiles while imagining the long overdue justice they were about to serve.

The herd of people gathered around his body. It was a slow slaughter that started off with taunting. Everyone took turns saying what they needed to say and attacking Mr. Lamorte however they wished. Violet was too far away to hear the words they spoke, but witnessed the crowd around him growing increasingly rowdy.

The group mauled him, pummeling him repeatedly with brute force; a strength they probably wouldn't have had under different circumstances. Their power increased as the years of oppression were released. The sound that filled the air was raw. It was desperate and frantic, and their hysteria echoed into the sky. They were savages, grunting and screaming like wild animals. All the years of torture and living in filth because of this man were coming to a head and there was no stopping their rage. They finally had the source of all their pain at their fingertips and the beating would not stop until Mr. Lamorte's heart did. A guttural cry came from one of the men before he made the final blow to Mr. Lamorte's skull. It was over and the night was silent again.

The crowd around Mr. Lamorte's dead body slowly dispersed. They no longer needed to hide in Violet's sewer, so they wandered aimlessly, locked in a distant mindset as their adrenaline gradually dissipated.

Violet crawled back into her sewer. She hugged Colin and let his innocence fill the air around them. She wanted to feel innocent again, but that was impossible. Any fragments of her childhood still remaining before tonight were stolen by the horror she just witnessed.

"What happened?" Colin asked, his voice scared as Violet began to shake. He kept his arms around her and tried to console her. This was backwards: *she* needed to be strong for *him.* Snapping out of her shock, she pulled herself together.

"Mr. Lamorte is dead."

"Dead?" Colin asked, breaking free of their hug. "How?"

"Murdered by the people who were hiding down here with us. They got rid of him for good." Her timid reaction at good news made him uneasy and confused. "It's a good thing," she said, addressing the confusion in his eyes. He nodded.

"What do we do now?"

"I don't know what happens next, but we are a team until the end. I'll never leave you."

"I won't leave you either."

They hugged and Violet was revived with a newfound strength that stemmed from Colin.

Chapter 52

Maila made it back to the cloud the solidifiers formulated in time. It was massive. She was exhausted but did her best to keep her energy up a little while longer. As an expert climithe she was a crucial part of this undertaking. The winds had to be powerful enough to push the song at its full volume through the smog. If it didn't echo through every nook and crack of North America, it might not affect every Debauched person living there.

Drue called out directions.

"We need all expert climithes stationed along the sides of the inner circle. Those on the outside will be in charge of keeping us moving in the direction of the city. Celia, Fallon, and I will be gliding above, letting you know which way to steer. Once you're in your spots, I will let you know if you are located on the north, south, east, or west side of the cloud."

"Alright," Jorban said. "See you on the other side." He and Kalline headed toward the cloud's outer edge. The rest of the group headed for the inner circle. Philo had his arm around his daughter but no one spoke.

"Expert climithes," Drue continued, looking at Philo, Mira, Windee, and Huck. "Please take your places on the secondary cloud stationed above the beach. There, you will continually push the song toward us as we carry it to the city."

The experts departed and Maila was left alone with the other climithes at the inner circle.

"Mai," an old, raspy voice came from behind Maila. Madivel was limping toward her.

Happiness filled Maila as she stepped away from her parents to talk to her. She gave her old friend a huge hug.

"I can't tell you how happy I was to learn you were still alive. Best day I've had in a while."

Maila squeezed her tighter in appreciation then let go.

"Why are you limping?"

"I was on a cloud next to the Axis when it got hit. Some debris flew into my leg and sliced me up pretty good. But I can't complain. I'm lucky to be alive."

"I'm very glad you're okay. There is so much I need to be filled in on once this is over."

"Yes, but for now, this mission you put into action is our priority." Madivel gave Maila a wink and a proud smile.

If she only knew the mission I just came back from! Maila thought, wishing there was time to tell her now.

Then, out of the corner of her eye, she saw Darrow. He was back to his normal self and helping his father get everything in order. She took a deep breath to even her nerves before approaching him. Before she got the chance to proceed, he turned his attention in her direction and noticed her, too. An overjoyed grin crossed his face and he glided to meet her where she stood. Upon contact, Darrow wrapped her in an embrace and held her like he'd never let go. They said nothing and let their hug soothe any residual trauma that remained. The relief of his embrace was overwhelming and extinguished every doubt that sparked while she was in Tier. His touch steadied the frantic heartbeat and panicked breathing she grew to accept as normal. It left Maila speechless and bewildered. When she reentered Ayren she thought her body realigned, but it hadn't. In undetected silence, her heart still ached, and she never noticed it until this moment.

When the hug ended, they opened their mouths to speak and spit out apologies in unison. They smiled at each other, relieved that they didn't need to hash out the terrible details to make sure the other understood their part in the miscommunication, or how they hurt one another. They both recognized where their faults lie and did not need to waste another word on the past.

"I missed you," Maila said, staring up at him.

"I don't think there are any words in existence to explain the anguish I felt when I thought I lost you forever. None that would do it proper justice anyway."

She understood what he meant. Saying she missed him didn't seem like enough either.

"I'm very glad we are together again."

"I'm very glad you're not dead!" he said, playfully. They both smiled. "I'm happy you're here with me, too." His tone shifted from lighthearted to reflective. "It's ironic that you brought about all these changes in Ayren. It was always my intent to do this, to make things right, and my main motivation was always you. Every time you asked me for the truth I became more determined to fix the laws so I could give it to you." Darrow took a deep breath. "I was trying to change the world for you."

"We can change it together," Maila smiled. She never needed a savior, but was glad to know that Darrow would always be there for her.

"Everything is so different now." He exhaled like he'd been holding his breath for years. "Though it happened in a strange fashion and was recklessly executed," he raised his eyebrows at her mischievousness, "your bravery and determination brought about the change the gliders couldn't initiate for centuries. You never settled for less than you deserved and I am so proud of you."

"Does that mean you'll be my ally now?" She teased him but meant it whole-heartedly. She was thrilled that he could see the positives within the sorrow she caused. He was very in tune with who she was at her core. The whole ordeal was a mistake, one they could both own some blame for, and making errors was inherently human. Despite the vast amount of time the Elements spent separating themselves from their ancestry, they still originated from humanity and could not escape the ancient characteristics intertwined into their genetics. She was guarded, he was stubborn. She was impulsive, he was controlling. He was not blind to the darkness accompanying their light, but he loved her anyway, without end. He would not give up on her, nor she him.

"Absolutely," Darrow smiled.

"Great, we've got a lot of work to do."

There was much to take care of after they attempted the forgetting spell. Her goals were set on the future and making the world a place that was not divided in half. There was innocence within the evil and conflicts within the good. Maila hoped to bring resolve to both halves.

She took her spot along the inner circle and Darrow joined his parents above. Everyone waited for the next instruction from Drue. After he finished assigning locations to each person, he addressed the group.

"Now, we wait until we hear the song. It's very important to keep the song grounded. We cannot let it carry up to us. If it does the magic will affect us as well. Just keep pushing the wind downward and out."

"How will we know if it has worked?" a woman called out.

"The Tierannites said they would be able to determine that."

Nobody raised any other questions. The space among the cloud remained still; only a nervous silence surrounded them as they waited.

Drue circled above the cloud, watching the massive group of Tierannites filter onto the beach. Once they were in place below, they held hands and formed a huge circle on the beach. Within that circle, smaller circles took shape, until the space inside the largest circumference was filled with bodies. In unison, they tilted their heads toward the sky. The sound was faint, but it was there. Drue took this as his cue.

"Start your winds!"

At once, everyone worked together to create a strong gust beneath the cloud. As the wind became stronger, the cloud turned an ominous shade of gray. Everyone in Ayren pushed harder, making their creation more powerful.

"North side, lighten up," Drue called down.

As they softened their stream, the cloud moved north toward the Debauched city. Creating the wind was tiring, but Maila used every ounce of strength she had left to keep her current strong. This plan had to work. With Mr. Lamorte dead and the rest of the Debauched population forgetting what happened, the war would end.

She could almost hear the song they carried. It was peaceful and soft, a hypnotic harmony of reverie. She stopped listening and stayed focused on the wind stream below her.

Hundreds of pale white arms hung over the side of the cloud as the Ayrenese worked their magic. Many shut their eyes in order to focus, including Maila, but after a few minutes she opened them to observe the masterpiece they were crafting. To her dismay, it was a mess. Instead of working as a cohesive unit, they operated without awareness for the greater whole. This lack of vision created a chaotic clutter of air currents below and the different streams weren't connecting. Each individual wind stream clashed against those near it, creating a violent gale.

"Everyone, open your eyes!" Maila shouted over the loud rumble. "We need to make our airstreams flow together seamlessly into one wind, not a hundred different currents."

People along the inner circle opened their eyes and saw what Maila was talking about. The winds they created were colliding against each other. Aware of the mistake, everyone refocused and attempted to thread their stream into their neighbor's. As they did so, the aggressive and unmanageable gale calmed and started to cooperate.

Happy with the change, Maila closed her eyes again and focused on the part of the breeze she conjured. She transitioned into the cerebral state that connected her mentally and physically with the wind she conceived. Its calm power rang throughout her entire being.

They traveled closer to the Debauched city carrying the Tierannite's song. It wouldn't be long before the melody filtered through the entire continent and their enemy forgot they existed beyond the smog.

Chapter 53

Violet sat in the sewer, legs crossed, watching Colin sleep. She still wanted to be rescued, wanted a way out, but as more time passed she wondered if Maila or Zyleh were ever going to come back.

She contemplated walking into the darkness with her flashlight to see if she could determine where the strangers from the other side of the world entered.

She could go now, but leaving Colin alone after all that happened felt wrong. The murder was gruesome and Violet was still disturbed. Not because Mr. Lamorte was dead, but because of the gory nature in which it happened. Colin may not need her company right now, but she needed his. The problem was that her only opportunity to explore was while he slumbered. Since she didn't tell him about the people from the other side of the smog, she couldn't explore while he was awake. He'd ask questions and she didn't want to get his hopes up yet.

He rustled gently and occasionally mumbled to himself. Violet worried he was having nightmares. He already endured so much in his short life and she hoped things would get better for him now that he was with her. She did her best to give him love and support like his real family would, but he still missed them terribly.

She sat with her back against the cold brick wall. Though she tried to suppress her hopes, she constantly found herself waiting to feel the warm breeze. This time it would signify the possibility of escaping this hell.

As thoughts of freedom filled her mind, a gentle flush of warm air brushed the side of her face. She sat up immediately, heart racing. Was it the same warmth that accompanied the outsiders whenever they entered her home? She wasn't sure if she imagined it or if it really happened, the sensation stopped as quickly as it came.

Every breath she took was filled with anticipation as she waited for it to happen again. She couldn't wait, her hopes were too high. Violet picked up her flashlight and journeyed into the darkness. It didn't take long before she came across the source.

A tall boy stood in front of her. He looked just like Zyleh; same green eyes and shaggy brown hair, but it wasn't him. This boy had a skinnier face and less muscle. There was also kindness behind his eyes.

"Who are you?" she demanded.

"Phelix. Are you Violet?"

"Yes," she said hesitantly, unsure why a new stranger had come looking for her. She expected to see the same two from the other day.

Phelix examined Violet with wide, amazed eyes.

"You're beautiful," he said in awe.

"What?" she asked, taken aback. She didn't know why, but this made her angry. She backed away and touched her face, embarrassed by the compliment. She never thought much about her appearance and having someone, especially a boy her own age, bring it up made her uncomfortable. The only time she ever saw her reflection was in glass windows or puddles.

"Why have you come?" she insisted.

Phelix tried to mirror her defensive tone, but fumbled over his words.

"How did you know I was here? Zyleh said you wouldn't be expecting me."

"The warm breeze."

"The what?"

"Every time I feel the warm breeze, it's followed by a distant voice giving me warnings or a run-in with one of you." Phelix wore a perplexed expression, "Don't you know what the warm breeze is?"

He shrugged, "It must be the result of us opening the passageway between your world and ours. The air is very different from where I come."

Violet nodded, that's what she assumed.

"Why are you here?" she insisted again. She had her mind set on escaping and needed to know if her prayer was about to be answered.

"My brother sent me here. Zyleh, you met him. You are going to have to trust me, I'm here to help."

"Help with what? Are you rescuing us from this place?"

"No, not yet. I can't tell you what is about to happen, it would defeat the purpose. Just trust me. Sit down."

She scrunched her nose in aggravation but did as instructed. He sat down across from her.

"I'm going to put my hands over your ears when the time is right and do a small chant. Listen only to me. If you hear anything else, ignore it and focus on me."

"Is this going to transport me to another world?" she asked earnestly.

Phelix laughed.

"No, I don't work in the business of teleportation."

She gave him a stern look and continued her thought.

"Because if it is, I need to go get Colin. He will need to come too."

"Who is Colin?" he asked. There was a hint of jealousy in his voice that Violet did not notice.

"He's my little brother," she said, liking the idea of having a family member again. "When I leave, he has to come too."

"He will be fine," Phelix's troubled tone disappeared after hearing her explanation, "and you aren't going anywhere yet. Everything needs to happen in the proper order. Just trust me."

"Alright," she said. She was hesitant but chose to believe this new stranger. "I'm putting my faith in you."

"I won't let you down." The inflection in his voice calmed her. His words were genuine and she no longer had the innate urge to doubt him.

He placed his large palms over her ears. As soon as they settled in place, everything became quiet. He leaned in close so their noses almost touched and the warmth of his breath induced goose bumps on her arms. He began muttering foreign words in a melodic rhythm. With his hands over her ears, all she could hear were his muffled mumblings.

Phelix stared into her bright blue eyes as he spoke in a language she couldn't understand. On most occasions, a situation like this would make her feel wildly uncomfortable, but with him she felt at ease.

She did as he said and ignored everything except him. Through the flesh and bone earmuffs, she was confident all she heard was Phelix, and even he was barely audible.

They continued to sit face to face for longer than Violet could count. Every time she tried to count the seconds that passed, she found herself counting the freckles on his nose instead.

She didn't know why this was necessary, or what it meant, but she liked the sound of his voice. It was soothing. Unaware of its compelling capabilities, she let his repetitive mantra take hold of her consciousness.

He watched her grow hazy from the power of his chant. As he hypnotized her into a state of peaceful unconsciousness, he wondered if he was doing the right thing. He was forcing her to remember the fleeting hope she acquired after seeing Zyleh and Maila. He was enabling the false hope of survival outside this city to continue. She could never leave this place. Tier was the only Element she could physically survive in and none of his fellow Tierannites would ever allow her to live among them. Only a few hours ago, her people were on their land, initiating war, and killing his people. To have any member of the Debauched in their home as a guest would be blasphemous. And as much as his father promoted peace, equality, and understanding, the damage caused by the Debauched was too recent to overlook.

Violet was nothing like the Debauched soldiers sent to Tier, nothing like the many decrepit humans he was forced to fight and kill. His heart contracted as he now understood why Maila wanted to save her. She was young and innocent. She *could* be saved.

Phelix's task suddenly felt burdensome: he was forcing Violet to remember everything. To remember him. To remember Zyleh and Maila. To remember there was a brighter and better place that she could never reach beyond her dismal city. His assignment was to preserve her memory and while at first that seemed noble, it now seemed cruel. When her face flickered with hope upon finding him in the darkness, guilt was all he felt. She believed they would save her when in reality, they couldn't. Forcing her to remember wasn't noble, it was a curse. A heartless and selfish act meant to satisfy only their needs. Perhaps he ought to let the chant within the winds take her, too. Let it cleanse her memory like everyone else in this city. Perhaps letting her forget was the kindest gift he could give her.

He shook his head knowing he could not break the promise he made to his brother and jeopardize the lives of those in Tier, Ayren, Ahi, and Coralen. Phelix sighed. If he had to do this, if he had to force her to hold on to the weight of her memories, he certainly would not let her carry it alone.

He kept his hands over her ears and kissed her forehead briefly during a pause in the chant. He wasn't sure how he would save her but he wouldn't let her down. She put her faith in him and in return, he would find a way to prove himself worthy of that honor. Unbeknownst to either of them, a silent promise was made in that moment that Phelix would move mountains to keep.

Chapter 54

She woke up on her dirty sleeping bag consumed in a cold sweat. Nightmares were normal, but this one felt like a memory. In fact, she was sure it had been real: the boy's green eyes, his warm hands upon her face, his soft lips kissing her forehead. But then it all went black and all she could see was her own gruesome murder after falling from the sky. The people of the city did this to her. They ripped her life away. *No they didn't,* she thought to herself. She looked down at her hands to remind herself she was still alive. That part of the memory was a nightmare, but it felt familiar. *Lamorte.* He's the one who was murdered.

Colin sat in the corner, crying for his mother. Violet could do nothing to console him. He woke up a new boy, one without any memory of her.

The boy was supposed to save them, but what had he done instead? Colin didn't know who she was anymore. He didn't remember Mr. Lamorte's boot camp. He stood crying in the shadows for hours, refusing to let her comfort him. Where did the foreign boy go? Phelix. His name was Phelix. Why did he do this to her? She trusted them, she trusted him. She put all her faith into them and now everything was worse than before. His voodoo stripped her of the only person she still cared for. Colin was petrified and inconsolable, asking for his parents and brother,

Dax. They were most likely dead, but when Violet tried to remind him of that, he sobbed with fury and called her a liar. He threw a fit and accused her of kidnapping him.

What had Phelix done? Her heart contracted violently as her already tattered world crumbled into tinier pieces. If there was an explanation, she prayed for it to come soon because she did not trust that her fragile heart could handle this new break. She inexplicably lost Colin, the only person she loved and trusted. They woke up to madness. One of them had lost their minds and she couldn't determine who the victim was yet. They were supposed to be safe, supposed to escape the smog. The freedom that sat at the edge of her fingertips yesterday vanished in her sleep. Their chance at a better life was stolen from them with no note explaining why.

The answers will come, she thought, *the answers will come.* She repeated this over and over inside her head, hoping to make it true. Her stability was on the fritz and she was having trouble distinguishing reality from nightmares. She was confident it all happened, but maybe that only meant she had gone insane. Colin was living proof that her memory could not be trusted.

She sat on the sewer floor waiting for a sign: a warm breeze to reassure her of all that happened up to this point, or a voice to call out to her from the darkness of the sewer tunnel. She no longer trusted herself. She no longer trusted sleep and what it concealed from her. If this madness was not explained, if it did not make sense to her by the time she laid down to sleep again, she feared she would not make it through another night. The anxiety of this nightmare was sure to strangle her as she slumbered.

Then it happened. Her prayers were answered. The warm breeze came again and tears of joy rolled down Violet's cheeks. They came back for her. She hadn't lost her mind and there would be an explanation to the puzzle she woke up to. If they caused this, surely they could also fix it. Violet got up and entered the shadows of the sewer, positive there was a reason behind this confusion. She ran into the darkness, confident once again in the hope of tomorrow.

Thank you for reading *Evo: The Elements*—I hope you enjoyed the story! If you have a moment, please consider leaving a review on Amazon. All feedback is greatly appreciated!

Amazon Author Account:
www.amazon.com/author/nicolineevans

Instagram:
www.instagram.com/nicolinenovels

Facebook:
www.facebook.com/nicoline.eva

Twitter:
www.twitter.com/nicolineevans

To learn more about my other novels, please visit my official author website:
www.nicolineevans.com